BEYOND ARMAGEDDON

Beyond Armageddon

EDITED BY
Walter M. Miller, Jr. and
Martin H. Greenberg

POSTSCRIPT TO THE INTRODUCTION BY
Martin H. Greenberg

UNIVERSITY OF NEBRASKA PRESS • LINCOLN

∞

First Nebraska paperback printing: 2006

Library of Congress Cataloging-in-Publication Data
Beyond Armageddon / edited by Walter M. Miller, Jr. and Martin H. Greenberg;
postscript to the introduction by Martin H. Greenberg.—Bison Books ed.
p.   cm.
ISBN-13: 978-0-8032-8315-2 (pbk.: alk. paper)
ISBN-10: 0-8032-8315-6 (pbk.: alk. paper)
1. Science fiction, American.   2. War stories, American.   3. Nuclear warfare—
Fiction.   I. Miller, Walter M., 1923–   II. Greenberg, Martin Harry.
PS648.S3B52   2006
813'.0876208358—dc22   2005032954

This Bison Books edition follows the original in beginning chapter 1 on arabic
page 17; no material has been omitted.

SALVADOR, by Lucius Shepard, copyright © 1984 by Mercury Press, Inc. Reprinted by
permission. THE STORE OF THE WORLDS, by Robert Sheckley, copyright © 1959 by
Robert Sheckley. Reprinted by permission of Kirby McCauley Ltd. THE BIG FLASH,
by Norman Spinrad, copyright © 1969 by Damon Knight. Reprinted by permission of
the author. LOT, by Ward Moore, copyright © 1953 by Fantasy House, Inc.; copyright
© renewed 1981 by Mercury Press, Inc. Reprinted by permission of Virginia Kidd.
DAY AT THE BEACH, by Carol Emshwiller, copyright © 1959 by Mercury Press, Inc.
Reprinted by permission of the author and the author's agent, Virginia Kidd. THE
WHEEL, by John Wyndham, copyright © 1952 by Standard Magazines, Inc.; copyright
© renewed 1980. Reprinted by permission of the agents for the author's estate, the
Scott Meredith Literary Agency, Inc., 845 Third Avenue, New York NY 10022. JODY
AFTER THE WAR, by Edward Bryant, copyright © 1972 by Damon Knight. Reprinted

Acknowledgments appearing on text page 387 constitute as extension of this page.

Case 101: Ch'iu-Ch'iu's Firestorm

A monk asked old Abbot Ch'iu-Ch'iu, "When the firestorm at the end of the world sweeps through, and everything is burned up, does the Buddha Nature burn with it?"

"Hand me a light," said Ch'iu-Ch'iu.

The student touched a taper to the charcoal footwarmer and gave it to him. Ch'iu-Ch'iu set the student's robe on fire, then yelled, "Put it out! Put it out!"

Concerning this case, Brother Pseudo comments:
>By firelight the patchrobe monk puts his question,
>Yet he sees not the blazes all about him.
>When did the world end for him?
>Wasn't it only yesterday?
>Bah! His farts add fuel to the fire!

from THE YELLOW CLIFF RECORD

Alibi

You ask where have I been for twenty-five years.
I will tell you.
I live here in the swamp.
I live here to save my hide.
There is a bounty on it.
I have a little brown pussy in the swamp.
Her name is Eva.
She thinks she is a psychiatrist.
I keep her on an island and
I feed her snake-meat to make her fat.
My name is really Adolf Hitler.
My hide is valuable.
Have you priced a good alligator bag lately?

I lie in the water with my eyeballs at the surface. I can grab the swimming snakes in my teeth that way. I save snake-meat for Eva and leave it on the shore. She will be good when she gets fat. Once there were knives and forks. I ate only vegetables and dairy products in those days, except when Frau Goering cooked Jewish sauerbraten for Hermann and me. You did not know sauerbraten is Jewish? It depends on who is the ingredient. My name is Hitler, Adolf. I shot myself in the mother. Now I live in the swamp with a little brown pussy named Eva. Sieg heil!

Walter M. Miller, Jr.

CONTENTS

BEYOND ARMAGEDDON

FOREWARNING

A Little Hell

The President is on record as agreeing with Jerry Falwell that a mysterious Megawar called "Armageddon" of uncertain future date may be about to terminate history. That, coupled with his joking remark that the bombing of the Evil Empire would begin in five minutes, suggests to me an anthology of stories about what happens to us *after* that mysterious Megawar scheduled by some biblical interpreters to begin, probably soon, at the small town of Megiddo (once called "Armageddon" by Greeks), which is at present in Israel on the West Bank. It's not a wholly implausible site just now for the beginning of a thermonuclear termination of the history of the planet.

So I picked through thousands of pages—it seems to me—of science fiction stories, sent to me by Martin Greenberg, about the aftermath of a Megawar at the end of the world, and lo, not a single one of them dealt with seven-horned beasts or the harlot that sits on the seven hills or the fate of Reagan and Falwell (or Gorbachev) when all the saints are lifted up into the skies at the time of the Great Rapture. So, seen as an effort to capitalize on the recent fervor for apocalyptic nuclear politics, this story-search would have to be judged a failure. Evidently, Fundamentalists don't write fantasy or science fiction, and might shrink from the suggestion that Saint John was writing it in Revelations ("Close Encounters of the Last Kind"?).

But we found twenty-one pretty good stories about a Megawar and its survivors toward the end of history. It can't be the *real* Armageddon, of course: there isn't any Rapture afterward, and the book begins in Central America, not on the West Bank.

Actually, in times of cataclysm, churches are filled with the newly pious, as they are beginning to fill today, but this is not reflected, either, in the post-Megawar fiction which I have seen. Nobody can fairly accuse us of excluding stories involving religion or politics from this book, or of avoiding controversy. In one story, the young hero is a priest (and the son of a priest), but not of any now-known persuasion. In two others, clergymen are minor characters, but they aren't of the friendly sort. Some other stories are so religiously human ("Jody after the War," for example) that anyone who thinks God became a human being at Bethlehem might find them religious—if he has no weightier matters such as Armageddon and the Book of Revelations in mind. Symbolically, one might say the book begins with the Fall and ends with the damnation of a homesick Faust. Along the way, "Lot" provides new insight into an old story from Genesis, and the rites of spring are celebrated in an ancient way in "The Feast of Saint Janis."

It's just as well that we not try to compete with John's Revelations and the motion picture *Threads*—both state-of-the-art in portraying cataclysm, religious or thermonuclear. We'd lose. This book is about people.

The Gamesmen and the Game

In war, as in a game of any kind, the idea of an acceptable risk can be quantified by assigning a positive or negative numerical value, often in money or lives, to each of all possible outcomes of a decision—how much do you win or lose?—and the value of each outcome is then multiplied by the estimated probability of its actually happening. The sum of the probabilities must be unity. The sum of the products is called the "expectation," and may turn out to be either plus or minus, a gain or a loss. The sum represents what you could expect to gain or lose *on the average* if you played the same decision an infinite number of times with the same odds. Run the same procedure for each of your full range of decisions, and you can arrive at an optimum strategy.

This game is routinely played by electric utilities, the Pentagon, the Kremlin, pension fund investment managers, and maybe even a few racetrack bettors. But when human extinction (as a result of a decision) is assigned a probability, however small, and a *finite* negative value, however large, and these two quantities are multiplied, and added to a list of other such products to obtain the expectation for a given political or military decision, the statistician and his employer should be detected, apprehended, and led away in straitjackets to the nearest lobotomy ward. Such people are not just running loose in Washington and Moscow, they're running things. And their game goes on because to assign human extinction an *infinitely* negative value would mean quitting the game altogether—not even the mathematics works with an infinity that destroys the game and the gamesmen—and would rule out any decision except really cooperating to make Megawar impossible.

Anybody but a comedian who can talk about the threat of human extinction without raising a little hell must be sick.

Megawar?—why another barbaric neologism? Well, the word *Holocaust* with a capital *H* refers to the mass murder of Jews living in Europe during World War II. But the word without the capital has come to mean the effect of a full-scale nuclear war, and there is within science fiction a subcategory usually called "post-holocaust fiction," from which we have chosen some worthy stories. I myself have used the word *holocaust* in refering to the effect of a thermonuclear exchange, so I do not urge others (except the book's publicist) to avoid this usage. But the diminishing memory of *the* Holocaust is being further blurred at a Nazi cemetery in Germany this week by an aged and fuzzy American President, and I prefer not contributing to this dangerous forgetfulness through careless use of the word. In this book I'll usually refer to the "war" at the end of civilization by a neologism, *Megawar*, except when the image of holocaust as a whole burnt offering comes to mind.

By the way, letters from readers enraged by the editorial text of this book should be addressed only to Walter Miller, Jr., and not to Martin Greenberg (who did nearly all the really hard work in excavating stories to consider for this anthology). The editorial *we* usually means "Miller," unless the selection of stories is part of the predicate.

The Layout of Armageddon

This book by twenty authors was begun in 1937 and took forty-eight years to complete. Most stories included here have this in common: the writers were looking toward and beyond an ultimate "war," the Megawar, and imagining what it would be like to find oneself alive afterwards. But each writer was looking ahead from one particular viewpoint during the history of half a century, and his vision was shaped by his times. For example, the nuclear-winter hypothesis is too recent an idea to play a role in *any* of these stories—although, curiously, Poul Anderson, writing in 1946, alludes to *Fimbulwinter*. There is no general agreement among these writers as to the extent of Megawar's destruction, nor is there any reason why there should be. The motion picture *Threads* has set the most recent benchmark for future thermonuclear horror entertainment, but the benchmark is not applicable to such stories from the past as these. Like Poul Anderson, Stephen Vincent Benét (who is perhaps best known for "The Devil and Daniel Webster") never heard of nuclear winter. Furthermore when Benét wrote "By the Waters of Babylon" he had never heard of atomic bombs, since he died in 1943. And yet, curiously, Benét alludes to "fire from the sky in the Great Burning," and to a poison that lingers in the ground of a shattered city.

While it took these authors forty-eight years to write the book, it took the editors only a few weeks to collect the book's scattered parts, separate them from other good post-Megawar stories that don't quite belong here, and arrange them in a sort of, well, an arrangement. The order is not always chronological, except near the beginning. In the first story, Megawar is only in the making; in the second, it's all in the mind, as is one version of quantum mechanics; in the third, it's consciously planned; in the fourth, it's off to a slow start. But it's all over by the beginning of the fifth story; and after the fourth story, bombs fall only in survivors' nightmares. The actual Megawar happens offstage, between stories, and the rest is about the survivors, the orphans of a pyschopathic civilization. Mood, rather than chronology, governs arrangement toward the middle of the book, but the last two stories wind things down again, and Jim Aikin (who was not necessarily thinking of Megawar's aftermath at all) leaves no doubt that the last story in the book will be the last story in the world worth telling or believing.

The stories have more in common among themselves than a Megawar in the background. There is a nostalgia for things lost that reminds me of ancient underworld myth, and many of the stories we have examined while putting the book together seem to be modern recurrences of that myth, whether or not the settings are subterranean. We have omitted all but one of the many literal underworld stories of extended survival in onetime fallout shelters, but in many others the quality of sadness and the yearning for ancient days and ancient ways remind one of the sighing shades in Virgil's Hades and Dante's Hell. The underworld mood is there even without the underworld setting, because post-Megawar stories are about an afterlife. Survivors don't really live in such a world; they haunt it. Only Ellison, with tongue deeply in cheek, suggests that it might be paradise downstairs for a young Aeneas and his underworld Dido, but *facilis descensus Averni,* sucker.

Perhaps the book as a whole, because of juxtapositions, implies something about human destiny that no author in it really intended to say, but if so, it's something I can't define, and if I could, I'd probably disagree with it to the extent that it underestimates the horror of Megawar. I think most of these authors have underestimated it, as I did myself in my own post-Megawar novel, published a quarter of a century ago. The focus today of our working-model image of Megawar has been sharpened by new data since most of these stories were written. We have computer models of what can happen.

Because the twenty authors wrote it while half a century was passing, it seems worthwhile to glance back at the whole period of time that brackets their work, and I'll do some of this backward-glancing while introducing individual stories. The same time-brackets include everything in the nonfictional world from the middle of the Great Depression, the Spanish Civil War, and the conquest of Ethiopia, through World War II and subsequent heroic police actions, culminating most recently in our glorious conquest of Grenada (nothing is newer at the time of this writing—except a strong odor of exploding cordite in Central America; see the first story).

World events are bound to be on the mind of a science-fiction writer, who must wonder whether the plausibility of his near-future plot will survive history's surprises at least until the story is published. And of course the Bomb does affect the way we look at everything. Owning the Bomb is the world's biggest and most expensive form of advertising, the message being "Don't tread on us." And the really insane thing about it is that this advertising is directed more to the American people than to people of the world, for whom the message becomes, "Don't tread on those criminal lunatics, unless you know you can kill them all, as you probably can if you're clever." The advertising at home is supposed to make us feel safe. A paranoid mating call always gets a paranoid answer. But of course it's all very enriching to war industries and stud generals, a combo one ex-general warned us about, and it encourages R&D, although a joint Soviet-American trip to Mars and beyond would encourage it as well or better.

Perhaps it's evil as well as crazy to talk of human extinction without raising a little hell. It's also not very helpful to raise hell without offering alternatives.

A Japanese Paradigm

The world at first glance seems full of petty dictators eager to obtain nuclear, chemical, or bacteriologial means of vengeance or conquest. We've been terrified by the possibility of nuclear proliferation because of a knee-jerk answer to the question, "What would really happen if we sold two or three 50-kiloton bombs to any little government that feels the need for nukes and has the cash to pay?" "Something horrible!" is the reflexive answer, but I'm a lot more afraid of Reagan, Gorbachev, & Co. than I am of, say, a mini-nuclear state headed by Muammar al-Qaddafi or Fidel Castro.

I think there is at least a small chance that the global nuclear Megawar that is assumed by the authors of most stories in this book will never come to pass. A *very* small chance.

A hope lies in the Third World. For forty years now the results of the karma which we cast at Hiroshima and Nagasaki have unfolded and enmeshed us like fish in an expanding nuclear net. History seems as irreversible as entropy. We keep adding to our karma to counter the results of previous karma, and soon India, Libya, Israel, Pakistan, Iran, South Africa, and Argentina will have nuclear "bargaining chips," no matter what we do. The Bomb cannot be un-invented, and nonproliferation agreements will not for long deter small, angry nations from developing uranium or plutonium warheads. What then?

In *Giving up the Gun*[1], Noel Perrin tells how medieval Japan abandoned firearms for two centuries when, after ninety-six years of using guns with devastating effect in feudal war, the gentlemen warriors of that isolated society gradually realized that matchlocks in the hands of peasants made them the military equals of the lordly Samurai. A typical *daimyo* came to detest the great equalizer as he watched famous knights blown off their horses at a hundred yards by bullets from his own or his enemy's conscripted riffraff. Feudal Japan, after developing its own thriving firearms industry, without much fanfare laid down the gun and returned to the sword until Commodore Perry came. They *did* melt down a lot of guns for erecting a big iron Buddha, but firearms, rather than being strictly banned, just faded away. Wars were nearly as bloody without them, but a gentleman could count on being killed only by another gentleman thereafter. Can you believe in men willing to trade guns for swords? This is like water running uphill. This is entropy decreasing in a local enclave. This is repealing social and economic history. This can't happen, but it did. Could this Japanese paradigm be applicable on a global scale when small riffraff nations begin to acquire their own nuclear equalizers to become small superpowers in their own right? Perrin's history of firearms in Japan suggests the question. One trouble, of course, is that not all small nations are the equivalent of hired riffraff. Some are—we have ours and they have theirs.

Will the present superpowers, when confronted with a growing league of nuclear jihad states and atomic banana republics, become as reasonable about abandoning the Bomb as the Samurai about abandoning the gun? Building Maginot Lines in the sky is no help against bombs small enough to be smuggled onto a beach like a bale of marijuana and carried to Washington in a knapsack by a hitchhiker. The Germans came around the Maginot Line on motorcycles in 1940—a ploy that one element of today's society still commemorates by wearing swastikas on their motorcycle helmets. The nuclear warriors will get around the star-wars Maginot in small boats and up the beaches, across Mexican and Canadian borders in

[1]Boulder, Co: Shambhala, 1980.

Volkswagens and Piper Cubs. A bomb that weighs sixty-eight pounds is indeed the new equalizer among nations. When will the first one explode, and where? It might plausibly happen a year or two before the first big nuclear disarmament agreement. Will it happen in a big city, with a yield of 0.5 hiroshimas? There will be no star-wars defense against it. Perhaps it *must* happen for the personal edification of people too young to have been involved in the national celebration of the cremation of two cities that preceded V-J Day, who lack either of guilt or rationalization of guilt deriving from personal memories of the week that piled up so much American karma. (See J. G. Ballard's "The Terminal Beach.")

I have my own modest proposal. It seems to me that if Muammar and Fidel and Zia and Stroessner and the Iroquois Nation and the Hairy Ainu had a few small bombs, the superpowers would suddenly yearn for real nuclear disarmament. The small powers will get the weapons, sooner or later. Perhaps we should side with inevitability at this point. That is often the Taoist way: let the water flow downhill as it will anyway, let entropy increase, maybe even help it along.

Why don't we junk the nonproliferation treaty, and then conduct a unilateral partial disarmament by selling all warheads smaller than a megaton to needy Third World nations, thus eliminating the budget deficit. To the *really* needy, by golly! Let's with characteristic American generosity give the bombs away. Every member of the UN gets a free American mini-bomb. After the giveaway, we invite the other multimegaton nations, by now hysterical, to sit down with us and all our new, little kiloton "friends" and talk things over. The Union of Concerned Scientists and fellow peaceniks will not like hearing that proliferation is not the problem but the solution, and Reaganite fundamentalists will deem such a solution less Taoist than Maoist, although the preacher of that very Taoist Sermon on the Mount himself elsewhere said, "If thou wilt be perfect, go, sell what thou hast, and give to the poor...and come follow me."

And why not? It makes no sense to think that humanity as a whole has more to fear from nuclear weapons in the hands of poor governments than rich governments, just because we're subjects of one of the rich ones.

There will be two sides in Megawar, all right, but the two sides are not going to be two nations. One side is the two mutually hostile governments, who have become politically, economically, and militarily dependent on each other's hostility to keep stud generals and defense contractors and commissars busy: that side is the mad, transpolar duality which may at any time commit itself and the human race to the *casus belli* when the odds are infinite. The *other* side in the Megawar is the rest of the human race. In this corner, we have the champion, militaristic Government. In the other corner, we have the challenger, all targeted people of the planet. But there isn't much of a challenge yet. Where *is* the challenger? What if they gave a peace and nobody came?

Once Megawar is launched, nationality ceases to exist. The ultimate atrocity has been committed, and every politician and military man who participated is thenceforward at war with the whole people of Earth, and all her various lifeforms. He is a world-killer. Every participant in the strike or counterstrike of Megawar, of whatever nationality, will have made himself a criminal, an enemy of the human race who might well hope for Nuremberg justice, if anyone is left alive to administer it, instead of the justice that overtook Mussolini when his countrymen hung him by his heels from a rail beside his girl friend and cut him up some before and after death. Some Rapture! If Megawar is committed by the superpowers, how long will survivors keep the illusion that somehow "our" government is less our enemy then than "their" government, or that they are different from us? Not long, I think—just until we look at the color of the dirty uniforms of looters and rapists who prowl in the aftermath of the clinical death of the planet (see "A Boy and His Dog") while waiting for cellular death to come.

More than one fearless leader has said, "If we ever have to use the nukes, it means we've failed." Is he a weenie? Failed what? Not having to? If using them is failure, then what is success? If a retaliatory strike means human extinction, and if surrendering after a first strike means human survival, by what other yardstick will our fearless leader measure success and failure, and *whose* success or failure—that of his ego, or of my two pre-kindergarten grandsons who live a few miles from a nuclear submarine slip (one of "ours")? If our fearless leader responds in kind to a first strike, my grandsons have failed indeed. Did somebody ask whether I would prefer them red to dead? No, asshole, there are other options; I would prefer them alive as rebels against whatever thanatotropic militarist government is then reigning, including that of red-white-and-blue fascist Nicaraguaphobes.

I'm writing these paragraphs on the fortieth anniversary of the total collapse of an insane Germany, a nation whose people had chosen a crazy leader and then deified the madman as their living Wotan, and, being possessed, went on to live out the story of the twilight and damnation of their half-forgotten devil-gods. A sentimental people, the Germans. We're sentimental too. I never met the Waffen SS, honored by Reagan this week at Bitburg (I had a fantasy-cartoon in mind that day: the President with his hand over his heart saying, *"Ich bin ein Waffen Bitburger"*), but I did on several occasions at various altitudes get sky-pocked messages from the Hermann Goering Panzer Division, whose 88-mm antiaircraft gunners were the nastiest shits in Italy, as far as I'm concerned, and the hottest shots. I still have a piece of their shrapnel I dug out of the fuselage a few inches from my ass the day I found out what cordite smells like. They killed a friend of mine. Why should I prefer Germans to Russians, whatever kind of government either of them chooses? Personal memories aside, der Waffen RR has made symbolic peace with mass murderers this week, and it's a bad omen. It's a bad omen too that 70 percent of the American people and 95 per cent of the Russian people approve of the way their rulers rule. Megawar needs the consent of the governed, and we have already given conditional consent. See Spinrad's "The Big Flash" for the transition to full consent.

Logos, Thanatos, Agape

If Megawar comes, it will come because human reason has finally and permanently prevailed over human compassion on a global scale, putting itself and the reasoner forever out of business. The world of the myriad things will have conquered the One forever. It's a possibility allowed for only in the theology of Vikings.

We worship reason in the West, partly because it has made us rich, and partly because we are heirs of the ancient Mediterranean civilization, not that of China or the Andes. "In the beginning was the Logos," wrote John, "...and the Logos was God." More than "word," *Logos* is the logic behind words—reason—which was supposed by some Greeks to be the original cause of the things-reasoned-about. John, an ex-stoic, identified God the Son with the divine Reason that brought the universe into being. "Through Him, all things were made which were made." The subjugation of all human mental activity to reason, to that orderly babble from the slight bulge in the left human temporal lobe, has been our tradition in the West ever since the Stoa, and the secularization of science strengthened rather than weakened that tradition, as Logos, through science, added a rich mathematical metaphor to the ordinary logical metaphor of grammar. But reason cuts apart, divides, separates. It also erects a screen of symbols between the thinker and the One. Reason has made us poor in compassion and rich in spirit *(animus)*.

Much of what we have historically considered quite reasonable, however, can be seen in hindsight as coldly murderous and banally evil. The development of the Bomb was a triumph of intellect. The decisions of the Inquisition were carefully reasoned. The behavior of Adolf Eichmann was rational. Scientists who plug for better weapons systems are impeccable in their left-brained thought. And why not trust Reason, which has bestowed such material blessings, if Reason is indeed the Son of God?

Because, in the myth of Genesis, Logos-Reason was the Snake, not the Savior. It was the ability to think in categories, the fruit of the tree of knowledge of good and evil, product of the Fall. This of course is heresy, but not an original one. The Gnostics, once a Western sect, were convinced that the world was created by the bad guys, and this is one Western tradition that the Church has repressed: the idea that whoever created the world was a rather stupid and arrogant fellow, Yaldabaoth, who made a lot of mistakes before Wisdom (Sophia) set him straight. In the beginning was the word, and the word was, for Gnostics, a pack of lies with which Yaldabaoth (or the Archons) deceived himself and his creatures.

Logos *does*, in a way, create the object-world, as a dark mirror between us and the One. A quark is an idea at first, and not a thing; it acquires thingness when a physicist chooses a noun *quark* to label an invariance in his calculations; until that moment, that universe which Zen Buddhists call "the myriad things" never included quarks. (Nor was there gravity before Newton; things just fell.) The other universe, "the One," is without form and void, as always. But through Logos, by name and description, has a thing been created: "Let there be *quark!*" Why? Because the rest of the myriad (and

Logos-created) things seem to harmonize better among themselves when quark's "existence" is recognized. Because it looks good in the green room of mind, hung there to hide broken plaster. *Dog* in the mind of a baby comes into being in a way not dissimilar to the creation of *quark* in the mind of a physicist; on the basis of interesting, observed behavior without the One, a name rings out: Bow-wow. And lo, dog is made. The fleas bite baby. The feel of the flea-bite is *tathata,* suchness, and so is the infant's wailing. Later "Fwees bite baby!" creates *fleas* through Logos. This is the way of the Fall, I think. This is the hereditary eating of the tree of knowledge of good and evil: learning how to talk, and to think in syllogisms, and do Boolean algebra. What makes it the Fall is not the acquisition of reason, but the displacement by reason of the original activity of seeing and hearing "the One," the void, the silence into which the Word will be spoken, in which babies and cats and mystical adepts carry on an existence we all once knew and forgot about when we learned to talk and think.

This original unbroken unity, this Tao, this God, this One, is not the enemy of reason, but the very mother of reason. We are, however, weaned. We forget what the world is like in the instant before it is apprehended by Logos.

And this algebra and this forgetfulness is by now haunting our genes like original sin. Before birth, babies are preparing for speech. Memory begins with speech, memory is reinforced and organized in the categories of speech. Before Logos, the memory-world is void and without form; there is only suchness, or Tao. After Logos brings rational speech, only rarely is the world void and without form, and then only for accomplished monks or yogins who have learned to live as infants (or cats) again in the silence of suchness. The rest of us live in the world of the myriad words-made-things, or things-made-words, the illusory world, the world of shadows in Plato's cave, the world of birth-and-death: *samsara,* created of, by, and through the Logos, discriminating Reason.

I point to the West's idolization of Logos, not to disparage science, for this idolatry preceded modern science by many centuries, but to preface the assertion that sometimes the use of reason is so inappropriate as to be either laughably or criminally insane, and that we need to learn to sacrifice reason when it's crazy to be rational. We recognize this need immediately in connection with sex; the logician who tries to be logical in the boudoir has always been good material for comedy. The only way to use logic in connection with sex is to avoid sex, if possible, and except for religious celibates, that's sad. Death is another subject inaccessible to reason, and so Dr. Strangelove, who insisted on using reason while the world faced global extinction, was also funny. Strangelovian logic is hilarious even in a straight Air Force study of the post-Megawar viability of paper money.

The West's idolatry of Logos—of reason, of order, of logic, of law, of science, of domination—has spread to the world. "Follow learning [Logos] and you pick up something new every day," said Lao-tzu. "Follow the Tao and you throw something away every day." You get indoor plumbing and TV sets for pursuing Logos. In pursuit of Tao you sit in the shade watching the waterfall, at least until an industrial or cultural revolution puts you in jail.

In the eighties, the dangerous ideological quarrel intensifies. The quarrel between Communist and Christian ideologues is strife internal to the same Church-of-the-Logos, and such internal quarrels have usually been the deadliest kind, fueled by theological hatred. If the disputes between the doomsday nations were merely economic and political, they might stop short of Megawar, but an *odium theologicum* exists between materialist logolatry and theist logolatry. The Marxist ideologue in the Kremlin and the Christian Fundamentalist ideologue here at home share a passion and an apocalyptic expectation of the other's impending extinction or damnation according two oddly symmetrical scenarios for the end of the world. Christianity has a script for the destruction of the world. Communism has a script for the destruction of Christianity and Capitalism. The directors of the play are following both scripts meticulously. Actors on neither side show a spirit of rebellion against the directors. There seems to be growing enthusiasm for the extremist bibliolatric churches and ministers who believe the imminent future is literally mapped out by the Book of Revelations, consistent with their belief that Genesis is literal history. This is the Christianity not of Agape, not even of Logos, but of Thanatos!

"In the beginning was the *Tao*," begins a Chinese translation of the Gospel of John (the *other* John), "and the *Tao* was with God, and the *Tao* was God." I prefer this translation to the Greek original, but it is really not what John, the Stoic, had in mind. It's an improvement, but translators are not supposed to make improvements. Contradicting this translation is the very first line of Lao-tzu's *Tao Te Ching*: "The Tao which can be communicated is not the eternal Tao." The tao which *can* be communicated is precisely the Logos, the word, the way of human discourse, logic, mathematics, science, law. Great indeed is the Logos, "the mother of the myriad things," Lao calls it. The mother, that is, of the communal human universe (as against, say, the communal universe deriving from dolphin speech); far greater is Tao, the way of Silence, the One, in which beats the compassionate heart. It is the Silence without which no Word can be spoken, the Emptiness without which no form can appear. It is the silent Night outside the glaring and roaring city of man, to which one in extremity may at last turn in recognition and spread wide his arms to her: *O Mother Chaos!* Save us from the outcome of our own mad Reason!

Walter M. Miller, Jr.
May, 1985

POSTSCRIPT TO THE INTRODUCTION
Martin H. Greenberg

Walter Miller died by his own hand in 1996 after decades, and perhaps a lifetime, of depression. His nearly forty stories and his great masterpiece, *A Canticle for Leibowitz*, were all he gave us, with virtually nothing after 1959, the year he turned thirty-seven.

We began work on *Beyond Armageddon* in late 1983, and it was published in 1985. Walt took it very seriously, rejecting some stories and writing extensively for the book. In fact, his introduction and notes constitute most of his published work after the seminal *A Canticle for Leibowitz* was released in 1959 and the publication of its sequel, *Saint Leibowitz and the Wild Horse Woman* (finished by Terry Bisson), in 1997.

Like any great science fiction writer, Walt was ahead of his time—just consider his discussion of Jerry Falwell and the rise of apocalyptic religious visions in the introduction to this book. He saw and feared the rise of fundamentalist religious movements before most people were even aware of them, although he didn't believe that religious fundamentalists would ever write science fiction or fantasy. On this last point he would be proved wrong by the publication of Tim LaHaye and Jerry Jenkins's *Left Behind* in 1996, which spawned a series of novels that have sold well over sixty million copies, becoming a publishing phenomenon and a subgenre of commercial fantasy.

One of Walt's great concerns was nuclear proliferation, which he believed would make nuclear war inevitable: in *Beyond Armageddon* he listed the countries he thought would soon have nuclear weapons, and he was largely correct. Among the countries he included are India, Israel, Pakistan, and South Africa, all of which have or are believed to have nuclear weapons today;

Libya, which has apparently dismantled its nuclear program; and Iran, which is believed to be only a few years away from developing nuclear weapons. On his list of future nuclear powers, only Argentina does not (apparently) have a current program dedicated to developing a weapon of mass destruction. The next couple of decades may well determine if our next generation bears witness to a nuclear exchange.

Nuclear holocaust was Walt's fear and that of his generation—fear of the Cold War turning hot. For a brief period the collapse of the Soviet Union promised a reprieve from the anxiety that spawned the bulk of these stories, but it was not to be: the rise of Islamic terrorism and the Internet, which provided the information for homegrown radiological, chemical, and biological devices, meant that the fear—and the response of writers to that fear—would continue.

Just consider the following, all of which were released since our anthology was first published: Japanese manga and anime such as *Akira* and *Fist of the North Star*; long-running series such as *Deathlands* by James Axler and *The Survivalist* by Jerry Ahern; numerous games such as *Battlefield: Apocalypse* and the *Fallout* series; and novels, films, and television series of enormously varying quality, from Margaret Atwood's *The Handmaid's Tale* and Sheri Tepper's *The Gate to Women's Country*, to *Cyborg* and similar films, to *The Terminator* and its sequels, to David Brin's wonderful *The Postman* (the novel, not the film).

But as Walter Miller knew all too well, tragedy is always personal, and I would like to dedicate this new edition of *Beyond Armageddon* to the writers of the stories in this anthology who are no longer with us:

Robert Abernathy
Poul Anderson
Ward Moore
Edgar Pangborn
Rog Phillips (Roger P. Graham)
John Wyndham
Roger Zelazny

1

For the most part, this book is about the aftermath of Megawar, but in a frequent speculative scenario, the last "war" in the world, rather than beginning with sneak megabangs by a superpower, escalates from a murderous scuffle where both sides are out of bounds—in a place such as Iran, Cuba, Pakistan, Nicaragua; the scuffle builds through angry frustration to a few rounds of kiloton-level tactical violence, and thence to the insane confrontation: the last called bluff.

Lucius Shepard's "Salvador" represents—here within the framework of this book more than Shepard intended—that small, pre-Megawar scuffle that lights the fuse, and it is not about the Megawar itself but about the Fundamental Weapon in war of any scale. "Ultimate" weapons become obsolete and are replaced by even more ultimate weapons, but the Fundamental Weapon, never obsolete this side of extinction, with which a society wages war on another, is always biological: the young human being trained to kill. Mother's lament, "I didn't raise my boy to be a soldier," is, if not hypocrisy, beside the point. She raises him in this society, and farms him out for training as a grunt at age five. His peer group raises him to be a soldier, urged on by motion picture, television, and toy industries (she can now buy him a cuddlesome little velvet "Nukie," a cute bomb with an American flag tailfin and its own tabletop silo). Grade school in my community (1929–1934) had a lot in common with Marine boot camp, and it hadn't changed much by the time my children attended the same county school system in the fifties. A bumper sticker from the Age of

Protest said, "What if they gave a war and nobody came?" Fat chance, even without conscription. It's like asking: What if they gave a schoolyard fist-fight and nobody came? And miss all that excited howling, shoving, and maybe blood? (See Jim Aikin's "My Life in the Jungle.")

The suicide rate among teenagers is higher than among adults, and more than one kid has joined up as a substitute for killing himself to escape emotional, social, or economic impoverishment. Dantzler was drafted, but no matter. The purpose of boot training is to arouse the impulse to suicide and then to turn it outward. The death wish is reversible as to direction. But how about when the Fundamental Weapon comes home? Is there a way to beat a sword like Dantzler into a plowshare?

SALVADOR
By Lucius Shepard

Three weeks before they wasted Tecolutla, Dantzler had his baptism of fire. The platoon was crossing a meadow at the foot of an emerald-green volcano, and being a dreamy sort, he was idling along, swatting tall grasses with his rifle barrel and thinking how it might have been a first-grader with crayons who had devised this elementary landscape of a perfect cone rising into a cloudless sky, when cap-pistol noises sounded on the slope. Someone screamed for the medic, and Dantzler dove into the grass, fumbling for his ampules. He slipped one from the dispenser and popped it under his nose, inhaling frantically; then, to be on the safe side, he popped another—"a double helpin' of martial arts," as DT would say—and lay with his head down until the drugs had worked their magic. There was dirt in his mouth, and he was afraid.

Gradually his arms and legs lost their heaviness, and his heart rate slowed. His vision sharpened to the point that he could see not only the pinpricks of fire blooming on the slope, but also the figures behind them, half-obscured by brush. A bubble of grim anger welled up in his brain, hardened by a fierce resolve, and he started moving toward the volcano. By the time he reached the base of the cone, he was all rage and reflexes. He spent the next forty minutes spinning acrobatically through the thickets, spraying shadows with bursts of his M–18; yet part of his mind remained distant from the action, marveling at his efficiency, at the comic-strip enthusiasm he felt for the task of killing. He shouted at the men he shot, and he shot them many more times than was necessary, like a child playing soldier.

"Playin' my ass!" DT would say. "You just actin' natural."

DT was a firm believer in the ampules; though the official line was that they contained tailored RNA compounds and pseudo-endorphins modified to an inhalant form, he held the opinion that they opened a man up to his inner nature. He was big, black, with heavily muscled arms and crudely stamped features, and he had come to the Special Forces direct from prison, where he had done a stretch for attempted murder; the palms of his hands were covered by jail tattoos—a pentagram and a horned monster. The words DIE HIGH were painted on his helmet. This was his second tour in Salvador, and Moody—who was Dantzler's buddy—said the drugs had addled DT's brains, that he was crazy and gone to hell.

"He collects trophies," Moody had said. "And not just ears like they done in 'Nam."

When Dantzler had finally gotten a glimpse of the trophies, he had been appalled. They were kept in a tin box in DT's pack and were nearly unrecognizable; they looked like withered brown orchids. But despite his revulsion, despite the fact that he was afraid of DT, he admired the man's capacity for survival and had taken to heart his advice to rely on the drugs.

On the way back down the slope, they discovered a live casualty, an Indian kid about Dantzler's age, nineteen or twenty. Black hair, adobe skin, and heavy-lidded brown eyes. Dantzler, whose father was an anthropologist and had done field work in Salvador, figured him for a Santa Ana tribesman; before leaving the States, Dantzler had pored over his father's notes, hoping this would give him an edge, and had learned to identify the various regional types. The kid had a minor leg wound and was wearing fatigue pants and a faded COKE ADDS LIFE T-shirt. This T-shirt irritated DT no end.

"What the hell you know 'bout Coke?" he asked the kid as they headed for the chopper that was to carry them deeper into Morazan

Province. "You think it's funny or somethin'?" He whacked the kid in the back with his rifle butt, and when they reached the chopper, he slung him inside and had him sit by the door. He sat beside him, tapped out a joint from a pack of Kools, and asked, "Where's Infante?"

"Dead," said the medic.

"Shit!" DT licked the joint so it would burn evenly. "Goddamn beaner ain't no use 'cept somebody else know Spanish."

"I know a little," Dantzler volunteered.

Staring at Dantzler, DT's eyes went empty and unfocused. "Naw," he said. "You don't know no Spanish."

Dantzler ducked his head to avoid DT's stare and said nothing; he thought he understood what DT meant, but he ducked away from the understanding as well. The chopper bore them aloft, and DT lit the joint. He let the smoke out his nostrils and passed the joint to the kid, who accepted gratefully.

"*Que sabor!*" he said, exhaling a billow; he smiled and nodded, wanting to be friends.

Dantzler turned his gaze to the open door. They were flying low between the hills, and looking at the deep bays of shadow in their folds acted to drain away the residue of the drugs, leaving him weary and frazzled. Sunlight poured in, dazzling the oil-smeared floor.

"Hey, Dantzler!" DT had to shout over the noise of the rotors. "Ask him whass his name!"

The kid's eyelids were drooping from the joint, but on hearing Spanish he perked up; he shook his head, though, refusing to answer. Dantzler smiled and told him not to be afraid.

"Ricardo Quu," said the kid.

"Kool!" said DT with false heartiness. "Thass my brand!" He offered his pack to the kid.

"*Gracias, no.*" The kid waved the joint and grinned.

"Dude's named for a godamn cigarette," said DT disparagingly, as if this were the height of insanity.

Dantzler asked the kid if there were more soldiers nearby, and once again received no reply, but apparently sensing in Dantzler a kindred soul, the kid leaned forward and spoke rapidly, saying that his village was Santander Jimenez, that his father was—he hesitated—a man of power. He asked where they were taking him. Dantzler returned a stony glare. He found it easy to reject the kid, and he realized later this was because he had already given up on him.

Latching his hands behind his head, DT began to sing—a wordless melody. His voice was discordant, barely audible above the rotors; but the tune had a familiar ring, and Dantzler soon placed it. The theme from *Star Trek*. It brought back memories of watching TV with his sister, laughing at the low-budget aliens and Scotty's Actors' Equity accent. He gazed out the door again. The sun was behind the hills, and the hillsides were unfeatured blurs of dark green smoke. Oh, God, he wanted to be home, to be anywhere but Salvador! A couple of the guys joined in the singing at DT's urging, and as the volume swelled, Dantzler's emotion peaked. He was on the verge of tears, remembering tastes and sights, the way his girl Jeanine had smelled, so clean and fresh, not reeking of sweat and perfume like the whores around Ilopango—finding all this substance in the banal touchstone of his culture and the illusions of the hillsides rushing past. Then Moody tensed beside him, and he glanced up to learn the reason why.

In the gloom of the chopper's belly, DT was as unfeatured as the hills—a black presence ruling them, more the leader of a coven than a platoon. The other two guys were singing their lungs out, and even the kid was getting into the spirit of things. "*Musica!*" he said at one point, smiling at everybody, trying to fan the flame of good feeling. He swayed to the rhythm and essayed a "la-la" now and again. But no one else was responding.

The singing stopped, and Dantzler saw that the whole platoon was staring at the kid, their expressions slack and dispirited.

"Space!" shouted DT, giving the kid a little shove. "The final frontier!"

The smile had not yet left the kid's face when he toppled out the door. DT peered after him; a few seconds later, he smacked his hand against the floor and sat back, grinning. Dantzler felt like screaming, the stupid horror of the joke was so at odds with the languor of his homesickness. He looked to the others for reaction. They were sitting with their heads down, fiddling with trigger guards and pack straps, studying their bootlaces, and seeing this, he quickly imitated them.

*   *   *

Morazan Province was spook country. Santa Ana spooks. Flights of birds had been reported to attack pistols; animals appeared at the perimeters of campsites and vanished when you shot them; dreams afflicted everyone who ventured there. Dantzler could not testify to the birds and animals, but he did have a recurring dream. In it the kid DT had killed was pinwheeling down through a golden fog, his T-shirt visible against the rolling backdrop, and sometimes a voice would boom out of the fog, saying, "You are killing my son." No, no, Dantzler would reply; it wasn't me, and besides, he's already dead. Then he would wake covered with sweat, groping for his rifle, his heart racing.

But the dream was not an important terror, and he assigned it no significance. The land was far more terrifying. Pine-forested ridges that stood out against the sky like fringes of electrified hair; little trails winding off into thickets and petering out, as if what they led to had been magicked away; gray rock faces along which they were forced to walk, hopelessly exposed to ambush. There were innumerable booby traps set by the guerillas, and they lost several men to rockfalls. It was the emptiest place of Dantzler's experience. No people, no animals, just a few hawks circling the solitudes between the ridges. Once in a while they found tunnels, and these they blew with the new gas grenades; the gas ignited the rich concentrations of hydrocarbons and sent flame sweeping through the entire system. DT would praise whoever had discovered the tunnel and would estimate in a loud voice how many beaners they had "refried." But Dantzler knew they were traversing pure emptiness and burning empty holes. Days, under debilitating heat, they humped the mountains, traveling seven, eight, even ten klicks up trails so steep that frequently the feet of the guy ahead of you would be on a level with your face; nights, it was cold, the darkness absolute, the silence so profound that Dantzler imagined he could hear the great humming vibration of the earth. They might have been anywhere or nowhere. Their fear was nourished by the isolation, and the only remedy was "martial arts."

Dantzler took to popping the pills without the excuse of combat. Moody cautioned him against abusing the drugs, citing rumors of bad side effects and DT's madness; but even he was using them more and more often. During basic training, Dantzler's D.I. had told the boots that the drugs were available only to the Special

Forces, that their use was optional; but there had been too many instances of lackluster battlefield performance in the last war, and this was to prevent a reoccurrence.

"The chickenshit infantry should take 'em," the D.I. had said. "You bastards are brave already. You're born killers, right?"

"Right, sir!" they had shouted.

"What are you?"

"Born killers, sir!"

But Dantzler was not a born killer; he was not even clear as to how he had been drafted, less clear as to how he had been manipulated into the Special Forces, and he had learned that nothing was optional in Salvador, with the possible exception of life itself.

The platoon's mission was reconnaissance and mop-up. Along with other Special Forces platoons, they were to secure Morazan prior to the invasion of Nicaragua; specifically, they were to proceed to the village of Tecolutla, where the Sandinista patrol had recently been spotted, and following that, they were to join up with the 1st Infantry and take part in the offensive against León, a provincial capital just across the Nicaraguan border. As Dantzler and Moody walked together, they frequently talked about the offensive, how it would be good to get down into flat country; occasionally they talked about the possibility of reporting DT, and once, after he had lead them on a forced night march, they toyed with the idea of killing him. But most often they discussed the ways of the Indians and the land, since this was what had caused them to become buddies.

Moody was slightly built, freckled, and red-haired; his eyes had the "thousand-yard stare" that came from too much war. Dantzler had seen winos with such vacant, lusterless stares. Moody's father had been in 'Nam, and Moody said it had been worse than Salvador because there had been no real commitment to win; but he thought Nicaragua and Guatemala might be the worst of all, especially if the Cubans sent in troops as they had threatened. He was adept at locating tunnels and detecting booby traps, and it was for this reason Dantzler had cultivated his friendship. Essentially a loner, Moody had resisted all advances until learning of Dantzler's father; thereafter he had buddied up, eager to hear about the field notes, believing they might give him an edge.

"They think the land has animal traits," said Dantzler one day as they climbed along a ridgetop. "Just like some kinds of fish look like plants or sea bottom, parts of the land look like plain ground, jungle...whatever. But when you enter them, you find you've entered the spirit world, the world of the *Sukias*."

"What's *Sukias*?" asked Moody.

"Magicians." A twig snapped behind Dantzler, and he spun around, twitching off the safety of his rifle. It was only Hodge—a lanky kid with the beginnings of a beer gut. He stared hollow-eyed at Dantzler and popped an ampule.

Moody made a noise of disbelief. "If they got magicians, why ain't they winnin'? Why ain't they zappin' us off the cliffs?"

"It's not their business," said Dantzler. "They don't believe in messing with worldly affairs unless it concerns them directly. Anyway, these places—the ones that look like normal land but aren't—they're called...." He drew a blank on the name. "*Aya*-something. I can't remember. But they have different laws. They're where your spirit goes to die after your body dies."

"Don't they got no heaven?"

"Nope. It just takes longer for your spirit to die, and so it goes to one of these places that's between everything and nothing."

"Nothin'," said Moody disconsolately, as if all his hopes for an afterlife had been dashed. "Don't make no sense to have spirits and not have no heaven."

"Hey," said Dantzler, tensing as wind rustled the pine boughs. "They're just a bunch of damn primitives. You know what their sacred drink is? Hot chocolate! My old man was a guest at one of their funerals, and he said they carried cups of hot chocolate balanced on these little red towers and acted like drinking it was going to wake them to the secrets of the universe." He laughed, and the laughter sounded tinny and psychotic to his own ears. "So you're going to worry about fools who think hot chocolate's holy water?"

"Maybe they just like it," said Moody. "Maybe somebody dyin' just give 'em an excuse to drink it."

But Dantzler was no longer listening. A moment before, as they emerged from pine cover onto the highest point of the ridge, a stony scarp open to the winds and providing a view of rumpled mountains and valleys extending to the horizon, he had popped an ampule. He felt so strong, so full of righteous purpose and controlled fury, it seemed only the sky was around him, that he was still ascending, preparing to do battle with the gods themselves.

Tecolutla was a village of white-washed stone tucked into a notch between two hills. From above, the houses—with their black windows and doorways—looked like an unlucky throw of dice. The streets ran uphill and down, diverging around boulders. Bougainvilleas and hibiscus speckled the hillsides, and there were tilled fields on the gentler slopes. It was a sweet, peaceful place when they arrived, and after they had gone it was once again peaceful; but its sweetness had been permanently banished. The reports of Sandinistas had proved accurate, and though they were casualties left behind to recuperate, DT had decided their presence called for extreme measures. Fu gas, frag grenades, and such. He had fired an M–60 until the barrel melted down, and then had manned the flamethrower. Afterward, as they rested atop the next ridge, exhausted and begrimed, having radioed in a chopper for resupply, he could not get over how one of the houses he had torched had resembled a toasted marshmallow.

"Ain't that how it was, man?" he asked, striding up and down the line. He did not care if they agreed about the house; it was a deeper question he was asking, one concerning the ethics of their actions.

"Yeah," said Dantzler, forcing a smile. "Sure did."

DT grunted with laughter. "You *know* I'm right, don'tcha man?"

The sun hung directly behind his head, a golden corona rimming a black oval, and Dantzler could not turn his eyes away. He felt weak and weakening, as if threads of himself were being spun loose and sucked into the blackness. He popped three ampules prior to the firefight, and his experience of Tecolutla had been a kind of mad whirling dance through the streets, spraying erratic bursts that appeared to be writing weird names on the walls. The leader of the Sandinistas had worn a mask—a gray face with a surprised hole of a mouth and pink circles around the eyes. A ghost face. Dantzler had been afraid of the mask and had poured round after round into it. Then, leaving the village, he had seen a small girl standing beside the shell of the last house, watching them, her colorless rag of a dress tattering in the breeze. She had been a victim of that malnutrition disease, the one that paled your skin and whitened your hair and left you retarded. He could not recall the name of the disease—things like names were slipping away from him—nor could he believe anyone had survived, and for a moment he had thought the spirit of the village had come out to mark their trail.

That was all he could remember of Tecolutla, all he wanted to remember. But he knew he had been brave.

Four days later, they headed up into a cloud forest. It was the dry season, but dry season or not, blackish gray clouds always shrouded these peaks. They were shot through by ugly glimmers of lightning, making it seem that malfunctioning neon signs were hidden beneath them, advertisements for evil. Everyone was jittery, and Jerry LeDoux—a slim, dark-haired Cajun kid—flat-out refused to go.

"It ain't reasonable," he said. "Be easier to go through the passes."

"We're on recon, man! You think the beaners be waitin' in the passes, wavin' their white flags?" DT whipped his rifle into firing position and pointed it at LeDoux. "C'mon, Louisiana man. Pop a few, and you feel different."

As LeDoux popped the ampules, DT talked to him.

"Look at it this way, man. This is your big adventure. Up there it be like all them animals shows on the tube. The savage kingdom, the unknown. Could be like Mars or somethin'. Monsters and shit, with big red eyes and tentacles. You wanna miss that, man? You wanna miss bein' the first grunt on Mars?"

Soon LeDoux was raring to go, giggling at DT's rap.

Moody kept his mouth shut, but he fingered the safety of his rifle and glared at DT's back. When DT turned to him, however, he relaxed. Since Tecolutla he had grown taciturn, and there seemed to be a shifting of lights and darks in his eyes, as if something were scurrying back and forth behind them. He had taken to wearing banana leaves on his head, arranging them under his helmet so the frayed ends stuck out the sides like strange green hair. He said this was camouflage, but Dantzler was certain it bespoke some secretive, irrational purpose. Of course DT had noticed Moody's spiritual erosion, and as they prepared to move out, he called Dantzler aside.

"He done found someplace inside his head that feel good to him," said DT. "He's tryin' to curl up into it, and once he do that he ain't gon' be responsible. Keep an eye on him."

Dantzler mumbled his assent, but was not enthused.

"I know he your fren', man, but that don't mean shit. Not the way things are. Now me, I don't give a damn 'bout you personally. But I'm your brother-in-arms, and thass somethin' you can count on... y'understand."

To Dantzler's shame, he did understand.

They had planned on negotiating the cloud forest by nightfall, but they had underestimated the difficulty. The vegetation beneath the clouds was lush—thick, juicy leaves that mashed underfoot, tangles of vines, trees with slick, pale bark and waxy leaves—and the visibility was only about fifteen feet. They were gray wraiths passing through grayness. The vague shapes of the foliage reminded Dantzler of fancifully engraved letters, and for a while he entertained himself with the notion that they were walking among the half-formed phrases of a constitution not yet manifest in the land. They barged off the trail, losing it completely, becoming veiled in spider webs and drenched by spills of water; their voices were oddly muffled, the tag ends of words swallowed up. After seven hours of this, DT reluctantly gave the order to pitch camp. They set electric lamps around the perimeter so they could see to string the jungle hammocks; the beam of light illuminated the moisture in the air, piercing the murk with jeweled blades. They talked in hushed tones, alarmed by the eerie atmosphere. When they had done with the hammocks, DT posted four sentries—Moody, Le-Doux, Dantzler, and himself. Then they switched off the lamps.

It grew pitch-dark, and the darkness was picked out by plips and plops, the entire spectrum of dripping sounds. To Dantzler's ears they blended into a gabbling speech. He imagined tiny Santa Ana demons talking about him, and to stave off paranoia he popped two ampules. He continued to pop them, trying to limit himself to one every half hour, but he was uneasy, unsure where to train his rifle in the dark, and he exceeded his limit. Soon it began to grow light again, and he assumed that more time had passed than he had thought. That often happened with the ampules—it was easy to lose yourself in being alert, in the wealth of perceptual detail available to your sharpened senses. Yet on checking his watch, he saw it was only a few minutes after two o'clock. His system was too inundated with the drugs to allow panic, but he twitched his head from side-to-side in tight little arcs to determine the source of the brightness. There did not appear to be a single source; it was simply that filaments of the cloud were gleaming, casting a diffuse golden glow, as if they were elements of a nervous system coming to life. He started to call out, then held back. The others must have seen the light, and they had given no cry; they probably had a good reason for their silence. He scrunched down flat, pointing his rifle out from the campsite.

Bathed in the golden mist, the forest had acquired an alchemic beauty. Beads of water glittered with gemmy brilliance; the leaves and vines and bark were gilded. Every surface shimmered with light...everything except a fleck of blackness hovering between two of the trunks, its size gradually increasing. As it swelled in his vision, he saw it had the shape of a bird, its wings beating, flying toward him from an inconceivable distance—inconceivable, because the dense vegetation did not permit you to see very far in a straight line, and yet the bird was growing larger with such slowness that it must have been coming from a long way off. It was not really flying, he realized; rather, it was as if the forest were painted on a piece of paper, as if someone were holding a lit match behind it and burning a hole, a hole that maintained the shape of a bird as it spread. He was transfixed, unable to react. Even when it had blotted out half the light, when he lay before it no bigger than a mote in relation to its huge span, he could not move or squeeze the trigger. And then the blackness swept over him. He had the sensation of being borne along at incredible speed, and he could no longer hear the dripping of the forest.

"Moody!" he shouted. "DT!"

But the voice that answered belonged to neither of them. It was hoarse, issuing from every part of the surrounding blackness, and he recognized it as the voice of his recurring dream.

"You are killing my son," it said. "I have led you here, to this *ayahuamaco*, so he may judge you."

Dantzler knew to his bones the voice was that of the *Sukia* of the village of Santander Jimenez. He wanted to offer a denial, to explain his innocence, but all he could manage was, "No." he said it tearfully, hopelessly, his forehead resting on his rifle barrel. Then his mind gave a savage twist, and his soldiery self regained control. He ejected an ampule from his dispenser and popped it.

The voice laughed—malefic, damning laughter whose vibrations shuddered Dantzler. He opened up with the rifle, spraying fire in all directions. Filigrees of golden holes appeared in the blackness, tendrils of mist coiled through them. He kept on firing until the blackness shattered and fell in jagged sections toward him. Slowly. Like shards of black glass dropping through water. He emptied the rifle and flung himself flat, shielding his head with his arms, expecting to be sliced into bits; but nothing touched him. At last he peeked between his arms; then—amazed, because the forest was now a uniform lustrous yellow—he rose to his knees. He scraped his hand on one of the crushed leaves beneath him, and blood welled from the cut. The broken fibers of the leaf were as stiff as wires. He stood, a giddy trickle of hysteria leaking up from the bottom of his soul. It was no forest, but a building of solid gold worked to resemble a forest—the sort of conceit that might have been fabricated for the child of an emperor. Canopied by golden leaves, columned by slender golden trunks, carpeted by golden grasses. The water beads were diamonds. All the gleam and glitter soothed his apprehension; here was something out of a myth, a habitat for princesses and wizards and dragons. Almost gleeful, he turned to the campsite to see how the others were reacting.

Once, when he was nine years old, he had sneaked into the attic to rummage through the boxes and trunks, and he had run across an old morocco-bound copy of *Gulliver's Travels*. He had been taught to treasure old books, and so he had opened it eagerly to look at the illustrations, only to find that the centers of the pages had been eaten away, and there, right in the heart of the fiction, was a nest of larvae. Pulpy, horrid things. It had been an awful sight, but one unique in his experience, and he might have studied those crawling scraps of life for a very long time if his father had not interrupted. Such a sight was now before him, and he was numb with it.

They were all dead. He should have guessed they would be; he had given no thought to them while firing his rifle. They had been struggling out of their hammocks when the bullets hit, and as a result, they were hanging half-in, half-out, their limbs dangling, blood pooled beneath them. The veils of golden mist made them look dark and mysterious and malformed, like monsters killed as they emerged from their cocoons. Dantzler could not stop staring, but he was shrinking inside himself. It was not his fault. That thought kept swooping in and out of a flock of less acceptable thoughts; he wanted to stay put, to be true, to alleviate the sick horror he was beginning to feel.

"What's your name?" asked a girl's voice behind him.

She was sitting on a stone about twenty feet away. Her hair was a tawny shade of gold, her skin a half-tone lighter, and her dress was cunningly formed out of the mist. Only her eyes were real. Brown, heavy-lidded eyes—they were at variance with the rest of her face, which had the fresh, unaffected beauty of an American teenager.

"Don't be afraid," she said, and patted the ground, inviting him to sit beside her.

He recognized the eyes, but it was no matter. He badly needed the consolation she could offer; he walked over and sat down. She let him lean his head against her thigh.

"What's your name?" she repeated.

"Dantzler," he said. "John Dantzler." And then he added, "I'm from Boston. My father's..." It would be too difficult to explain about anthropology. "He's a teacher."

"Are there many soldiers in Boston?" She stroked his cheek with a golden finger.

The caress made Dantzler happy. "Oh, no," he said. "They hardly know there's a war going on."

"This is true?" she said, incredulous.

"Well, they *do* know about it, but it's just news on the TV to them. They've got more pressing problems. Their jobs, families."

"Will you let them know about the war when you return home?" she asked. "Will you do that for me?"

Dantzler had given up hope of returning home, of surviving, and her assumption that he would do both acted to awaken his gratitude. "Yes," he said fervently. "I will."

"You must hurry," she said. "If you stay in the *ayahuamaco* too long, you will never leave. You must find the way out. It is a way not of directions or trails, but of events."

"Where is this place?" he asked, suddenly aware of how much he had taken it for granted.

She shifted her leg away, and if he had not caught himself on the stone, he would have fallen. When he looked up, she had vanished. He was surprised that her disappearance did not alarm him; in reflex he slipped out a couple of ampules, but after a moment's reflection he decided not to use them. It was impossible to slip them back into the dispenser, so he tucked them into the interior webbing of his helmet for later. He doubted he would need them, though. He felt strong, competent, and unafraid.

Dantzler stepped carefully between the hammocks, not wanting to brush against them; it might have been his imagination, but they seemed to be bulged down lower than before, as if death had weighed out heavier than life. That heaviness was in the air, pressuring him. Mist rose like golden steam from the corpses, but the sight no longer affected him—perhaps because the mist gave the illusion of being their souls. He picked up a rifle with a full magazine and headed off into the forest.

The tips of the golden leaves were sharp, and he had to ease past them to avoid being cut; but he was at the top of his form, moving gracefully, and the obstacles barely slowed his pace. He was not even anxious about the girl's warning to hurry; he was certain the way out would soon present itself. After a minute or so, he heard voices and after another few seconds, he came to a clearing divided by a stream, one so perfectly reflecting that its banks appeared to enclose a wedge of golden mist. Moody was squatting to the left of the stream, staring at the blade of his survival knife and singing under his breath—a wordless melody that had the erratic rhythm of a trapped fly. Beside him lay Jerry LeDoux, his throat slashed from ear to ear. DT was sitting on the other side of the stream; he had been shot just above the knee, and though he had ripped up his shirt for bandages and tied off the leg with a tourniquet, he was not in good shape. He was sweating, and the gray chalky pallor infused his skin. The entire scene had the weird vitality of something that had materialized in a magic mirror, a bubble of reality enclosed within a gilt frame.

DT heard Dantzler's footfalls and glanced up. "Waste him!" he shouted, pointing at Moody.

Moody did not turn from contemplation of the knife. "No," he said, as if speaking to someone whose image was held in the blade.

"Waste him, man!" screamed DT. "He killed LeDoux!"

"Please," said Moody to the knife. "I don't want to."

There was blood clotted on his face, more blood on the banana leaves sticking out of his helmet.

"Did you kill Jerry?" asked Dantzler; while he addressed the question to Moody, he did not relate to him as an individual, only as part of a design whose messages he had to unravel.

"Jesus Christ! Waste him!" DT smashed his fist against the ground in frustration.

"O.K.," said Moody. With an apologetic look, he sprang to his feet and charged Dantzler, swinging the knife.

Emotionless, Dantzler stitched a line of fire across Moody's chest; he went sideways into the bushes and down.

"What the hell was you waitin' for!" DT tried to rise, but winced and fell back. "Damn! Don't know if I can walk."

"Pop a few," Dantzler suggested mildly.

"Yeah. Good thinkin', man." DT fumbled for his dispenser.

Dantzler peered into the bushes to see where Moody had fallen. He felt nothing, and this pleased him. He was weary of feeling.

DT popped an ampule with a flourish, as if making a toast, and inhaled. "Ain't you gon' to do some, man?"

"I don't need them," said Dantzler. "I'm fine."

The stream interested him; it did not reflect the mist, as he had supposed, but was itself a seam of the mist.

"How many you think they was?" asked DT.

"How many what?"

"Beaners, man! I wasted three or four after they hit us, but I couldn't tell how many they was."

Dantzler considered this in light of his own interpretation of events and Moody's conversation with the knife. It made sense. A Santa Ana kind of sense.

"Beats me," he said. "But I guess there's less than there used to be."

DT snorted. "You got *that* right!" He heaved to his feet and limped to the edge of the stream. "Gimme a hand across."

Dantzler reached out to him, but instead of taking his hand, he grabbed his wrist and pulled him off balance. DT teetered on his good leg, then toppled and vanished beneath the mist. Dantzler had expected him to fall, but he surfaced instantly, mist clinging to his skin. Of course, thought Dantzler; his body would have to die before his spirit would fall.

"What you doin', man?" DT was more disbelieving than enraged.

Dantzler planted a foot in the middle of his back and pushed him down until his head was submerged. DT bucked and clawed at the foot and managed to come to his hands and knees. Mist slithered from his eyes, his nose, and he choked out the words "...kill you...." Dantzler pushed him down again; he got into pushing him down and letting him up, over and over. Not so as to torture him. Not really. It was because he had suddenly understood the nature of the *ayahuamaco's* laws, that they were approximations of normal laws, and he further understood that his actions had to approximate those of someone jiggling a key in a lock. DT was the key to the way out, and Dantzler was jiggling him, making sure all the tumblers were engaged.

Some of the vessels in DT's eyes had burst, and the whites were occluded by films of blood. When he tried to speak, mist curled from his mouth. Gradually his struggles subsided; he clawed runnels in the gleaming yellow dirt of the bank and shuddered. His shoulders were knobs of black land floundering in a mystic sea.

For a long time after DT sank from view, Dantzler stood beside the stream, uncertain of what was left to do and unable to remember a lesson he had been taught. Finally, he shouldered his rifle and walked away from the clearing. Morning had broken, the mist had thinned, and the forest had regained its usual coloration. But he scarcely noticed these changes, still troubled by his faulty memory. Eventually he let it slide—it would all come clearer sooner or later. He was just happy to be alive. After a while he began to kick his rifle in a carefree fashion against the weeds

When the 1st Infantry poured across the Nicaraguan border and wasted León, Dantzler was having a quiet time at the VA hospital in Ann Arbor, Michigan; and at the precise moment the bulletin was flashed nationwide, he was sitting in the lounge, watching the American League playoffs between Detroit and Texas. Some of the patients ranted at the interruption, while others shouted them down, wanting to hear the details. Dantzler expressed no reaction whatsoever. He was solely concerned with being a model patient; however, noticing that one of the staff was giving him a clinical stare, he added his weight on the side of the baseball fans. He did not want to appear too controlled. The doctors were as suspicious of that sort of behavior as they were of its contrary. But the funny thing was—at least it was funny to Dantzler—that his feigned annoyance at the bulletin was an exemplary proof of his control, his expertise at moving through life the way he had moved through the golden leaves of the cloud forest. Cautiously, gracefully, efficiently. Touching nothing, and being touched by nothing. That was the lesson he had learned—to be as perfect a counterfeit of a man as the *ayahuamaco* had been of the land; to adopt the various stances of a man, and yet, by virtue of his distance from things human, to be all the more prepared for the onset of crisis or a call to action. He saw nothing aberrant in this; even the doctors would admit that men were little more than organized pretense. If he was different from other men, it was only that he had a deeper awareness of the principles on which his personality was founded.

When the battle of Managua was joined, Dantzler was living at home. His parents had urged him to go easy in readjusting to civilian life, but he had immediately gotten a job as a management trainee in a bank. Each morning he would drive to work and spend a controlled, quiet eight hours; each night he would watch TV with his mother, and before going to bed, he would climb to the attic and inspect the trunk containing his souvenirs of war—helmet, fatigues, knife, boots. The doctors had insisted he face his experiences, and this ritual was his way of following their instructions. All in all, he was quite pleased with his progress, but he still had problems. He had not been able to force himself to venture out at night, remembering too well the darkness in the cloud forest, and he had rejected his friends, refusing to see them or answer their calls—he was not secure with the idea of friendship. Further, despite his methodical approach to life, he was prone to a nagging restlessness, the feeling of a chore left undone.

One night his mother came into his room and told him that an old friend Phil Curry, was on the phone. "Please talk to him, Johnny," she said. "He's been drafted, and I think he's a little scared."

The word "drafted" struck a responsive chord in Dantzler's soul, and after brief deliberation, he went downstairs and picked up the receiver.

"Hey," said Phil. "What's the story, man? Three months, and you don't even give me a call."

"I'm sorry," said Dantzler. "I haven't been feeling so hot."

"Yeah, I understand." Phil was silent a moment. "Listen, man. I'm leavin', y'know, and we're havin' a big send-off at Sparky's. It's goin' on right now. Why don't you come down?"

"I don't know."

"Jeanine's here, man. Y'know, she's still crazy 'bout you, talks 'bout you alla time. She don't go out with nobody."

Dantzler was unable to think of anything to say.

"Look," said Phil, "I'm pretty weirded out by this soldier shit. I hear it's pretty bad down there. If you got anything you can tell me 'bout what it's like, man, I'd 'preciate it."

Dantzler could relate to Phil's concern, his desire for an edge, and besides, it felt right to go. Very right. He would take some precautions against the darkness.

"I'll be there," he said.

It was a foul night, spitting snow, but Sparky's parking lot was jammed. Dantzler's mind was flurried like the snow, crowded like the lot—thoughts whirling in, jockeying for position, melting away. He hoped his mother would not wait up, he wondered if Jeanine still wore her hair long, he was worried because the palms of his hands were unnaturally warm. Even with the car windows rolled up, he could hear loud music coming from inside the club. Above the door the words SPARKY'S ROCK CITY were being spelled out a letter at a time in red neon, and when the spelling was complete, the letters flashed off and on and a golden neon explosion bloomed around them. After the explosion, the entire sign went dark for a split second, and the big ramshackle building seemed to grow large and merge with the black sky. He had an idea it was watching him, and he shuddered—one of those sudden lurches downward of that kind that take you just before you fall asleep. He knew the people inside did not intend him any harm, but he also knew that places have a way of changing people's intent, and he did not want to be caught off guard. Sparky's might be such a place, might be a huge black presence camouflaged by neon, its true substance one with the abyss of the sky, the phosphorescent snowflakes jittering in his headlights, the wind keening through the side vent. He would have liked very much to drive home and forget about his promise to Phil; however, he felt a responsibility to explain about the war. More than a responsibility, an evangelistic urge. He would tell them about the kid falling out of the chopper, the white-haired girl in Tecolutla, the emptiness. God, yes! How you went down chock-full of ordinary American thoughts and dreams, memories of smoking weed and chasing tail and hanging out and freeway flying with a case of something cold, and how you smuggled back a human-shaped container of pure Salvadorian emptiness. Primo grade. Smuggled it back to the land of silk and money, of mindfuck video games and topless tennis matches and fast-food solutions to the nutritional problem. Just a taste of Salvador would banish all those trivial obsessions. Just a taste. It would be easy to explain.

Of course, some things beggared explanation.

He bent down and adjusted the survival knife in his boot so the hilt would not rub against his calf. From his coat pocked he withdrew the two ampules he had secreted in his helmet that long-ago night in the cloud forest. As the neon explosion flashed once more, glimmers of gold coursed along their shiny surfaces. He did not think he would need them; his hand was steady, and his purpose was clear. But to be on the safe side, he popped them both.

2

I knew and loved a kid a lot like Dantzler. Didn't everybody?

There might be *one* world in which the trail through Tecolutla leads to nuclear Armageddon, and quite another world in which the same trail twists and winds its way into global peace. The trail seems somehow to depend on human choice, and the next story is about such a choice.

Jonathan Schell wrote: "The extra worlds offered by science fiction may provide us with an escape in imagination from the tight trap that our species is caught in in reality."[1]

Maybe. At Sheckley's "Store" these extra worlds are even offered for sale, but judge for yourself about the "trap" and the "escape" and the "reality." The deal reminds me of Schrödinger's cat.

The "many-worlds" interpretation of quantum mechanics, as an alternative to the "orthodox" Copenhagen interpretation, was seriously proposed by three physicists named Everett, Wheeler, and Graham, and cropped up in a professional paper by Everett about two years before Sheckley's story was published in 1959. The Everett–Wheeler–Graham theory holds that the "wave function" of quantum mechanics, which represents all the possibilities of the outcome of an experimental observation and which is usually said to "collapse" when the act of observation itself actualizes only *one* of the many possibilities, is a physical reality which continues after the observation, but in separate

[1]Jonathan Schell, *The Fate of the Earth* (New York: Avon, 1980).

discrete universes, in each of which exists a new version of the observer who sees the occurrence of one of the other possibilities defined by the wave function. There is no "collapse" of the function, but a realization of all its possibilities by fissioning universes.[2]

Is the wave-function a physical reality itself, or is it only a mathematical fiction which ceases to exist when an unobserved reality is "realized" by the act of observation? In the famous "Schrödinger's Cat" thought-experiment, a cat is placed in a box without windows, and the box contains a lethal device which may be triggered (or not) by a random event, such as an occasional pulse from a cosmic-ray detector. As time passes, the probability mounts that the cat inside the box is dead, but without actually opening the box, the situation can only be described in terms of probability, something like the wave function. When the box is opened, the cat is seen to be either dead or alive. The probability has become unity, actualized by the observation. The wave function collapses. But according to the many-worlds interpretation there is no collapse; the act of opening the box actualizes *both* possibilities, causing the universe to branch. One universe contains the observer and the dead cat; the other universe contains an observer-counterpart and a purring kitty-counterpart. That's according to the Everett–Wheeler–Graham line of reasoning. Sound crazy to you? Try the "orthodox" interpretation of quantum mechanics, if you think orthodoxy any the less mind-boggling. Or try shopping for a better world at Sheckley's store. You'll see why a patron of that establishment reminds me of Schrödinger's boxed cat. The difference is that the patron has a choice of outcomes. Or has he?

THE STORE OF THE WORLDS
by Robert Sheckley

Mr. Wayne came to the end of the long, shoulder-high mound of gray rubble, and there was the Store of the Worlds. It was exactly

[2]See Gary Zukav's *The Dancing Wu Li Masters* (New York: Bantam) for a nonmathematical description of the conceptual difficulties in reconciling the results of quantum mechanics with our commonsense ideas of the world(s).

as his friends had described: a small shack constructed of bits of lumber, parts of cars, a piece of galvanized iron, and a few rows of crumbling bricks, all daubed over with a watery blue paint.

He glanced back down the long lane of rubble to make sure he hadn't been followed. He tucked his parcel more firmly under his arm; then, with a little shiver at his own audacity, he opened the door and slipped inside.

"Good morning," the proprietor said.

He, too, was exactly as described: a tall, crafty-looking old fellow with narrow eyes and downcast mouth. His name was Tompkins. He sat in an old rocking chair, and perched on the back of it was a blue-and-green parrot. There was one other chair in the store, and a table. On the table was a rusted hypodermic.

"I've heard about your store from friends," Mr. Wayne said.

"Then you know my price," Tompkins said."Have you brought it?"

"Yes," said Mr. Wayne, holding up his parcel. "All my worldly goods. But I want to ask first—"

"They always want to ask," Tompkins said to the parrot, who blinked. "Go ahead, ask."

"I want to know what really happens."

Tompkins sighed. "What happens is that: I give you an injection which knocks you out. Then, with the aid of certain gadgets which I have in the back of the store, I liberate your mind."

Tompkins smiled as he said that, and his silent parrot seemed to smile, too.

"What happens then?" Mr. Wayne asked.

"Your mind, liberated from its body, is able to choose from the countless probability worlds which the earth casts off in every second of its existence."

Grinning now, Tompkins sat up in his rocking chair and began to show signs of enthusiasm.

"Yes, my friend, though you might not have suspected it, from the moment this battered earth was born out of the sun's fiery womb, it cast off its alternate-probability worlds. Worlds without end, emanating from events large and small; every Alexander and every amoeba creating worlds, just as ripples will spread in a pond no matter how big or how small the stone you throw. Doesn't every object cast a shadow? Well, my friend, the earth itself is four-dimensional; therefore it casts three-dimensional shadows, solid re-flections of itself, through every moment of its being. Millions, billions of earths! An infinity of earths! And your mind, liberated by me, will be able to select any of these worlds and live upon it for a while."

Mr. Wayne was uncomfortably aware that Tompkins sounded like a circus barker, proclaiming marvels that simply couldn't exist. But, Mr. Wayne reminded himself, things had happened within his own lifetime which he would never have believed possible. Never! So perhaps the wonders that Tompkins spoke of were possible, too.

Mr. Wayne said, "My friends also told me—"

"That I was an out-and-out fraud?" Tompkins asked.

"Some of them *implied* that," Mr. Wayne said cautiously. "But I try to keep an open mind. They also said—"

"I know what your dirty-minded friends said. They told you about the fulfillment of desire. Is that what you want to hear about?"

"Yes," said Mr. Wayne. "They told me that whatever I wished for—whatever I wanted—"

"Exactly," Tompkins said. "The thing could work in no other way. There are the infinite worlds to choose among. Your mind chooses and is guided only by desire. Your deepest desire is the only thing that counts. If you have been harboring a secret dream of murder—"

"Oh, hardly, hardly!" cried Mr. Wayne.

"—then you will go to a world where you *can* murder, where you can roll in blood, where you can outdo de Sade or Nero or whoever your idol may be. Suppose it's power you want? Then you'll choose a world where you are a god, literally and actually. A bloodthirsty Juggernaut, perhaps, or an all-wise Buddha."

"I doubt very much if I—"

"There are other desires, too," Tompkins said. "All heavens and all hells will be open to you. Unbridled sexuality. Gluttony, drunk-enness, love, fame—anything you want."

"Amazing!" said Mr. Wayne.

"Yes," Tompkins agreed. "Of course, my little list doesn't exhaust all the possibilities, all the combinations and permutations of desire. For all I know, you might want a simple, placid, pastoral existence on a South Sea island among idealized natives."

"That sounds more like me," Mr. Wayne said with a shy laugh.

"But who knows?" Tompkins asked. "Even you might not know what your true desires are. They might involve your own death."

"Does that happen often?" Mr. Wayne asked anxiously.

"Occasionally."

"I wouldn't want to die," Mr. Wayne said.

"It hardly ever happens," Tompkins said, looking at the parcel in Mr. Wayne's hands.

"If you say so.... But how do I know all this is real? Your fee is extremely high; it'll take everything I own. And for all I know, you'll give me a drug and I'll just *dream!* Everything I own just for a— shot of heroin and a lot of fancy words!"

Tompkins smiled reassuringly. "The experience has no druglike quality about it. And no sensation of a dream, either."

"If it's *true,*" Mr. Wayne said a little petulantly, "why can't I stay in the world of my desire for good?"

"I'm working on that," Tompkins said. "That's why I charge so high a fee—to get materials, to experiment. I'm trying to find a way of making the transition permanent. So far I haven't been able to loosen the cord that binds a man to his own earth—and pulls him back to it. Not even the great mystics could cut that cord, except with death. But I still have my hopes."

"It would be a great thing if you succeeded," Mr. Wayne said politely.

"Yes, it would!" Tompkins cried with a surprising burst of passion. "For then I'd turn my wretched shop into an escape hatch! My process would be free then, free for everyone! Everyone could go to the earth of his desires, the earth that really suited him and leave *this* damned place to the rats and worms—"

Tompkins cut himself off in midsentence and became icy calm. "But I fear my prejudices are showing. I can't offer a permanent escape from this world yet, not one that doesn't involve death. Perhaps I never will be able to. For now, all I can offer you is a vacation, a change, a taste of another world and a look at your own desires. You know my fee. I'll refund if it the experience isn't satisfactory."

"That's good of you," Mr. Wayne said quite earnestly. "But there's that other matter my friends told me about. The ten years off my life."

"That can't be helped," Tompkins said, "and can't be refunded.

My process is a tremendous strain on the nervous system, and life expectancy is shortened accordingly. That's one of the reasons why our so-called government has declared my process illegal."

"But they don't enforce the ban very firmly," Mr. Wayne said.

"No. Officially the process is banned as a harmful fraud. But officials are men, too. They'd like to leave this earth, just like everyone else."

"The cost," Mr. Wayne mused, gripping his parcel tightly. "And ten years off my life! For the fulfillment of my secret desires.... Really, I must give this some thought."

"Think away," Tompkins said indifferently.

All the way home Mr. Wayne thought about it. When his train reached Port Washington, Long Island, he was still thinking. And driving his car from the station to his house, he was still thinking about Tompkins's crafty old face, and worlds of probability, and the fulfillment of desire.

But when he stepped inside his home, those thoughts had to stop. Janet, his wife, wanted him to speak sharply to the maid, who had been drinking again. His son, Tommy, wanted help with the sloop, which was to be launched tomorrow. And his baby daughter wanted to tell about her day in kindergarten.

Mr. Wayne spoke pleasantly but firmly to the maid. He helped Tommy put the final coat of copper paint on the sloop's bottom, and he listened to Peggy tell her adventures in the playground.

Later, when the children were in bed and he and Janet were alone in their living room, she asked him if something was wrong.

"Wrong?"

"You seem to be worried about something," Janet said. "Did you have a bad day at the office?"

"Oh, just the usual sort of thing..."

He certainly was not going to tell Janet, or anyone else, that he had taken the day off and gone to see Tompkins in his crazy old Store of the Worlds. Nor was he going to speak about the right every man should have, once in his lifetime, to fulfill his most secret desires. Janet, with her good common sense, would never understand that.

The next days at the office were extremely hectic. All of Wall

Street was in a mild panic over events in the Middle East and in Asia, and stocks were reacting accordingly. Mr. Wayne settled down to work. He tried not to think of the fulfillment of desire at the cost of everything he possessed, with ten years of his life thrown in for good measure. It was crazy! Old Tompkins must be insane!

On weekends he went sailing with Tommy. The old sloop was behaving very well, taking practically no water through her bottom seams. Tommy wanted a new suit of racing sails, but Mr. Wayne sternly rejected that. Perhaps next year, if the market looked better. For now, the old sails would have to do.

Sometimes at night, after the children were asleep, he and Janet would go sailing. Long Island Sound was quiet then and cool. Their boat glided past the blinking buoys, sailing toward the swollen yellow moon.

"I *know* something's on your mind," Janet said.

"Darling, please!"

"Is there something you're keeping from me?"

"Nothing!"

"Are you sure? Are you absolutely sure?"

"Absolutely sure."

"Then, put your arms around me. That's right..."

And the sloop sailed itself for a while.

Desire and fulfillment....But autumn came and the sloop had to be hauled. The stock market regained some stability, but Peggy caught the measles. Tommy wanted to know the difference between ordinary bombs, atom bombs, hydrogen bombs, cobalt bombs and all the other kinds of bombs that were in the news. Mr. Wayne explained to the best of his ability. And the maid quit unexpectedly.

Secret desires were all very well. Perhaps he *did* want to kill someone or live on a South Sea island. But there were responsibilities to consider. He had two growing children and the best of wives.

Perhaps around Christmastime....

But in midwinter there was a fire in the unoccupied guest room due to defective wiring. The firemen put out the blaze without much damage, and no one was hurt. But it put any thought of Tompkins out of his mind for a while. First the bedroom had to be repaired, for Mr. Wayne was very proud of his gracious old house.

Business was still frantic and uncertain due to the international situation. Those Russians, those Arabs, those Greeks, those Chinese. The intercontinental missiles, the atom bombs, the Sputniks.... Mr. Wayne spent long days at the office and sometimes evenings, too. Tommy caught the mumps. A part of the roof had to be reshingled. And then already it was time to consider the spring launching of the sloop.

A year had passed, and he'd had very little time to think of secret desires. But perhaps next year. In the meantime...

"Well?" said Tompkins. "Are you all right?"

"Yes, quite all right," Mr. Wayne said. He got up from the chair and rubbed his forehead.

"Do you want a refund?" Tompkins asked.

"No. The experience was quite satisfactory."

"They always are," Tompkins said, winking lewdly at the parrot. "Well, what was yours?"

"A world of the recent past," Mr. Wayne said.

"A lot of them are. Did you find out about your secret desire? Was it murder? Or a South Sea island?"

"I'd rather not discuss it," Mr. Wayne said pleasantly but firmly.

"A lot of people won't discuss it with me," Tompkins said sulkily. "I'll be damned if I know why."

"Because—well, I think the world of one's secret desire seems sacred, somehow. No offense.... Do you think you'll ever be able to make it permanent? The world of one's choice, I mean?"

The old man shrugged his shoulders. "I'm trying. If I succeed, you'll hear about it. Everyone will."

"Yes, I suppose so." Mr. Wayne undid his parcel and laid its contents on the table. The parcel contained a pair of army boots, a knife, two coils of copper wire, and three small cans of corned beef.

Tompkins's eyes glittered for a moment. "Quite satisfactory," he said. "Thank you."

"Good-bye," said Mr. Wayne. "And thank *you*."

Mr. Wayne left the shop and hurried down to the end of the lane of gray rubble. Beyond it, as far as he cold see, lay flat fields of rubble, brown and gray and black. Those fields, stretching to every horizon, were made of the twisted corpses of buildings, the shattered remnants of trees and the fine white ash that once was human flesh and bone.

"Well," Mr. Wayne said to himself, "at least we gave as good as we got."

His year in the past had cost him everything he owned and ten years of life thrown in for good measure. Had it been a dream? It was still worth it! But now he had to put away all thought of Janet and the children. That was finished, unless Tompkins perfected his process. Now he had to think about his own survival.

He picked his way carefully through the rubble, determined to get back to the shelter before dark, before the rats came out. If he didn't hurry, he'd miss the evening potato ration.

3 _____

How do you spell relief? S-E-X? D-E-A-T-H? In 1941, I met a graduate student in chemistry—I'll call him "Homer Hamhocks"—who was fully conscious of his desire to make the world a wasteland, and I think he was hoping the Chemistry Department would let him make the extermination of mankind (or maybe just womankind) the subject of his doctoral research. He made this his ambition for the understandable reason that his involuntary sexual orientation was not fully appreciated on this planet. He's had forty-four years to work on the project since then, unless he's chewed a cyanide cap by now, and I do worry that he may have contributed something in chemistry or genetics to the advancement of the doomsday clock. Jesse Helms has been doing his Chicken Little routine because the Russians are splicing cobra-venom genes into common disease organisms, he says, and wants us to do it too. Catch a common bug, die of venom. True or not, Homer would have loved that idea, as he must have loved the Bomb. Of course, if the Everett–Wheeler–Graham theory is correct, there's a world in which Homer has come out of the closet and relinquished the grudge by now. We're safer if that world is our own. Homer was a genius, or so he told me.

While Mr. Wayne's unconscious (and Homer's conscious) attachment to Thanatos is shared by many, the sentiment expressed by General Chapman in the following story—"We'd like to get it all over with, one way or another"—is not yet consciously the desire of the majority, at least not to the extent of offering the consent of the

46

governed to those willing to risk Megawar. But that can be fixed by clever PR men, according to Norman Spinrad, who wrote "The Big Flash" back when Nixon was still in the White House and while our grunts were still dying in Vietnam. However, the story plays just as well today with Ronald Reagan in the cast and with the Central America of Lucius Shephard (first story in the book) as the problem in the background, begging for a nuclear solution. Spinrad's plot is as intricate as that of a novel, and the characters and viewpoints change so abruptly that the story should be read with careful attention to these permutations, lest the identity of the villain be overlooked.

THE BIG FLASH
by Norman Spinrad

T minus 200 days...and counting...

They came on freaky for my taste—but that's the name of the game: freaky means a draw in the rock business. And if the Mandala was going to survive in L.A., competing with a network-owned joint like The American Dream, I'd just have to hold my nose and out-freak the opposition. So after I had dug the Four Horsemen for about an hour, I took them into my office to talk turkey.

I sat down behind my Salvation Army desk (the Mandala is the world's most expensive shoestring operation) and the Horsemen sat down on the bridge chairs sequentially, establishing the group's pecking order.

First, the head honcho, lead guitar and singer, Stony Clarke—blonde shoulder-length hair, eyes like something in a morgue when he took off his steel-rimmed shades, a reputation as a heavy acid-head and the look of a speed-freak behind it. Then Hair, the drummer, dressed like a Hell's Angel, swastikas and all, a junkie, with fanatic eyes that were a little too close together, making me wonder whether he wore swastikas because he grooved behind the Angel thing or made like an Angel because it let him groove behind the swastika in public. Number three was a cat who called himself Super Spade and wasn't kidding—he wore earrings, natural hair, a

Stokeley Carmichael sweatshirt, and on a thong around his neck a shrunken head that had been whitened with liquid shoe polish. He was the utility infielder: sitar, base, organ, flute, whatever. Number four, who called himself Mr. Jones, was about the creepiest cat I had ever seen in a rock group, and that is saying something. He was their visuals, synthesizer and electronics man. He was at least forty, wore Early Hippy clothes that looked like they had been made by Sy Devore, and was rumored to be some kind of Rand Corporation dropout. There's no business like show business.

"Okay, boys," I said, "you're strange, but you're my kind of strange. Where you worked before?"

"We ain't, baby," Clarke said. "We're the New Thing. I've been dealing crystal and acid in the Haight. Hair was drummer for some plastic group in New York. The Super Spade claims it's the reincarnation of Bird and it don't pay to argue. Mr. Jones, he don't talk too much. Maybe he's a Martian. We just started putting our thing together."

One thing about this business, the groups that don't have square managers, you can get cheap. They talk too much.

"Groovy," I said. "I'm happy to give you guys your start. Nobody knows you, but I think you got something going. So I'll take a chance and give you a week's booking. One a.m. to closing, which is two, Tuesday through Sunday, four hundred a week."

"Are you Jewish?" asked Hair.

"What?"

"Cool it," Clarke ordered. Hair cooled it. "What it means," Clarke told me, "is that four hundred sounds like pretty light bread."

"We don't sign if there's an option clause," Mr. Jones said.

"The Jones-thing has a good point," Clarke said. "We do the first week for four hundred, but after that it's a whole new scene, dig?"

I didn't feature that. If they hit it big, I could end up not being able to afford them. But on the other hand four hundred was light bread, and I needed a cheap closing act pretty bad.

"Okay," I said. "But a verbal agreement that I get first crack at you when you finish the gig."

"Word of honor," said Stony Clarke.

That's this business—the word of honor of an ex-dealer and speedfreak.

T minus 199 days ... and counting ...

Being unconcerned with ends, the military mind can be easily manipulated, easily controlled, and easily confused. Ends are defined as those goals set by civilian authority. Ends are the conceded province of civilians; means are the province of the military, whose duty it is to achieve the ends set for it by the most advantageous applications of the means at its command.

Thus the confusion over the war in Asia among my uniformed clients at the Pentagon. The end has been duly set: eradication of the guerrillas. But the civilians have overstepped their bounds and meddled in means. The Generals regard this as unfair, a breach of contract, as it were. The Generals (or the faction among them most inclined to paranoia) are beginning to see the conduct of the war, the political limitation on means, as a ploy of the civilians for performing a putsch against their time-honored prerogatives.

This aspect of the situation would bode ill for the country, were it not for the fact that the growing paranoia among the Generals has enabled me to manipulate them into presenting both my scenarios to the President. The President has authorized implementation of the major scenario, provided that the minor scenario is successful in properly molding public opinion.

My major scenario is simple and direct. Knowing that the poor flying weather makes our conventional airpower, with its dependency on relative accuracy, ineffectual, the enemy has fallen into the pattern of grouping his forces into larger units and launching punishing annual offensives during the monsoon season. However, these larger units are highly vulnerable to tactical nuclear weapons, which do not depend upon accuracy for effect. Secure in the knowledge that domestic political considerations preclude the use of nuclear weapons, the enemy will once again form into division-sized units or larger during the next monsoon season. A parsimonious use of tactical nuclear weapons, even as few as twenty one-hundred-kiloton bombs, employed simultaneously and in an advantageous pattern, will destroy a minimum of two hundred thousand enemy troops, or nearly two-thirds of his total force, in a twenty-four-hour period. The blow will be crushing.

The minor scenario, upon whose success the implementation of the major scenario depends, is far more sophisticated, due to its subtler goal: public acceptance of, or, optimally, even public clamor for, the use of tactical nuclear weapons. The task is difficult, but my scenario is quite sound, if somewhat exotic, and with the full, if to-some-extent-clandestine support of the upper military hierarchy, certain civil government circles, and the decision makers in key aerospace corporations, the means now at my command would seem adequate. The risks, while statistically significant, do not exceed an acceptable level.

T minus 189 days . . . and counting . . .

The way I see it, the network deserved the shafting I gave them. They shafted me, didn't they? Four successful series I produce for those bastards, and two bomb out after thirteen weeks and they send me to the salt mines! A discotheque, can you imagine they make me producer at a lousy discotheque! A remittance man they make me, those schlockmeisters. Oh, those schnorrers made the American Dream sound like a kosher deal—twenty percent of the net, they say. And you got access to all our sets and contract players, it'll make you a rich man, Herm. And like a yuk, I sign, being broke at the time, without reading the fine print. I should know they've set up the American Dream as a tax loss? I should know that I've *gotta* use their lousy sets and stiff contract players and have it written off against my gross? I should know their shtick is to run the American Dream at a loss and then do a network TV show out of the joint from which I don't see a penny? So I end up running the place for them at a paper loss, living on salary, while the network rakes it in off the TV show that I end up paying for out of my end.

Don't bums like that deserve to be shafted? It isn't enough they use me as a tax loss patsy, they gotta tell me who to book! "Go sign the Four Horsemen, the group that's packing them in at the Mandala," they say. "We want them on *A Night With The American Dream.* They're hot."

"Yeah, they're hot," I say, "which means they'll cost a mint. I can't afford it."

They show me more fine print—next time I read the contract

with a microscope. I *gotta* book whoever they tell me to and I gotta absorb the cost of my books! It's enough to make a Litvak turn anti-semit.

So I had to go to the Mandala to sign up these hippies. I made sure I didn't get there till twelve-thirty so I wouldn't have to stay in that nuthouse any longer than necessary. Such a dive! What Bernstein did was take a bankrupt Hollywood-Hollywood club on the Strip, knock down all the interior walls and put up this monster tent inside the shell. Just thin white screening over two-by-fours. Real shlock. Outside the tent, he's got projectors, lights, speakers, all the electronic mumbo jumbo and inside is like being surrounded by movie screens. Just the tent and the bare floor, not even a real stage, just a platform on wheels they shlepp in and out of the tent when they change groups.

So you can imagine he doesn't draw exactly a class crowd. Not with the American Dream up the street being run as a network tax loss. What they got is the smelly, hard-core hippies I don't let in the door and the kind of j.d. high school kids that think it's smart to hang around putzes like that. A lot of dope-pushing goes on. The cops don't like the place and the rousts draw professional trouble-makers.

A real den of iniquity—I felt like I was walking onto a Casbah set. The last group had gone off and the Horsemen hadn't come on yet, so what you had was this crazy tent filled with hippies, half of them on acid or pot or amphetamine or for all I know Ajax, high school would-be hippies, also mostly stoned and getting ugly, and a few crazy schwartzes looking to fight cops. All of them standing around waiting for something to happen, and about ready to make it happen. I stood near the door, just in case. As they say, "the vibes were making me uptight."

All of a sudden the house lights go out and it's black as a network executive's heart. I hold my hand on my wallet—in this crowd, tell me there are no pickpockets. Just the pitch-black and dead silence for what, ten beats, something crawling along my bones, but I know it's some kind of subsonic effect and not my imagination, because all the hippies are standing still and you don't hear a sound.

Then from a monster speaker so loud you feel it in your teeth, a heartbeat, but heavy, slow, half-time like maybe a whale's heart.

The thing crawling along my bones seems to be synchronized with the heartbeat and I feel almost like I am that big dumb heart beating there in the darkness.

Then a dark red spot—so faint it's almost infrared—hits the stage which they have wheeled out. On the stage are four uglies in crazy black robes—you know, like the Grim Reaper wears—with that ugly red light all over them like blood. Creepy. Boom-ba-boom. Boom-ba-boom. The heartbeat still going, still that subsonic bone-crawl and the hippies are staring at the Four Horsemen like mesmerized chickens.

The bass player, a regular jungle-bunny, picks up the rhythm of the heartbeat. Dum-da-dum. Dum-da-dum. The drummer beats it out with earsplitting rim-shots. Then the electric guitar, tuned like a strangling cat, makes with horrible heavy chords. Whang-ka-whang. Whang-ka-whang.

It's just awful, I feel it in my guts, my bones; my eardrums are just like some great big throbbing vein. Everybody is swaying to it, I'm swaying to it. Boom-ba-boom. Boom-ba-boom.

Then the guitarist starts to chant in rhythm with the heartbeat, in a hoarse, shrill voice like somebody dying: "*The* big flash . . . The big *flash* . . ."

And the guy at the visuals console diddles around and rings of light start to climb the walls of the tent, blue at the bottom becoming green as they get higher, then yellow, orange and finally as they become a circle on the ceiling, eye-killing neon-red. Each circle takes exactly one heartbeat to climb the wall.

Boy, what an awful feeling! Like I was a tube of toothpaste being squeezed in rhythm till the top of my head felt like it was gonna squirt up with those circles of light through the ceiling.

And then they start to speed it up gradually. The same heartbeat, the same rim-shots, same chords, same circles, same bass, same subsonic bone-crawl, but just a little faster. . . . Then faster! Faster!

Thought I would die! Knew I would die! Heart beating like a lunatic. Rim-shots like a machine gun. Circles of light sucking me up the walls, into that red neon hole.

Oy, incredible! Over and over faster and faster till the voice was a scream and the heartbeat a boom and the rim-shots a whine and the guitar howled feedback and my bones were jumping out of my body—

Every spot in the place came on and I went blind from the sudden light—

An awful explosion-sound came over every speaker, so loud it rocked me on my feet—

I felt myself squirting out of the top of my head and loved it.

Then:

The explosion became a rumble—

The light seemed to run together into a circle on the ceiling, leaving everything else black.

And the circle became a fireball.

The fireball became a slow-motion film of an atomic bomb cloud as the rumbling died away. Then the picture faded into a moment of total darkness and the house lights came on.

What a number!

Gevalt, what an act!

So after the show, when I got them alone and found out they had no manager, not even an option to the Mandala, I thought faster than I ever had in my life.

To make a long story short and sweet, I gave the network the royal screw. I signed the Horsemen to a contract that made me their manager and gave me twenty percent of their take. Then I booked them into the American Dream at ten thousand a week, wrote a check as proprietor of the American Dream, handed the check to myself as manager of the Four Horsemen, then resigned as a network flunky, leaving them with a ten thousand bag and me with twenty percent of the hottest group since the Beatles.

What the hell, he who lives by the fine print shall perish by the fine print.

T minus 148 days ... and counting ...

"You haven't seen the tape yet, have you, B.D.?" Jake said. He was nervous as hell. When you reach my level in the network structure, you're used to making subordinates nervous, but Jake Pitkin was head of network continuity, not some office boy, and certainly should be used to dealing with executives at my level. Was the rumor really true?

We were alone in the screening room. It was doubtful that the projectionist could hear us.

"No, I haven't seen it yet," I said. "But I've heard some strange stories."

Jake looked positively deathly. "About the tape?" he said.

"About you, Jake," I said, deprecating the rumor with an easy smile. "That you don't want to air the show."

"It's true, B.D.," Jake said quietly.

"Do you realize what you're saying? Whatever our personal tastes—and I personally think there's something unhealthy about them—the Four Horsemen are the hottest thing in the country right now and that dirty little thief Herm Gellman held us up for a quarter of a million for an hour show. It cost another two hundred thousand to make it. We've spent another hundred thousand on promotion. We're getting top dollar from the sponsors. There's over a million dollars one way or the other riding on that show. That's how much we blow if we don't air it."

"I know that, B.D.," Jake said. "I also know this could cost me my job. Think about that. Because knowing all that, I'm still against airing the tape. I'm going to run the closing segment for you. I'm sure enough that you'll agree with me to stake my job on it."

I had a terrible feeling in my stomach. I have superiors too and The Word was that *A Trip With The Four Horsemen* would be aired, period. No matter what. Something funny was going on. The price we were getting for commercial time was a precedent and the sponsor was a big aerospace company which had never bought network time before. What really bothered me was that Jake Pitkin had no reputation for courage; yet here he was laying his job on the line. He must be pretty sure I would come around to his way of thinking or he wouldn't dare. And though I couldn't tell Jake, I had no choice in the matter whatsoever.

"Okay, roll it," Jake said into the intercom mike. "What you're going to see," he said as the screening room lights went out, "is the last number."

On the screen:

A shot of empty blue sky, with soft, lazy electric guitar chords behind it. The camera pans across a few clouds to an extremely long shot on the sun. As the sun, no more than a tiny circle of light, moves into the center of the screen, a sitar-drone comes in behind the guitar.

Very slowly, the camera begins to zoom in on the sun. As the image of the sun expands, the sitar gets louder and the guitar begins to fade and a drum starts to give the sitar a beat. The sitar gets louder, the beat gets more pronounced and begins to speed up as the sun continues to expand. Finally, the whole screen is filled with unbearably bright light behind which the sitar and drum are in a frenzy.

Then over this, drowning out the sitar and drum, a voice like a sick thing in heat: *"Brighter...than a thousand suns..."*

The light dissolves into a close-up of a beautiful dark-haired girl with huge eyes and moist lips, and suddenly there is nothing on the sound track but soft guitar and voices crooning low: *"Brighter ...Oh God, it's brighter...brighter...than a thousand suns..."*

The girl's face dissolves into a full shot of the Four Horsemen in their Grim Reaper robes and the same melody that had played behind the girl's face shifts into a minor key, picks up whining, reverberating electric guitar chords and a sitar-drone and becomes a dirge: *"Darker...the world grows darker..."*

And a series of cuts in time to the dirge:

A burning village in Asia strewn with bodies—

"Darker...the world grows darker..."

The corpse-heap at Auschwitz—

"Until it gets so dark..."

A gigantic auto graveyard with gaunt Negro children dwarfed in the foreground—

"I think I'll die..."

A Washington ghetto in flames with the Capitol misty in the background—

"...before the daylight comes..."

A jump-cut to an extreme close-up on the lead singer of the Horsemen, his face twisted into a mask of desperation and ecstasy. And the sitar is playing double-time, the guitar is wailing and he is screaming at the top of his lungs: *"But before I die, let me make that trip before the nothing comes..."*

The girl's face again, but transparent, with a blinding yellow light shining through it. The sitar beat gets faster and faster with the guitar whining behind it and the voice is working itself up into a howling frenzy: *"...the last big flash to light my sky..."*

Nothing but the blinding light now—

"...and zap! the world is done..."

An utterly black screen for a beat that becomes black fading to blue at a horizon—

"...but before we die let's dig that high that frees us from our binds...that blows all cool that ego-drool and burns us from our mind...the last big flash, mankind's last gas, the trip we can't take twice..."

Suddenly, the music stops dead for a half a beat. Then:

The screen is lit up by an enormous fireball—

A shattering rumble—

The fireball coalesces into a mushroom-pillar cloud as the roar goes on. As the roar begins to die out, fire is visible inside the monstrous nuclear cloud. And the girl's face is faintly visible superimposed over the cloud.

A soft voice, amplified over the roar, obscenely reverential now: Brighter...great God, it's brighter...brighter than a thousand suns..."

And the screen went blank and the lights came on.

I looked at Jake. Jake looked at me.

"That's sick," I said. "That's really sick."

"You don't want to run a thing like that, do you, B.D.?" Jake said softly.

I made some rapid mental calculations. The loathsome thing ran something under five minutes...it could be done...

"You're right, Jake," I said. "We won't run a thing like that. We'll cut it out of the tape and squeeze in another commercial at each break. That should cover the time."

"You don't understand," Jake said. "The contract Herm rammed down our throats doesn't allow us to edit. The show's a package— all or nothing. Besides, the whole show's like that."

"All like that? What do you mean, all like that?"

Jake squirmed in his seat. "Those guys are...well, perverts, B.D.," he said.

"Perverts?"

"They're...well, they're in love with the atom bomb or something. Every number leads up to the same thing."

"You mean...they're all like that?"

"You got the picture, B.D.," Jake said. "We run an hour of that or we run nothing at all."

"Jesus."

I knew what I wanted to say. Burn the tape and write off the million dollars. But I also knew it would cost me my job. And I knew that five minutes after I was out the door, they would have someone in my job who would see things their way. Even my superiors seemed to be just handing down The Word from higher up. I had no choice. There was no choice.

"I'm sorry, Jake," I said. "We run it."

"I resign," said Jake Pitkin, who had no reputation for courage.

T minus 10 days ... and counting ...

"It's a clear violation of the Test-Ban Treaty," I said.

The Undersecretary looked as dazed as I felt. "We'll call it a peaceful use of atomic energy, and let the Russians scream," he said.

"It's insane."

"Perhaps," the Undersecretary said. "But you have your orders, General Carson, and I have mine. From higher up. At exactly eight fifty-eight p.m. local time on July fourth, you will drop a fifty-kiloton atomic bomb on the designated ground zero at Yucca Flats."

"But the people ... the television crew ..."

"Will be at least two miles outside the danger zone. Surely, SAC can manage that kind of accuracy under 'laboratory conditions.'"

I stiffened. "I do not question the competence of any bomber crew under my command to perform this mission," I said. "I question the reason for the mission. I question the sanity of the orders."

The Undersecretary shrugged, smiled weakly. "Welcome to the club."

"You mean you don't know what this is all about either?"

"All I know is what was transmitted to me by the Secretary of Defense, and I got the feeling he doesn't know everything, either. You know that the Pentagon has been screaming for the use of tactical nuclear weapons to end the war in Asia—you SAC boys have been screaming the loudest. Well, several months ago, the President conditionally approved a plan for the use of tactical weapons during the next monsoon season."

I whistled. The civilians were finally coming to their senses. Or were they?

"But what does that have to do with—?"

"Public opinion," the Undersecretary said. "It was conditional upon a drastic change in public opinion. At the time the plan was approved, the polls showed that seventy-eight point eight percent of the population opposed the use of tactical nuclear weapons, nine point eight percent favored their use and the rest were undecided or had no opinion. The President agreed to authorize the use of tactical nuclear weapons by a date, several months from now, which is still top secret, provided that by that date at least sixty-five percent of the population approved their use and no more than twenty percent actively opposed it."

"I see.... Just a ploy to keep the Joint Chiefs quiet."

"General Carson," the Undersecretary said, "apparently you are out of touch with the national mood. After the first Four Horsemen show, the polls showed that twenty-five percent of the population approved the use of nuclear weapons. After the second show, the figure was forty-one percent. It is now forty-eight percent. Only thirty-two percent are now actively opposed."

"You're trying to tell me that a rock group—"

"A rock group and the cult around it. It's become a national hysteria. There are imitators. Haven't you seen those buttons?"

"The ones with a mushroom cloud on them that say 'Do it'?"

The Undersecretary nodded. "Your guess is as good as mine whether the National Security Council just decided that the Horsemen hysteria could be used to mold public opinion, or whether the Four Horsemen were their creatures to begin with. But the results are the same either way—the Horsemen and the cult around them have won over precisely that element of the population which was most adamantly opposed to nuclear weapons: hippies, students, dropouts, draft-age youth. Demonstrations against the war and against nuclear weapons have died down. We're pretty close to that sixty-five percent. Someone—perhaps the President himself—has decided that one more big Four Horsemen show will put us over the top."

"The President is behind this?"

"No one else can authorize the detonation of an atomic bomb, after all," the Undersecretary said. "We're letting them do the show live from Yucca Flats. It's being sponsored by an aerospace company heavily dependent on defense contracts. We're letting them truck in a live audience. Of course the government is behind it.''

"And SAC drops an A-bomb as the show-stopper?"

"Exactly."

"I saw one of those shows," I said. "My kids were watching it. I got the strangest feeling... I almost wanted that red telephone to ring...."

"I know what you mean," the Undersecretary said. "Sometimes I get the feeling that whoever's behind this has gotten caught up in the hysteria themselves... that the Horsemen are now using whoever was using them... a closed circle. But I've been tired lately. The war's making us all so tired. If only we could get it all over with...."

"We'd all like to get it over with one way or the other," I said.

T minus 60 minutes...and counting...

I had orders to muster *Blackfish*'s crew for the live satellite relay of *The Four Horsemen's Fourth.* Superficially, it might seem strange to order the whole Polaris fleet to watch a television show, but the morale factor involved was quite significant.

Polaris subs are frustrating duty. Only top sailors are chosen and a good sailor craves action. Yet if we are ever called upon to act, our mission will have been a failure. We spend most of our time honing skills that must never be used. Deterrence is a sound strategy but a terrible drain on the men of the deterrent forces—a drain exacerbated in the past by the negative attitude of our countrymen toward our mission. Men who, in the service of their country, polish their skills to a razor edge and then must refrain from exercising them have a right to resent being treated as pariahs.

Therefore the positive change in the public attitude toward us that seems to be associated with the Four Horsemen has made them mascots of a kind to the Polaris fleet. In their strange way they seem to speak for us and to us.

I chose to watch the show in the missile control center, where a full crew must always be ready to launch the missiles on five-minute notice. I have always felt a sense of communion with the duty watch in the missile control center that I cannot share with the other men under my command. Here we are not Captain and crew but mind and hand. Should the order come, the will to fire the missiles will be mine and the act will be theirs. At such a moment, it will be good not to feel alone.

All eyes were on the television set mounted above the main console as the show came on and...

The screen was filled with a whirling spiral pattern, metallic yellow on metallic blue. There was a droning sound that seemed part sitar and part electronic and I had the feeling that the sound was somehow coming from inside my head and the spiral seemed etched directly on my retinas. It hurt mildly, yet nothing in the world could have made me turn away.

Then two voices, chanting against each other:

"Let it all come in...."

"Let it all come out...."

"In...out...in...out...in...out..."

My head seemed to be pulsing—in-*out*, in-*out*, in-*out*—and the spiral pattern began to pulse color-changes with the words: yellow-on-blue (in)...green-on-red (*out*)...In-*out*-in-*out*-in-*out*....

In the screen...*out* my head....I seemed to be beating against some kind of invisible membrane between myself and the screen as if something were trying to embrace my mind and I were fighting it....But why was I fighting it?

The pulsing, the chanting, got faster and faster till *in* could not be told from *out* and negative spiral afterimages formed in my eyes faster than they could adjust to the changes, piled up on each other faster and faster till it seemed my head would explode—

The chanting and the droning broke and there were the Four Horsemen, in their robes, playing on some stage against a backdrop of clear blue sky. And a single voice, soothing now: *"You are in...."*

Then the view was directly above the Horsemen and I could see that they were on some kind of circular platform. The view moved slowly and smoothly up and away and I saw that the circular stage was atop a tall tower; around the tower and completely circling it was a huge crowd seated on desert sands that stretched away to an empty infinity.

"And we are in and they are in...."

I was down among the crowd now; they seemed to melt and flow like plastic, pouring from the television screen to enfold me....

"And we are all in here together...."

A strange and beautiful feeling... the music got faster and wilder, ecstatic... the hull of the *Blackfish* seemed unreal... the crowd was swaying to it around me... the distance between myself and the crowd seemed to dissolve... I was there... they were here.... We were transfixed....

"*Oh yeah, we are all in here together... together....*"

T minus 45 minutes... and counting...

Jeremy and I sat staring at the television screen, ignoring each other and everything around us. Even with the short watches and the short tours of duty, you can get to feeling pretty strange down here in a hole in the ground under tons of concrete; just you and the guy with the other key, with nothing to do but think dark thoughts and get on each other's nerves. We're all supposed to be as stable as men can be, or so they tell us, and they must be right because the world's still here. I mean, it wouldn't take much—just two guys on the same watch over the same three Minutemen flipping out at the same time, turning their keys in the dual lock, pressing the three buttons... Pow! World War III!

A bad thought, the kind we're not supposed to think or I'll start watching Jeremy and he'll start watching me and we'll get a paranoid feedback going.... But that can't happen; we're too stable, too responsible. As long as we remember that it's healthy to feel a little spooky down here, we'll be all right.

But the television set is a good idea. It keeps us in contact with the outside world, keeps it real. It'd be too easy to start thinking that the missile control center down here is the only real world and that nothing that happens up there really matters.... Bad thought!

The Four Horsemen... somehow these guys help you get it all out. I mean that feeling that it might be better to release all that tension, get it all over with. Watching the Four Horsemen, you're able to go with it without doing any harm, let it wash over you and then through you. I suppose they are crazy; they're all the human craziness in ourselves that we've got to keep very careful watch over down here. Letting it all come out watching the Horsemen makes it surer that none of it will come out down here. I guess that's why a lot of us have taken to wearing those "Do it" buttons off duty. The brass doesn't mind; they seem to understand that it's the kind of inside sick joke we need to keep us functioning.

Now that spiral thing they had started the show with—and the droning—came back on. Zap! I was right back in the screen again, as if the commerical hadn't happened.

"We are all in here together...."

And then a close-up of the lead singer, looking straight at me, as close as Jeremy and somehow more real. A mean-looking guy with something behind his eyes that told me he knew where everything lousy and rotten was at.

A bass began to thrum behind him and some kind of electronic hum that set my teeth on edge. He began playing his guitar, mean and low-down. And singing in that kind of drop-dead tone of voice that starts brawls in bars:

"I stabbed my mother and I mugged my paw...."

A riff of heavy guitar-chords echoed the words mockingly as a huge swastika (red-on-black, black-on-red) pulsed like a naked vein on the screen—

The face of the Horsemen, leering—

"Nailed my sister to the toilet door...."

Guitar behind the pulsing swastika—

"Drowned a puppy in a ce-ment machine.... Burned a kitten just to hear it scream...."

On the screen, just a big fire burning in slow-motion, and the voice became a slow, shrill, agonized wail:

"Oh God, I've got this red-hot fire burning in the marrow of my brain....

"Oh yes, I got this fire burning...in the stinking marrow of my brain....

"Gotta get me a blowtorch...and set some naked flesh on flame...."

The fire dissolved into the face of a screaming Oriental woman, who ran through a burning village clawing at the napalm on her back.

"I got this message...boiling in the bubbles of my blood....A man ain't nothing but a fire burning...in a dirty glob of mud...."

A film-clip of a Nuremburg rally: a revolving swastika of marching men waving torches—

Then the leader of the Horsemen superimposed over the twisted flaming cross:

Don't you hate me, baby, can't you feel somethin' screaming in your mind?

"*Don't you hate me, baby, feel me drowning you in slime!*"

Just the face of the Horsemen howling hate—

"*Oh yes, I'm a monster, mother....*"

A long view of the crowd around the platform, on their feet, waving arms, screaming soundlessly. Then a quick zoom in and a kaleidoscope of faces, eyes feverish, mouths open and howling—

"*Just call me—*"

The face of the Horseman superimposed over the crazed faces of the crowd—

"*Mankind!*"

I looked at Jeremy. He was toying with the key on the chain around his neck. He was sweating. I suddenly realized that I was sweating too and that my own key was throbbing in my hand alive....

T minus 13 minutes... and counting...

A funny feeling, the Captain watching the Four Horsemen here in the *Blackfish's* missile control center with us. Sitting in front of my console watching the television set with the Captain kind of breathing down my neck.... I got the feeling he knew what was going through me and I couldn't know what was going through him ... and it gave the fire inside me a kind of greasy feel I didn't like....

Then the commercial was over and that spiral-thing came on again and whoosh! it sucked me right back into the television set and I stopped worrying about the Captain or anything like that....

Just the spiral going yellow-blue, red-green, and then starting to whirl and whirl, faster and faster, changing colors and whirling, whirling, whirling....And the sound of a kind of Coney Island carousel tinkling behind it, faster and faster and faster, whirling and whirling and whirling, flashing red-green, yellow-blue, and whirling, whirling, whirling....

And this big hum filling my body and whirling, whirling, whirling....My muscles relaxing, going limp, whirling, whirling, whirling, all limp, whirling, whirling, whirling, oh so nice, just whirling, whirling....

And in the center of the flashing spiraling colors, a bright dot of colorless light, right at the center, not moving, not changing, while the whole world went whirling and whirling in colors around it, and the humming was coming from the spinning colors and the dot was humming its song to me....

The dot was a light way down at the end of a long, whirling, whirling tunnel. The humming started to get a little louder. The bright dot started to get a little bigger. I was drifting down the tunnel toward it, whirling, whirling, whirling....

T minus 11 minutes...and counting...

Whirling, whirling, whirling down a long, long tunnel of pulsing colors, whirling, whirling, toward the circle of light way down at the end of the tunnel.... How nice it would be to finally get there and soak up the beautiful hum filling my body and then I could forget that I was down here in this hole in the ground with a hard brass key in my hand, just Duke and me, down here in a cave under the ground that was a spiral of flashing colors, whirling, whirling toward the friendly light at the end of the tunnel, whirling, whirling....

T minus 10 minutes...and counting...

The circle of light at the end of the whirling tunnel was getting bigger and bigger and the humming was getting louder and louder and I was feeling better and better and the *Blackfish's* missile control center was getting dimmer and dimmer as the awful weight of command got lighter and lighter, whirling, whirling, and I felt so good I wanted to cry, whirling, whirling....

T minus 9 minutes...and counting...

Whirling, whirling...I was whirling, Jeremy was whirling, the hole in the ground was whirling, and the circle of light at the end of the tunnel whirled closer and closer and—I was through! A place filled with yellow light. Pale metal-yellow light. Then pale metallic blue. Yellow. Blue. Yellow. Blue. Yellow-blue-yellow-blue-yellow-blue-yellow...

Pure light pulsing...and pure sound droning. And just the *feeling* of letters I couldn't read between the pulses—not-yellow and not-blue—too quick and too faint to be visible, but important, very important....

And then a voice that seemed to be singing from inside my head, almost as if it were my own:

"Oh, oh, oh...don't I really wanna know....Oh, oh, oh...don't I really wanna know...."

The world pulsing, flashing around those words I couldn't read, couldn't quite read, had to read, could *almost* read....

"Oh, oh, oh...great God I really wanna know...."

Strange amorphous shapes clouding the blue-yellow-blue flickering universe, hiding the words I had to read....Dammit, why wouldn't they get out of the way so I could find out what I had to know!

"Tell me tell me tell me tell me tell me....Gotta know gotta know gotta know gotta know...."

T minus 7 minutes...and counting...

Couldn't read the words! Why wouldn't the Captain let me read the words?

And that voice inside me: *"Gotta know...gotta know...gotta know why it hurts me so...."* Why wouldn't it shut up and let me read the words? Why wouldn't the words hold still? Or just slow down a little? If they'd slow down a little, I could read them and then I'd know what I had to do....

T minus 6 minutes...and counting...

I felt the sweaty key in the palm of my hand....I saw Duke stroking his own key. Had to know! Now—through the pulsing blue-yellow-blue light and the unreadable words that were building up an awful pressure in the back of my brain—I could see the Four Horsemen. They were on their knees, crying, looking up at something and begging: *"Tell me tell me tell me tell me...."*

Then soft billows of rich red-and-orange fire filled the world and a huge voice was trying to speak. But it couldn't form the words. It stuttered and moaned—

The yellow-blue-yellow flashing around the words I couldn't read—the same words, I suddenly sensed, that the voice of the fire was trying so hard to form—and the Four Horsemen on their knees begging: *"Tell me tell me tell me...."*

The friendly warm fire trying so hard to speak—

"Tell me tell me tell me tell me...."

T minus 4 minutes...and counting...

What were the words? What was the order? I could sense my men silently imploring me to tell them. After all, I was their Captain, it was my duty to tell them. It was my duty to find out!

"Tell me tell me tell me..." the robed figures on their knees implored through the flickering pulse in my brain and I could almost make out the words...almost....

"Tell me tell me tell me...." I whispered to the warm orange fire that was trying so hard but couldn't quite form the words. The men were whispering it too: "Tell me tell me...."

T minus 3 minutes...and counting...

The question burning blue and yellow in my brain. WHAT WAS THE FIRE TRYING TO TELL ME? WHAT WERE THE WORDS I COULDN'T READ?

Had to unlock the words! Had to find the key!

A key....*The* key! THE KEY! And there was the lock that imprisoned the words, right in front of me! Put the key in the lock....I looked at Jeremy. Wasn't there some reason, long ago and far away, why Jeremy might try to stop me from putting the key in the lock?

But Jeremy didn't move as I fitted the key into the lock....

T minus 2 minutes...and counting...

Why wouldn't the Captain tell me what the order was? The fire knew, but it couldn't tell. My head ached from the pulsing, but I couldn't read the words.

"Tell me tell me tell me..." I begged.

Then I realized that the Captain was asking too.

T minus 90 seconds...and counting...

"*Tell me tell me tell me...*" the Horsemen begged. And the words I couldn't read were a fire in my brain.

Duke's key was in the lock in front of us. From very far away, he said: "We have to do it together."

Of course...our keys...our keys would unlock the words!

I put my key into the lock. One, two, three, we turned our keys together. A lid on the console popped open. Under the lid were three red buttons. Three signs on the console lit up in red letters: ARMED.

T minus 60 seconds...and counting...

The men were waiting for me to give some order. I didn't know what the order was. A magnificent orange fire was trying to tell me but it couldn't get the words out.... Robed figures were praying to the fire....

Then, through the yellow-blue flicker that hid the words I had to read, I saw a vast crowd encircling a tower. The crowd was on its feet begging silently—

The tower in the center of the crowd became the orange fire that was trying to tell me what the words were—

Became a great mushroom of billowing smoke and blinding orange-red glare....

T minus 30 seconds...and counting...

The huge pillar of fire was trying to tell Jeremy and me what the words were, what we had to do. The crowd was screaming at the cloud of flame. The yellow-blue flicker was getting faster and faster behind the mushroom cloud. I could almost read the words! I could see that there were two of them!

T minus 20 seconds...and counting...

Why didn't the Captain tell us? I could almost see the words!

Then I heard the crowd around the beautiful mushroom cloud shouting: "DO IT! DO IT! DO IT! DO IT! DO IT!"

T minus 10 seconds...and counting...
"DO IT! DO IT! DO IT! DO IT! DO IT! DO IT! DO IT!"
What did they want me to do? Did Duke know?

9

The men were waiting! What was the order? They hunched over the firing controls, waiting....The firing controls....?"
"DO IT! DO IT! DO IT! DO IT! DO IT!"

8

"DO IT! DO IT! DO IT! DO IT! DO IT!": the crowd screaming. "Jeremy!" I shouted. "I can read the words!"

7

My hands hovered over my bank of firing buttons....
"DO IT! DO IT! DO IT! DO IT!" the words said.
Didn't the Captain understand?

6

"What do they want us to do, Jeremy?"

5

Why didn't the mushroom cloud give the order? My men were waiting! A good sailor craves action.
Then a great voice spoke from the pillar of fire: "DO IT...DO IT ...DO IT..."

4

"There's only one thing we can do down here, Duke."

3

"The order, men! Action! Fire!"

2

Yes, yes, yes! Jeremy—

1

I reached for my bank of firing buttons. All along the console, the men reached for their buttons. But I was too fast for them! I would be first!

0   .

THE BIG FLASH

4 _____

The electromagnetic pulse will finally zap that high-kilowatt audio-visual gear and reduce the noise level. Now the fun of survival can begin. Let's take a holiday from such heavy concern with our rat race against the doomsday clock, now past midnight anyway, and join Ward Moore's Jimmon family for an outing in the country while warheads fall on cities. I remembered reading "Lot" when it first appeared in 1953, and the fact that Marty Greenberg mentioned it in our first discussion last year prompted my quick acceptance of his invitation to co-edit this book. Feminists may find this version of the Lot family's adventures after leaving Sodom more compatible with intuition than the account in Genesis, whose editors perhaps felt they had to go for a certain patriarchal slant to avoid offending the all-male readership of those times.

LOT
by Ward Moore

Mr. Jimmon even appeared elated, like a man about to set out on a vacation.

"Well, folks, no use waiting any longer. We're all set. So let's go."

There was a betrayal here; Mr. Jimmons was not the kind of man who addressed his family as "folks."

"David, you're sure...?"

Mr. Jimmon merely smiled. This was quite out of character; customarily he reacted to his wife's habit of posing unfinished questions—after seventeen years the unuttered and larger part of the queries were always instantly known to him in some mysterious way, as though unerringly projected by the key in which the introduction was pitched, so that not only the full wording was communicated to his mind, but the shades and implications which circumstance and humor attached to them—with sharp and querulous defense. No matter how often he resolved to stare quietly or use the still more effective, Afraid I didn't catch your meaning, dear, he had never been able to put his resolution into force. Until this moment of crisis. Crisis, reflected Mr. Jimmon, still smiling and moving suggestively toward the door, crisis changes people. Brings out underlying qualities.

It was Jir who answered Molly Jimmon, with the adolescent's half-whine of exasperation. "Aw, furcrysay, mom, what's the idea? The highways'll be clogged tight. What's the good figuring out everything heada time and having everything all set if you're going to start all over again at the last minute? Get a grip on yourself and let's go."

Mr. Jimmon did not voice the reflexive, That's no way to talk to your mother. Instead he thought, not unsympathetically, of woman's slow reaction time. Asset in childbirth, liability behind the wheel. He knew Molly was thinking of the house and all the things in it: her clothes and Erika's, the TV set—so sullenly ugly now, with the electricity gone—the refrigerator in which the food would soon begin to rot and stink, the dead stove, the cellarful of cases of canned stuff for which there was no room in the station wagon. And the Buick, blocked up in the garage, with the air thoughtfully let out of the tires and the battery hidden.

Of course the house would be looted. But they had known that all along. When they—or rather he, for it was his executive's mind and training which were responsible for the Jimmons' preparation against this moment—planned so carefully and providentially, he had weighed property against life and decided on life. No other decision was possible. "Aren't you at least going to phone Pearl and Dan?"

Now why in the world, thought Mr. Jimmon, completely above petty irritation, should I call Dan Davisson? (Because of course it's *Dan* she means—My Old Beau. Oh, he was nobody then, just an impractical dreamer without a penny to his name; it wasn't for years that he was recognized as a Mathematical Genius; now he's a professor and all sorts of things—but she automatically says Pearl-and-Dan, not Dan.) What can Dan do with the square root of minus nothing to offset M equals whatever it is, at this moment? Or am I supposed to ask if Pearl has all her diamonds? Query, why doesn't Pearl wear pearls? Only diamonds? My wife's friend, heh heh, but even the subtlest intonation won't label them when you're entertaining an important client and Pearl and Dan.

And why should I phone? What sudden paralysis afflicts her? Hysteria?

"No," said Mr. Jimmon. "I did not phone Pearl and Dan."

Then he added, relenting. "Phone's been out since."

"But," said Molly.

She's hardly going to ask me to drive into town. He selected several answers in readiness. But she merely looked toward the telephone helplessly (she ought to have been fat, thought Mr. Jimmon, really she should, or anyway plump; her thinness gives her that air of competence), so he amplified gently, "They're unquestionably all right. As far away from it as we are."

Wendell was already in the station wagon. With Waggie hidden somewhere. Should have sent the dog to the humane society; more merciful to have it put to sleep. Too late now; Waggie would have to take his chance. There were plenty of rabbits in the hills above Malibu; he had often seen them quite close to the house. At all events there was no room for a dog in the wagon, already loaded to within a pound of its capacity.

Erika came in briskly from the kitchen, her brown jodhpurs making her appear at first glance even younger than fourteen. But only at first glance; then the swell of hips and breasts denied the childishness the jodhpurs seemed to accent.

"The water's gone, mom. There's no use sticking around any longer."

Molly looked incredulous. "The water?"

"Of course the water's gone," said Mr. Jimmon, not impatiently, but rather with satisfaction in his own foresight. "If it didn't get the aqueduct, the mains depend on pumps. Electric pumps. When the electricity went, the water went too."

"But the water," repeated Molly, as though this last catastrophe was beyond all reason—even the outrageous logic which It brought in its train.

Jir slouched past them and outside. Erika tucked in a strand of hair, pulled her jockey cap downward and sideways, glanced quickly at her mother and father, then followed. Molly took several steps, paused, smiled vaguely in the mirror, and walked out of the house.

Mr. Jimmons patted his pockets; the money was all there. He didn't even look back before closing the front door and rattling the knob to be sure the lock had caught. It had never failed, but Mr. Jimmon always rattled it anyway. He strode to the station wagon, running his eyes over the springs to reassure himself again that they really hadn't overloaded it.

The sky was overcast; you might have thought it one of the regular morning high fogs if you didn't know. Mr. Jimmon faced southeast, but It had been too far away to see anything. Now Erika and Molly were in the front seat; the boys were in the back, lost amid the neatly packed stuff. He opened the door on the driver's side, got in, turned the key, and started the motor. Then he said casually over his shoulder, "Put the dog out, Jir."

Wendell protested, too quickly, "Waggie's not here."

Molly exclaimed, "Oh, David..."

Mr. Jimmon said patiently, "We're losing pretty valuable time. There's no room for the dog; we have no food for him. If we had room we could have taken more essentials; those few pounds might mean the difference."

"Can't find him," muttered Jir.

"He's not here. I tell you he's not here," shouted Wendell, tearful voiced.

"If I have to stop the motor and get him myself we'll be wasting still more time and gas." Mr. Jimmon was still detached, judicial. "This isn't a matter of kindness to animals. It's life and death."

Erika said evenly, "Dad's right, you know. It's the dog or us. Put him out, Wend."

"I tell you—" Wendell began.

"Got him!" exclaimed Jir. "Okay, Waggie! Outside and good luck."

The spaniel wriggled ecstatically as he was picked up and put out through the open window. Mr. Jimmon raced the motor, but it didn't drown out Wendell's anguish. He threw himself on his brother, hitting and kicking. Mr. Jimmon took his foot off the gas, and as soon as he was sure the dog was away from the wheels, eased the station wagon out of the driveway and down the hill toward the ocean.

"Wendell, Wendell, stop," pleaded Molly. "Don't hurt him, Jir."

Mr. Jimmon clicked on the radio. After a preliminary hum, clashing static crackled out. He pushed all five buttons in turn varying the quality of unintelligible sound. "Want me to try?" offered Erika. She pushed the manual button and turned the knob slowly. Music dripped out.

Mr. Jimmon grunted. "Mexican station. Try something else. Maybe you can get Ventura."

They rounded a tight curve. "Isn't that the Warbinns'?" asked Molly.

For the first time since It happened Mr. Jimmon had a twinge of impatience. There was no possibility, even with the unreliable eye of shocked excitement, of mistaking the Warbinns' blue Mercury. No one else on Rambla Catalina had one anything like it, and visitors would be most unlikely now. If Molly would apply the most elementary logic!

Besides, Warbinn had stopped the blue Mercury in the Jimmon driveway five times every week for the past two months—ever since they had decided to put the Buick up and keep the wagon packed and ready against this moment—for Mr. Jimmon to ride with him to the city. Of course it was the Warbinns'.

"...advised not to impede the progress of the military. Adequate medical staffs are standing by at all hospitals. Local civilian defense units are taking all steps in accordance..."

"Santa Barbara," remarked Jir, nodding at the radio with an expert's assurance.

Mr. Jimmon slowed, prepared to follow the Warbinns down to 101, but the Mercury halted and Mr. Jimmon turned out to pass it. Warbinn was driving and Sally was in the front seat with him; the back seat appeared empty except for a few things obviously hastily thrown in. No foresight, thought Mr. Jimmon.

Warbinn waved his hand vigorously out the window and Sally shouted something.

"...*panic will merely slow rescue efforts. Casualties are much smaller than originally reported...*"

"How do they know?" asked Mr. Jimmon, waving politely at the Warbinns.

"Oh, David, aren't you going to stop? They want something."

"Probably just to talk."

"...*to retain every drop of water. Emergency power will be in operation shortly. There is no cause for undue alarm. General...*"

Through the rearview mirror Mr. Jimmon saw the blue Mercury start after them. He had been right then, they only wanted to say something inconsequential. At a time like this.

At the junction with U.S. 101 five cars blocked Rambla Catalina. Mr. Jimmon set the handbrake, and steadying himself with the open door, stood tiptoe twistedly, trying to see over the cars ahead. 101 was solid with traffic which barely moved. On the southbound side of the divided highway a stream of vehicles flowed illegally north.

"Thought everybody was figured to go east," gibed Jir over the other side of the car.

Mr. Jimmon was not disturbed by his son's sarcasm. How right he'd been to rule out the trailer. Of course the bulk of the cars were headed eastward as he'd calculated; this sluggish mass was nothing compared with the countless ones which must now be blocking the roads to Pasadena, Alhambra, Garvey, Norwalk. Even the northbound refugees were undoubtedly taking 99 or regular 101—the highway before them was really 101 Alternate—he had picked the most feasible exit.

The Warbinns drew up alongside. "Hurry didn't do you much good," shouted Warbinn, leaning forward to clear his wife's face.

Mr. Jimmon reached in and turned off the ignition. Gas was going to be precious. He smiled and shook his head at Warbinn; no use pointing out that he'd got the inside lane by passing the Mercury, with a better chance to seize the opening on the highway when it came. "Get in the car, Jir, and shut the door. Have to be ready when this breaks."

"If it ever does," said Molly. "All that rush and bustle. We might just as well..."

Mr. Jimmon was conscious of Warbinn's glowering at him and

resolutely refused to turn his head. He pretended not to hear him yell. "Only wanted to tell you you forgot to pick up your bumper jack. It's in front of our garage."

Mr. Jimmon's stomach felt empty. What if he had a flat now? Ruined, condemned. He knew a burning hate for Warbinn—incompetent borrower, bad neighbor, thoughtless, shiftless, criminal. He owed it to himself to leap from the station wagon and seize Warbinn by the throat...

"What did he say, David? What is Mr. Warbinn saying?"

Then he remembered it was the jack from the Buick; the station wagon's was safely packed where he could get at it easily. Naturally he would never have started out on a trip like this without checking so essential an item. "Nothing," he said, "nothing at all."

"...plane dispatches indicate target was the Signal Hill area. Minor damage was done to Long Beach, Wilmington, and San Pedro. All nonmilitary air traffic warned from Mines Field..."

The smash and crash of bumper and fender sounded familiarly on the highway. From his lookout station he couldn't see what had happened, but it was easy enough to reconstruct the impatient jerk forward that caused it. Mr. Jimmon didn't exactly smile, but he allowed himself a faint quiver of internal satisfaction. A crash up ahead would make things worse, but a crash behind—and many of them were inevitable—must eventually create a gap.

Even as he thought this, the first car at the mouth of Rambla Catalina edged onto the shoulder of the highway. Mr. Jimmon slid back in and started the motor, inching ahead after the car in front, gradually leaving the still uncomfortable proximity of the Warbinns.

"Got to go to the toilet," announced Wendell abruptly.

"Didn't I tell you—! Well, hurry up! Jir, keep the door open and pull him in if the car starts to move."

"I can't go here."

Mr. Jimmon restrained his impulse to snap, Hold it in then. Instead he said mildly, "This is a crisis, Wendell. No time for niceties. Hurry."

"...the flash was seen as far north as Ventura and as far south as Newport. An eyewitness who had just arrived by helicopter..."

"That's what we should have had," remarked Jir. "You thought of everything except that."

"That's no way to speak to your father," admonished Molly.

"Aw, heck, mom, this is a crisis. No time for niceties."

"You're awful smart, Jir," said Erika. "Big, tough, brutal man."

"Go down, brat," returned Jir, "your nose needs wiping."

"As a matter of record," Mr. Jimmon said calmly, "I thought of both plane and helicopter and decided against them."

"I can't go. Honest, I just can't go."

"Just relax, darling," advised Molly. "No one is looking."

"...fires reported in Compton, Lynwood, South Gate, Harbor City, Lomita, and other spots are now under control. Residents are advised not to attempt to travel on the overcrowded highways as they are much safer in their homes or places of employment. The civilian defense..."

The two cars ahead bumped forward. "Get in," shouted Mr. Jimmon.

He got the left front tire of the station wagon on the asphalt shoulder—the double lane of concrete was impossibly far ahead— only to be blocked by the packed procession. The clock on the dash said 11:04. Nearly five hours since It happened, and they were less than two miles from home. They could have done better walking. Or on horseback.

"...All residents of the Los Angeles area are urged to remain calm. Local radio service will be restored in a matter of minutes, along with electricity and water. Reports of fifth column activities have been greatly exaggerated. The FBI has all known subversives under..."

He reached over and shut it off. Then he edged a daring two inches farther on the shoulder, almost grazing an aggressive Cadillac packed solid with cardboard cartons. On his left a Model A truck shivered and trembled. He knew, distantly and disapprovingly, that it belonged to two painters who called themselves man and wife. The truck bed was loaded high with household goods; poor, useless things no looter would bother to steal. In the cab the artists passed a quart beer bottle back and forth. The man waved it genially at him; Mr. Jimmon nodded discouragingly back.

The thermometer on the mirror showed 90. Hot all right. Of course if they ever got rolling... I'm thirsty, he thought; probably suggestion. If I hadn't seen the thermometer. Anyway I'm not going to paw around in back for the canteen. Forethought. Like the arms. He cleared his throat. "Remember there's an automatic in the glove compartment. If anyone tries to open the door on your side, use it."

"Oh, David, I..."

Ah, humanity. Nonresistance, Gandhi. I've never shot at anything but a target. At a time like this. But they don't understand.

"I could use the rifle from back here," suggested Jir. "Can I, dad?"

"I can reach the shotgun," said Wendell. "That's better at close range."

"Gee, you men are brave," jeered Erika. Mr. Jimmon said nothing; both shotgun and rifle were unloaded. Foresight again.

He caught the hiccuping pause in the traffic instantly, gratified at his smooth coordination. How far he could proceed on the shoulder before running into a culvert narrowing the highway to the concrete he didn't know. Probably not more than a mile at most, but at least he was off Rambla Catalina and on 101.

He felt tremendously elated. Successful.

"Here we go!" He almost added, Hold on to your hats.

Of course the shoulder too was packed solid, and progress, even in low gear, was maddening. The gas consumption was something he did not want to think about; his pride in the way the needle of the gauge caressed the F shrank. And gas would be hard to come by in spite of his pocketful of ration coupons. Black market.

"Mind if I try the radio again?" asked Erika, switching it on.

Mr. Jimmon, following the pattern of previous success, insinuated the left front tire onto the concrete, eliciting a disapproving squawk from the Pontiac alongside.

"... *sector was quiet. Enemy losses are estimated...*"

"Can't you get something else?" asked Jir. "Something less dusty?"

"Wish we had TV in the car," observed Wendell. "Joe Tellifer's old man put a set in the back seat of their Chrysler."

"Dry up, squirt," said Jir. "Let the air out of your head."

"Jir."

"Oh, mom, don't pay attention! Don't you see that's what he wants?"

"Listen, brat, if you weren't a girl, I'd spank you."

"You mean, If I wasn't your sister. You'd probably enjoy such childish sex play with any other girl."

"Erika!"

Where do they learn it? marveled Mr. Jimmon. These progressive schools. Do you suppose...?

He edged the front wheel farther in exultantly, taking advantage of a momentary lapse of attention on the part of the Pontiac's driver. Unless the other went berserk with frustration and rammed into him, he practically had a cinch on a car length of the concrete now.

"Here we go!" he gloried. "We're on our way."

"Aw, if I was driving we'd be halfway to Oxnard by now."

"Jir, that's no way to talk to your father."

Mr. Jimmon reflected dispassionately that Molly's ineffective admonitions only spurred Jir's sixteen-year-old brashness, already irritating enough in its own right. Indeed, if it were not for Molly, Jir might...

It was of course possible—here Mr. Jimmon braked just short of the convertible ahead—Jir wasn't just going through a "difficult" period (What was particularly difficult about it? he inquired, in the face of all the books Molly suggestively left around on the psychological problems of growth. The boy had everything he could possibly want.) but was the type who, in different circumstances drifted well into—well, perhaps not exactly juvenile delinquency, but...

"...in the Long Beach—Wilmington—San Pedro area. Comparison with that which occurred at Pittsburgh reveals that this morning's was in every way less serious. All fires are now under control and all the injured are now receiving medical attention..."

"I don't think they're telling the truth," stated Mrs. Jimmon.

He snorted. He didn't think so either, but by what process had she arrived at that conclusion?

"I want to hear the ball game. Turn on the ball game, Rick," Wendell demanded.

Eleven sixteen, and rolling northward on the highway. Not bad, not bad at all. Foresight. Now if he could only edge his way leftward to the southbound strip they'd be beyond the Santa Barbara bottleneck by two o'clock.

"The lights," exclaimed Molly, "the taps!"

Oh no, thought Mr. Jimmon, not that too. Out of the comic strips.

"Keep calm," advised Jir. "Electricity and water are both off—remember?"

"I'm not quite an imbecile yet, Jir. I'm quite aware everything went off. I was thinking of the time it went back on."

"Furcrysay, mom, you worrying about next month's bills now?"

Mr. Jimmon, nudging the station wagon ever leftward, formed

the sentence: You'd never worry about bills, young man, because you never have to pay them. Instead of saying it aloud, he formed another sentence: Molly, your talent for irrelevance amounts to genius. Both sentences gave him satisfaction.

The traffic gathered speed briefly, and he took advantage of the spurt to get solidly in the left-hand lane, right against the long island of concrete dividing the north- from the south-bound strips. "That's using the old bean, dad," approved Wendell.

Whatever slight pleasure he might have felt in his son's approbation was overlaid with exasperation. Wendell, like Jir, was more Manville than Jimmon; they carried Molly's stamp on their faces and minds. Only Erika was a true Jimmon. Made in my own image, he thought pridelessly.

"I can't help but think it would have been at least courteous to get in touch with Pearl and Dan. At least *try*. And the Warbinns...

The gap in the concrete divider came sooner than he anticipated and he was on the comparatively unclogged southbound side. His foot went down on the accelerator and the station wagon grumbled earnestly ahead. For the first time Mr. Jimmon became aware how tightly he'd been gripping the wheel; how rigid the muscles in his arms, shoulders, and neck had been. He relaxed partway as he adjusted to the speed of the cars ahead and the speedometer needle hung just below 45, but resentment against Molly (at least courteous), Jir (no time for niceties), and Wendell (not to go), rode up in the saliva under his tongue. Dependent. Helpless. Everything on him. Parasites.

At intervals Erika switched on the radio. News was always promised immediately, but little was forthcoming, only vague, nervous attempts to minimize the extent of the disaster and soothe listeners with allusions to civilian defense, military activities on the ever advancing front, and comparison with the destruction of Pittsburgh, so vastly much worse than the comparatively harmless detonation at Los Angeles. Must be pretty bad, thought Mr. Jimmon; cripple the war effort...

"I'm hungry," said Wendell.

Molly began stirring around, instructing Jir where to find the sandwiches. Mr. Jimmon thought grimly of how they'd have to adjust to the absence of civilized niceties; bread and mayonnaise and lunch meat. Live on rabbit, squirrel, abalone, fish. When Wendell grew hungry he'd have to get his own food. Self-sufficiency. Hard and tough.

At Oxnard the snarled traffic slowed them to a crawl again. Beyond, the juncture with the main highway north kept them at the same infuriating pace. It was long after two when they reached Ventura, and Wendell, who had been fidgeting and jumping up and down in the seat for the past hour, proclaimed, "I'm tired of riding."

Mr. Jimmon set his lips. Molly suggested, ineffectually, "Why don't you lie down, dear?"

"Can't. Way this crate is packed, ain't room for a grasshopper."

"Verry funny. Verrrry funny," said Jir.

"Now, Jir, leave him alone! He's just a little boy."

At Carpinteria the sun burst out. You might have thought it the regular dissipation of the fog, only it was almost time for the fog to come down again. Should he try the San Marcos Pass after Santa Barbara, or the longer, better way? Flexible plans, but...Wait and see.

It was four when they got to Santa Barbara and Mr. Jimmon faced concerted though unorganized rebellion. Wendell was screaming with stiffness and boredom; Jir remarked casually to no one in particular that Santa Barbara was the place they were going to beat the bottleneck oh yeh; Molly said, Stop at the first clean-looking gas station. Even Erika added, "Yes, dad, you'll really have to stop."

Mr. Jimmon was appalled. With every second priceless and hordes of panic-stricken refugees pressing behind, they would rob him of all the precious gains he'd made by skill, daring, judgment. Stupidity and shortsightedness. Unbelievable. For their own silly comfort—good lord, did they think they had a monopoly on bodily weaknesses? He was cramped as they and wanted to go as badly. Time and space which could never be made up. Let them lose this half hour and it was quite likely they'd never get out of Santa Barbara.

"If we lose a half hour now we'll never get out of here."

"Well, now, David, that wouldn't be utterly disastrous, would it? There are awfully nice hotels here and I'm sure it would be more comfortable for everyone than your idea of camping in the woods, hunting and fishing..."

He turned off State; couldn't remember name of the parallel street, but surely less traffic. He controlled his temper, not heroically, but desperately. "May I ask how long you would propose to stay in one of these awfully nice hotels?"

"Why, until we could go home."

"My dear Molly..." What could he say? My dear Molly, we are never going home, if you mean Malibu? Or: My dear Molly, you just don't understand what is happening?

The futility of trying to convey the clear picture in his mind. Or any picture. If she could not of herself see the endless mob pouring out of Los Angeles, searching frenziedly for escape and refuge, eating up the substance of the surrounding country in ever-widening circles, crowding, jam-packing, overflowing every hotel, boarding-house, lodging, or private home into which they could edge, agonizedly bidding up the price of everything until the chaos they brought with them was indistinguishable from the chaos they were fleeing—if she could not see all this instantly and automatically, she could not be brought to see it at all. Any more than the other aimless, planless, improvident fugitives could see it.

So, my dear Molly; nothing.

Silence gave consent to continued expostulation. "David, do you really mean you don't intend to stop at *all?*"

Was there any point in saying, Yes, I do? He set his lips still more tightly and once more weighed San Marcos Pass against the coast route. Have to decide now.

"Why, the time we're waiting here, just waiting for the cars up ahead to move would be enough."

Could you call her stupid? He weighed the question slowly and justly, alert for the first jerk of the massed cars all around. Her reasoning was valid and logical if the laws of physics and geometry were suspended. (Was that right—physics and geometry? Body occupying two different positions at the same time?) It was the facts which were illogical—not Molly. She was just exasperating.

By the time they were halfway to Gaviota or Goleta—Mr. Jimmon could never tell them apart—foresight and relentless sternness began to pay off. Those who had left Los Angeles without preparation and in panic were dropping out or slowing down, to get gas or oil, repair tires, buy food, seek rest rooms. The station wagon was steadily forging ahead.

He gambled on the old highway out of Santa Barbara. Any kind of obstruction would block its two lanes; if it didn't he would be beating the legions on the wider, straighter road. There were stretches now where he could hit 50; once he sped a happy half-mile at 65.

Now the insubordination crackling all around gave indication of simultaneous explosion. "I really," began Molly, and then discarded this for a fresher, firmer start. "David, I don't understand how you can be so utterly selfish and inconsiderate."

Mr. Jimmon could feel the veins in his forehead begin to swell, but this was one of those rages that didn't show.

"But, dad, would ten minutes ruin everything?" asked Erika.

"Monomania," muttered Jir. "Single track. Like Hitler."

"I want my dog," yelped Wendell. "Dirty old dog-killer."

"Did you ever hear of cumulative—" Erika had addressed him reasonably; surely he could make her understand? "Did you ever hear of cumulative..." What was the word? Snowball rolling downhill was the image in his mind. "Oh, what's the use?"

The old road rejoined the new; again the station wagon was fitted into the traffic like parquetry. Mr. Jimmon, from an exultant, un-fettered—almost—65 was imprisoned in a treadmill set at 38. Keep calm; you can do nothing about it, he admonished himself. Need all your nervous energy. Must be wrecks up ahead. And then, with a return of satisfaction: if I hadn't used strategy back there we'd have been with those making 25. A starting-stopping 25.

"It's fantastic," exclaimed Molly. "I could almost believe Jir's right and you've lost your mind."

Mr. Jimmons smiled. This was the first time Molly had ever openly showed disloyalty before the children or sided with them in their presence. She was revealing herself. Under pressure. Not the pressure of events; her incredible attitude at Santa Barbara had demonstrated her incapacity to feel that. Just pressure against the bladder.

"No doubt those left behind can console their last moments with pride in their sanity." The sentence came out perfectly formed, with none of the annoying pauses or interpolated "ers" or "mmphs" which could, as he knew from unhappy experience, flaw the most crushing rejoinders.

"Oh, the end can always justify the means for those who want it that way."

"Don't they restrain people—"

"That's enough, Jir!"

Trust Molly to return quickly to fundamental hypocrisy; the automatic response—his mind felicitously grasped the phrase, conditioned reflex—to the customary stimulus. She had taken an explicit stand against his common sense, but her rigid code—honor thy father; iron rayon the wrong side; register and vote; avoid scenes; only white wine with fish; never rehire a discharged servant—quickly substituted pattern for impulse. Seventeen years.

The road turned away from the ocean, squirmed inland and uphill for still slower miles, abruptly widened into a divided, four-lane highway. Without hesitation Mr. Jimmon took the southbound side; for the first time since they had left Rambla Catalina his foot went down to the floorboards and with a sigh of relief the station wagon jumped into smooth, ecstatic speed.

Improvisation and strategy again. And, he acknowledged generously, the defiant example this morning of those who'd done the same thing in Malibu. Now, out of reestablished habit the other cars kept to the northbound side even though there was nothing coming south. Timidity, routine, inertia. Pretty soon they would realize sheepishly that there were neither traffic nor traffic cops to keep them off, but it would be miles before they had another chance to cross over. By that time he would have reached the comparatively uncongested stretch.

"It's dangerous, David."

Obey the law. No smoking. Keep off the grass. Please adjust your clothes before leaving. Trespassers will be. Picking California wild flowers or shrubs is forbidden. Parking 45 min. Do not.

She hadn't put the protest in the more usual form of a question. Would that technique have been more irritating? *Isn't it dangerous Day-vid?* His calm conclusion: it didn't matter.

"No time for niceties," chirped Jir.

Mr. Jimmon tried to remember Jir as a baby. All the bad novels he had read in the days when he read anything except *Time* and *The New Yorker*, all the movies he'd seen before they had a TV set, always prescribed such retrospection as a specific for softening the present. If he could recall David Alonzo Jimmon, Junior, at six months, helpless and lovable, it should make Jir more acceptable by discovering some faint traces of the one in the other.

But though he could re-create in detail the interminable, disgusting, trembling months of that initial pregnancy (had he really

been afraid she would die?) he was completely unable to reconstruct the appearance of his firstborn before the age of...It must
have been at six that Jir had taken his baby sister out for a walk
and lost her. (Had Molly permitted it? He still didn't know for sure.)
Erika hadn't been found for four hours.

The tidal screeching of sirens invaded and destroyed his thoughts.
What the devil...? His foot lifted from the gas pedal as he slewed
obediently to the right, ingrained reverence surfacing at the sound.

"I told you it wasn't safe! Are you really trying to kill us all?"

Whipping over the rise ahead, a pair of motorcycles crackled.
Behind them snapped a long line of assorted vehicles, fire trucks
and ambulances mostly, interspersed here and there with olive-drab
army equipment. The cavalcade flicked down the central white line,
one wheel in each lane. Mr. Jimmon edged the station wagon as
far over as he could; it still occupied too much room to permit the
free passage of the onrush without compromise.

The knees and elbows of the motorcycle policemen stuck out
widely, reminding Mr. Jimmon of grasshoppers. The one on the
near side was headed straight for the station wagon's left front fender;
for a moment Mr. Jimmon closed his eyes as he plotted the un-
swerving course, knifing through the crustlike steel, bouncing lightly
on the tires, and continuing unperturbed. He opened them to see
the other officer shoot past, mouth angrily open in his direction
while the one straight ahead came to a skidding stop.

"Going to get it now," gloated Wendell.

An old-fashioned parent, one of the horrible examples held up
to shuddering moderns like himself, would have reached back and
relieved his tension by clouting Wendell across the mouth. Mr.
Jimmon merely turned off the motor.

The cop was not indulging in the customary deliberate and om-
inous performance of slowly dismounting and striding toward his
victim with ever more menacing steps. Instead he got off quickly
and covered the few feet to Mr. Jimmon's window with unimpres-
sive speed.

Heavy goggles concealed his eyes; dust and stubble covered his
face. "Operator's license!"

Mr. Jimmon knew what he was saying, but the sirens and the
continuous rustle of the convoy prevented the sound from coming
through. Again the cop deviated from the established routine; he

did not take the proffered license and examine it incredulously before drawing out his pad and pencil, but wrote the citation, glancing up and down from the card to Mr. Jimmon's hand.

Even so, the last of the vehicles—*San Jose F.D.*—passed before he handed the summons through the window to be signed. "Turn around and proceed in the proper direction," he ordered curtly, pocketing the pad and buttoning his jacket briskly.

Mr. Jimmon nodded. The officer hesitated, as though waiting for some limp excuse. Mr. Jimmon said nothing.

"No tricks," said the policeman over his shoulder. "Turn around and proceed in the proper direction."

He almost ran to his motorcycle, and roared off, twisting his head for a final stern frown as he passed, siren wailing. Mr. Jimmon watched him dwindle in the rearview mirror and then started the motor. "Gonna lose a lot more than you gained," commented Jir.

Mr. Jimmon gave a last glance in the mirror and moved ahead, shifting into second. "David!" exclaimed Molly, horrified, "you're not turning around!"

"Observant," muttered Mr. Jimmon, between his teeth.

"Dad, you can't get away with it," Jir decided judicially.

Mr. Jimmon's answer was to press the accelerator down savagely. The empty highway stretched invitingly ahead; a few hundred yards to their right they could see the northbound lanes ant-clustered. The sudden motion stirred the traffic citation on his lap, floating it down to the floor. Erika leaned forward and picked it up.

"Throw it away," ordered Mr. Jimmon.

Molly gasped. "You're out of your mind."

"You're a fool," stated Mr. Jimmon calmly. "Why should I save that piece of paper?"

"Isn't what you told the cop." Jir was openly jeering now.

"I might as well have, if I'd wanted to waste conversation. I don't know why I was blessed with such a stupid family—"

"May be something in heredity after all."

If Jir had said it out loud, reflected Mr. Jimmon, it would have passed casually as normal domestic repartee, a little ill-natured perhaps, certainly callow and trite, but not especially provocative. Muttered, so that it was barely audible, it was an ultimate defiance. He had read that far back in prehistory, when the young males felt their strength, they sought to overthrow the rule of the Old Man and usurp his place. No doubt they uttered a preliminary growl or screech as challenge. They were not very bright, but they acted in a pattern; a pattern Jir was apparently following.

Refreshed by placing Jir in proper Neanderthal setting, Mr. Jimmon went on, "—none of you seem to have the slightest initiative or ability to grasp reality. Tickets, cops, judges, juries mean nothing anymore. There is no law now but the law of survival."

"Aren't you being dramatic, David?" Molly's tone was deliberately aloof adult to excited child.

"I could hear you underline words, dad," said Erika, but he felt there was no malice in her gibe.

"You mean we can do anything we want now? Shoot people? Steal cars and things?" asked Wendell.

"There, David! You see?"

Yes, I see. Better than you. Little savage. This is the pattern. What will Wendell—and the thousands of other Wendells (for it would be unjust to suppose Molly's genes and domestic influence unique)—be like after six months of anarchy? Or after six years?

Survivors, yes. And that will be about all: naked, primitive, ferocious, superstitious savages. Wendell can read and write (but not so fluently as I or any of our generation at his age); how long will he retain the tags and scraps of progressive schooling?

And Jir? Detachedly Mr. Jimmon foresaw the fate of Jir. Unlike Wendell, who would adjust to the new conditions, Jir would go wild in another sense. His values were already set; they were those of television, high school dating, comic strips, law and order. Released from civilization, his brief future would be one of guilty rape and pillage until he fell victim to another youth or gang bent the same way. Molly would disintegrate and perish quickly. Erika...

The station wagon flashed along the comparatively unimpeded highway. Having passed the next crossover, there were now other vehicles on the southbound strip, but even on the northbound one, crowding had eased.

Furiously Mr. Jimmon determined to preserve the civilization in Erika. (He would teach her everything he knew [including the insurance business?])...ah, if he were some kind of scientist, now— not the Dan Davisson kind, whose abstract speculations seemed always to prepare the way for some new method of destruction, but the... Franklin? Jefferson? Watt? protect her night and day from the refugees who would be roaming the hills south of Monterey. The rifle ammunition, properly used—and he woud see that no one but himself used it—would last years. After it was gone— presuming fragments and pieces of a suicidal world hadn't pulled itself miraculously together to offer a place to return to—there were the two hunting bows whose steel-tipped shafts could stop a man as easily as a deer or mountain lion. He remembered debating long, at the time he had first begun preparing for It, how many bows to order, measuring their weight and bulk against the other precious freight and deciding at last that two was the satisfactory minimum. It must have been in his subconscious mind all along that of the whole family Erika was the only other person who could be trusted with a bow.

"There will be," he spoke in calm and solemn tones, not to Wendell, whose question was now left long behind, floating on the gas-greasy air of a sloping valley growing with live oaks, but to a large, impalpable audience, "There will be others who will think that because there is no longer law or law enforcement—"

"You're being simply fantastic!" She spoke more sharply than he had ever heard her in front of the children. "Just because It happened to Los Angeles—"

"And Pittsburgh."

"All right. And Pittsburgh, doesn't mean that the whole United States has collapsed and everyone in the country is running frantically for safety."

"Yet," added Mr. Jimmon firmly, "yet, do you suppose they are going to stop with Los Angeles and Pittsburgh, and leave Gary and Seattle standing? Or even New York and Chicago? Or do you imagine Washington will beg for armistice terms while there is the least sign of organized life left in the country?"

"We'll wipe Them out first," insisted Jir in patriotic shock. Wendell backed him up with a machine gun "brrrrr."

"Undoubtedly. But it will be the last gasp. At any rate it will be years, if at all in my lifetime, before stable communities are reestablished—"

"David, you're raving."

"Reestablished," he repeated. "So there will be many others who'll also feel that the dwindling of law and order is license to kill people and steal cars 'and things.' Naked force and cunning will be the only means of self-preservation. That was why I picked out a spot where I felt survival would be easiest; not only because of wood and water, game and fish, but because it's nowhere near the main highways, and so unlikely to be chosen by any great number."

"I wish you'd stop harping on that insane idea. You're just a little too old and flabby for pioneering. Even when you were younger you were hardly the rugged, outdoor type."

No, thought Mr. Jimmon, I was the sucker type. I would have gotten somewhere if I'd stayed in the bank, but like a bawd you pleaded; the insurance business brought in the quick money for you to give up your job and have Jir and the proper home. If you'd got rid of it as I wanted. Flabby, *Flabby!* Do you think your scrawniness is so enticing?

Controlling himself, he said aloud, "We've been through all this. Months ago. It's not a question of physique, but of life."

"Nonsense. Perfect nonsense. Responsible people who really know its effects... Maybe it was advisable to leave Malibu for a few days or even a few weeks. And perhaps it's wise to stay away from the larger cities. But a small town or village, or even one of those ranches where they take boarders—"

"Aw, mom, you agreed. You know you did. What's the matter with you anyway? Why are you acting like a drip?"

"I want to go and shoot rabbits and bears like dad said," insisted Wendell.

Erika said nothing, but Mr. Jimmon felt he had her sympathy; the boy's agreement was specious. Wearily he debated going over the whole ground again, patiently pointing out that what Molly said might work in the Dakotas or the Great Smokies but was hardly operative anywhere within refugee range of the Pacific Coast. He had explained all this many times, including the almost certain impossibility of getting enough gasoline to take them into any of the reasonably safe areas; that was why they'd agreed on the region below Monterey, on California State Highway 1, as the only logical goal.

A solitary car decorously bound in the legal direction interrupted his thoughts. Either crazy or has mighty important business, he decided. The car honked disapprovingly as it passed, hugging the extreme right of the road.

Passing through Buellton the clamor again rose for a pause at a filling station. He conceded inwardly that he could afford ten or fifteen minutes without strategic loss since by now they must be among the leaders of the exodus; ahead lay little more than the normal travel. However, he had reached such a state of irritated frustration and consciousness of injustice that he was willing to endure unnecessary discomfort himself in order to inflict a longer delay on them. In fact it lessened his own suffering to know the delay was needless, that he was doing it, and that his action was a just—if inadequate—punishment.

"We'll stop this side of Santa Maria," he said. "I'll get gas there."

Mr. Jimmon knew triumph: his forethought, his calculations, his generalship had justified themselves. Barring unlikely mechanical failure—the station wagon was in perfect shape—or accident—and the greatest danger had certainly passed—escape was now practically assured. For the first time he permitted himself to realize how unreal, how romantic the whole project had been. As any attempt to evade the fate charted for the multitude must be. The docile mass perished; the headstrong (but intelligent) individual survived.

Along with triumph went an expansion of his prophetic vision of life after reaching their destination. He had purposely not taxed the cargo capacity of the wagon with transitional goods; there was no tent, canned luxuries, sleeping bags, lanterns, candles, or any of the paraphernalia of camping midway between the urban and nomadic life. Instead, besides the weapons, tackle, and utensils, there was in miniature the List for Life on a Desert Island: shells and cartridges, lures, hooks, nets, gut, leaders, flint and steel, seeds, traps, needles and thread, government pamphlets on curing and tanning hides and the recognition of edible weeds and fungi, files, nails, a judicious stock of simple medicines. A pair of binoculars to spot intruders. No coffee, sugar, flour; they would begin living immediately as they would have to in a month or so in any case, on the old, half-forgotten human cunning.

"Cunning," he said aloud.

"What?"

"Nothing. Nothing."

"I still think you should have made an effort to reach Pearl and Dan."

"The telephone was dead, Mother."

"At the moment, Erika. You can hardly have forgotten how often the lines have been down before. And it never takes more than half an hour till they're working again."

"Mother, Dan Davisson is quite capable of looking after himself."

Mr. Jimmons shut out the rest of the conversation so completely he didn't know whether there was any more to it or not. He shut out the intense preoccupation with driving, with making speed, with calculating possible gains. In the core of his mind, quite detached from everything about him, he examined and marveled.

Erika. The cool, inflexible, adult tone. Almost indulgent, but so dispassionate as not to be. One might have expected her to be exasperated by Molly's silliness, to have answered impatiently, or not at all.

Mother. Never in his recollection had the children ever called her anything but mom. The "Mother" implied—oh, it implied a multitude of things. An entirely new relationship, for one. A relationship of aloofness, or propriety without emotion. The ancient stump of the umbilical cord, black and shriveled, had dropped off painlessly.

She had not bothered to argue about the telephone or point out the gulf between "before" and now. She had not even tried to touch Molly's deepening refusal of reality. She had been ... indulgent.

Not "Uncle Dan," twitteringly imposed false avuncularity, but striking through it (and the facade of "Pearl and") and aside (when I was a child I ... something ... but now I have put aside childish things); the wealth of implicit assertion. Ah, yes, Mother, we all know the pardonable weakness and vanity; we excuse you for your constant reminders, but Mother, with all deference, we refuse to be forced any longer to be parties to middle-age's nostalgic flirtatiousness. One could almost feel sorry for Molly.

... middle-age's nostalgic flirtatiousness ...

... nostalgic ...

Metaphorically Mr. Jimmon sat abruptly upright. The fact that he was already physically in this position made the transition, while invisible, no less emphatic. The nostalgic flirtatiousness of middle age implied—might imply—memory of something more than mere coquetry. Molly and Dan.

It all fitted together so perfectly it was impossible to believe it untrue. The impecunious young lovers, equally devoted to Dan's genius, realizing marriage was out of the question (he had never denied Molly's shrewdness; as for Dan's impracticality, well, impracticality wasn't necessarily uniform or consistent. Dan had been practical enough to marry Pearl and Pearl's money) could have renounced...

Or not renounced at all?

Mr. Jimmon smiled; the thought did not ruffle him. Cuckoo, cuckoo. How vulgar, how absurd. Suppose Jir were Dan's? A blessed thought.

Regretfully he conceded the insuperable obstacle of Molly's conventionality. Jir was the product of his own loins. But wasn't there an old superstition about the image in the woman's mind at the instant of conception? So, justly and rightly Jir was not his. Nor Wendy, for that matter. Only Erika, by some accident. Mr. Jimmon felt free and lighthearted.

"Get gas at the next station," he bulletined.

"The next one with a clean rest room," Molly corrected.

Invincible. The Earth Mother, using men for her purposes: reproduction, clean rest rooms, nourishment, objects of culpability, *Better Homes and Gardens.* The bank was my life; I could have gone far but: Why, David—they pay you less than the janitor! It's ridiculous. And: I can't understand why you hesitate; it isn't as though it were a different type of work.

No, not different; just more profitable. Why didn't she tell Dan Davisson to become an accountant; that was the same type of work, just more profitable? Perhaps she had and Dan had simply been less befuddled. Or amenable. Or stronger in purpose? Mr. Jimmon probed his pride thoroughly and relentlessly without finding the faintest twinge of retrospective jealousy. Nothing like that mattered now. Nor, he admitted, had it for years.

Two close-peaked hills gulped the sun. He toyed with the idea of crossing to the northbound side now that it was uncongested and there were occasional southbound cars. Before he could decide the divided highway ended.

"I hope you're not planning to spend the night in some horrible motel," said Molly. "I want a decent bath and a good dinner."

Spend the night. Bath. Dinner. Again calm sentences formed in his mind, but they were blown apart by the unbelievable, the monumental obtuseness. How could you say, it is absolutely essential to drive till we get there? When there were no absolutes, no essentials in her concepts? My dear Molly, I—.

"No," he said, switching on the lights.

Wendy, he knew, would be the next to kick up a fuss. Till he fell mercifully asleep. If he did. Jir was probably debating the relative excitements of driving all night and stopping in a strange town. His voice would soon be heard.

The lights of the combination wayside store and filling station burned inefficiently, illuminating the deteriorating false front brightly and leaving the gas pumps in shadow. Swallowing regret at finally surrendering to mechanical and human need, and so losing the hard-won position, relaxing even for a short while the fierce initiative that had brought them through in the face of all probability, he pulled the station wagon alongside the pumps and shut off the motor. About halfway—the worst half, much the worst half— to their goal. Not bad.

Molly opened the door on her side with stiff dignity. "I certainly wouldn't call this a *clean* station." She waited for a moment, hand still on the window, as though expecting an answer.

"Crummy joint," exclaimed Wendell, clambering awkwardly out.

"Why not?" asked Jir. "No time for niceties." He brushed past his mother, who was walking slowly into the shadows.

"Erika," began Mr. Jimmon, in a half-whisper.

"Yes, dad?"

"Oh . . . never mind. Later."

He was not himself quite sure what he had wanted to say, what exclusive, urgent message he had to convey. For no particular reason he switched on the interior light and glanced at the packed orderliness of the wagon. Then he slid out from behind the wheel.

No sign of the attendant, but the place was certainly not closed. Not with the lights on and the hoses ready. He stretched, and walked slowly, savoring the comfortably painful uncramping of his muscles, toward the crude outhouse labeled MEN. Molly, he thought, must be furious.

When he returned, a man was leaning against the station wagon. "Fill it up with ethyl," said Mr. Jimmon pleasantly, "and check the oil and water."

The man made no move. "That'll be five bucks a gallon." Mr. Jimmon thought there was an uncertain tremor in his voice.

"Nonsense; I've plenty of ration coupons."

"Okay." The nervousness was gone now, replaced by an ugly truculence. "Chew'm up and spit'm in your gas tank. See how far you can run on them."

The situation was not unanticipated. Indeed, Mr. Jimmon thought with satisfaction of how much worse it must be closer to Los Angeles; how much harder the gouger would be on later supplicants as his supply of gasoline dwindled. "Listen," he said, and there was reasonableness rather than anger in his voice, "we're not out of gas. I've got enough to get to Santa Maria, even to San Luis Obispo."

"Okay. Go on then. Ain't stopping you."

"Listen. I understand your position. You have a right to make a profit in spite of government red tape."

Nervousness returned to the man's speech. "Look, whyn't you go on? There's plenty other stations up ahead."

The reluctant bandit. Mr. Jimmon was entertained. He had fully intended to bargain, to offer $2 a gallon, even to threaten with the pistol in the glove compartment. Now it seemed mean and niggling even to protest. What good was money now? "All right," he said, "I'll pay you five dollars a gallon."

Still the other made no move. "In advance."

For the first time Mr. Jimmon was annoyed; time was being wasted. "Just how can I pay you in advance when I don't know how many gallons it'll take to fill the tank?"

The man shrugged.

"Tell you what I'll do. I'll pay for each gallon as you pump it. In advance." He drew out a handful of bills; the bulk of his money was in his wallet, but he'd put the small bills in his pockets. He handed over a five. "Spill the first one on the ground or in a can if you've got one."

"How's that?"

Why should I tell him; give him ideas? As if he hadn't got them already. "Just call me eccentric," he said. "I don't want the first gallon from the pump. Why should you care? It's just five dollars more profit."

For a moment Mr. Jimmon thought the man was going to refuse, and he regarded his foresight with new reverence. Then he reached behind the pump and produced a flatsided tin in which he inserted the flexible end of the hose. Mr. Jimmon handed over the bill, the man wound the handle round and back—it was an ancient gas pump such as Mr. Jimmon hadn't seen for years—and lifted the drooling hose from the can.

"Minute," said Mr. Jimmon.

He stuck two fingers quickly and delicately inside the nozzle and smelled them. Gas all right, not water. He held out a ten-dollar bill. "Start filling."

Jir and Wendell appeared out of the shadows. "Can we stop at a town where there's a movie tonight?"

The handle turned, a cog-toothed rod crept up and retreated, gasoline gurgled into the tank. Movies, thought Mr. Jimmon, handing over another bill; movies, rest rooms, baths, restaurants. Gouge apprehensively lest a scene be made and propriety disturbed. In a surrealist daydream he saw Molly turning the crank, grinding him on the cogs, pouring his essence into insatiable Jir and Wendell. He held out $20.

Twelve gallons had been put in when Molly appeared. "You have a phone here?" he asked casually. Knowing the answer from the blue enameled sign not quite lost among less sturdy ones advertising soft drinks and cigarettes.

"You want to call the cops?" He didn't pause in his pumping.

"No. Know if the lines to L.A."—Mr. Jimmon loathed the abbreviation—"are open yet?" He gave him another ten.

"How should I know?"

Mr. Jimmon beckoned his wife around the other side of the wagon, out of sight. Swiftly but casually he extracted the contents of his wallet. The 200 dollar bills made a fat lump. "Put this in your bag," he said. "Tell you why later. Meantime why don't you try and get Pearl and Dan on the phone? See if they're okay?"

He imagined the puzzled look on her face. "Go on," he urged. "We can spare a minute while he's checking the oil."

He thought there was a hint of uncertainty in Molly's walk as she went toward the store. Erika joined her brothers. The tank gulped: gasoline splashed on the concrete. "Guess that's it."

The man became suddenly brisk as he put up the hose, screwed the gas cap back on. Mr. Jimmon had already disengaged the hood; the man offered the radiator a squirt of water, pulled up the oil gauge, wiped it, plunged it down, squinted at it under the light, and said, "Oil's OK."

"All right," said Mr. Jimmon. "Get in, Erika."

Some of the lights shone directly on her face. Again he noted how mature and self-assured she looked. Erika would survive— and not as a savage either. The man started to wipe the windshield. "Oh, Jir," he said casually, "run in and see if your mother is getting her connection. Tell her we'll wait."

"Aw, furcrysay. I don't see why I always—"

"And ask her to buy a couple of boxes of candy bars if they've got them. Wendell, go with Jir, will you?"

He slid in behind the wheel and closed the door gently. The motor started with hardly a sound. As he put his foot on the clutch and shifted into low he thought Erika turned to him with a startled look. As the station wagon moved forward, he was sure of it.

"It's all right, Erika," said Mr. Jimmon. "I'll explain later." He'd have lots of time to do it.

5 _____

When they found the corpse of the elder Ms. Lot as dry and salty as a country ham in that evaporated brine pit beside the road from Sodom, did anybody perform an autopsy? Was there an inquest? The Bible doesn't really say God did it to her, only that He warned her. "And his wife, looking back, was turned into a pillar of salt." Thud.

You'll be spared the details of the nuclear war out of which the rest of these stories grow. The state of the art in thermonuclear horror-entertainment at the time of this writing is still the motion picture *Threads*. All the nuclear bombs in this book have already been dropped, except in the memories of certain characters. What will it be like after the end of the world?

Like the Jimmons, Carol Emshwiller's family have fuel problems on their holiday at the beach four years after Megawar. Among other worries, the concern about genetic damage or infertility begins to show, a concern that turns up again and again in post-Megawar fiction, and several times in this book.

DAY AT THE BEACH
by Carol Emshwiller

"It's Saturday," the absolutely hairless woman said, and she pulled at her frayed green kerchief to make sure it covered her head. "I sometimes forget to keep track of the days, but I marked three more off on the calendar because I think that's how many I forgot, so this *must* be Saturday."

Her name was Myra and she had neither eyebrows nor lashes nor even a faint, transparent down along her cheeks. Once she had had long, black hair, but now, looking at her pink, bare face, one would guess she had been a redhead.

Her equally hairless husband, Ben, sprawled at the kitchen table waiting for breakfast. He wore red plaid Bermuda shorts, rather faded, and a tee shirt with a large hole under the arm. His skull curved above his staring eyes more naked-seeming than hers because he wore no kerchief or hat.

"We used to always go out on Saturdays," she said, and she put a bowl of oatmeal at the side of the table in front of a youth chair.

Then she put the biggest bowl between her husband's elbows.

"I have to mow the lawn this morning," he said. "All the more so if it's Saturday."

She went on as if she hadn't heard. "A day like today we'd go to the beach. I forget a lot of things, but I remember that."

"If I were you, I just wouldn't think about it." Ben's empty eyes finally focused on the youth chair and he turned then to the open window behind him and yelled, "Littleboy, Littleboy," making the sound run together all L's and Y. "Hey, it's breakfast, Boy," and under his breath he said, "He won't come."

"But I *do* think about it. I remember hot dogs and clam chowder and how cool it was days like this. I don't suppose I even have a bathing suit around any more."

"It wouldn't be like it used to be."

"Oh, the sea's the same. That's one thing sure. I wonder if the boardwalk's still there."

"Hah," he said. "I don't have to see it to know it's all gone for firewood. It's been four winters now."

She sat down, put her elbows on the table and stared at her bowl. "Oatmeal," she said, putting in that one word everything she felt about the beach and wanting to go there.

"It's not that I don't want to do better for you," Ben said. He touched her arm with the tips of his fingers for just a moment. "I wish I could. And I wish I could have hung on to that corned beef hash last time, but it was heavy and I had to run and there was a fight on the train and I lost the sugar, too. I wonder which bastard has it now."

"I know how hard you try, Ben. I do. It's just sometimes everything comes on you at once, especially when it's a Saturday like this. Having to get water way down the block and that only when there's electricity to run the pump, and this oatmeal; sometimes it's just once too often, and then, most of all, you commuting in all that danger to get food."

"I make out. I'm not the smallest one on that train."

"God, I think that everyday. Thank God, I say to myself, or where would we be now. Dead of starvation that's where."

She watched him leaning low over his bowl, pushing his lips out and making a sucking sound. Even now she was still surprised to see how long and naked his skull arched, and she had an impulse, seeing it there so bare and ugly and thinking of the commuting, to cover it gently with her two hands, to cup it and make her hands do for his hair; but she only smoothed at her kerchief again to make sure it covered her own baldness.

"Is it living, though? Is it living, staying home all the time, hiding like, in this house? Maybe it's the rest of them, the dead ones, that are lucky. It's pretty sad when a person can't even go to the beach on a Saturday."

She was thinking the one thing she didn't want to do most of all was to hurt him. No, she told herself inside, sternly. Stop it right now. Be silent for once and eat, and, like Ben says, don't think; but she was caught up in it somehow and she said, "You know, Littleboy never did go to the beach yet, not even once, and it's only nine miles down," and she knew it would hurt him.

"Where is Littleboy?" he said and yelled again out the window. "He just roams."

"It isn't as if there were cars to worry about any more, and have you seen how fast he is and how he climbs so good for three and a half? Besides, what can you do when he gets up so early?"

He was finished eating now and he got up and dipped a cup of water from the large pan on the stove and drank it. "I'll take a look," he said. "He won't come when you call."

She began to eat finally, watching him out the kitchen window and listening to him calling. Seeing him hunched forward and squinting because he had worn glasses before and his last pair had been broken a year ago. Not in a fight, because he was careful not to wear them commuting even then, when it wasn't quite so bad. It was Littleboy who had done it, climbed up and got them himself from the very top drawer, and he was a whole year younger. Next thing she knew they were on the floor, broken.

Ben disappeared out of range of the window and Littleboy came darting in as though he had been huddling by the door behind the arborvitae all the time.

He was the opposite of his big, pink and hairless parents, with thick and fine black hair growing low over his forehead and extending down the back of his neck so far that she always wondered if it ended where hair used to end before, or whether it grew too far down. He was thin and small for his age, but strong-looking and wiry with long arms and legs. He had a pale, olive skin, wide, blunt features and a wary stare, and he looked at her now, waiting to see what she would do.

She only sighed, lifted him and put him in his youth chair and kissed his firm, warm cheek, thinking, what beautiful hair, and wishing she knew how to cut it better so he would look neat.

"We don't have any more sugar," she said, "but I saved you some raisins," and she took down a box and sprinkled some on his cereal.

Then she went to the door and called, "He's here, Ben. He's here." And in a softer voice she said, "The pixy." She heard Ben answer with a whistle and she turned back to the kitchen to find Littleboy's oatmeal on the floor in a lopsided oval lump, and him, still looking at her with wise and wary brown eyes.

She knelt down first, and spooned most of it back into the bowl. Then she picked him up rather roughly, but there was gentleness to the roughness, too. She pulled at the elastic topped jeans and gave him two hard, satisfying slaps on bare buttocks. "It isn't as if we had food to waste," she said, noticing the down that grew along his backbone and wondering if that was the way three year olds had been before.

He made an Aaa, Aaa, but didn't cry, and after that she picked him up and held him so that he nuzzled into her neck in the way she liked. "Aaa," he said again, more softly, and bit her just above the collar bone.

She dropped him down, letting him kind of slide with her arms still around him. It hurt and she could see there was a shallow, half-inch piece bitten right out.

"He bit me again," she shouted, hearing Ben at the door. "He bit me. A real piece out even, and look, he has it in his mouth still."

"God, what a..."

"Don't hurt him. I already slapped him good for the floor and three is a hard age." She pulled at Ben's arm. "It says so in the books. Three is hard, it says." But she remembered it really said that three was a beginning to be cooperative age.

He let go and Littleboy ran out of the kitchen back toward the bedrooms.

She took a deep breath. "I've just got to get out of this house. I mean really away."

She sat down and let him wash the place and cross two bandaids over it. "Do you think we could go? Do you think we could go just one more time with a blanket and a picnic lunch? I've just got to do *something*."

"All right. All right. You wear the wrench in your belt and I'll wear the hammer, and we'll risk taking the car."

She spent twenty minutes looking for bathing suits and not finding them, and then she stopped because she knew it didn't really matter, there probably wouldn't be anyone there.

The picnic was simple enough. She gathered it together in five minutes, a precious can of tuna fish and hard, homemade biscuits baked the evening before when the electricity had come on for a while, and shriveled, worm-eaten apples, picked from neighboring trees and hoarded all winter in another house that had a cellar.

She heard Ben banging about in the garage, measuring out gas from his cache of cans, ten miles' worth to put in the car and ten miles' worth in a can to carry along and hide someplace for the trip back.

Now that he had decided they would go, her mind began to be full of what-ifs. Still, she thought, she would *not* change her mind. Surely once in four years was not too often to risk going to the beach. She had thought about it all last year too, and now she was going and she would enjoy it.

She gave Littleboy an apple to keep him busy and she packed the lunch in the basket, all the time pressing her lips tight together, and she said to herself that she was *not* going to think of any more what-ifs, and she *was* going to have a good time.

Ben had switched after the war from the big-finned Dodge to a small and rattly European car. They fitted into it cozily, the lunch in back with the army blanket and a pail and shovel for playing in the sand, and Littleboy in front on her lap, his hair brushing her cheek as he turned, looking out.

They started out on the empty road. "Remember how it was before on a weekend?" she said, and laughed. "Bumper to bumper, they called it. We didn't like it then."

A little way down they passed an old person on a bicycle, in jeans and a bright shirt with the tail out. They couldn't tell if it was a man or a woman, but the person smiled and they waved and called, "Aaa."

The sun was hot, but as they neared the beach there began to be a breeze and she could smell the sea. She began to feel as she had the very first time she had seen it. She had been born in Ohio and she was twelve before she had taken a trip and come out on the wide, flat, sunny sands and smelled this smell.

She held Littleboy tight though it made him squirm, and she leaned against Ben's shoulder. "Oh, it's going to be fun!" she said. "Littleboy, you're going to see the sea. Look darling, keep watching, and smell. It's delicious." And Littleboy squirmed until she let go again.

Then, at last, there was the sea, and it *was* exactly as it had always been, huge and sparkling and making a sound like . . . no, *drowning out* the noises of wars. Like the black sky with stars, or the cold and stolid moon, it dwarfed even what had happened.

They passed the long, brick bathhouses, looking about as they always had, but the boardwalks between were gone, as Ben had said, not a stick left of them.

"Let's stop at the main bathhouse."

"No," Ben said. "We better keep away from those places. You can't tell who's in there. I'm going way down beyond."

She was glad, really, especially because at the last bathhouse she thought she saw a dark figure duck behind the wall.

They went down another mile or so, then drove the car off behind some stunted trees and bushes.

"Nothing's going to spoil this Saturday," she said, pulling out the picnic things, "just nothing. Come, Littleboy" She kicked off her shoes and started running for the beach, the basket bouncing against her knee.

Littleboy slipped out of his roomy sneakers easily, and scampered after her. "You can take your clothes off," she told him. "There's nobody here at all."

When Ben came, later, after hiding the gas, she was settled, flat on the blanket in old red shorts and a halter, and still the same green kerchief, and Littleboy, brown and naked, splashed with his pail in the shallow water, the wetness bringing out the hairs along his back.

"Look," she said, "nobody as far as you can see and you can see so far. It gives you a different feeling from home. You know there are people here and there in the houses, but here, it's like we were the only ones, and here it doesn't even matter. Like Adam and Eve, we are, just you and me and our baby."

He lay on his stomach next to her. "Nice breeze," he said.

Shoulder to shoulder they watched the waves and the gulls and Littleboy, and later they splashed in the surf and then ate the lunch and lay watching again, lazy, on their stomachs. And after a while she turned on her back to see his face. "With the sea it doesn't matter at all," she said and she put her arm across his shoulder. "And we're just part of everything, the wind and the earth and the sea too, my Adam."

"Eve," he said and smiled and kissed her and it was a longer kiss than they had meant. "Myra. Myra."

"There's nobody but us."

She sat up. "I don't even know a doctor since Press Smith was killed by those robbing kids and I'd be scared."

"We'll find one. Besides, you didn't have any trouble. It's been so damn long." She pulled away from his arm. "And I love you. And Littleboy, he'll be way over four by the time we'd have another one."

She stood up and stretched and then looked down the beach and Ben put a hand around her ankle. She looked down the other way. "Somebody's coming," she said, and then he got up too.

Far down, walking in a business-like way on the hard, damp part of the sand, three men were coming toward them.

"You got your wrench?" Ben asked. "Put it under the blanket and sit down by it, but keep your knees under you."

He put his tee shirt back on, leaving it hanging out, and he hooked the hammer under his belt in back, the top covered by the shirt. Then he stood and waited for them to come.

They were all three bald and shirtless. Two wore jeans cut off at the knees and thick belts, and the other had checked shorts and a red leather cap and a pistol stuck in his belt in the middle of the front at the buckle. He was older. The others looked like kids and they held back as they neared and let the older one come up alone. He was a small man, but looked tough. "You got gas," he said, a flat-voiced statement of fact.

"Just enough to get home."

"I don't mean right here. You got gas at home is what I mean."

Myra sat stiffly, her hand on the blanket on top of where the wrench was. Ben was a little in front of her and she could see his curving, forward-sloping shoulders and the lump of the hammer-head at the small of his back. If he stood up straight, she thought, and held his shoulders like they ought to be, he would look broad and even taller and he would show that little man, but the other had the pistol. Her eyes kept coming back to its shining black.

Ben took a step forward. "Don't move," the little man said. He shifted his weight to one leg, looking relaxed, and put his hand on his hip near the pistol. "Where you got the gas to get you home? Maybe we'll come with you and you might lend us a little of that gas you got there at your house. Where'd you hide the stuff to get you back, or I'll let my boys play a bit with your little one and you might not like it."

Littleboy, she saw, had edged down, away from them, and he crouched now, watching with his wide-eyed stare. She could see the tense, stringy muscles along his arms and legs and he reminded her of gibbons she had seen at the zoo long ago. His poor little face looks old, she thought, too old for three years. Her fingers closed over the blanket-covered wrench. They'd better not hurt Littleboy.

She heard her husband say, "I don't know." "Oh, Ben," she said, "oh, Ben."

The man made a motion and the two youths started out, but Littleboy had started first, she saw. She pulled at her wrench and then had to stop and fumble with the blanket, and it took a long time because she kept her eyes on Littleboy and the two others chasing.

She heard a shout and a grunt beside her. "Oh, Ben," she said again, and turned, but it was Ben on top attacking the other, and the small man was trying to use his pistol as a club but he had hold of the wrong end for that, and Ben had the hammer and he was much bigger.

He was finished in a minute. She watched, empty-eyed, the whole of it, holding the wrench in a white-knuckled hand in case he needed her.

Afterward, he moved from the body into a crouching run, hammer in one hand and pistol, by the barrel, in the other. "You stay here," he shouted back.

She looked at the sea for a few minutes, and listened to it, but her own feelings seemed more important than the stoic sea now. She turned and followed, walking along the marks where the feet had swept at the soft sand.

Where the bushes began she saw him loping back. "What happened?"

"They ran off when they saw me after them with the other guy's gun. No bullets though. You'll have to help look now."

"He's lost!"

"He won't come when you call. We'll just have to look. He could be way out. I'll try that and you stay close and look here. The gas is buried under that bush there, if you need it."

"We've got to find him, Ben. He doesn't know his way home from here."

He came to her and kissed her and held her firmly across the shoulders with one arm. She could feel his muscles bunch into her neck as hard almost as the head of his hammer that pressed against her arm. She remembered a time four years ago when his embrace had been soft and comfortable. He had had hair then, but he had been quite fat, and now he was hard and bald, having gained something and lost something.

He turned and started off, but looked back and she smiled and nodded to show him she felt better from his arm around her and the kiss.

I would die if anything happened and we would lose Littleboy, she thought, but mostly I would hate to lose Ben. Then the world would really be lost altogether, and everything would be ended.

She looked, calling in a whisper, knowing she had to peer under each bush and watch behind and ahead for scampering things. He's so small when he huddles into a ball and he can sit so still. Sometimes I wish there was another three-year-old around to judge him by. I forget so much about how it used to be, before. Sometimes I just wonder about him.

"Littleboy, Littleboy. Mommy wants you," she called softly. "Come. There's still time to play in the sand and there are apples left." She leaned forward, and her hand reached to touch the bushes.

Later the breeze began to cool and a few clouds gathered. She shivered in just her shorts and halter, but it was mostly an inner coldness. She felt she had circled, hunting, for well over an hour, but she had no watch, and at a time like this she wasn't sure of her judgment. Still, the sun seemed low. They should go home soon. She kept watching now, too, for silhouettes of people who might *not* be Ben or Littleboy, and she probed the bushes with her wrench with less care. Every now and then she went back to look at the blanket and the basket and the pail and shovel, lying alone and far from the water, and the body there, with the red leather cap beside it.

And then, when she came back another time to see if all the things were still there, undisturbed, she saw a tall, two-headed seeming monster walking briskly down the beach, and one head, bouncing directly over the other one, had hair and was Littleboy's.

The sunset was just beginning. The rosy glow deepened as they neared her and changed the colors of everything. The red plaid of Ben's shorts seemed more emphatic. The sand turned orangeish. She ran to meet them, laughing and splashing her feet in the shallow water, and she came up and held Ben tight around the waist and Littleboy said, "Aaa."

"We'll be home before dark," she said. "There's even time for one last splash."

They packed up finally while Littleboy circled the body by the blanket, touching it sometimes until Ben slapped him for it and he went off and sat down and made little cat sounds to himself.

He fell asleep in her lap on the way home, lying forward against her with his head at her neck the way she liked. The sunset was deep, with reds and purples.

She leaned against Ben. "The beach always makes you tired," she said. "I remember that from before too. I'll be able to sleep tonight."

They drove silently along the wide empty parkway. The car had no lights, but that didn't matter.

"We did have a good day after all," she said. "I feel renewed."

"Good," he said.

It was just dark as they drove up to the house. Ben stopped the car and they sat a moment and held hands before moving to get the things out.

"We had a good day," she said again. "And Littleboy saw the sea." She put her hand on the sleeping boy's hair, gently so as not to disturb him and then she yawned. "I wonder if it really *was* Saturday."

6 _____

Man's feelings about his own technology have never been unmixed.
Religious sects have rejected all new-fangled gadgets and continue to
live as if culturally frozen in the last century. I heard many expressions
of disdain for technology during the back-to-the-Earth movement of the
sixties, especially at the only shantytown hippie commune I was
privileged to visit, where the women pulled the plow, the water was
pumped by hand, and organic gardening manuals were studied under
kerosene lamps. If so many people manage to dislike technology in
times of peace and prosperity, think how many survivors of Megawar
might blame not only the politicians but the scientists and technicians
who gave them weapons, and really turn back the clock. But a
rejection of technology is not a return to innocence, and does not
imply a subordination of Logos to Tao, or logic to compassion.

THE WHEEL
by John Wyndham

The old man sat on his stool and leaned back against the whitened
wall. He had upholstered the stool elegantly with a hare skin because there didn't seem to be much between his own skin and his

108

bones these days. It was exclusively his stool, and recognized in the farmstead as such. The strands of a whip that he was supposed to be plaiting drooped between his bent fingers, but, because the stool was comfortable and the sun was warm, his fingers had stopped moving and his head was nodding.

The yard was empty save for a few hens that pecked more inquisitively than hopefully in the dust, but there were sounds that told of others who had not the old man's leisure for siesta. From round the corner of the house came the occasional plonk of an empty bucket as it hit the water, and its scrape on the sides of the well as it came up full. In the shack across the yard a dull pounding went on rhythmically and soporifically. The old man's head fell further forward as he drowsed.

Presently, from beyond the rough enclosing wall there came another sound, slowly approaching. A rumbling and a rattling, with an intermittent squeaking. The old man's ears were no longer sharp, and for some minutes it failed to disturb him. Then he opened his eyes and, locating the sound, sat staring incredulously toward the gateway. The sound drew closer, and a boy's head showed above the wall. He grinned at the old man, an expression of excitement in his eyes. He did not call out, but moved a little faster until he came to the gate. There he turned into the yard proudly towing behind him a box mounted on four wooden wheels.

The old man got up suddenly from his seat, alarm in every gesture. He waved both arms at the boy as though he would push him back. The boy stopped. His expression of gleeful pride faded into astonishment. He stared at the old man who was waving him away so urgently. While he still hesitated, the old man continued to shoo him off with one hand while he placed the other on his own lips, and started to walk toward him. Reluctantly and bewilderedly the boy turned, but too late. The pounding in the shed stopped. A middle-aged woman appeared in the doorway. Her mouth was open to call, but the words did not come. Her jaw dropped slackly, her eyes seemed to bulge, then she crossed herself, and screamed....

The sound split the afternoon peace. Behind the house the bucket fell with a clatter, and a young woman's head showed round the corner. Her eyes widened. She crammed the back of one hand across her mouth, and crossed herself with the other. A young man appeared in the stable doorway, and stood there transfixed. Another girl came pelting out of the house with a little girl behind her. She stopped as suddenly as if she had run into something. The little girl stopped too, vaguely alarmed by the tableau, and clinging to her skirt.

The boy stood quite still with all their gaze upon him. His bewilderment began to give way to fright at the expression in their eyes. He looked from one horrified face to another until his gaze met the old man's. What he saw there seemed to reassure him a little—or to frighten him less. He swallowed. Tears were not far away as he spoke:

"Gran, what's the matter? What are they all looking at me like that for?"

As if the sound of his voice had released a spell the middle-aged woman came to life. She reached for a hayfork which leaned against the shack wall. Raising its points toward the boy she walked slowly in between him and the gate. In a hard voice she said:

"Go on! Get in the shed!"

"But, ma—" the boy began.

"Don't you dare call me that now," she told him.

In the tense lines of her face the boy could see something that was almost hatred. His own face screwed up, and he began to cry.

"Go on," she repeated harshly. "Get in there."

The boy backed away, a picture of bewildered misery. Then, suddenly, he turned and ran into the shed. She shut the door on him, and fastened it with a peg. She looked round at the rest as though defying them to speak. The young man withdrew silently into the gloom of the stable. The two young women crept away, taking the little girl with them. The woman and the old man were left alone.

Neither of them spoke. The old man stood motionless, regarding the box where it stood on its wheels. The woman suddenly put her hands up to her face. She made little moaning noises as she swayed, and the tears came trickling out between her fingers. The old man turned. His face was devoid of all expression. Presently she recovered herself a little.

"I never would have believed it. My own little David!" she said.

"If you'd not screamed, nobody need have known," said the old man.

His words took some seconds to sink in. When they did, her expression hardened again.

"Did you show him how?" she asked, suspiciously.

He shook his head.

"I'm old, but I'm not crazy," he told her. "And I'm fond of Davie," he added.

"You're wicked, though. That was a wicked thing you just said."

"It was true."

"I'm a God-fearing woman. I'll not have evil in my house—whatever shape it comes in. And when I see it I know my duty."

The old man drew breath for a reply, but checked it. He shook his head. He turned and went back to his stool, looking, somehow, older than before.

There was a tap on the door. A whispered *Sh!* For a moment Davie saw a square of night sky with a dark shape against it. Then the door closed again.

"You had your supper, Davie?" a voice asked.

"No, gran. Nobody's been."

The old man grunted.

"Thought not. Scared of you, all of 'em. Here, take this. Cold chicken, it is."

Davie's hand sought and found what the other held out to him. He gnawed on a leg while the old man moved about in the dark, searching for somewhere to sit. He found it, and let himself down with a sigh.

"This is a bad business, Davie boy. They've sent for the priest. He'll be along tomorrow."

"But I don't understand, gran. Why do they all act like I've done something wrong?"

"Oh, Davie!" said his grandfather, reproachfully.

"Honest, I don't, gran."

"Come now, Davie. Every Sunday you go to church, and every time you go, you pray. What do you pray?"

The boy gabbed a prayer. After a few moments the old man stopped him.

"There," he said. "That last bit."

"Preserve us from the Wheel?" Davie repeated, wonderingly. "What *is* the Wheel, gran? It must be something terrible bad, I know, 'cos when I ask them they just say it's wicked, and not to talk of it. But they don't say what it is."

The old man paused before he replied, then he said:

"That box you got out there. Who told you to fix it that way?"

"Why, nobody, gran. I just reckon it'd move easier that way. It does, too."

"Listen, Davie. Those things you put on the side of it—they're *wheels.*"

It was some time before the boy's voice came back out of the darkness. When it did, it sounded bewildered.

"What, those round bits of wood? But they can't be, gran. That's all they are—just round bits of wood. But the Wheel—that's something awful, terrible, something everybody's scared of."

"All the same, that's what they are." The old man ruminated awhile. "I'll tell you what's going to happen tomorrow, Davie. In the morning the priest will come here to see your box. It'll be still there because nobody dares to touch it. He'll sprinkle some water on it and say a prayer just to make it safe to handle. Then they'll take it into the field and make a fire under it, and they'll stand round singing hymns while it burns.

"Then they'll come back, and take you down to the village, and ask you questions. They'll ask you what the Devil looked like when he came to you, and what he offered to give you if you'd use the Wheel."

"But there wasn't any Devil, gran."

"That don't matter. If they think there was, then sooner or later you'll be telling them there was, *and* just how he looked when you saw him. They've got ways...Now what you got to do is act innocent. You got to say you found that box just the way it is now. You didn't know what it was, but you just brought it along on account of it would make good firewood. That's your story, and you've got to stick to it. 'F you stick to it, no matter what they do, *maybe* you'll get through okay."

"But gran, what is there that's so bad about the Wheel? I just can't understand."

The old man paused more lengthily than before.

"Well, it's a long story, Davie—and it all began a long, long while ago. Seems like in those days everybody was happy and good and suchlike. Then one day the Devil came along and met a man and told him that he could give him something to make him as strong as a hundred men, an' make him to run faster than the wind, an' fly higher than the birds. Well, the man said that'd be mighty fine, an' what did the Devil want for it? And the Devil said he didn't want a thing—not just then. And so he gave the man the Wheel.

"By and by, after the man had played around with the Wheel awhile he found out a whole lot of things about it: how it would make other Wheels, and still more Wheels, and do all the things the Devil had said, with a whole heap more."

"What, it'd fly, 'n everything?" said the boy.

"Sure. It did all those things. And it began to kill people, too—one way and another. Folks put more and more Wheels together the way the Devil told them, and they found they could do a whole lot bigger things, and kill more people, too. And they couldn't stop using the Wheel then on account of they would have starved if they had.

"Well, that was just what the Devil wanted. He'd got 'em cinched, you see. Pretty near everything in the world was depending on Wheels, and things got worse and worse, and the old Devil just lay back an' laughed to see what his Wheel was doing. Then things got terrible bad. I don't know quite the way it happened, but things got so terrible worse that wasn't scarcely anybody left alive—only just a few, like it had been after the Flood. An' they was near finished."

"And all that was on account of the Wheel?"

"Uh-huh—leastways, it couldn't have happened without it. Still, somehow they made out. They built shacks, an' planted corn, an' by an' by the Devil met a man and started talking about his Wheel again. Now this man was very old and very wise and very god-fearing, so he said to the Devil: 'No. You go right back to Hell,' and then he went all around warning everybody about the Devil and his wheel, and got 'em all plumb scared.

"But the old Devil don't give up that easy. He's mighty tricky, too. There's time when a man gets an idea that turns out to be pretty nearly a Wheel—maybe like rollers, or screws, or somethin'—but it'll just pass so long as it ain't fixed in the middle. Yes, he keeps along trying, an' now and then he does tempt a man into making a

Wheel. Then the priest comes and they burn the Wheel. And they take the man away. And to stop him making any more Wheels, and to discourage any other folk, they burn him too."

"They b-burn him?" stammered the boy.

"That's what they do. So you see why you got to say you *found* it, and stick to that."

"Maybe if I promised never to make another—?"

"That wouldn't be no good, Davie. They're all scared of the Wheel, and when men are scared they get angry and cruel. No, you gotta keep to it."

The boy thought for some moments, then he said:

"What about ma? She'll know. I had that box off her yesterday. Does it matter?"

The old man grunted. He said, heavily:

"Yes, it does matter. Women do a lot of pretending to be scared— but once they do scare, they scare more horribly than men. And your ma's dead scared."

There was a long silence in the darkness of the shed. When the old man spoke again, it was in a calm, quiet voice.

"Listen, Davie lad. I'm going to tell you something. And you're going to keep it to yourself—not tell a soul till maybe you're an old man like me?"

"Sure, gran, 'f you say."

"I'm tellin' you because you found out about the Wheel for yourself. There'll always be boys like you who do. There've got to be. You can't kill an idea the way they try to. You can keep it down awhile, but sooner or later it'll come out. Now what you've got to understand is that the Wheel's *not* evil. Never mind what the scared men all tell you. No discovery is good or evil until men make it that way. Think about that, Davie boy. One day they'll start to use the Wheel again. I hoped it would be in my time, but—well, maybe it'll be in yours. When it does come, don't you be one of the scared ones; be one of the ones that's going to show 'em how to use it better than they did last time. It's not the Wheel—it's fear that's evil, Davie. Remember that."

He stirred in the darkness. His feet clumped on the hard earth floor.

"Reckon it's time I was gettin' along. Where are you, boy?"

His groping hand found Davie's shoulder, and then rested a moment on his head.

"God bless you, Davie. And don't worry any more. It's goin' to be all right. You trust me?"

"Yes, gran."

"Then you go to sleep. There's some hay in the corner there."

The glimpse of dark sky showed briefly again. Then the sound of the old man's feet shuffled across the yard into silence.

When the priest arrived he found a horror-stricken knot of people collected in the yard. They were gazing at an old man who worked away with a mallet and pegs on a wooden box. The priest stood, scandalized.

"Stop!" he cried. "In the name of God, stop!"

The old man turned his head toward him. There was a grin of crafty senility on his face.

"Yesterday," he said, "I was a fool. I only made four wheels for it. Today I am a wise man—I am making two more wheels so that it will run half as easily again."

They burned the box, as he had said they would. Then they took him away.

In the afternoon a small boy whom everyone had forgotten turned his eyes from the column of smoke that rose in the direction of the village, and hid his face in his hands.

"I'll remember, gran. I'll remember. It's only fear that's evil," he said, and his voice choked in his tears.

7

You can count on the priest to be quite logical about the matter, I believe. He doesn't just follow the Logos, he enforces it.

Reason and compassion are not natural enemies, just natural strangers. They coexist in most scientists, most priests, most all of us. But compassion is just *not* a theorem of the Logos. Wyndham's priest reminds me of another one, his opposite in most ways, a most civilized and humane man of the cloth and also of science, the late Jesuit geobiologist Pierre Teilhard de Chardin. In 1946 he wrote an *étude* called "Some Reflections on the Spiritual Repercussions of the Atom Bomb"[1] in which he reproved those scientists who, on the eve of the first atomic explosion, felt moral qualms because by then a military victory was in sight *without* the weapon, and who wanted to stop the experiment, to suppress the knowledge. In his little essay, Teilhard does not mention the "spiritual repercussions" of Hiroshima and Nagasaki, and makes no comment on the decision to use the weapon. That the know-how of bomb building could never have been suppressed is certain. It seems strange to me that a faithful priest of Christ could let his admiration for scientific "progress" lead him to devalue the moral qualms of fellow scientists belatedly shrinking from the genocide implicit in their own invention. Teilhard was a deeply spiritual man, who as a thinker nevertheless sometimes carried the idea of an incarnate Logos to a near-idolatrous extreme as the goal of

[1]Which became a chapter of his book *The Future of Man* (New York: Harper & Row, 1964).

116

evolution. Compassion and the worship of progress seem not very compatible, but it is clear from his other work that, when he was not praising progress, Teilhard was a compassionate man. My admiration for the French Jesuit, who suffered the censorship if not the censure of his own church, is not diminished by his strange little étude, but the "spiritual repercussions of the atomic bomb" are better summed up in the soul of a Jody than in strange hymns to man's mastery over matter.

JODY AFTER THE WAR
by Edward Bryant

Light lay bloody on the mountainside. From our promontory jutting above the scrub pine, we looked out over the city. Denver spread from horizon to horizon. The tower of the U.S. Capitol Building caught the sun blindingly. We watched the contrail of a Concorde II jetliner making its subsonic approach into McNicholls Field, banking in a sweeping curve over the pine-lined foothills. Directly below us, a road coiled among rocks and trees. A campfire fed smoke into the November air. The wind nudged the smoke trail our way and I smelled the acrid tang of wood smoke. We watched the kaleidoscope of cloud shadows crosshatch the city.

Jody and I sat close, my arm around her shoulders. No words, no facial expressions as afternoon faded out to dusk. My feet gradually went to sleep.

"Hey."

"Mmh?" she said, startled.

"You look pensive."

Her face stayed blank.

"What are you thinking?"

"I'm not. I'm just feeling." She turned back to the city. "What are you thinking?"

"Uh, not much," I said. Lie; I'd been thinking about survivors. "Well, thinking how beautiful you are." Banal, but only half an evasion. I mean she *was* beautiful. Jody was imprinted in my mind the first time I saw her, when I peered up out of the anesthetic fog and managed to focus on her standing beside my hospital bed: the half-Indian face with the high cheekbones. Her eyes the color of dark smoke. I couldn't remember what she'd worn then. Today she wore faded blue jeans and a blue chambray work shirt, several sizes too large. No shoes. Typically, she had climbed the mountain barefoot.

Without looking back at me, she said, "You were thinking more than that."

I hesitated. I flashed a sudden mental image of Jody's face the way she had described it in her nightmares: pocked with red and black spots that oozed blood and pus, open sores that gaped where her hair had grown, her skin...

Jody squeezed my hand. It was as if she were thinking, that's all right, Paul, if you don't want to talk to me now, that's fine.

I never was any good with evasions, except perhaps with myself. Survivors. Back after the A-bombings of Hiroshima and Nagasaki, the Japanese had called them *hibakusha*—which translates roughly as "sufferers." Here in America we just called them survivors, after the Chinese suicided their psychotic society in the seventies, and destroyed most of urban America in the process. I guess I was lucky; I was just a kid in the middle of Nevada when the missiles hit. I'd hardly known what happened east of the Mississippi and west of the Sierras. But Jody had been with her parents somewhere close to Pittsburgh. So she became a survivor; one of millions. Most of them weren't even hurt in the bombings. Not physically.

Jody was a survivor. And I was lonely. I had thought we could give each other something that would help. But I wasn't sure anymore. I wondered if I had a choice after all. And I was scared.

Jody leaned against me and shared the warmth of my heavy windbreaker. The wind across the heaped boulders of the mountainside was chill, with the sun barely down. Jody pressed her head under my chin. I felt the crisp hair against my jaw. She rested quietly for a minute, then turned her face up toward mine.

"Remember the first time?"

"Here?"

She nodded. "A Sunday like this, only not so cold. I'd just gotten in from that Hayes Theatre assignment in Seattle when you phoned. I hadn't even unpacked. Then you called and got me up here for a picnic." She smiled. In the new shadows her teeth were very white. "What a god-awful time."

That picnic. A summer and about fourteen hundred miles had separated us while she set up PR holograms of *Hamlet* and I haunted Denver phone booths.

Then here on the mountainside we'd fought bitterly. We had hurt each other with words and Jody had begun to cry and I'd held her. We kissed and barbed words stopped. Through her tears, Jody whispered that she loved me and I told her how much I loved her. That was the last time either of us said those words. Funny how you use a word so glibly when you don't really understand it; then switch to euphemisms when you do.

"You're very far away."

"It's nothing." I fished for easy words. "The usual," I said. "My future with Ma Bell, going back to school, moving to Seattle to try writing for the network." Everything but—*Liar!* sneered something inside. Why didn't you include damaged chromosomes in the list, and leukemia, and paranoia, and frigidity, and...? *Shut up!*

"Poor Paul," Jody said. "Hemmed in. Doesn't know which way to turn. For Christmas I think I'll get you a lifesize 'gram from *Hamlet*. I know a guy at the Hayes who can get me one."

"Hamlet, right. That's me." I lightly kissed her forehead. "There, I feel better. You ought to be a therapist."

Jody looked at me strangely and there was a quick silence I couldn't fill.

She smiled then and said, "All right, I'm a therapist. Be a good patient and eat. The thermos won't keep the coffee hot all night."

She reached into the canvas knapsack I'd packed up the mountain and took out the thermos and some foil parcels. "Soybeef," she said, pointing to the sandwiches. "The salt's in with the hardboiled eggs. There's cake for dessert."

Filling my stomach was easier than stripping my soul, so I ate. But the taste in my mouth when I thought about Jody fixing meals all the rest of our lives. Food for two, three times a day, seven days a week, an average of thirty days a...Always unvarying. Always food for two. God, I wanted children! I concentrated on chewing.

After the meal, we drank beer and watched the city below as five million Denverites turned on their lights. I knew I was getting too high too fast when I confused pulling the tabs off self-cooling beer cans with plucking petals from daisies.

She loves me.

Funny how melodrama crops up in real life. *My* life. Like when I met her.

It was about a year before, when I'd just gotten a job with Mountain Bell as a SMART—that's their clever acronym for Service Maintenance and Repair Trainee. In a city the size of Denver there are more than half a million public pay phones, of which at least a third are out of order at any given time; vandals mostly, sometimes mechanical failure. Someone has to go out and spotcheck the phones, then fix the ones that are broken. That was my job. Simple.

I'd gone into a bad area, Five Points, where service was estimated to be eighty percent blanked out. I should have been smart enough to take a partner along, or maybe to wear blackface. But I was a lot younger then. I ended up on a bright Tuesday afternoon, sprawled in my own blood on the sidewalk in front of a grocery store after a Chicago gang had kicked the hell out of me.

After about an hour somebody called an ambulance. Jody. On the phone I'd just repaired before I got stomped. She'd wandered by with a field crew on some documentary assignment, snapping holograms of the poverty conditions.

She loves me not.

I remembered what we'd quarreled about in September. Back in early August a friend of Jody's and mine had come back from Seattle. He was an audio engineer who'd worked free-lance with the Hayes Theatre. He'd seen Jody.

"Man, talk about wild!" my friend said. "She must've got covered by everything with pants from Oregon to Vancouver." He looked at my face. "Uh, you have something going with her?"

She loves me.

"What's so hard to understand?" Jody had said. "Didn't you ever meet a survivor before? Didn't you ever think about survivors? What it's like to see death so plainly all around?" Her voice was low and very intense. "And what about feeling you ought never to have babies, and not wanting even to come close to taking the chance?" Her voice became dull and passionless. "Then there was Seattle, Paul, and there's the paradox. The only real defense against death is not to feel. But I *want* to feel sometimes and that's why—" She broke off and began to cry. "Paul, that's why there were so many of them. But they couldn't—I can't make it. Not with anyone."

Confused, I held her.

"I want you."

And it didn't matter which of us had said that first.

She loves me not.

"Why don't you ever say what you think?"

"It's easy," I said, a little bitter. "Try being a lonely stoic all your life. It gets to be habit after a while."

"You think I don't know?" She rolled over, turned to the wall. "I'm trying to get through." Her voice was muffled by the blankets.

"Yeah. Me too."

She sat up suddenly, the sheets falling away from her. "Listen! I told you it would be like this. You can have me. But you have to accept what I am."

"I will."

Neither of us said anything more until morning.

She loves me.

Another night she woke up screaming. I stroked her hair and kissed her face lightly.

"Another one?"

She nodded.

"Bad?"

"Yes."

"You want to talk about it?"

There was hesitation, then a slow nod.

"I was in front of a mirror in some incredibly baroque old bedroom," she said. "I was vomiting blood and my hair was coming out and falling down on my shoulders. It wound around my throat and I couldn't breathe. I opened my mouth and there was blood running from my gums. And my skin—it was completely covered with black and red pustules. They—" She paused and closed her eyes. "They were strangely beautiful." She whimpered. "The worst—" She clung to me tightly. "Oh, God! The worst part was that I was pregnant."

She roughly pushed herself away and wouldn't let me try to comfort her. She lay on her back and stared at the ceiling. Finally, childlike, she took my hand. She held my fingers very tight all the rest of the night.

She loves me not.

But she did, I thought. She does. In her own way, just as you love her. It's never going to be the way you imagined it as a kid. But you love her. Ask her. Ask her now.

"What's going on?" Jody asked, craning her neck to look directly below our ledge. Far down we saw a pair of headlights, a car sliding around the hairpin turns in the foothills road. The whine of a racing turbine rasped our ears.

"I don't know. Some clown in a hurry to park with his girl."

The car approached the crest of a hill and for an instant the headlights shone directly at us, dazzling our eyes. Jody jerked back and screamed. "The sun! So bright! God, Pittsburgh—" Her strength seemed to drain; I lowered her gently to the ledge and sat down beside her. The rock was rough and cold as the day's heat left. I couldn't see Jody's face, except as a blur in the darkness. There was light from the city and a little from the stars, but the moon hadn't risen.

"Please kiss me."

I kissed her and used the forbidden words. "I love you."

I touched her breast; she shivered against me and whispered something I couldn't quite understand. A while later my hand touched the waist of her jeans and she drew away.

"Paul, no."

"Why not?" The beer and my emotional jag pulsed in the back of my skull. I ached.

"You know."

I knew. For a while she didn't say anything more, nor did I. We felt tension build its barrier. Then she relaxed and put her cheek against mine. Somehow we both laughed and the tension eased.

Ask her. And I knew I couldn't delay longer. "Damn it," I said, "I still love you. And I know what I'm getting into." I paused to breathe. "After Christmas I'm taking off for Seattle. I want you to marry me there."

I felt her muscles tense. Jody pulled away from me and got to her feet. She walked to the end of the ledge and looked out beyond the city. She turned to face me and her hands were clenched.

"I don't know," she said. "At the end of summer I'd have said 'no' immediately. Now—"

I sat silent.

"We'd better go," she said after a while, her voice calm and even. "It's very late."

We climbed down from the rocks then, with the November chill a well of silence between us.

8_____

Guilt trips, so chic in the sixties, are out of fashion these days, at least until the next national disaster. Playing word-games, I once asked a literary lady for the opposite of *innocence*. "Sophistication" was her ready reply. (I forget where I swiped this. It works only on a certain type of victim, and may be an exclusive test for the type.) About three rounds later, I asked for the opposite of *guilt*. She hesitated too long, then ventured, "Sanity? Health?"

That's why guilt trips fell out of fashion. When I reminded her that the opposite of guilt is innocence, she thumped her knee and said "Shit!"—annoyed by the confrontation with so crude, so legalistic a duality as objective innocence and objective guilt. This may have something to do with the following story, which, like Shepard's "Salvador," is about the Fundamental Weapon, in a time of forging plowshares. It may be perceived differently by readers old enough to remember the mini-holocausts at Hiroshima and Nagasaki than by readers not yet past their mid-fifties. While it's true that the young today have unprecedented audio-visual access to the history of this century, nevertheless a forty-year-old documentary lacks the impact of a current event which put kinks in your personal lifestyle. I remember *celebrating* Hiroshima. Harry Truman gave it to me and my new wife as a wedding present. We really appreciated it after the shock wore off. It meant I would be discharged by October 1945, and would not, after all, have to go back into combat, this time in the Pacific. I did

124

not rejoice in the hundreds of kilodeaths among the enemy, whom my society had been persuading me to hate, but those deaths seemed to me a side effect; the purpose of the Bomb was to get me out of the Army Air Corps, and the radio was helping to soothe any uneasiness by playing the Battle Hymn of the Republic and making patriotic announcements. Victory was glorious and everybody got drunk. ("Every victory should be celebrated as a wake," said Lao-tzu, who was not an Irishman.) Harry Truman always denied any remorse about that wedding gift. Ballard's old warrior makes a similar denial, but he's very nostalgic. Meet Hydrogen Man, come home at last, long after the Megawar (here conceived to be a *mini*-Megawar).

THE TERMINAL BEACH
J. G. Ballard

At night, as he lay asleep on the floor of the ruined bunker, Traven heard the waves breaking along the shore of the lagoon, reminding him of the deep Atlantic rollers on the beach at Dakar, where he had been born, and of waiting in the evenings for his parents to drive home along the corniche road from the airport. Overcome by this long-forgotten memory, he woke uncertainly from the bed of old magazines on which he slept and ran towards the dunes that screened the lagoon.

Through the cold night air he could see the abandoned Super-fortresses lying among the palms, beyond the perimeter of the emergency landing field three hundred yards away. Traven walked through the dark sand, already forgetting where the shore lay, although the atoll was only half a mile in width. Above him, along the crests of the dunes, the tall palms leaned into the dim air like the symbols of some cryptic alphabet. The landscape of the island was covered by strange ciphers.

Giving up the attempt to find the beach, Traven stumbled into a set of tracks left years earlier by a large caterpillar vehicle. The heat released by one of the weapon tests had fused the sand, and the double line of fossil imprints, uncovered by the evening air,

wound its serpentine way among the hollows like the footfalls of
an ancient saurian.

Too weak to walk any further, Traven sat down between the tracks.
With one hand he began to excavate the wedgeshaped grooves from
a drift into which they disappeared, hoping that they might lead
him towards the sea. He returned to the bunker shortly before dawn,
and slept through the hot silences of the following noon.

The Blocks

As usual on these enervating afternoons, when not even the faintest
breath of offshore breeze disturbed the dust, Traven sat in the shadow
of one of the blocks, lost somewhere within the center of the maze.
His back resting against the rough concrete surface, he gazed with
a phlegmatic eye down the surrounding aisles and at the line of
doors facing him. Each afternoon he left his cell in the abandoned
camera bunker and walked down into the blocks. For the first half
an hour he restricted himself to the perimeter aisle, now and then
trying one of the doors with the rusty key in his pocket—he had
found it among the litter of smashed bottles in the isthmus of sand
separating the testing ground from the airstrip—and then, inevitably, with a sort of drugged stride, he set off into the center of the
blocks, breaking into a run and darting in and out of the corridors,
as if trying to flush some invisible opponent from his hiding place.
Soon he would be completely lost. Whatever his efforts to return
to the perimeter, he found himself once more in the center.

Eventually he would abandon the task, and sit down in the dust,
watching the shadows emerge from their crevices at the foot of the
blocks. For some reason he always arranged to be trapped when
the sun was at zenith—on Eniwetok, a thermonuclear noon.

One question in particular intrigued him: "What sort of people
would inhabit this minimal concrete city?"

The Synthetic Landscape

"This island is a state of mind," Osborne, one of the biologists
working in the old submarine pens, was later to remark to Traven.

The truth of this became obvious to Traven within two or three weeks of his arrival. Despite the sand and the few anemic palms, the entire landscape of the island was synthetic, a man-made artifact with all the associations of a vast system of derelict concrete motorways. Since the moratorium on atomic tests, the island had been abandoned by the Atomic Energy Commission, and the wilderness of weapon aisles, towers, and blockhouses ruled out any attempt to return it to its natural state. (There were also stronger unconscious motives, Tavern recognized, for leaving it as it was: if primitive man felt the need to assimilate events in the external world to his own psyche, twentieth-century man had reversed this process—by this Cartesian yardstick, the island at least *existed*, in a sense true of few other places.)

But apart from a few scientific workers, no one yet felt any wish to visit the former testing ground, and the naval patrol boat anchored in the lagoon had been withdrawn five years before Traven's arrival. Its ruined appearance, and the associations of the island with the period of the Cold War—what Traven had christened the 'Pre-Third'—were profoundly depressing, an Auschwitz of the soul whose mausoleums contained the mass graves of the still undead. With the Russo-American *détente* this nightmarish chapter of history had been gladly forgotten.

The Pre-Third

> The actual and potential destructiveness of the atomic bomb plays straight into the hands of the Unconscious. The most cursory study of the dream-life and fantasies of the insane shows that ideas of world-destruction are latent in the unconscious mind. Nagazaki destroyed by the magic of science is the nearest man has yet approached to the realisation of dreams that even during the safe immobility of sleep are accustomed to develop into nightmares of anxiety.
>
> Glover: War, Sadism and Pacifism

The Pre-Third: the period had been characterized in Traven's mind above all by its moral and psychological inversions, by its sense of the whole of history, and in particular of the immediate future—the two decades, 1945–65—suspended from the quivering volcano's lip of World War III. Even the death of his wife and six-year-old son in a motor accident seemed only part of this immense synthesis of the historical and psychic zero, the frantic highways where each morning they met their deaths the advance causeways to the global armegeddon.

Third Beach

He had come ashore at midnight, after a hazardous search for an opening in the reef. The small motorboat he had hired from an Australian pearl-diver at Charlotte Island subsided into the shallows, its hull torn by the sharp coral. Exhausted, Traven walked through the darkness among the dunes, where the dim outlines of bunkers and concrete towers loomed between the palms.

He woke the next morning into bright sunlight, lying half-way down the slope of a wide concrete beach. This ringed what appeared to be an empty reservoir or target basin, some two hundred feet in diameter, part of a system of artificial lakes built down the center of the atoll. Leaves and dust choked the waste grilles, and a pool of warm water two feet deep lay in the center, reflecting a distant line of palms.

Traven sat up and took stock of himself. This brief inventory, which merely confirmed his physical identity, was limited to little more than his thin body in its frayed cotton garments. In the context of the surrounding terrain, however, even this collection of tatters seemed to possess a unique vitality. The emptiness of the island, and the absence of any local fauna, were emphasized by the huge sculptural forms of the target basins let into its surface. Separated from each other by narrow isthmuses, the lakes stretched away along the curve of the atoll. On either side, sometimes shaded by the few palms that had gained a precarious purchase in the cracked cement, were roadways, camera towers, and isolated blockhouses, together forming a continuous concrete cap upon the island, a functional megalithic architecture as grey and minatory (and apparently as ancient, in its projection into, and from, time future) as any of Assyria and Babylon.

The series of weapons tests had fused the sand in layers, and the pseudogeological strata condensed the brief epochs, microseconds in duration, of the thermonuclear age. "The key to the past lies in the present." Typically the island inverted this geologist's maxim.

Here the key to the present lay in the future. The island was a fossil of time future, its bunkers and blockhouses illustrating the principle that the fossil record of life is one of armor and the exo-skeleton.

Traven knelt in the warm pool and splashed his shirt and trousers. The reflection revealed the watery image of a thinly bearded face and gaunt shoulders. He had come to the island with no supplies other than a small bar of chocolate, expecting that in some way the island would provide its own sustenance. Perhaps, too, he had identified the need for food with a forward motion in time, and that with his return to the past, or at most into a zone of non-time, this need would be obviated. The privations of the previous six months, during his journey across the Pacific, had reduced his always thin body to that of a migrant beggar, held together by little more than the preoccupied gaze in his eye. Yet this emaciation, by stripping away the superfluities of the flesh, seemed to reveal an inner sinewy toughness, an economy and directness of movement.

For several hours he wandered about, inspecting one bunker after another for a convenient place to sleep. He crossed the remains of a small landing strip, next to a dump where a dozen B–29's lay across one another like dead reptile birds.

The Corpses

Once he entered a small street of metal shacks, containing a cafeteria, recreation rooms, and shower stalls. A wrecked jukebox lay half-buried in the sand behind the cafeteria, its selection of records still in their rack.

Further along, flung into a small target basin fifty yards from the shacks, were the bodies of what at first he thought were the inhabitants of this ghost town—a dozen life-size plastic models. Their half-melted faces, contorted to bleary grimaces, gazed up at him from the jumble of legs and torsos.

On either side of him, muffled by the dunes, came the sounds of waves, the great rollers on the seaward side breaking over the reefs, and onto the beaches within the lagoon. However, he avoided the sea, hesitating before any rise that might take him within its sight. Everywhere the camera towers offered him a convenient aerial view of the confused topography of the island, but he avoided their rusting ladders.

He soon realized that however confused and random the block-houses and camera towers might seem, their common focus dominated the landscape and gave to it a unique perspective. As Traven noticed when he sat down to rest in the window slit of one of the blockhouses, all these observation posts occupied positions on a series of concentric perimeters, moving in tightening arcs towards the inmost sanctuary. This ultimate circle, below ground zero, remained hidden beyond a line of dunes a quarter of a mile to the west.

The Terminal Bunker

After sleeping for a few nights in the open, Traven returned to the concrete beach where he had woken on his first morning on the island, and made his home—if the term could be applied to that damp crumbling hovel—in a camera bunker fifty yards from the target lakes. The dark chamber between the thick canted walls, tomblike though it might seem, gave him a sense of physical reassurance. Outside, the sand drifted against the sides, half-burying the narrow doorway, as if crystallizing the immense epoch of time that had elapsed since the bunker's construction. The narrow rectangles of the five camera slits, their shapes and positions determined by the instruments, studded the east wall like cryptic ideograms. Variations of these ciphers decorated the walls of the other bunkers. In the morning, if Traven was awake, he would always find the sun divided into five emblematic beacons.

Most of the time the chamber was filled only by a damp gloomy light. In the control tower at the landing field Traven found a collection of discarded magazines, and used these to make a bed. One day, lying in the bunker shortly after the first attack of beriberi, he pulled out a magazine pressing into his back and found inside it a full-page photograph of a six-year-old girl. This blonde-haired child, with her composed expression and self-immersed eyes, filled him with a thousand painful memories of his son. He pinned the page to the wall and for days gazed at it through his reveries.

For the first few weeks Traven made little attempt to leave the bunker, and postponed any further exploration of the island. The symbolic journey through its inner circles set its own times of arrival and departure. He evolved no routine for himself. All sense of time soon vanished; his life became completely existential, an absolute break separating one moment from the next like two quantal events. Too weak to forage for food, he lived on the old ration packs he found in the wrecked Superfortresses. Without any implements, it took him all day to open the cans. His physical decline continued, but he watched his spindling arms and legs with indifference.

By now he had forgotten the existence of the sea and vaguely assumed the atoll to be part of some continuous continental table. A hundred yards away to the north and south of the bunker a line of dunes, topped by the palisade of enigmatic palms, screened the lagoon and sea, and the faint muffled drumming of the waves at night had fused with his memories of war and childhood. To the east was the emergency landing field and the abandoned aircraft. In the afternoon light their shifting rectangular shadows would appear to writhe and pivot. In front of the bunker, where he sat, was the system of target lakes, the shallow basins extending across the center of the atoll. Above him the five apertures looked out upon this scene like the tutelary deities of some futuristic myth.

The Lakes and the Specters

The lakes had been designed originally to reveal any radiobiological changes in a selected range of flora and fauna, but the specimens had long since bloomed into grotesque parodies of themselves and been destroyed.

Sometimes in the evenings, when a sepulchral light lay over the concrete bunkers and causeways, and the basins seemed like ornamental lakes in a city of deserted mausoleums, abandoned even by the dead, he would see the specters of his wife and son standing on the opposite bank. Their solitary figures appeared to have been watching him for hours. Although they never moved, Traven was sure they were beckoning to him. Roused from his reverie, he would stumble across the dark sand to the edge of the lake and wade through the water, shouting at the two figures as they moved away hand in hand among the lakes and disappeared across the distant causeways.

Shivering with cold, Traven would return to the bunker and lie on the bed of old magazines, waiting for their return. The image of their faces, the pale lantern of his wife's cheeks, floated on the river of his memory.

The Blocks (II)

It was not until he discovered the blocks that Traven realized he would never leave the island.

At this stage, some two months after his arrival, Traven had exhausted the small cache of food, and the symptoms of beriberi had become more acute. The numbness in his hands and feet, and the gradual loss of strength, continued. Only by an immense effort, and the knowledge that the inner sanctum of the island still lay unexplored, did he manage to leave the paliasse of magazines and make his way from the bunker.

As he sat in the drift of sand by the doorway that evening, he noticed a light shining through the palms far into the distance around the atoll. Confusing this with the image of his wife and son, and visualizing them waiting for him at some warm hearth among the dunes, Traven set off towards the light. Within fifty yards he lost his sense of direction. He blundered about for several hours on the edges of the landing strip, and succeeded only in cutting his foot on a broken Coca-Cola bottle in the sand.

After postponing his search for the night, he set out again in earnest the next morning. As he moved past the towers and block-houses the heat lay over the island in an unbroken mantle. He had entered a zone devoid of time. Only the narrowing perimeters of the bunkers warned him that he was crossing the inner field of the fire-table.

He climbed the ridge which marked the furthest point in his previous exploration of the island. The plain beyond was covered with target aisles and explosion breaks. On the gray walls of the recording towers, which rose into the air like obelisks, were the faint outlines of human forms in stylized postures, the flash-shadows of the target community burned into the cement. Here and there, where the concrete apron had cracked, a line of palms hung precariously in the motionless air. The target lakes were smaller, filled with the broken bodies of plastic dummies. Most of them still lay in the inoffensive domestic postures into which they had been placed before the tests.

Beyond the furthest line of dunes, where the camera towers began to turn and face him, were the tops of what seemed to be a herd of square-backed elephants. They were drawn up in precise ranks in a hollow that formed a shallow corral.

Traven advanced towards them, limping on his cut foot. On either side of him the loosening sand had excavated the dunes, and several of the blockhouses tilted on their sides. This plain of bunkers stretched for some quarter of a mile. To one side the half-submerged hulks of a group of concrete shelters, bombed out onto the surface in some earlier test, lay like the husks of the abandoned wombs that had given birth to this herd of megaliths.

The Blocks (III)

To grasp something of the vast number and oppressive size of the blocks, and their impact upon Traven, one must try to visualize sitting in the shade of one of these concrete monsters, or walking about in the center of this enormous labyrinth which extended across the central table of the island. There were some two thousand of them, each a perfect cube fifteen feet in height, regularly spaced at ten-yard intervals. They were arranged in a series of tracts, each composed of two hundred blocks, inclined to one another and to the direction of the blast. They had weathered only slightly in the years since they were first built, and their gaunt profiles were like the cutting faces of an enormous die-plate, designed to stamp out huge rectilinear volumes of air. Three of the sides were smooth and unbroken, but the fourth, facing away from the direction of the blast, contained a narrow inspection door.

It was this feature of the blocks that Traven found particularly disturbing. Despite the considerable number of doors, by some freak of perspective only those in a single aisle were visible at any point within the maze, the rest obscured by the intervening blocks. As he walked from the perimeter into the center of the massif, line upon line of the small metal doors appeared and receded, a world of closed exits concealed behind endless corners.

Approximately twenty of the blocks, those immediately below

ground zero, were solid, the walls of the remainder of varying thicknesses. From the outside they appeared to be of uniform solidity.

As he entered the first of the long aisles, Traven felt his step lighten; the sense of fatigue that had dogged him for so many months begin to lift. With their geometric regularity and finish, the blocks seemed to occupy more than their own volume of space, imposing on him a mood of absolute calm and order. He walked on into the center of the maze, eager to shut out the rest of the island. After a few random turns to the left and right, he found himself alone, the vistas to the sea, lagoon and island closed.

Here he sat down with his back against one of the blocks, the quest for his wife and son forgotten. For the first time since his arrival at the island the sense of dissociation prompted by its fragmenting landscape began to recede.

One development he did not expect. With dusk, and the need to leave the blocks and find food, he realized that he had lost himself. However he retraced his steps, struck out left or right at an oblique course, oriented himself around the sun and pressed on resolutely north or south, he found himself back at his starting point. Despite his best efforts, he was unable to make his way out of the maze. That he was aware of his motives gave him little help. Only when hunger overcame the need to remain did he manage to escape.

Abandoning his former home near the aircraft dump, Traven collected together what canned food he could find in the waist turret and cockpit lockers of the Superfortresses and pulled them across the island on a crude sledge. Fifty yards from the perimeter of the blocks he took over a tilting bunker, and pinned the fading photograph of the blond-haired child to the wall beside the door. The page was falling to pieces, like his fragmenting image of himself. Each evening when he woke he would eat uneagerly and then go out into the blocks. Sometimes he took a canteen of water with him and remained there for two or three days.

Traven: In Parentheses

Elements in a quantal world:
>The terminal beach
>The terminal bunker
>The blocks

The landscape is coded.

Entry points into the future = levels in a spinal landscape = zones of significant time.

The Submarine Pens

This precarious existence continued for the following weeks. As he walked out to the blocks one evening, he again saw his wife and son, standing among the dunes below a solitary tower, their faces watching him calmly. He realized that they had followed him across the island from their former haunt among the dried-up lakes. Once again he saw the beckoning light, and he decided to continue his exploration of the island.

Half a mile further along the atoll he found a group of four submarine pens, built over an inlet, now drained, which wound through the dunes from the sea. The pens still contained several feet of water, filled with strange luminescent fish and plants. A warning light winked at intervals from a metal tower. The remains of a substantial camp, only recently vacated, stood on the concrete pier outside. Greedily Traven heaped his sledge with the provisions stacked inside one of the metal shacks. With this change of diet the beriberi receded, and during the next days he returned to the camp. It appeared to be the site of a biological expedition. In a field office he came across a series of large charts of mutated chromosomes. He rolled them up and took them back to his bunker. The abstract patterns were meaningless, but during his recovery he amused himself by devising suitable titles for them. (Later, passing the aircraft dump on one of his forays, he found the half-buried jukebox, and tore the list of records from the selection panel, realizing that these were the most appropriate captions for the charts. Thus embroidered, they took on many layers of cryptic associations.)

Traven Lost Among the Blocks

August 5. Found the man Traven. A strange derelict figure, hiding in a bunker in the deserted interior of the island. He is suffering from severe exposure and malnutrition, but is unaware of this, or, for that matter, of any other events in the world around him....

He maintains that he came to the island to carry out some scientific project—unstated—but I suspect that he understands his real motives and the unique role of the island.... In some way its landscape seems to be involved with certain unconscious notions of time, and in particular with those that may be a repressed premonition of our own deaths. The attractions and dangers of such an architecture, as the past has shown need no stressing.

August 6. He has the eyes of the possessed. I would guess that he is neither the first, nor the last, to visit the island.

—from Dr. C. Osborne, *Eniwetok Diary.*

With the exhaustion of his supplies, Traven remained within the perimeter of the blocks almost continuously, conserving what strength remained to him to walk slowly down their empty corridors. The infection in his right foot made it difficult for him to replenish his supplies from the stores left by the biologists, and as his strength ebbed he found progressively less incentive to make his way out of the blocks. The system of megaliths now provided a complete substitute for those functions of his mind which gave to it its sense of the sustained rational order of time and space, his awareness kindled from levels above those of his present nervous system (if the automatic system is dominated by the past, the cerebro-spinal reaches towards the future). Without the blocks his sense of reality shrank to little more than the few square inches of sand beneath his feet.

On one of his last ventures into the maze, he spent all night and much of the following morning in a futile attempt to escape. Dragging himself from one rectangle of shadow to another, his leg as heavy as a club and apparently inflamed to the knee, he realized that he must soon find an equivalent for the blocks or he would end his life within them, trapped within this self-constructed mausoleum as surely as the retinue of Pharaoh.

He was sitting exhausted somewhere within the center of the system, the faceless lines of the tomb-booths receding from him, when the sky was slowly divided by the drone of a light aircraft. This passed overhead, and then, five minutes later, returned. Seizing his opportunity, Traven struggled to his feet and made his exit from the blocks, his head raised to follow the glistening exhaust trail.

As he lay down in the bunker he dimly heard the aircraft return and carry out an inspection of the site.

A Belated Rescue

"Who are you?" A small sandy-haired man was peering down at him with a severe expression, then put away a syringe in his valise. "Do you realize you're on your last legs?"

"Traven... I've had some sort of accident. I'm glad you flew over."

"I'm sure you are. Why didn't you use our emergency radio? Anyway, we'll call the Navy and have you picked up."

"No..." Traven sat up on one elbow and felt weakly in his hip pocket. "I have a pass somewhere. I'm carrying out research."

"Into what?" The question assumed a complete understanding of Traven's motives. Traven lay in the shade beside the bunker, and drank weakly from a canteen as Dr. Osborne dressed his foot. "You've also been stealing our stores."

Traven shook his head. Fifty yards away the blue and white Cessna stood on the concrete apron like a large dragonfly. "I didn't realize you were coming back."

"You must be in a trance."

The young woman at the controls of the aircraft climbed from the cockpit and walked over to them, glancing at the gray bunkers and blocks. She seemed unaware of or uninterested in the decrepit figure of Traven. Osborne spoke to her over his shoulder, and after a downward glance at Traven she went back to the aircraft. As she turned Traven rose involuntarily, recognizing the child in the photograph he had pinned to the wall. Then he remembered that the magazine could not have been more than four or five years old.

The engine of the aircraft started. It turned onto one of the roadways and took off into the wind.

The young woman drove over by jeep that afternoon with a small camp bed and a canvas awning. During the intervening hours Traven had slept, and woke refreshed when Osborne returned from his scrutiny of the surrounding dunes.

"What are you doing here?" the young woman asked as she secured one of the guy-ropes to the bunker.

"I'm searching for my wife and son," Traven said.

"They're on this island?" Surprised, but taking the reply at face value, she looked around her. "Here?"

"In a manner of speaking."

After inspecting the bunker, Osborne joined them. "The child in the photograph. Is she your daughter?"

"No." Traven tried to explain. "She's adopted *me*."

Unable to make sense of his replies, but accepting his assurances that he would leave the island, Osborne and the young woman returned to their camp. Each day Osborne returned to change the dressing, driven by the young woman, who seemed to grasp the role cast for her by Traven in his private mythology. Osborne, when he learned of Traven's previous career as a military pilot, assumed that he was a latter-day martyr left high and dry by the moratorium on thermonuclear tests.

"A guilt complex isn't an indiscriminate supply of moral sanctions. I think you may be overstretching your's."

When he mentioned the name Eatherly, Traven shook his head.

Underterred, Osborne pressed: "Are you sure you're not making similar use of the image of Eniwetok—waiting for your pentecostal wind?"

"Believe me, Doctor, no," Traven replied firmly. "For me the H-Bomb is a symbol of absolute freedom. Unlike Eatherly I feel it's given me the right—the obligation, even—to do anything I choose."

"That seems strange logic," Osborne commented. "Aren't we at least responsible for our physical selves?"

Traven shrugged. "Not now, I think. After all, aren't we in effect men raised from the dead?"

Often, however he thought of Eatherly: the prototypal Pre-Third Man, dating the Pre-Third from August 6, 1945, carrying a full load of cosmic guilt.

Shortly after Traven was strong enough to walk again he had to be rescued from the blocks for a second time. Osborne became less conciliatory.

"Our work is almost complete," he warned Traven. "You'll die here. Traven, what are you looking for?"

To himself Traven said: the tomb of the unknown civilian, *Homo hydrogenensis*, Eniwetok Man. To Osborne he said: "Doctor, your laboratory is at the wrong end of this island."

"I'm aware of that, Traven. There are rarer fish swimming in your head than in any submarine pen."

On the day before they left Traven and the young woman drove over to the lakes where he had first arrived. As a final present from Osborne, an ironic gesture unexpected from the elderly biologist, she had brought the correct list of legends for the chromosome charts. They stopped by the derelict jukebox and she pasted them on to the selection panel.

They wandered among the supine wrecks of the Superfortresses. Traven lost sight of her, and for the next ten minutes searched in and out of the dunes. He found her standing in a small amphitheater formed by the sloping mirrors of a solar energy device, built by one of the visiting expeditions. She smiled to him as he stepped through the scaffolding. A dozen fragmented images of herself were reflected in the broken panes. In some she was sans head, in others multiples of her raised arms circled her like those of a Hindu goddess. Exhausted, Traven turned away and walked back to the jeep.

As they drove away he described his glimpses of his wife and son. "Their faces are always calm. My son's particularly, although he was never really like that. The only time his face was grave was when he was being born—then he seemed millions of years old."

The young woman nodded. "I hope you find them." As an afterthought she added: "Dr. Osborne is going to tell the Navy you're here. Hide somewhere."

Traven thanked her. When she flew away from the island for the last time he waved to her from his seat beside the blocks.

The Naval Party

When the search party came for him Traven hid in the only logical place. Fortunately the search was perfunctory, and was called off after a few hours. The sailors had brought a supply of beer with them, and the search soon turned into a drunken ramble. On the walls of the recording towers Traven later found balloons of obscene dialogue chalked into the mouths of the shadow figures, giving their postures the priapic gaiety of the dancers in cave drawings.

The climax of the party was the ignition of a store of gasoline in an underground tank near the airstrip. As he listened, first to the megaphones shouting his name, the echoes receding among the dunes like the forlorn calls of dying birds, then to the boom of the explosion and the laughter as the landing craft left, Traven felt a premonition that these were the last sounds he would hear.

He had hidden in one of the target basins, lying down among the bodies of the plastic dummies. In the hot sunlight their deformed faces gaped at him sightlessly from the tangle of limbs, their blurred smiles like those of the soundlessly laughing dead. Their faces filled his mind as he climbed over the bodies and returned to the bunker.

As he walked towards the blocks he saw the figures of his wife and son standing in his path. They were less than ten yards from him, their white faces watching him with a look of almost over-whelming expectancy. Never had Traven seen them so close to the blocks. His wife's pale features seemed illuminated from within, her lips parted as if in greeting, one hand raised to take his own. His son's grave face, with its curiously fixed expression, regarded him with the same enigmatic smile of the girl in the photograph.

"Judith! David!" Startled, Traven ran forwards to them. Then, in a sudden movement of light, their clothes turned into shrouds, and he saw the wounds that disfigured their necks and chests. Appalled, he cried out to them. As they vanished he fled into the safety and sanity of the blocks.

The Catechism of Goodbye

This time he found himself, as Osborne had predicted, unable to leave the blocks.

Somewhere in the shifting center of the maze, he sat with his back against one of the concrete flanks, his eyes raised to the sun. Around him the lines of cubes formed the horizons of his world. At times they would appear to advance towards him, looming over him like cliffs, the intervals between them narrowing so that they were little more than an arm's length apart, a labyrinth of narrow corridors running between them. Then they would recede from him, sepa-rating from each other like points in an expanding universe, until the nearest line formed an intermittent palisade along the horizon.

Time had become quantal. For hours it would be noon, the shad-ows contained within the motionless bulk of the blocks, the heat reverberating off the concrete floor. Abruptly he would find it was early afternoon or evening, the shadows everywhere like pointing fingers.

"Goodbye, Eniwetok," he murmured.

Somewhere there was a flicker of light, as if one of the blocks, like a counter on an abacus, had been plucked away.

"Goodbye, Los Alamos." Again a block seemed to vanish. The corridors around him remained intact, but somewhere, Traven was convinced, in the matrix superimposed on his mind, a small interval of neutral space had been punched.

Goodbye, Hiroshima.

Goodbye, Alamogordo.

Goodbye, Moscow, London, Paris, New York....

Shuttles flickered, a ripple of integers. Traven stopped, accepting the futility of this megathlon farewell. Such a leave-taking required him to fix his signature on every one of the particles in the universe.

Total Noon: Eniwetok

The blocks now occupied positions on an endlessly revolving circus wheel. They carried him upwards, to heights from which he could see the whole island and the sea, and then down again through the opaque disc of the floor. From here he looked up at the undersurface of the concrete cap, an inverted landscape of rectilinear hollows, the dome-shaped mounds of the lake-system, the thousands of empty cubic pits of the blocks.

"Goodbye, Traven"

To his disappointment he found that this ultimate act of rejection gained him nothing.

In an interval of lucidity, he looked down at his emaciated arms and legs propped loosely in front of him, the brittle wrists and hands covered with a lacework of ulcers. To his right was a trail of disturbed dust, the marks of slack heels.

In front of him lay a long corridor between the blocks, joining an oblique series a hundred yards away. Among these, where a narrow interval revealed the open space beyond, was a crescent-shaped shadow, poised in the air.

During the next half-hour it moved slowly, turning as the sun swung.

The outline of a dune.

*   *   *

Seizing on this cipher, which hung before him like a symbol on a shield, Traven pushed himself through the dust. He climbed precariously to his feet, and covered his eyes from all sight of the blocks.

Ten minutes later he emerged from the western perimeter. The dune whose shadow had guided him lay fifty yards away. Beyond it, bearing the shadow like a screen, was a ridge of limestone, which ran away among the hillocks of a wasteland. The remains of old bulldozers, bales of barbed wire, and fifty-gallon drums lay half buried in the sand.

Traven approached the dune, reluctant to leave this anonymous swell of sand. He shuffled around its edges, and then sat down in the shade by a narrow crevice in the ridge.

Ten minutes later he noticed that someone was watching him.

The Marooned Japanese

This corpse, whose eyes stared up at Traven, lay to his left at the bottom of the crevice. That of a man of middle age and powerful build, it lay on its side with its head on a pillow of stone, as if surveying the window of the sky. The fabric of the clothes had rotted to a gray tattered vestment, but in the absence of any small animal predators on the island the skin and musculature had been preserved. Here and there, at the angle of knee or wrist, a bony point shone through the leathery integument of the yellow skin, but the facial mask was still intact, and revealed a male Japanese of the professional classes. Looking down at the strong nose, high forehead, and broad mouth, Traven guessed that the Japanese had been a doctor or lawyer.

Puzzled as to how the corpse had found itself here, Traven slid a few feet down the slope. There were no radiation burns on the skin, which indicated that the Japanese had been there for less than five years. Nor did he appear to be wearing a uniform, so had not been a member of a military or scientific mission.

To the left of the corpse, within reach of his hand, was a frayed leather case, the remains of a map wallet. To the right was the bleached husk of a haversack, open to reveal a canteen of water and a small jerrican.

Greedily, the reflex of starvation making him for the moment ignore this discovery that the Japanese had deliberately chosen to die in the crevice, Traven slid down the slope until his feet touched the splitting soles of the corpse's shoes. He reached forward and seized the canteen. A cupful of flat water swilled around the rusting bottom. Traven gulped down the water, the dissolved metal salts cloaking his lips and tongue with a bitter film. He pried the lid and chewed at the tarry flakes. They filled his mouth with an almost intoxicating sweetness. After a few moments he felt light-headed and sat back beside the corpse. Its sightless eyes regarded him with unmoving compassion.

The Fly

(A small fly, which Traven presumes has followed him into the crevice, now buzzes about the corpse's face. Traven leans forward to kill it, then reflects that perhaps this minuscule sentry had been the corpse's faithful companion, in return fed on the rich liqueurs and distillations of its pores. Carefully, to avoid injuring the fly, he encourages it to alight on his wrist.)

DR. YASUDA: Thank you, Traven. (*The voice is rough, as if unused to conversation.*) In my position, you understand.

TRAVEN: Of course, Doctor. I'm sorry I tried to kill it. These ingrained habits, you know, they're not easy to shrug off. Your sister's children in Osaka in '44, the exigencies of war, I hate to plead them, most known motives are so despicable one searches the unknown in the hope that....

YASUDA: Please, Traven, do not be embarrassed. The fly is lucky to retain its identity for so long. That son you mourn, not to mention my own two nieces and nephew, did they not die each day? Every parent in the world mourns the lost sons and daughters of their past childhoods.

TRAVEN: You're very tolerant, Doctor. I wouldn't dare—

YASUDA: Not at all, Traven. I make no apologies for you. After all, each one of us is little more than the meager residue of the infinite unrealized possibilities of our lives. But your son and my nieces are fixed in our minds forever, their identities as certain as the stars.

TRAVEN: (*not entirely convinced*) That may be so, Doctor, but it leads to a dangerous conclusion in the case of this island. For instance, the blocks....

YASUDA: They are precisely to what I refer. Here among the blocks, Traven, you at last find the image of yourself free of time and space. This island is an ontological Garden of Eden; why try to expel yourself into a quantal world?

TRAVEN: Excuse me. *(The fly has flown back to the corpse's face and sits in one of the orbits, giving the good doctor an expression of quizzical beadiness. Reaching forward, Traven entices it onto his palm.)* Well, yes, these bunkers may be ontological objects, but whether this is the ontological fly seems doubtful. It's true that on this island it's the only fly, which is the next best thing.

YASUDA: You can't accept the plurality of the universe, Traven. Ask yourself, why? Why should this obsess you. It seems to me that you are hunting for the white leviathan, zero. The beach is a dangerous zone; avoid it. Have a proper humility; pursue a philosophy of acceptance.

TRAVEN: Then may I ask why you came here, Doctor?

YASUDA: To feed this fly. "What greater love—?"

TRAVEN: *(Still puzzling)* It doesn't really solve my problem. The blocks, you see....

YASUDA: Very well, if you must have it that way...

TRAVEN: But, Doctor—

YASUDA:*(Peremptorily)* Kill that fly!

TRAVEN: That's not an end, or a beginning. *(Hopelessly he kills the fly. Exhausted, he falls asleep beside the corpse.)*

The Terminal Beach

Searching for a piece of rope in the refuse dump behind the dunes, Traven found a bale of rusty wire. He unwound it, then secured a harness around the corpse's chest and dragged it from the crevice. The lid of a wooden crate served as a sledge. Traven fastened the corpse into a sitting position, and set off along the perimeter of the blocks. Around him the island was silent. The lines of palms hung in the sunlight, only his own motion varying the shifting ciphers of their crisscrossing trunks. The square turrets of the camera towers jutted from the dunes like forgotten obelisks.

An hour later, when Traven reached his bunker, he untied the wire cord he had fastened around his waist. He took the chair left for him by Dr. Osborne and carried it to a point midway between the bunker and the blocks. Then he tied the body of the Japanese to the chair, arranging the hands so that they rested on the wooden arms, giving the moribund figure a posture of calm repose.

This done to his satisfaction, Traven returned to the bunker and squatted under the awning.

As the next days passed into weeks, the dignified figure of the Japanese sat in his chair fifty yards from him, guarding Traven from the blocks. Their magic still filled Traven's reveries, but he now had sufficient strength to rouse himself and forage for food. In the hot sunlight the skin of the Japanese became more and more bleached, and sometimes Traven would wake at night to find the white sepulchral figure sitting there, arms resting at its sides, in the shadows that crossed the concrete floor. At these moments he would often see his wife and son watching him from the dunes. As time passed they came closer, and he would sometimes turn to find them only a few yards behind him.

Patiently Traven waited for them to speak to him, thinking of the great blocks whose entrance was guarded by the seated figure of the dead archangel, as the waves broke on the distant shore and the burning bombers fell through his dreams.

9_____

Ballard saw his post-mini-Megawar world as recovering quickly after little more than the loss of a few world capitals and population centers. But the real world was pretty much a wreck already when Poul Anderson wrote "Tomorrow's Children" right after World War II, and to me the story still has the smell of 1946 about it, when much of Old World, east and west, was picking itself up out of rubble, under the auspices of conquering overseers. Here the author enlarges the ruins of 1946 by a few orders of magnitude and brings it home as Megawar's aftermath, but the focus of concern is again that of Jody and Paul and Myra and Ben and Littleboy: the damage to human reproduction, as viewed from a global perspective.

TOMORROW'S CHILDREN
by Poul Anderson

> On the world's loom
> Weave the Norns doom,
> Nor may they guide it nor change.
> —Wagner, Siegfried

Ten miles up, it hardly showed. Earth was a cloudy green and brown blur, the vast vault of the stratosphere reaching changelessly out to spatial infinities, and beyond the pulsing engine there was silence and serenity no man could ever touch. Looking down, Hugh Drummond could see the Mississippi gleaming like a drawn sword, and its slow curve matched the contours shown on his map. The hills, the sea, the sun and wind and rain, they didn't change. Not in less than a million slow-striding years, and human efforts flickered too briefly in the unending night for that.

Farther down, though, and especially where cities had been— The lone man in the solitary stratojet swore softly, bitterly, and his knuckles whitened on the controls. He was a big man, his gaunt rangy form sprawling awkwardly in the tiny pressure cabin, and he wasn't quite forty. But his dark hair was streaked with gray, in the shabby flying suit his shoulders stooped, and his long homely face was drawn into haggard lines. His eyes were black-rimmed and sunken with weariness, dark and dreadful in their intensity. He'd seen too much, survived too much, until he began to look like most other people of the world. *Heir of the ages,* he thought dully.

Mechanically, he went through the motions of following his course. Natural landmarks were still there, and he had powerful binoculars to help him. But he didn't use them much. They showed too many broad shallow craters, their vitreous smoothness throwing back sunlight in the flat blank glitter of a snake's eye, the ground about them a churned and blasted desolation. And there were the worse regions of—deadness. Twisted dead trees, blowing sand, tumbled skeletons, perhaps at night a baleful blue glow of fluorescence. The bombs had been nightmares, riding in on wings of fire and horror to shake the planet with the death blows of cities. But the radioactive dust was worse than any nightmare.

He passed over villages, even small towns. Some of them were deserted, the blowing colloidal dust, or plague, or economic breakdown making them untenable. Others still seemed to be living a feeble half-life. Especially in the Midwest, there was a pathetic struggle to return to an agricultural system, but the insects and blights—

Drummond shrugged. After nearly two years of this, over the scarred and maimed planet, he should be used to it. The United States had been lucky. Europe, now—

Der Untergang des Abendlandes, he thought grayly. *Spengler foresaw the collapse of a topheavy civilization. He didn't foresee atomic bombs, radioactive-dust bombs, bacteria bombs, blight bombs—the bombs, the senseless inanimate bombs flying like monster insects over the shivering world. So he didn't guess the extent of the collapse.*

Deliberately he pushed the thoughts out of his conscious mind. He didn't want to dwell on them. He'd lived with them two years, and that was two eternities too long. And anyway, he was nearly home now.

The capital of the United States was below him, and he sent the stratojet slanting down in a long thunderous dive toward the mountains. Not much of a capital, the little town huddled in a valley of the Cascades, but the waters of the Potomac had filled the grave of Washington. Strictly speaking, there was no capital. The officers of the government were scattered over the country, keeping in precarious touch by plane and radio, but Taylor, Oregon, came as close to being the nerve center as any other place.

He gave the signal again on his transmitter, knowing with a faint spine-crawling sensation of the rocket batteries trained on him from the green of those mountains. When one plane could carry the end of a city, all planes were under suspicion. Not that anyone outside was supposed to know that that innocuous little town was important. But you never could tell. The war wasn't officially over. It might never be, with sheer personal survival overriding the urgency of treaties.

A light-beam transmitter gave him a cautious: "O.K. Can you land in the street?"

It was a narrow, dusty track between two wooden rows of houses, but Drummond was a good pilot and this was a good jet. "Yeah," he said. His voice had grown unused to speech.

He cut speed in a spiral descent until he was gliding with only the faintest whisper of wind across his ship. Touching wheels to the street, he slammed on the brake and bounced to a halt.

Silence struck at him like a physical blow. The engine stilled, the sun beating down from a brassy blue sky on the drabness of rude "temporary" houses, the total-seeming desertion beneath the impassive mountains—home! Hugh Drummond laughed, a short harsh bark with nothing of humor in it, and swung open the cockpit canopy.

There were actually quite a few people, he saw, peering from doorways and side streets. They looked fairly well fed and dressed, many in uniform, they seemed to have purpose and hope. But this, of course, was the capital of the United States of America, the world's most fortunate country.

"Get out—quick!"

The peremptory voice roused Drummond from the introspection into which those lonely months had driven him. He looked down at a gang of men in mechanics' outfits, led by a harassed-looking man in captain's uniform. "Oh—of course," he said slowly. "You want to hide the plane. And, naturally, a regular landing field would give you away."

"Hurry, get out, you infernal idiot! Anyone, *anyone* might come over and see—"

"They wouldn't get unnoticed by an efficient detection system, and you still have that," said Drummond, sliding his booted legs over the cockpit edge. "And anyway, there won't be any more raids. The war's over."

"Wish I could believe that, but who are you to say? Get a move on!"

The grease monkeys hustled the plane down the street. With an odd feeling of loneliness, Drummond watched it go. After all, it had been his home for—how long?

The machine was stopped before a false house whose whole front was swung aside. A concrete ramp led downward, and Drummond could see a cavernous immensity below. Light within it gleamed off silvery rows of aircraft.

"Pretty neat," he admitted. "Not that it matters any more. Probably it never did. Most of the hell came over on robot rockets. Oh, well." He fished his pipe from his jacket. Colonel's insignia glittered briefly as the garment flipped back.

"Oh...sorry, sir!" exclaimed the captain. "I didn't know—"

"'S O.K. I've gotten out of the habit of wearing a regular uniform. A lot of places I've been, an American wouldn't be very popular." Drummond stuffed tobacco into his briar, scowling. He hated to think how often he'd had to use the Colt at his hip, or even the machine guns in his plane, to save himself. He inhaled smoke gratefully. It seemed to drown out some of the bitter taste.

"General Robinson said to bring you to him when you arrived, sir," said the captain. "This way, please."

*   *   *

They went down the street, their boots scuffing up little acrid clouds of dust. Drummond looked sharply about him. He'd left very shortly after the two-month Ragnarok which had tapered off when the organization of both sides broke down too far to keep on making and sending the bombs, and maintaining order with famine and disease starting their ghastly ride over the homeland. At that time, the United States was a cityless, anarchic chaos, and he'd had only the briefest of radio exchanges since then, whenever he could get a long-range set still in working order. They'd made remarkable progress meanwhile. How much, he didn't know, but the mere existence of something like a capital was sufficient proof.

Robinson— His lined face twisted into a frown. He didn't know the man. He'd been expecting to be received by the President, who had sent him and some others out. Unless the others had—No, he was the only one who had been in eastern Europe and western Asia. He was sure of that.

Two sentries guarded the entrance to what was obviously a converted general store. But there were no more stores. There was nothing to put in them. Drummond entered the cool dimness of an antechamber. The clatter of a typewriter, the Wac operating it—He gaped and blinked. That was—impossible! Typewriters, secretaries—hadn't they gone out with the whole world, two years ago? If the Dark Ages had returned to Earth, it didn't seem—*right*—that there should still be typewriters. It didn't fit, didn't—

He grew aware that the captain had opened the inner door for him. As he stepped in, he grew aware of how tired he was. His arm weighed a ton as he saluted the man behind the desk.

"At ease, at ease." Robinson's voice was genial. Despite the five stars on his shoulders, he wore no tie or coat, and his round face was smiling. Still, he looked tough and competent underneath. To run things nowadays, he'd have to be.

"Sit down, Colonel Drummond." Robinson gestured to a chair near his and the aviator collapsed into it, shivering. His haunted eyes traversed the office. It was almost well enough outfitted to be a prewar place.

Prewar! A word like a sword, cutting across history with a brutality of murder, hazing everything in the past until it was a vague golden glow through drifting, red-shot black clouds. And—only two years. *Only two years!* Surely sanity was meaningless in a world of such nightmare inversions. Why, he could barely remember Barbara and the kids. Their faces were blotted out in a tide of other visages— starved faces, dead faces, human faces become beastformed with want and pain and eating throttled hate. His grief was lost in the agony of the world, and in some ways he had become a machine himself.

"You look plenty tired," said Robinson.

"Yeah...yes, sir—"

"Skip the formality. I don't go for it. We'll be working pretty close together, can't take time to be diplomatic."

"Uh-huh. I came over the North Pole, you know. Haven't slept since— Rough time. But, if I may ask, you—" Drummond hesitated.

"I? I suppose I'm President. Ex officio, pro tem, or something. Here, you need a drink." Robinson got bottle and glasses from a drawer. The liquor gurgled out in a pungent stream. "Prewar Scotch. Till it gives out I'm laying off this modern hooch. *Gambai.*"

The fiery, smokey brew jolted Drummond to wakefulness. Its glow was pleasant in his empty stomach. He heard Robinson's voice with a surrealistic sharpness:

"Yes, I'm at the head now. My predecessors made the mistake of sticking together, and of traveling a good deal in trying to pull the country back into shape. So I think the sickness got the President, and I now it got several others. Of course, there was no means of holding an election. The armed forces had almost the only organization left, so we had to run things. Berger was in charge, but he shot himself when he learned he'd breathed radiodust. Then the command fell to me. I've been lucky."

"I see." It didn't make much difference. A few dozen more deaths weren't much, when over half the world was gone. "Do you expect to—continue lucky?" A brutally blunt question, maybe, but words weren't bombs.

"I do." Robinson was firm about that. "We've learned by experience, learned a lot. We've scattered the army, broken it into small outposts at key points throughout the country. For quite a while, we stopped travel altogether except for absolute emergencies, and then with elaborate precautions. That smothered the epidemics. The microorganisms were bred to work in crowded areas, you know.

They were almost immune to known medical techniques, but without hosts and carriers they died. I guess natural bacteria ate up most of them. We still take care in traveling, but we're fairly safe now."

"Did any of the others come back? There were a lot like me, sent out to see what really had happened to the world."

"One did, from South America. Their situation is similar to ours, though they lacked our tight organization and have gone further toward anarchy. Nobody else returned but you."

It wasn't surprising. In fact, it was a cause for astonishment that anyone had come back. Drummond had volunteered after the bomb erasing St. Louis had taken his family, not expecting to survive and not caring much whether he did. Maybe that was why he had.

"You can take your time in writing a detailed report," said Robinson, "but in general, how are things over there?"

Drummond shrugged. "The war's over. Burned out. Europe has gone back to savagery. They were caught between America and Asia, and the bombs came both ways. Not many survivors, and they're starving animals. Russia, from what I saw, has managed something like you've done here, though they're worse off than we. Naturally, I couldn't find out much there. I didn't get to India or China, but in Russia I heard rumors— No, the world's gone too far into disintegration to carry on war."

"Then we can come out in the open," said Robinson softly. "We can really start rebuilding. I don't think there'll ever be another war, Drummond. I think the memory of this one will be carved too deeply on the race for us ever to forget."

"Can you shrug it off that easily?"

"No, no, of course not. Our culture hasn't lost its continuity, but it's had a terrific setback. We'll never wholly get over it. But—we're on our way up again."

The general rose, glancing at his watch. "Six o'clock. Come on, Drummond, let's get home."

"Home?"

"Yes, you'll stay with me. Man, you look like the original zombie. You'll need a month or more of sleeping between clean sheets, of home cooking and home atmosphere. My wife will be glad to have you; we see almost no new faces. And as long as we'll work together, I'd like to keep you handy. The shortage of competent men is terrific."

* * *

They went down the street, an aide following. Drummond was again conscious of the weariness aching in every bone and fiber of him. A home—after two years of ghost towns, of shattered chimneys above blood-dappled snow, of flimsy lean-tos housing starvation and death.

"Your plane will be mighty useful, too," said Robinson. "Those atomic-powered craft are scarcer than hens' teeth used to be." He chuckled hollowly, as at a rather grim joke. "Got you through close to two years of flying without needing fuel. Any other trouble?"

"Some, but there were enough spare parts." No need to tell of those frantic hours and days of slaving, of desperate improvisation with hunger and plague stalking him who stayed overlong. He'd had his troubles getting food, too, despite the plentiful supplies he'd started out with. He'd fought for scraps in the winters, beaten off howling maniacs who would have killed him for a bird he'd shot or a dead horse he'd scavenged. He hated that plundering, and would not have cared personally if they'd managed to destroy him. But he had a mission, and the mission was all he'd had left as a focal point for his life, so he'd clung to it with fanatic intensity.

And now the job was over, and he realized he couldn't rest. He didn't dare. Rest would give him time to remember. Maybe he could find surcease in the gigantic work of reconstruction. Maybe.

"Here we are," said Robinson.

Drummond blinked in new amazement. There was a car, camouflaged under brush, with a military chauffeur—a *car!* And in pretty fair shape, too.

"We've got a few oil wells going again, and a small patched-up refinery," explained the general. "It furnishes enough gas and oil for what traffic we have."

They got in the rear seat. The aide sat in front, a rifle ready. The car started down a mountain road.

"Where to?" asked Drummond a little dazedly.

Robinson smiled. "Personally," he said, "I'm almost the only lucky man on Earth. We had a summer cottage on Lake Taylor, a few miles from here. My wife was there when the war came, and stayed, and nobody came along till I brought the head officers here with me. Now I've got a home all to myself."

"Yeah...Yeah, you're lucky," said Drummond. He looked out the window, not seeing the sun-spattered woods. Presently he asked, his voice a little harsh: "How is the country really doing now?"

"For a while it was rough. Damn rough. When the cities went, our transportation, communication, and distribution systems broke down. In fact, our whole economy disintegrated, though not all at once. Then there was the dust and the plagues. People fled, and there was open fighting when overcrowded safe places refused to take in any more refugees. Police went with the cities, and the army couldn't do much patrolling. We were busy fighting the enemy troops that'd flown over the Pole to invade. We still haven't gotten them all. Bands are roaming the country, hungry and desperate outlaws, and there are plenty of Americans who turned to banditry when everything else failed. That's why we have this guard, though so far none have come this way.

"The insect and blight weapons just about wiped out our crops, and that winter everybody starved. We checked the pests with modern methods, though it was touch and go for a while, and next year got some food. Of course, with no distribution as yet, we failed to save a lot of people. And farming is still a tough proposition. We won't really have the bugs licked for a long time. If we had a research center as well equipped as those which produced the things—But we're gaining. We're gaining."

"Distribution—" Drummond rubbed his chin. "How about railroads? Horse-drawn vehicles?"

"We have some railroads going, but the enemy was as careful to dust most of ours as we were to dust theirs. As for horses, they were nearly all eaten that first winter. I know personally of only a dozen. They're on my place; I'm trying to breed enough to be of use, but—" Robinson smiled wryly—"by the time we've raised that many, the factories should have been going quite a spell."

"And so now—?"

"We're over the worst. Except for outlaws, we have the population fairly well controlled. The civilized people are fairly well fed, with some kind of housing. We have machine shops, small factories, and the like going, enough to keep our transportation and other mechanisms 'level.' Presently we'll be able to expand these, begin actually increasing what we have. In another five years or so, I guess, we'll be integrated enough to drop martial law and hold a general election. A big job ahead, but a good one."

The car halted to let a cow lumber over the road, a calf trotting at her heels. She was gaunt and shaggy, and skittered nervously from the vehicle into the brush.

"Wild," explained Robinson. "Most of the real wild life was killed off for food in the last two years, but a lot of farm animals escaped when their owners died or fled, and have run free ever since. They—" He noticed Drummond's fixed gaze. The pilot was looking at the calf. Its legs were half the normal length.

"Mutant," said the general. "You find a lot of such animals. Radiation from bombed or dusted areas. There are even a lot of human abnormal births." He scowled, worry clouding his eyes. "In fact, that's just about our worst problem. It—"

The car came out of the woods onto the shore of a small lake. It was a peaceful scene, the quiet waters like molten gold in the slanting sunlight, trees ringing the circumference and all about them the mountains. Under one huge pine stood a cottage, a woman on the porch.

It was like one summer with Barbara—Drummond cursed under his breath and followed Robinson toward the little building. It wasn't, it wasn't, it could never be. Not ever again. There were soldiers guarding this place from chance marauders, and— There was an odd-looking flower at his foot. A daisy, but huge and red and irregularly formed.

A squirrel chittered from a tree. Drummond saw that its face was so blunt as to be almost human.

Then he was on the porch, and Robinson was introducing him to "my wife, Elaine." She was a nice-looking young woman with eyes that were sympathetic on Drummond's exhausted face. The aviator tried not to notice that she was pregnant.

He was led inside, and reveled in a hot bath. Afterward there was supper, but he was numb with sleep by then, and hardly noticed it when Robinson put him to bed.

Reaction set in, and for a week or so Drummond went about in a haze, not much good to himself or anyone else. But it was surprising what plenty of food and sleep could do, and one evening Robinson came home to find him scribbling on sheets of paper.

"Arranging my notes and so on," he explained. "I'll write out the complete report in a month, I guess."

"Good. But no hurry." Robinson settled tiredly into an armchair. "The rest of the world will keep. I'd rather you'd just work at this off and on, and join my staff for your main job."

"O.K. Only what'll I do?"

"Everything. Specialization is gone; too few surviving specialists and equipment. I think your chief task will be to head the census bureau."

"Eh?"

Robinson grinned lopsidedly. "You'll be the census bureau, except for what few assistants I can spare you." He leaned forward, said earnestly: "And it's one of the most important jobs there is. You'll do for this country what you did for central Eurasia, only in much greater detail. Drummond, we have to *know*."

He took a map from a desk drawer and spread it out. "Look, here's the United States. I've marked regions known to be uninhabitable in red." His fingers traced out the ugly splotches. "Too many of 'em, and doubtless there are others we haven't found yet. Now, the blue X's are army posts." They were sparsely scattered over the land, near the centers of population groupings. "Not enough of those. It's all we can do to control the more or less well-off, orderly people. Bandits, enemy troops, homeless refugees—they're still running wild, skulking in the backwoods and barrens, and raiding whenever they can. And they spread the plague. We won't really have it licked till everybody's settled down, and that'd be hard to enforce. Drummond, we don't even have enough soldiers to start a feudal system for protection. The plague spread like a prairie fire in those concentrations of men.

"We have to *know*. We have to know how many people survived— half the population, a third, a quarter, whatever it is. We have to know where they are, and how they're fixed for supplies, so we can start up an equitable distribution system. We have to find all the small-town shops and labs and libraries still standing, and rescue their priceless contents before looters or the weather beat us to it. We have to locate doctors and engineers and other professional men, and put them to work rebuilding. We have to find the outlaws and round them up. We— I could go on forever. Once we have all that information, we can set up a master plan for redistributing population, agriculture, industry, and the rest more efficiently, for getting the country back under civil authority and police, for opening regular transportation and communication channels—for getting the nation back on its feet."

"I see," nodded Drummond. "Hitherto, just surviving and hanging on to what was left has taken precedence. Now you're in a position to start expanding, *if* you know where and how much to expand."

"Exactly," Robinson rolled a cigarette, grimacing. "Not much tobacco left. What I have is perfectly foul. Lord, that war was crazy!"

"All wars are," said Drummond dispassionately, "but technology advanced to the point of giving us a knife to cut our throats with. Before that, we were just beating our heads against the wall. Robinson, we can't go back to the old ways. We've *got* to start on a new track—a track of sanity."

"Yes. And that brings up—" The other man looked toward the kitchen door. They could hear the cheerful rattle of dishes there, and smell mouth-watering cooking odors. He lowered his voice. "I might as well tell you this now, but don't let Elaine know. She... she shouldn't be worried. Drummond, did you see our horses?"

"The other day, yes. The colts—"

"Uh-huh. There've been five colts born of eleven mares in the last year. Two of them were so deformed they died in a week, another in a few months. One of the two left has cloven hoofs and almost no teeth. The last one looks normal—so far. One out of eleven, Drummond."

"Were those horses near a radioactive area?"

"They must have been. They were rounded up wherever found and brought here. The stallion was caught near the site of Portland, I know. But if he were the only one with mutated genes, it would hardly show in the first generation, would it? I understand nearly all mutations are Mendelian recessives. Even if there were one dominant, it would show in all the colts, but none of these looked alike."

"Hm-m-m—I don't know much about genetics, but I do know hard radiation, or rather the secondary charged particles it produces, will cause mutation. Only mutants are rare, and tend to fall into certain patterns—"

"*Were* rare!" Suddenly Robinson was grim, something coldly frightened in his eyes. "Haven't you noticed the animals and plants? They're fewer than formerly, and... well, I've not kept count, but at least half those seen or killed have something wrong, internally or externally."

Drummond drew heavily on his pipe. He needed something to hang onto, in a new storm of insanity. Very quietly, he said: "In my college biology course, they told me the vast majority of mutations are unfavorable. More ways of not doing something than of doing it. Radiation might sterilize an animal, or might produce several degrees of genetic change. You could have mutation so violently lethal the possessor never gets born, or soon dies. You could have all kinds of more or less handicapping factors, or just random changes not making much difference one way or the other. Or in a few cases you might get something actually favorable, but you couldn't really say the possessor is a true member of the species. And favorable mutations themselves usually involve a price in the partial or total loss of some other function."

"Right." Robinson nodded heavily. "One of your jobs on the census will be to try and locate any and all who know genetics, and send them here. But your real task, which only you and I and a couple of others must know about, the job overriding all other considerations, will be to find the human mutants."

Drummond's throat was dry. "There've been a lot of them?" he whispered.

"Yes. But we don't know how many or where. We only know about those people who live near an army post, or have some other fairly regular intercourse with us, and they're only a few thousand all told. Among them, the birth rate has gone down to about half the prewar ratio. And over half the births they do have are abnormal."

"*Over half—*"

"Yeah. Of course, the violently different ones soon die, or are put in an institution we've set up in the Alleghenies. But what can we do with viable forms, if their parents still love them? A kid with deformed or missing or abortive organs, twisted internal structure, a tail, or something even worse...well, *it'll* have a tough time in life, but it can generally survive. And perpetuate itself—"

"And a normal-looking one might have some unnoticeable quirk, or a characteristic that won't show up for years. Or even a normal one might be carrying recessives, and pass them on— God!" The exclamation was half blasphemy, half prayer. "But how'd it happen? People weren't all near atom-hit areas."

"Maybe not, though a lot of survivors escaped from the outskirts. But there was that first year, with everybody on the move. One could pass near enough to a blasted region to be affected, without knowing it. And that damnable radiodust, blowing on the wind. It's got a long half-life. It'll be active for decades. Then, as in any collapsing culture, promiscuity was common. Still is. Oh, it's spread itself, all right."

"I still don't see why it spread itself so much. Even here—"

"Well, I don't know why it shows up here. I suppose a lot of the local flora and fauna came in from elsewhere. This place is safe. The nearest dusted region is three hundred miles off, with mountains between. There must be many such islands of comparatively normal conditions. We have to find them too. But elsewhere—"

"Soup's on," announced Elaine, and went from the kitchen to the dining room with a loaded tray.

The men rose. Grayly, Drummond looked at Robinson and said tonelessly: "O.K. I'll get your information for you. We'll map mutation areas and safe areas, we'll check on our population and resources, we'll eventually get all the facts you want. But—what are you going to do then?"

"I wish I knew," said Robinson haggardly. "I wish I knew."

Winter lay heavily on the north, a vast gray sky seeming frozen solid over the rolling white plains. The last three winters had come early and stayed long. Dust, colloidal dust of the bombs, suspended in the atmosphere and cutting down the solar constant by a deadly percent or two. There had even been a few earthquakes, set off in geologically unstable parts of the world by bombs planted right. Half of California had been ruined when a sabotage bomb started the San Andreas Fault on a major slip. And that kicked up still more dust.

Fimbulwinter, thought Drummond bleakly. *The doom of the prophecy. But no, we're surviving. Though maybe not as men—*

Most people had gone south, and there overcrowding had made starvation and disease and internecine struggle the normal aspects of life. Those who'd stuck it out up here, and had luck with their pest-ridden crops, were better off.

Drummond's jet slid above the cratered black ruin of the Twin Cities. There was still enough radioactivity to melt the snow, and the pit was like a skull's empty eye socket. The man sighed, but he was becoming calloused to the sight of death. There was so much of it. Only the struggling agony of life mattered any more.

He strained through the sinister twilight, swooping low over the unending fields. Burned-out hulks of farmhouses, bones of ghost towns, sere deadness of dusted land—but he'd heard travelers speak of a fairly powerful community up near the Canadian border, and it was up to him to find it.

A lot of things had been up to him in the last six months. He'd had to work out a means of search, and organize his few, overworked assistants into an efficient staff, and go out on the long hunt.

They hadn't covered the country. That was impossible. Their few planes had gone to areas chosen more or less at random, trying to get a cross section of conditions. They'd penetrated wildernesses of hill and plain and forest, establishing contact with scattered, still demoralized out-dwellers. On the whole, it was more laborious than anything else. Most were pathetically glad to see any symbol of law and order and the paradisical-seeming "old days." Now and then there was danger and trouble, when they encountered wary or sullen or outright hostile groups suspicious of a government they associated with disaster, and once there had even been a pitched battle with roving outlaws. But the work had gone ahead, and now the preliminaries were about over.

Preliminaries—It was a bigger job to find out exactly how matters stood than the entire country was capable of undertaking right now. But Drummond had enough facts for reliable extrapolation. He and his staff had collected most of the essential data and begun correlating it. By questioning, by observation, by seeking and finding, by any means that came to hand they'd filled their notebooks. And in the sketchy outlines of a Chinese drawing, and with the same stark realism, the truth was there.

Just this one more place, and I'll go home, thought Drummond for the—thousandth?— time. His brain was getting into a rut, treading the same terrible circle and finding no way out. *Robinson won't like what I tell him, but there it is.* And darkly, slowly: *Barbara, maybe it was best you and the kids went as you did. Quickly, cleanly, not even knowing it. This isn't much of a world. It'll never be our world again.*

He saw the place he sought, a huddle of buildings near the frozen shores of the Lake of the Woods, and his jet murmured toward the white ground. The stories he'd heard of this town weren't overly encouraging, but he supposed he'd get out all right. The others had his data anyway, so it didn't matter.

By the time he'd landed in the clearing just outside the village, using the jet's skis, most of the inhabitants were there waiting. In the gathering dusk they were a ragged and wild-looking bunch, clumsily dressed in whatever scraps of cloth and leather they had. The bearded, hard-eyed men were armed with clubs and knives and a few guns. As Drummond got out, he was careful to keep his hands away from his own automatics.

"Hello," he said. "I'm friendly."

"Y' better be," growled the big leader. "Who are you, where from, an' why?"

"First," lied Drummond smoothly, "I want to tell you I have another man with a plane who knows where I am. If I'm not back in a certain time, he'll come with bombs. But we don't intend any harm or interference. This is just a sort of social call. I'm Hugh Drummond of the United States Army."

They digested that slowly. Clearly, they weren't friendly to the government, but they stood in too much awe of aircraft and armament to be openly hostile. The leader spat. "How long you staying?"

"Just overnight, if you'll put me up. I'll pay for it." He held up a small pouch. "Tobacco."

Their eyes gleamed, and the leader said, "You'll stay with me. Come on."

Drummond gave him the bribe and went with the group. He didn't like to spend such priceless luxuries thus freely, but the job was more important. And the boss seemed thawed a little by the fragrant brown flakes. He was sniffing them greedily.

"Been smoking bark an' grass," he confided. "Terrible."

"Worse than that," agreed Drummond. He turned up his jacket collar and shivered. The wind starting to blow was bitterly cold.

"Just what y' here for?" demanded someone else.

"Well, just to see how things stand. We've got the government started again, and are patching things up. But we have to know where folks are, what they need, and so on."

"Don't want nothing t' do with the gov'ment," muttered a woman. "They brung all this on us."

"Oh, come now. We didn't ask to be attacked." Mentally, Drummond crossed his fingers. He neither knew nor cared who was to blame. Both sides, letting mutual fear and friction mount to hysteria—In fact, he wasn't sure the United States hadn't sent out the first rockets, on orders of some panicky or aggressive officials. Nobody was alive who admitted knowing.

"It's a jedgment o' God, for the sins o' our leaders," persisted the woman. "The plague, the fire-death, all that, ain't it foretold in the Bible? Ain't we living in the last days o' the world?"

"Maybe." Drummond was glad to stop before a long low cabin. Religious argument was touchy at best, and with a lot of people nowadays it was dynamite.

They entered the rudely furnished but fairly comfortable structure. A good many crowded in with them. For all their suspicion, they were curious, and an outsider in an aircraft was a blue-moon event these days.

Drummond's eyes flickered unobtrusively about the room, noticing details. Three women—that meant a return to concubinage. Only to be expected in a day of few men and strong-arm rule. Ornaments and utensils, tools and weapons of good quality—yes, that confirmed the stories. This wasn't exactly a bandit town, but it had waylaid travelers and raided other places when times were hard, and built up a sort of dominance of the surrounding country. That, too, was common.

There was a dog on the floor nursing a litter. Only three pups, and one of those was bald, one lacked ears, and one had more toes than it should. Among the wide-eyed children present, there were several two years old or less, and with almost no obvious exceptions, they were also different.

Drummond sighed heavily and sat down. In a way, this clinched it. He'd known for a long time, and finding mutation here, as far as any place from atomic destruction, was about the last evidence he needed.

He had to get on friendly terms, or he wouldn't find out much about things like population, food production, and whatever else there was to know. Forcing a smile to stiff lips, he took a flask from his jacket. "Prewar rye," he said. "Who wants a nip?"

"Do we!" The answer barked out in a dozen voices and words. The flask circulated, men pawing and cursing and grabbing to get at it. *Their homebrew must be pretty bad,* thought Drummond wryly.

The chief shouted an order, and one of his women got busy at the primitive stove. "Rustle you a mess o' chow," he said heartily. "An' my name's Sam Buckman."

"Pleased to meet you, Sam." Drummond squeezed the hairy paw hard. He had to show he wasn't a weakling, a conniving city slicker.

"What's it like, outside?" asked someone presently. "We ain't heard for so long—"

"You haven't missed much," said Drummond between bites. The food was pretty good. Briefly, he sketched conditions. "You're better off than most," he finished.

"Yeah. Mebbe so." Sam Buckman scratched his tangled beard. "What I'd give f'r a razor blade—! It ain't easy, though. The first year we weren't no better off 'n anyone else. Me, I'm a farmer, I kept some ears o' corn an' a little wheat an' barley in my pockets all that winter, even though I was starving. A bunch o' hungry refugees plundered my place, but I got away an' drifted up here. Next year I took an empty farm here an' started over."

Drummond doubted that it had been abandoned, but said nothing. Sheer survival outweighed a lot of considerations.

"Others came an' settled here," said the leader reminiscently. "We farm together. We have to; one man couldn't live by hisself, not with the bugs an' blight, an' the crops sproutin' into all new kinds, an' the outlaws aroun'. Not many up here, though we did beat off some enemy troops last winter." He glowed with pride at that, but Drummond wasn't particularly impressed. A handful of freezing starveling conscripts, lost and bewildered in a foreign enemy's land, with no hope of ever getting home, weren't formidable.

"Things getting better, though," said Buckman. "We're heading up." He scowled blackly, and a palpable chill crept into the room. "If 'twern't for the births—"

"Yes—the births. The new babies. Even the stock an' plants." It was an old man speaking, his eyes glazed with near-madness. "It's the mark o' the beast. Satan is loose in the world—"

"Shut up!" Huge and bristling with wrath, Buckman launched himself out of his seat and grabbed the oldster by his scrawny throat. "Shut up 'r I'll bash y'r lying head in. Ain't no son o' mine being marked by the devil."

"Or mine—" "Or mine—" The rumble of voices ran about the cabin, sullen and afraid.

"It's God's jedgment, I tell you!" The woman was shrilling again. "The end o' the world is near. Prepare f'r the second coming—"

"An' you shut up too, Mag Schmidt," snarled Buckman. He stood bent over, gnarled arms swinging loose, hands flexing, little eyes darting red and wild about the room. "Shut y'r trap an' keep it shut. I'm still boss here, an' if you don't like it you can get out. I still don't think that gunny-looking brat o' y'rs fell in the lake by accident."

The woman shrank back, lips tight. The room filled with a crackling silence. One of the babies began to cry. It had two heads.

Slowly and heavily, Buckman turned to Drummond, who sat immobile against the wall. "You see?" he asked dully. "You see how it is? Maybe it is the curse o' God. Maybe the world is ending. I dunno. I just know there's few enough babies, an' most o' them deformed. Will it go on? Will all our kids be monsters? Should we ... kill these an' hope we get some human babies? What is it? What to do?"

Drummond rose. He felt a weight as of centuries on his shoulders, the weariness, blank and absolute, of having seen that smoldering panic and heard that desperate appeal too often, too often.

"Don't kill them," he said. "That's the worst kind of murder, and anyway it'd do no good at all. It comes from the bombs, and you can't stop it. You'll go right on having such children, so you might as well get used to it."

By atomic-powered stratojet it wasn't far from Minnesota to Oregon, and Drummond landed in Taylor about noon the next day. This time there was no hurry to get his machine under cover, and up on the mountain was a raw scar of earth where a new airfield was slowly being built. Men were getting over their terror of the sky. They had another fear to face now, and it was one from which there was no hiding.

Drummond walked slowly down the icy main street to the central office. It was numbingly cold, a still, relentless intensity of frost eating through clothes and flesh and bone. It wasn't much better inside. Heating systems were still poor improvisations.

"You're back!" Robinson met him in the antechamber, suddenly galvanized with eagerness. He had grown thin and nervous, looking ten years older, but impatience blazed from him. "How is it? How is it?"

Drummond held up a bulky notebook. "All here," he said grimly. "All the facts we'll need. Not formally correlated yet, but the picture is simple enough."

Robinson laid an arm on his shoulder and steered him into the office. He felt the general's hand shaking, but he'd sat down and had a drink before business came up again.

"You've done a good job," said the leader warmly. "When the country's organized again, I'll see you get a medal for this. Your men in the other planes aren't in yet."

"No, they'll be gathering data for a long time. The job won't be finished for years. I've only got a general outline here, but it's enough. It's enough." Drummond's eyes were haunted again.

Robinson felt cold at meeting that too-steady gaze. He whispered shakily: "Is it—bad?"

"The worst. Physically, the country's recovering. But biologically, we've reached a crossroads and taken the wrong fork."

"What do you mean? *What do you mean?*"

Drummond let him have it then, straight and hard as a bayonet thrust. "The birth rate's a little over half the prewar," he said, "and about seventy-five percent of all births are mutant, of which possibly two-thirds are viable and presumably fertile. Of course, that doesn't include late-maturing characteristics, or those detectable by naked-eye observation, or the mutated recessive genes that must be carried by a lot of otherwise normal zygotes. And it's everywhere. There are no safe places."

"I see," said Robinson after a long time. He nodded, like a man struck a stunning blow and not yet fully aware of it. "I see. The reason—"

"Is obvious."

"Yes. People going through radioactive areas—"

"Why, no. That would only account for a few. But—"

"No matter. That fact's there, and that's enough. We have to decide what to do about it."

"And soon." Drummond's jaw set. "It's wrecking our culture. We at least preserved our historical continuity, but even that's going now. People are going crazy as birth after birth is monstrous. Fear of the unknown, striking at minds still stunned by the war and its immediate aftermath. Frustration of parenthood, perhaps the most basic instinct there is. It's leading to infanticide, desertion, despair, a cancer at the root of society. We've got to act."

"How? How?" Robinson stared numbly at his hands.

"I don't know. You're the leader. Maybe an educational campaign, though that hardly seems practicable. Maybe an acceleration of your program for re-integrating the country. Maybe—I don't know."

Drummond stuffed tobacco into his pipe. He was near the end of what he had, but would rather take a few good smokes than a lot of niggling puffs. "Of course," he said thoughtfully, "it's probably not the end of things. We won't know for a generation or more, but I rather imagine the mutants can grow into society. They'd better, for they'll outnumber the humans. The thing is, if we just let matters drift there's no telling where they'll go. The situation is unprecedented. We may end up in a culture of specialized variations, which would be very bad from an evolutionary standpoint. There may be fighting between mutant types, or with humans. Interbreeding may produce worse freaks, particularly when accumulated recessives start showing up. Robinson, if we want any say at all in what's going to happen in the next few centuries, we have to act quickly. Otherwise it'll snowball out of all control."

"Yes. Yes, we'll have to act fast. And hard." Robinson straightened in his chair. Decision firmed his countenance, but his eyes were staring. "We're mobilized," he said. "We have the men and the weapons and the organization. They won't be able to resist."

The ashy cold of Drummond's emotions stirred, but it was with a horrible wrenching of fear. "What are you getting at?" he snapped.

"Racial death. All mutants and their parents to be sterilized whenever and wherever detected."

"You're crazy!" Drummond sprang from his chair, grabbed Robinson's shoulders across the desk, and shook him. "You...why, it's impossible! You'll bring revolt, civil war, final collapse!"

"Not if we go about it right." There were little beads of sweat studding the general's forehead. "I don't like it any better than you, but it's got to be done or the human race is finished. Normal births a minority—" He surged to his feet, gasping. "I've thought a long time about this. Your facts only confirmed my suspicions. This tears it. Can't you see? Evolution has to proceed slowly. Life wasn't meant for such a storm of change. Unless we can save the true human stock, it'll be absorbed and differentiation will continue till humanity is a collection of freaks, probably intersterile. Or...there must be a lot of lethal recessives. In a large population, they can accumulate unnoticed till nearly everybody has them and then start emerging all at once. That'd wipe us out. It's happened before, in rats and other species. If we eliminate mutant stock now, we can still save the race. It won't be cruel. We have sterilization techniques which are quick and painless, not upsetting the endocrine balance. But it's got to be done." His voice rose to a raw scream, broke. "It's got to be done!"

Drummond slapped him, hard. He drew a shuddering breath, sat down, and began to cry, and somehow that was the most horrible sight of all. "You're crazy," said the aviator. "You've gone nuts with brooding alone on this the last six months, without knowing or being able to act. You've lost all perspective.

"We can't use violence. In the first place, it would break our tottering, cracked culture irreparably, into a mad-dog finish fight. We'd not even win it. We're outnumbered, and we couldn't hold down a continent, eventually a planet. And remember what we said once, about abandoning the old savage way of settling things, that never brings a real settlement at all? We'd throw away a lesson our noses were rubbed in not three years ago. We'd return to the beast— to ultimate extinction.

"And anyway," he went on very quietly, "it wouldn't do a bit of good. Mutants would still be born. The poison is everywhere. Normal parents will give birth to mutants, somewhere along the line. We just have to accept that fact, and live with it. The *new* human race will have to."

"I'm sorry." Robinson raised his face from his hands. It was a ghastly visage, gone white and old, but there was calm on it. "I—blew my top. You're right. I've been thinking of this, worrying and wondering, living and breathing it, lying awake nights, and when I finally sleep I dream of it. I...yes, I see your point. And you're right."

"It's O.K. You've been under a terrific strain. Three years with never a rest, and the responsibility for a nation, and now this—Sure, everybody's entitled to be a little crazy. We'll work out a solution, somehow."

"Yes, of course." Robinson poured out two stiff drinks and gulped his. He paced restlessly, and his tremendous ability came back in waves of strength and confidence. "Let me see—Eugenics, of course. If we work hard, we'll have the nation tightly organized inside of ten years. Then...well, I don't suppose we can keep the mutants from interbreeding, but certainly we can pass laws to protect humans and encourage their propagation. Since radical mutations would probably be intersterile anyway, and most mutants handicapped one way or another, a few generations should see humans completely dominant again."

Drummond scowled. He was worried. It wasn't like Robinson to be unreasonable. Somehow, the man had acquired a mental blind spot where this most ultimate of human problems was concerned. He said slowly, "That won't work either. First, it'd be hard to impose and enforce. Second, we'd be repeating the old *Herrenvolk* notion. Mutants are inferior, mutants must be kept in their place—to enforce that, especially on a majority, you'd need a full-fledged totalitarian state. Third, that wouldn't work either, for the rest of the world, with almost no exceptions, is under no such control and we'll be in no position to take over that control for a long time—generations. Before then, mutants will dominate everywhere over there, and if they resent the way we treat their kind here, we'd better run for cover."

"You assume a lot. How do you know those hundreds or thousands of diverse types will work together? They're less like each other than like humans, even. They could be played off against each other."

"Maybe. But *that* would be going back onto the old road of treachery and violence, the road to Hell. Conversely, if every not-quite-human is called a 'mutant,' like a separate class, he'll think he is, and act accordingly against the lumped-together 'humans.' No, the only way to sanity—to *survival*—is to abandon class prejudice and race hate altogether, and work as individuals. We're all...well, Earthlings, and subclassification is deadly. We all have to live together, and might as well make the best of it."

"Yeah...yeah, that's right too."

"Anyway, I repeat that all such attempts would be useless. All Earth is infected with mutation. It will be for a long time. The purest human stock will still produce mutants."

"Y-yes, that's true. Our best bet seems to be to find all such stock and withdraw it into the few safe areas left. It'll mean a small human population, but a *human* one."

"I tell you, that's impossible," clipped Drummond. "There is no safe place. Not one."

Robinson stopped pacing and looked at him as at a physical antagonist. "That so?" he almost growled. "Why?"

Drummond told him, adding incredulously, "Surely you knew that. Your physicists must have measured the amount of it. Your doctors, your engineers, that geneticist I dug up for you. You obviously got a lot of this biological information you've been slinging at me from him. They *must* all have told you the same thing."

Robinson shook his head stubbornly. "It can't be. It's not reasonable. The concentration wouldn't be great enough."

"Why, you poor fool, you need only look around you. The plants, the animals—Haven't there been any births in Taylor?"

"No. This is still a man's town, though women are trickling in and several babies are on the way—" Robinson's face was suddenly twisted with desperation. "Elaine's is due any time now. She's in the hospital here. Don't you see, our other kid died of the plague. This one's all we have. We want him to grow up in a world free of want and fear, a world of peace and sanity where he can play and laugh and become a man, not a beast starving in a cave. You and I are on our way out. We're the old generation, the one that wrecked the world. It's up to us to build it again, and then retire from it to let our children have it. The future's theirs. We've got to make it ready for them."

Sudden insight held Drummond motionless for long seconds. Understanding came, and pity, and an odd gentleness that changed his sunken bony face. "Yes," he murmured, "yes, I see. That's why you're working with all that's in you to build a normal, healthy world. That's why you nearly went crazy when this threat appeared. That...that's why you can't, just can't comprehend—"

He took the other man's arm and guided him toward the door. "Come on," he said. "Let's go see how your wife's making out. Maybe we can get her some flowers on the way."

The silent cold bit at them as they went down the street. Snow crackled underfoot. It was already grimy with town smoke and dust, but overhead the sky was incredibly clean and blue. Breath smoked whitely from their mouths and nostrils. The sound of men at work rebuilding drifted faintly between the bulking mountains.

"We couldn't emigrate to another planet, could we?" asked Robinson, and answered himself: "No, we lack the organization and resources to settle them right now. We'll have to make out on Earth. A few safe spots—there *must* be others besides this one—to house the true humans till the mutation period is over. Yes, we can do it."

"There are no safe places," insisted Drummond. "Even if there were, the mutants would still outnumber us. Does your geneticist have any idea how this'll come out, biologically speaking?"

"He doesn't know. His specialty is still largely unknown. He can make an intelligent guess, and that's all."

"Yeah. Anyway, our problem is to learn to live with the mutants, to accept anyone as—Earthling—no matter how he looks, to quit thinking anything was ever settled by violence or connivance, to build a culture of individual sanity. Funny," mused Drummond, "how the impractical virtues, tolerance and sympathy and generosity, have become the fundamental necessities of simple survival. I guess it was always true, but it took the death of half the world and the end of a biological era to make us see that simple little fact. The job's terrific. We've got half a million years of brutality and greed, superstition and prejudice, to lick in a few generations. If we fail, mankind is done. But we've got to try."

They found some flowers, potted in a house, and Robinson bought them with the last of his tobacco. By the time he reached the hospital, he was sweating. The sweat froze on his face as he walked.

The hospital was the town's biggest building, and fairly well equipped. A nurse met them as they entered.

"I was just going to send for you, General Robinson," she said. "The baby's on the way."

"How ... is she?"

"Fine, so far. Just wait here, please."

Drummond sank into a chair and with haggard eyes watched Robinson's jerky pacing. *The poor guy. Why is it expectant fathers are supposed to be so funny? It's like laughing at a man on the rack. I know, Barbara, I know.*

"They have some anesthetics," muttered the general. "They ... Elaine never was very strong."

"She'll be all right." *It's afterward that worries me.*

"Yeah—Yeah—How long, though, how long?"

"Depends. Take it easy." With a wrench, Drummond made a sacrifice to a man he liked. He filled his pipe and handed it over. "Here, you need a smoke."

"Thanks." Robinson puffed raggedly.

The slow minutes passed, and Drummond wondered vaguely what he'd do when—it—happened. It didn't have to happen. But the chances were all against such an easy solution. He was no psychologist. Best just to let things happen as they would.

The waiting broke at last. A doctor came out, seeming an inscrutable high priest in his white garments. Robinson stood before him, motionless.

"You're a brave man," said the doctor. His face, as he removed the mask, was stern and set. "You'll need your courage."

"She—" It was hardly a human sound, that croak.

"Your wife is doing well. But the baby—"

A nurse brought out the little wailing form. It was a boy. But his limbs were rubbery tentacles terminating in boneless digits.

Robinson looked, and something went out of him as he stood there. When he turned, his face was dead.

"You're lucky," said Drummond, and meant it. He'd seen too many other mutants. "After all, if he can use those hands he'll get along all right. He'll even have an advantage in certain types of work. It isn't a deformity, really. If there's nothing else, you've got a good kid."

"*If!* You can't tell with mutants."

"I know. But you've got guts, you and Elaine. You'll see this through, together." Briefly, Drummond felt an utter personal desolation. He went on, perhaps to cover that emptiness:

"I see why you didn't understand the problem. You *wouldn't*. It was a psychological block, suppressing a fact you didn't dare face. That boy is really the center of your life. You couldn't think the truth about him, so your subconscious just refused to let you think rationally on that subject at all.

"Now you know. Now you realize there's no safe place, not on all the planet. The tremendous incidence of mutant births in the first generation could have told you that alone. Most such new characteristics are recessive, which means both parents have to have it for it to show in the zygote. But genetic changes are random, except for a tendency to fall into roughly similar patterns. Four-leaved clovers, for instance. Think how vast the total number of such changes must be, to produce so many corresponding changes in a couple of years. Think how many, *many* recessives there must be, existing only in gene patterns till their mates show up. We'll just have to take our chances of something really deadly accumulating. We'd never know till too late."

"The dust—"

"Yeah. The radiodust. It's colloidal, and uncountable other radio-colloids were formed when the bombs went off, and ordinary dirt gets into unstable isotopic forms near the craters. And there are radiogases too, probably. The poison is all over the world by now, spread by wind and air currents. Colloids can be suspended indefinitely in the atmosphere.

"The concentration isn't too high for life, though a physicist told me he'd measured it as being very near the safe limit and there'll probably be a lot of cancer. But it's everywhere. Every breath we draw, every crumb we eat and drop we drink, every clod we walk on, the dust is there. It's in the stratosphere, clear on down to the surface, probably a good distance below. We could only escape by sealing ourselves in air-conditioned vaults and wearing spacesuits whenever we got out, and under present conditions that's impossible.

"Mutations were rare before, because a charged particle has to get pretty close to a gene and be moving fast before its electro-magnetic effect causes physico-chemical changes, and then that particular chromosome has to enter into reproduction. Now the charged particles, and the gamma rays producing still more, are everywhere. Even at the comparatively low concentration, the odds favor a given organism having so many cells changed that at least one will give rise to a mutant. There's even a good chance of like recessives meeting in the first generation, as we've seen. Nobody's safe, no place is free."

"The geneticist thinks some true humans will continue."

"A few, probably. After all, the radioactivity isn't too concentrated, and it's burning itself out. But it'll take fifty or a hundred years for the process to drop to insignificance, and by then the pure stock will be way in the minority. And there'll still be all those unmatched recessives, waiting to show up."

"You were right. We should never have created science. It brought the twilight of the race."

"I never said that. The race brought its own destruction, through misuse of science. Our culture was scientific anyway, in all except its psychological basis. It's up to us to take that last and hardest step. If we do, the race may yet survive."

Drummond gave Robinson a push toward the inner door. "You're exhausted, beat up, ready to quit. Go on in and see Elaine. Give her my regards. Then take a long rest before going back to work. I still think you've got a good kid."

Mechanically, the de facto President of the United States left the room. Hugh Drummond stared after him a moment, then went out into the street.

10 _____

Meanwhile, on the other side of the planet, in a part of Siberia altogether overlooked by Colonel Drummond...

Robert Abernathy tells the kind of story that seems to stir up archetypes, and like the story of Cain and Abel you know in your bones it's *true* whether it ever happened or not. I think of this story—which I had the pleasure of reading first in 1954—whenever I remember any of the harebrained studies that have come out of the Pentagon on how the remains of post-nuclear society might best be managed toward "recovery"; the value of money is a consideration in one such study. In Abernathy's "Heirs Apparent" the dispute between capitalism and collectivism is put into proper perspective for the world's last Communist and the world's last American entrepreneur, by forces far older than either of their warring systems, both now defunct, except in the mind of Comrade Bogomazov.

HEIRS APPARENT
By Robert Abernathy

Warily crouching, Bogomazov moved forward up the gentle slope. Above his head the high steppe-grass, the *kovýl'*, nodded its plumes in the chilly wind. He shivered.

All at once the wind brought again the wood-smoke smell, and his nostrils flared like a hunting animal's. With sudden recklessness he rose to his full height and looked eagerly across the grasslands that sloped to the river.

Down yonder, hugging the riverbank among scanty trees, was a cluster of crudely and newly built thatched huts. Bogomazov's hunger-keen eyes were quick to note the corral that held a few head of cattle, the pens that must mean poultry, as well as the brown swatches of plowed fields. The wanderer licked his lips, and his hand, almost of itself, unbuttoned the holster at his hip and loosened the pistol there.

But he controlled his urge to plunge ahead; he sank down to concealment in the grass again, and his tactician's glance swept over the scene, studying approaches, seeking human figures, signs of guards and readiness. He saw none, but still he did not move; only the habit of extreme caution had kept him alive this long and enabled him to travel a thousand miles across the chaos that had been Russia.

Presently two small figures emerged from one of the huts and went unhurriedly to the chicken pens, were busy there for a time, and returned. Bogomazov relaxed; it was almost certain now that he had not been seen. At last he obeyed his rumbling stomach and resumed his advance, though indirectly so as to take advantage of the terrain, stalking the village.

He was a strange, skulking figure—Nikolai Nikolayevich Bogomazov, onetime Colonel of the Red Army and Hero of the Soviet Union; now ragged and half naked, face concealed by a scraggly growth of beard, hair slashed awkwardly short across the forehead to prevent its falling into his eyes. His shoes had gone to pieces long ago and the rags he had wrapped around his feet in their place had worn through, leaving him barefoot; he did not know how to make shoes of bark, peasant-style. His army trousers flapped in shreds around his bony shanks. The torn khaki shirt he wore was of American manufacture, a trophy of the great offensive two years earlier that had carried the Russian armies halfway across Europe and through the Near East into Africa...those had been the great days: before the bitter realization that it would never be enough to defeat Western armies; after the destruction of the great cities and industries, to be sure, but before the really heavy bombardments had begun....

Bogomazov wormed his way forward, mouth watering, thinking of chickens.

He was close enough to his objective to hear contented poultry noises, and was thinking of how best to deal with the plaited reeds of the enclosure, when a voice behind him cried startledly, *"Oho!"*

The stalker instinctively rolled to one side, his pistol in his hand; then he saw that the man who had shouted was some yards away and backing nervously toward the nearby hovels—a stocky, shabby figure, broad face richly bearded; most important, he had no weapon. Bogomazov came to a quick decision; sheathing his gun, he got to his feet and called sharply, "Halt!"

The other froze at the tone of command, and stared sullenly at the armed scarecrow confronting him. Farther off a door banged and there were footsteps hurrying nearer. Bogomazov watched without a tremor as a half dozen other men and boys approached and stopped beside the first man, as if he stood on an invisible line. A couple of them carried rifles, but the lone interloper did not flinch. Not for the first time, he was gambling everything on a bluff. And these were merely peasants.

"What place is this?" he demanded in the same crisp voice of authority.

"Novoselye," one answered hesitantly. "The New Settlement."

"I can see as much. Who is responsible here?"

"Wait a minute," rumbled the big bearded man who had first spotted him. "How about telling us who you are and what you want?" He shuffled uneasily from one foot to another as the stranger's cold eyes raked him, but succeeded in maintaining a halfhearted air of defiance.

"My name doesn't matter for the present," said Bogomazov slowly. "What does matter is that I am a Communist."

He felt and saw the stiffening, the electric rise of tension, the furtive crawling look that came into the score of eyes upon him; and outwardly Bogomazov was cool, relaxed, but inwardly he was like a coiled spring. His hand hovered unobtrusively close to the pistol butt.

This was the die-cast. He knew personally of too many cases of Communists beaten, assassinated, lynched by those who should have followed their orders, during the storm of madness and despair on the heels of the great disasters, the storm that still went on....

Bogomazov had been too clever to be caught, just as he had been clever enough to realize in time, when three months ago the total breakdown of the civil authority had commenced to envelop the military as well, that in the north where he then was the northern winter now setting in would finish what the bombardments had begun. A thousand miles of southward trek lay behind him—from the lands where the blizzards would soon sweep in from Asia to blanket the blackened relics of the Old and New Russias, where the river Moskvá was making a new marsh of the immense shallow depression that had been the site of Moscow, where scarcely a dead tree, let alone a building, stood on all the plain that had once been ruled by Great Novgorod and greater Leningrad.

The man with the beard said warily, "What do you want of us ... Comrade?"

Bogomazov let out his breath in an inaudible sigh. He said curtly, "Are there any Communists among you?"

"No, Comrade."

"Then who is responsible?"

They looked at one another uneasily. The spokesman gulped and stammered, "The ... the American is responsible."

Bogomazov's composure was sorely tested. He frowned searchingly at the speaker, "You said—*amerikanets?*"

"*Da, tovarishch.*"

Bogomazov took a deep breath and two steps toward them. "All right. Take me to this American ... at once!"

The peasants faltered briefly, then moved to obey. As Bogomazov strode up the straggling village street in their midst, he was very much aware that a man with a rifle walked on either side of him— like a guard of honor or a prisoner's escort. Bogomazov left his holster flap unbuttoned. From the hovels some women and children peered out to watch as they passed; a whisper fluttered from hut to hut:"*Kommuníst prishól....*"

They stopped in front of a shed, built roughly like the other buildings, of hand-hewn boards. From inside came a rhythmic clanging of metal, and when Bogomazov stepped boldly through the open doorway he was met by a hot blast of air. A stone forge glowed brightly, and a man turned from it, shirtless and sweating, hammer still raised above an improvised anvil.

As the blacksmith straightened, mopping his forehead, Bogomazov saw at first glance that he was in truth an American or at least a Westerner; he had the typical—and hated—features, the long narrow face and jaw, the prominent nose like the beak of some predatory bird, the lanky loose-jointed build. The Russian word *amerikanets* means not only "American," but also, as a slang expression, "man who get things done, go-getter"; and it had passed through Bogomazov's mind that these peasants might have applied the term as a fanciful sort of title to some energetic leader risen from among them—but, no: the man before him was really one of the enemy.

With a smooth motion Bogomazov drew and leveled his pistol. He said, "You are under arrest in the name of the Soviet Government."

The other stared at his unkempt menacing figure with a curious grimace, as if he were undecided whether to laugh or cry. The pistol moved in a short, commanding arc; the hammer fell from opened fingers, thudding dully on the earthen floor.

Bogomazov sensed rather than saw the painful uncertainty of the armed men in the doorway; he didn't turn his head. "Keep your hands in sight," he ordered. "Stand over there." The man obeyed carefully; evidently he understood Russian.

"Now," said the Communist, "explain. What kind of infiltration have you been carrying on here?"

The American blinked at him, still wearing that ambiguous expression. He said mildly, his speech fluent though heavily accented, "At the moment when I was so rudely interrupted, I was trying to beat part of a gun mounting into a plowshare. We put in the fall wheat with the old-style wooden plows; a couple of iron shares will make the spring sowing a lot easier and more rewarding, and we may even be able to break some more land this fall."

"Stop evading! I asked you...Wait." Feeling intuitively that the psychological moment had come, Bogomazov gestured brusquely at the men in the doorway. "You may go. I will call when you are needed."

They shuffled their feet, fingered the rifles they held, and melted away.

The American smiled wryly. "You know how to handle these people, don't you?...But I wish you'd quit pointing that gun now. You aren't going to shoot me in any case until after you've questioned me, and I wouldn't advise you to then. I'm not a very good blacksmith, I admit, but I am the only person here who knows anything about farm management . . . unless you happen to be a stray *agronóm.*"

The Russian lowered the pistol and caressed its barrel with his other hand, his face expressionless. "Go on," he said. "I begin to see. You are a specialist who had turned his knowledge to account to obtain a position of leadership."

The other sighed. "You might say that, or you might say I was drafted. The original nucleus of this community was two light machine guns—abandoned after all the ammunition was used up in brushes with the *razbóiniki.* This group was footloose then; I persuaded them to strike south, since when winter came they'd have broken up or starved, and look for unblighted land to farm. As for me, I used to work for the United States Department of Agriculture; what I know about tractor maintenance doesn't do much good just now, but some of the rest is still applicable. I realized pretty early— after I walked away by myself from a crash landing near Tula—that my chances of survival alone, as an alien, would be practically zero. . . . My name, incidentally, is Leroy Smith—Smith means *kuznéts,* but I never thought I'd revert so far to type," he added with a glance at the smoldering forge.

"Go on, Smeet," said Bogomazov, still fondling the gun. "What have you accomplished?"

The American gave him a perplexed look. "Well . . . these people here aren't a very choice bunch. About half of them were factory hands—proletarians, you know—who've had to learn from the ground up. The rest were mostly low-grade collective farm workers—fair to mediocre at carrying out the foreman's orders, but lost when it comes to figuring out what to do next. That, of course, is where I come in." He eyed the Russian speculatively. "And you, as a lone survivor, must have talents that Novoselye can use. We ought to be able to make a deal."

"I," said Bogomazov flatly, "am a Communist."

Smith's eyes narrowed. "Oh, oh," he murmured under his breath. "I should have known it—the way he bulled in here, the way—"

"There will be no deal. As a specialist, you are useful. You will continue to be useful. You will remember that you are serving the Soviet State; any irregularity, any sabotage or wrecking activities— *I* will punish." He hefted the pistol.

The American said wearily, "Don't you realize that the Soviet State, the Communist Party, the war—all that's over and done with, kaput? And America too, I suppose—the last I heard our whole industrial triangle was a radioactive bonfire and Washington had been annexed to Chesapeake Bay. Here we're a handful of survivors trying to go on surviving."

"The war is not over. Did you think you could start a war and call it quits when you became nauseated with it?"

"We didn't start it."

In the light of the forge Bogomazov's eyes glittered with a color that matched the metal of the weapon he held. "You capitalists made your fundamental mistake through vulgar materialism. You thought you could destroy Communism by destroying the capital, the wealth and industry, and military power we had built up as a base in the Soviet Union. You didn't realize that our real capital was always—ourselves, the Communists. That's why we will inherit the earth, now that your war has shattered the old world!"

Smith watched him talk with a sort of dazed fascination, and then, the spell breaking, smiled faintly. "Before you go about inheriting the earth, it will be necessary to worry about lasting out the winter."

"Naturally!" snapped Bogomazov. He stepped back to the doorway, and called, "You there! Come on in." He singled out one of the armed peasants. "You will stand guard, to see that this foreigner does not escape or commit any acts of sabatoge, such as damaging tools. You will not listen to anything he may say. So long as he behaves properly, you will leave him strictly alone, understood?"

The man nodded violently. "Yes, Comrade."

"I am going to inspect the settlement. You, Smeet—back to making plowshares, and they had better be good!"

Winter closed down inexorably. Icy winds blew from the steppe—not the terrible fanged winds of the northern tundras, but freezing all the same; and on still days the smoke from the huts rose far into the bright frosty air, betraying the village's location to any chance marauders.

There was no help for that, but there was plenty of work to be done. Almost every day the forge was busy, and on the outskirts of Novoseleye hammers rang, where new houses were going up to relieve the settlement's crowding. It would have been good to have a stockade, too; but on the almost treeless plain it had become necessary to go dangerously far to find usable timber.

Bogomazov, making one of his frequent circuits of the village in company with Ivanov, his silent and caninely devoted fellow Communist who had strayed in a few weeks after him, halted to watch the construction. The American Smith was lending a hand on the job—at the moment, he had paused to show a former urban clerk how to use a hammer without bending precious nails.

Bogomazov watched for a minute in silence, then called, "Smeet!"

The American looked round, straightened and came toward them without haste. "What is it now?"

"I have been looking for you. Some of the cattle are sick; no one seems to know if it is serious. Do you know anything about veterinary medicine?"

"I've done a little cow doctoring—I was brought up on a farm. I'll take a look at them right away."

"Good." Watching the other turn to go, Bogomazov felt an uneasy though familiar surprise at the extent to which he and the settlement had come to rely on this outlander. Time and again, in greater or lesser emergencies calling for special skills, the only one who knew what to do—or the only one who would volunteer to try—had been this inevitable Smith.

There was an explanation for that, of course: from Smith's references to his prewar life in America, Bogomazov gathered that he had worked at one time or another at a remarkable variety of "specialties," moving from place to place and from job to job, in the chaotic capitalistic labor market, in a manner which would never have been tolerated in the orderly Soviet economic system.... As a result, he seemed to have done a little of everything and to know more than a little about everything.

And Bogomazov was aware that, behind his back, the villagers referred to the foreigner as "Comrade Specialist"—improperly giving him the title of honor, *tovarishch*, though he was not even a Soviet citizen, let alone a Party member....

That train of thought was a reminder, and Bogomazov called, "Wait! Another matter, when you have time...I am told that the stove in Citizen Vrachov's hut will not draw."

Smith turned, smiling. "That's all right. Vrachov's wife complained to me about it, and I've already fixed the flue."

Bogomazov stiffened. "She should not have gone to you. She should have reported the matter to me first."

The American's smile faded. "Oh... discipline, eh?"

"Discipline is essential," said Bogomazov flatly. Ivanov, at his elbow, nodded emphatic agreement.

"I suppose it is." Smith eyed them thoughtfully. "I've got to admit that you've accomplished some things I probably couldn't have done—like redistributing the housing space and cooking up a system of rationing to take the village through the winter—and making it stick."

"You could not have done those things because you are not a Communist," said Bogomazov with energy. "You are used to the 'impossibilities' of a dying society; but we are strong in the knowledge that history is on our side. There is nothing that a real Bolshevik cannot achieve!"

Ivanov nodded again.

"History," Smith said refectively, "is notorious for changing sides. I wonder if even a Bolshevik... But in the case of Vrachov's wife's chimney, your discipline seems rather petty."

The Russian drew visibly into himself. "Enough!" he said sharply. "You are to see to the cattle."

Smith shrugged slightly and turned away. "O.K.," he said. "*Volya vasha*—you're the boss."

A half-grown boy bolted headlong down the village street, feet ringing on the frost-hard ground. "*Razbóinike!*" he shrieked. "*Razbo-o-oiniki!*"

At the feared cry—"robbers!"—the inhabitants poured out of their dwellings like bees from a threatened hive, some snatching up axes, hoes, even sticks of firewood. No guns—one of Bogomazov's first acts after he had restored the Soviet authority in Novoselye had been to round up all the firearms, a motley collection of Russian and other makes, and store them safely in a stout shed under the protection of the village's only working padlock.

The villagers began to huddle together, hugging the shelter of their houses and staring anxiously eastward, at the farther banks of the frozen river. The boy who had given the alarm ran among them, pointing. Everyone saw the little black figures, men and horses, moving yonder, pacing up and down the snow-covered shore; and a concerted groan went up as one mounted man ventured testingly out onto the ice and, evidently found it strong enough.

To make things worse, the penned cattle, upset by the tumult, began bawling. That sound would carry clearly across the river, and would whet the appetites of the *razbóiniki*. The Novoselyane shivered, remembering all the tales of villages overrun and burned, the inhabitants driven off or slaughtered, remembering too their own collisions with such troops of marauders—remnants of revolted army units, of mobs that had escaped the cities' ruin, of dispersed Asian tribes—armed riffraff swept randomly together from heaven knows where, *izzá granítsy*, from beyond the frontiers even....

These *razbóiniki* were plainly numerous, and plainly, too, they were coming. Perhaps a hundred men, half of them mounted, were in sight, and on the skyline beyond the river the sharper-sighted glimpsed wagons, probably ox-drawn. The enemy were well organized, not merely casual looters. The Novoselyane gripped their improvised weapons—vaguely, frightenedly determined to show fight, but withal no more than sheep for the slaughter. A hulking young ex-factory worker mourned aloud, "*Bozhe moi*, if we only still had the machine guns..."

Then Bogomazov came striding down the street, flinging commands right and left as he went, commands that sent the villagers scurrying into an approximation of a defense line. He swore bitterly, wrestling with the frozen padlock on the shed where the guns had been stored; he got it open, and, together with Ivanov, began to run up and down the line passing out rifles and strict orders not to use them until word was given.

The mounted *razbóiniki* were approaching at a walk, in an uneven skirmish line across the ice.

Smith stood watching, hands tucked for warmth—he owned no mittens—into the pockets of the tattered flight jacket he still clung to. As Bogomazov hurried past, cradling a sniper's rifle equipped with telescopic sights, Smith remarked, "I used to be a pretty fair shot—"

"Keep out of the way!" snapped the Communist. He dropped to all fours, crept out onto the open slope beyond the row of houses, and lay sighting carefully. Behind the line Ivanov scurried from point to point, repeating the orders; "Hold your fire, and when you do shoot, aim for the horses in front. They have fewer horses than men; and if an enemy can once be persuaded that the front line is too dangerous, he will shortly have no front line...."

The hollow sound of the hooves came nearer, clear in the hush. Then Bogomazov's rifle cracked, and the lead horse reared, throwing its rider; the ice gave way beneath its hind feet, and it floundered. Guns began going off all along the line of houses as Bogomazov came wriggling back. The horsemen on the ice scattered, trotting and crouching low in the saddles, returning the fire. Bullets ricocheted screaming through the village, ripping splinters from walls and roofs.

Some of the *razbóiniki* were busied dragging their wounded or foundered comrades and their mounts back toward the farther shore, but off to the right a handful of horsemen broke into a reckless gallop across the groaning ice, making determinedly for the low bank above the village. Bogomazov, rifle slung, started in that direction, beckoning some of the defenders from the firing line and bellowing to the others: "Fire only at the ones still coming! Save your cartridges!"

The *razbóiniki* made the shore and bore down on Novoselye's flank, whooping, urging their unkempt ponies to a dead run. They were heading for the corral, hoping to smash the stockade around it and drive the cattle off; but when they were almost upon their objective bullets started snapping among them. One man spun from his saddle and went rolling along the frozen ground, and a horse sprawled headlong, pinning its rider. The others' nerve broke, and they wheeled and fled.

Bogomazov walked out, pistol ready, to inspect the casualties. The man who had been hit was already dead. Bogomazov fired twice with cool precision, finishing first the gasping, lung-shot horse and then the rider who lay stunned beneath it.

He told his men, "They may attack repeatedly. We will establish watches."

But the *razbóiniki* had had enough. After an anxious hour of watching the movements on the far side of the river, the villagers became aware that the enemy, horse, foot, and wagons, had reassembled in marching order and was streaming away southward. The Novoselyane laughed, wept with relief, and embraced one another; someone did an impromptu clog dance in the street.

Bogomazov entered the sooty one-room dwelling which, because of his occupancy, was known as the *nachál' naya izbá*, the "primary hut." He breathed the warm close air gratefully, beginning to shed his mittens and padded coat. Then he stopped short as he saw Smith warming his hands by the stove, a rifle slung over his shoulder. "Where did you get that?"

The American grinned. "One of the proletariat developed combat fatigue about ten seconds after the shooting started, so I filled in."

Bogomazov hesitated imperceptibly, then thrust his hand out. "Give it to me."

Slowly Smith unslung the weapon and handed it over. Bogomazov unloaded it, stuffed the cartridges into his pocket, opened the door of the *izbá* and called to a passing boy, "Here. You are responsible for delivering this rifle to Comrade Ivanov."

The youth hugged the rifle to him, looking adoringly at Bogomazov. "Yes, sir, Comrade General!"

Bogomazov started to speak, checked himself, and closed the door.

"So you're putting the guns under lock and key again."

"Naturally. Ivanov is attending to that now."

The American raised an eyebrow quizzically. "In my country's Constitution there is, or used to be, a provision safeguarding the people's right to keep and bear arms."

"The Soviet Constitution contains no such provision."

"Today, though, we might have been overrun and massacred if the enemy had approached less openly, and hadn't been seen in time for you to break out the guns."

Bogomazov sank wearily onto a bench by the fire and began unwinding the rags that served him as leggings. He said heavily, "*Mister* Smeet, you are neither a Russian nor a Communist, and you do not understand these people as I do. You had better leave administration to me, and devote yourself to those matters which you are expert in.... How is your work with the radio?"

Smith shook his head impatiently. "Nothing there—I can't raise any signals, maybe because there aren't any.... But the question of the guns is a secondary one. The main thing is—what are we going to do now?"

The Russian eyed him wonderingly. "What do you mean?"

"I came here to speak to you because the attack today confirmed a suspicion that's been growing on me for some time, ever since the first bandits raided through here in November.... Did you notice the organization these *razbóiniki* seemed to have? They were fairly well disciplined; they attacked from and fell back on a mobile camp, with wagons no doubt carrying their women and children, and with driven cattle. The population of their whole camp must be two or three times that of Novoselye."

"So? We beat them off. You saw that they proceeded south; the winter is too much for them, whereas we will sit it out snugly in our houses, so long as order is maintained and rations are conserved."

"But they'll be back in the spring."

"Perhaps. If so, we will be stronger by then."

"How stronger? We've very little rifle ammunition left, and before the spring crop comes in there's going to be trouble with malnutrition."

"The marauders are subject to the same troubles. In Lipy, only fifty kilometers from here, there is a man who knows how to make gunpowder."

"I could make gunpowder, for that matter—but damned if I know where to find any sulfur.... You miss the point. The signs of organization we saw indicate that these people, wherever they came from originally, have succeeded in taking to a nomadic way of life—a permanently roving existence. They'll be on us again next spring, without 'perhaps.'"

Bogomazov shrugged impatiently. "So, there are dangers. I am not losing sight of them. You had better concentrate on trying to establish radio communication."

The American said hotly, "You're still blind to what this development means! You ... Well, before this war some of our Western 'bourgeois' historians—naturally you wouldn't have read their writings—saw human history as a long struggle between two basically different ways of life, the two main streams of social evolution: Civilization and Nomadism. Civilization is a way of life based on agriculture—principally cereal crops—on fixed places of habitation, on comparatively stable social patterns whose highest form is the state. Nomadism, on the other hand, has as its economic foundation not fields, but herds; geographically, it rests not on settlements, villages, towns, cities, but on perpetual migration from pasture to pasture; socially, its typical higher form of organization is not the state, but the horde.

"Since written history began the boundary between Civilization and Nomadism has swayed back and forth as one or the other gained local advantage; but in general, during the historic period—really a very small part of the whole past of humanity—Civilization has been on the offensive. The last great onslaught from the nomad world was in the twelfth century—the Mongol conquests, which swept through this very region and brought about the period that your historians call the Tartar Yoke. By the eighteenth century the counterattack of Civilization had been so successful that the historian Gibbon—another bourgeois you probably haven't read—could rejoice that 'cannon and fortifications' had made Europe forever secure against any more such invasions. It looked as if Nomadism was through, due to disappear altogether.... But Civilization went on to invent the means of destroying itself: weapons indefinitely effective against the fixed installations that civilized life depends on, but of little consequence to the rootless nomad.

"And now—where are your cannons, your fortifications, your coal mines and steel mills, your nitrogen-fixing and sulfuric-acid plants? When you discount these raiders as nuisances, you're still living in a world that just died a violent death. We no longer have the whole of Civilization backing us up; we're on our own!"

Bogomazov had listened with half-shut eyes, soaking up the fire's warmth. "Then you think Civilization is finished?"

"No! But I think that what's left of it will have to fall back and regroup. You and we, the Americans and Russians—we fought our war for the control of Civilization, and very nearly wrecked it in the process; but on both sides we were and are on the side of Civilization. That's what counts now.... What's out situation here? According to the scanty liaison we've achieved, there are a number of other settlements like this up and down the river, scattered seeds trying to take root again. From the east, toward the Caspian, there's no news at all, and westward, in the Ukraine, reports tell of nothing but wandering bands—the blights the planes spread interdicted agriculture throughout that region for some years to come.

"In the spring the *razbóiniki* will be on us again—and perhaps in the meantime their fragmentary groups will have coalesced into bigger and more formidable hordes. With their rediscovered technique of Nomadic life, they'll be expanding into the vacuum created by the internal collapse of the civilized world, as the Huns and their kindred did when the Roman Empire fell....I think we have no choice but to migrate west as soon as the spring crop is in. This country here can no longer be held for Civilization; for one thing it's too badly devastated, and for another it's all one huge plain, natural Nomad country. The Eurasian plain extends through northern Europe, clear across Germany and France; we should move south to look for a more favorable geography. It might be possible to make a stand in the Crimea, but it's said the radioactivity is very bad there; either the Balkans or Italy, with their mountains, should probably be our ultimate objective."

Bogomazov sat up straight, looking hard at Smith. He frowned. "You are suggesting—that Russia be abandoned to the *razbóiniki?*"

"Exactly. That will be the result in any case: I'm suggesting that we save ourselves while we've got time."

The Communist's eyes narrowed, with a peculiar glitter; he was motionless and silent for a moment, then he barked with humorless laughter. "You want a lecture a Marxist on history! I know history. Do you know that this is the very region where took place the events told in the *Tale of Igor's Host;* the same region where Prince Dmitri Donskói overthrew the Golden Horde? And you tell me to retreat from a handful of bandits! Do you know—"

"I don't see what the bygone glories of Holy Russia have to do either with Marxism or with preserving Civilization," Smith interrupted dryly.

The other rose to his feet, rocking on them like an undersized but infuriated bear, and glared hotly at the American's lanky figure. He shouted, "Will you be quiet, before I—"

The door slammed open, letting in a cold blast, and in it stood Ivanov breathing hard. He gasped, "Comrade Bogomazov! There are two rifles missing!"

In a flash Bogomazov was himself again, reaching for his coat. "Two? I'll investigate, and whoever is trying to hide—"

"Beg pardon, Comrade Bogomazov, but it's worse that that. Vasya and Mishka the Frog—that is, Citizens Rudin and Bagryanov—are gone with the rifles."

"The young fools..." Bogomazov plunged through the doorway, still struggling into his coat. Smith followed more slowly; when he caught up, the Communist was in the center of a knot of villagers, furiously interrogating a shawl-wrapped old woman who was bitterly weeping.

"Where did they go? Which way?" demanded Bogomazov.

The old woman, mother of one of the missing youths, only sniffled repeatedly: "*Ushlí v razboíniki*...they went to the robbers...."

The Communist wheeled from her in disgust, fists clenching uselessly at his sides. Smith said conversationally, "You'll never catch them now. There you see the effect of another weapon in Nomadism's arsenal."

"What in the devil's name are you talking about?"

"Psychological warfare. Those young fellows, finding guns in their hands and adventure in their hearts, deserted Civilization and its dreary chores for a more romantic-looking life."

Bogomazov grunted angrily, "Ideological nonsense! Russians have always run off to join the robbers. It's in their nature."

"Exactly. As boys in my country used to head West in hopes of becoming cowboys. I wonder what's happening in the American West now.... Men have always tended to rebel against civilized restraints and hanker after the nomad's free, picturesque existence; and when the restraints are loosened, they may bolt."

"We can do without that pair. And you—" Bogomazov eyed the American stonily and spoke with deliberate emphasis. "You'll not repeat these notions of yours to anyone else—understood?" Without awaiting any response, he turned on his heel and stalked away toward the *nachál' naya izbá*.

Smith gazed somberly after him, knowing that further argument would be useless. The decision was made—to stand and fight it out here.

Spring came with the thunderous breakup of the river ice, with the sluicing of thawed water that made the prairie a trackless wilderness of mud for a time, with the pushing of new green everywhere on the vast rolling plains and, less densely, in the fields that last fall had been so painfully broken and seeded.

Spring came with foreboding, that somehow waxed apace with the hope that returning green life wakens in all living. Smith had kept his ideas to himself; but the Novoselyane whispered among themselves. Those who had been city dwellers had nothing but a formless and unfocused fear of the great windy spaces, the silences, the night noises of birds and water creatures along the marshy river brim; but the peasants had their immemorial stories, raised up from the depths of a tradition as deep as race memory, given new and frightening meanings. Over their heads had come and gone serfdom, emancipation, serfdom again under the name of collectivization, and finally the apocalyptic swallowing up of the world of cities that they had never quite understood or trusted . . . and they remembered other things.

They knew that in the old days the greening swells beyond the river had been the edge of the world, the Tartar steppe, out of which the khans had ridden to see the Russian princes grovel and bring tribute before the horse-tail standards. The grandiose half-finished works of the Fifth Five-Year Plan were strewn wreckage there now, and it came to their mind that perhaps it was the Tartar steppe again. They remembered the ancient sorrows of the Slavs, the woes that are told in the Russian Primary Chronicle. They spoke darkly of the Horde of Mamai, which in Russian speech has passed into proverbs; and of the *obry*, whose name now means "ogres," but who historically were the nomad Avars, that took to herding human cattle even into the heart of Europe. . . .

When the Communists were not watching them, they studied signs in the flight of migrating birds and the cries of night fowl. Somehow all the portents were evil.

There were more tangible reasons for alarm. News filtered in of settlements downriver raided and laid waste by wandering bands, whose numbers and ferocity no doubt grew mightily in the telling. Bogomazov succeeded in suppressing or minimizing most of these reports, but not all, nor could trailing smoke smudges in the southern sky one bright afternoon be concealed. . . .

Bogomazov sensed the slow rise of dark superstitious fear around him, and he moved about the village, the faithful Ivanov trotting at his heels, scolding, coaxing, exhorting, all to scant avail; to combat the villagers' fears was like wrestling with an amorphous thing in a nightmare. Once upon a time a local administrator could have reached for the telephone and conjured up an impressive caravan of Party officials in shiny automobiles, with uniforms, medals and manners which would leave the yokels for many weeks incapable of saying anything but "Yes, Comrade." Or he might have pointed to airplanes droning across the sky as visible signs of the omnipotence of the Soviet State. But now there was no telephone, and all that flew was the migrant birds, passing northward day after day as if fleeing from some terror in the south.

"We are on our own now," thought Bogomazov, then scowled as he remembered that the American had said it.

The end came suddenly.

Smith had gone out with a half dozen peasants to inspect the growing wheat. All at once they looked up and saw, across the narrow width of a field, a little group of horsemen, no more than their own number, quietly sitting on their shaggy ponies, watching. How they had come up so silently and unseen was a mystery; it was as if the world had changed to that fairy-tale plenum of possibilities in which armed bands spring up from seed sown in the earth.

These watchers carried a bizarre mixture of modern and primitive armament; some had rifles, but cavalry sabers dangled against their thighs, and some bore spears whose hammered iron points flashed in the sun.

The two parties were motionless, confronting one another for a minute or two like strangers from different worlds. Then the interlopers wheeled about without haste and trotted away over a rise.

"Come on!" said Smith quietly, and set out at a run for the village.

Bogomazov, face impassive, heard the news that the danger was again upon them. He produced his key and opened the padlocked shed door—and stood frozen in dismay, for the shed was empty. Someone had employed the winter's leisure to tunnel under a side wall and remove all the guns.

"Who did this?" shouted the Communist at the villagers assembling in the square.

"Not I, Comrade..."

"It wasn't I, Comrade..."

Uniformly, the peasant faces reflected the transparent guilt of naughty children.

"Very well!" said Bogomazov bitterly. "You're all in it. You've stolen the guns and hidden them, in the thatch, under the floor, no matter where. But now, bring them out—do you hear?"

They stirred uneasily, but did not move to obey.

"Apparently," said a sardonic voice, "the Soviet Constitution has been amended."

"You!...Were *you* behind this thievery?"

"Certainly not," said Smith. "They don't trust me too far either—they have a hazy notion that I'm one of your kind, one of the rulers they hate but haven't learned to do without."

He swung around and said, without raising his voice, to the men nearest: "You've taken the guns for your own protection—if you intend to use them that way, now's the time. The main body of the *razbóiniki* won't be far behind the scouting party we saw. Do you propose to defend yourselves, the houses you've built and the fields you've plowed?"

They murmured among themselves, and began to drift off by twos and threes. Presently men were emerging from all the huts, awkwardly carrying the missing rifles.

It was all of a taut hour before they had sight again of the enemy, but for a good part of that hour they heard the mournful creaking of wagons in the steppe, out of view beyond the higher ground. The sound was disembodied, sourceless, seeming to come from nowhere and everywhere.

The men of Novoselye clustered in uneasy groups, waiting, fingering their weapons unsteadily. Bogomazov took charge, ordering them here and there, lashing the village into a posture of defense; they obeyed him, but halfheartedly, with the look of dumb driven cattle on their faces.

One moment there was no sign of the foe save for the creaking of unseen wheels. The next, a dozen mounted figures were briefly silhouetted along the skyline, dipped down the green wave of the grassy slope toward the fields, and were followed by others and yet others, till—to eyes wavering in beginning panic—the whole hillside seemed sliding down in an avalanche of men and horses.

"Steady!" snapped Bogomazov. "Hold your fire—"

Abruptly one man let his rifle fall and turned, sobbing, to flee; it was Ivanov, the other Communist. Bogomazov intercepted him in two long strides and felled him with a full-armed blow, the pistol weighting his hand.

"Get up, get back to your post!" he spat into the dazed and bloody face.

But the villagers had already begun to fall back down the street, in a concerted tide of fear that threatened momentarily to become a total rout.

Smith, looming conspicuous by his height among them, shouting in a carrying voice, *"Don't drop your guns! We'll* make a stand in the square!" The American materialized at Bogomazov's side and wrenched urgently at his arm, dragging him, dazed with fury and disappointment, after the retreating mob. "Come on! If we can hold the men together for a few minutes, maybe we can still rally them."

The *razbóiniki* were jogging across the planted ground, trampling ruthlessly over the new wheat. From the street's other end rose a cry, "Here they come!" and almost simultaneously someone screamed and pointed across the river, where a third troop had come into view on the opposite bank, as if posted to cut off the last possible escape.

As the invaders, with jingling bridles and clattering hooves, swept from two sides into Novoselye, its able-bodied inhabitants huddled in the square; those who still clutched their weapons and those without wore the same look of hopeless waiting for an expected blow.

The *razbóiniki* closed in cautiously. Their leader, a squat leathery-looking man with a wide Kalmyk face, rode near; he reined in and looked down expressionlessly—at the Novoselyane. He said loudly, in stumbling Russian, "We—not want kill you. You give up—we burn village, go. Be peace." He repeated, "Peace!" watching for their response with almost a benevolent air, the while he tightened the strap of his slung rifle—it was his most prized possession, a German rifle that could hit targets at a thousand yards, and he had no intention of wasting his few remaining cartridges in close fighting. An old saber hung loose in its sheath at his side.

Smith pushed forward and spoke slowly and distinctly: "We too desire peace, between your people and ours. Why should we fight and waste lives, when so few are left after the great war? You are wanderers, we farm the land—only a little of the land, so there is room for both of us."

He watched the stolid Asiatic face keenly for any hint of response. Did the *razbóinik* leader realize that the villagers wouldn't fight, that—so far as this outpost was concerned—the resistance of Civilization was at an end?

"Village—bad," the Kalmyk declared, with unhelpful gestures. "Build houses, plow land—then, *boom!* No good..." He gave up, and half turned in the saddle, beckoning to a young man with Slavic features. The latter advanced a couple of paces, and said glibly in Russian:

"The *vozhd'* means that it is dangerous to live in towns. If people live in towns, sooner or later the American bombers come, many are killed and others sickened with burns and bowels turning to water; the death blows even across the steppes and kills animals and men.... We cannot allow you to live in such danger. So we will burn this town, and in return for the favor we do you we will take only half the cattle, and such ammunition as you may have that will fit the guns we possess; for the rest, you may keep your arms and movable property, and go freely where you like. Whoever may wish to join us is welcome."

"Your terms are too hard," said Smith steadily. "And you—"

He was interrupted. Bogomazov, pale with determination, thrust him aside and shouted in a voice of command, "That man is a traitor to the motherland! Citizens, follow me!"

The pistol in his hand roared, but in the instant as he aimed the young spokesman had thrown himself flat over his horse's neck. Simultaneously the Kalmyk leader leaned far out of the saddle, and his saber descended like a silent flash of lightning.

The villagers on one side, the raiders on the other, stared unmoving, unmoved, at the fallen man. Smith bent over him, almost under the nervously dancing feet of the Kalmyk's pony.

Bogomazov made a great effort to rise, and failed. His eyes looked unfocusedly up into the American's face; his expression was one of incredulity.

He strove to speak, choking on blood. Smith leaned close, and thought he understood the dying man's last words, uttered with that look of dazed wonder: *"Even a Bolshevik..."*

The nomad spokesman rode forward again, red in the face, and shouted fiercely, "Are there any more dissenters?"

Smith stood up and faced them. The game was lost and the enemy knew it now, but he still had to try the last card he possessed. He said tensely, "You are mistaken. The American bombers aren't coming any more."

"How can you know?"

"Because I myself am an American."

There was a dead hush, in which Smith heard clearly the noise of a carbine's hammer being drawn back. The Kalmyk's slanted eyes rested inscrutably upon him. Then the man grinned under his straggling mustache, and said something, a rapid string of Asiatic syllables.

"The *vozhd'* says: 'That may or may not be true. To him you seem to be a man much like other men.'"

"But—" Smith began.

"*But* we're taking no chances. We burn the village in half an hour; you have that long to assemble your goods. Those who wish to move on with us will signify by gathering in the field yonder. *Kryshka*—that's all!"

Smith let his hands fall to his sides. Some of the villagers had already begun to drift toward the indicated assembly point.

Some way out in the steppe there was a *kurgán*, an ancient grass-grown burial mound of some forgotten people. Civilizations, wars and disasters had passed it by and it was the same. It was the highest point for many miles. From it Smith watched the glowing embers of the New Settlement.

All around was the plain, immense and darkening in the spring twilight. Thousands of miles, months of footsore march, it must be to reach any place where there would be a doubtful security and a chance to begin anew. Time and space—once man had conquered them, but now man was a rare animal again in a world where time and space mocked him. Smith wondered: Would they be conquered again in his own lifetime, or that of his grandchildren? Bogomazov had been lucky in a way; his training had enabled him to disbelieve what he knew to be true, so that he had never been forced to recognize the meaning of what had happened—or had he, there at the end?

In the west the horizon was empty, or at least his eyes could no longer make out against the sunset the black specks of the westward-marching horde. About half of the uprooted villagers had gone with it—with few exceptions, those who had come originally from the cities, the factories; the peasants remained. They were encamped now about the ancient mound.

Behind Smith a voice asked plaintively, "Comrade American— what will we do? Some of us think we should go on south, to-ward..."

"Don't bother me now!" Smith said harshly; then, as the man drew back abashed: "Tomorrow...we'll see, tomorrow."

The retreating feet were soundless on the grassy slope. Down by the river the last sparks were dying. Somewhere far off in the steppe shuddered a mournful cry that Smith did not know—perhaps it was the howl of a wolf. In the west the light faded, and night fell with the darkness sweeping on illimitable wings out of Asia.

11_____

Another problem among science fiction's post-Megawar survivors, besides sickness, violence, sterility, impotence, mutation, and miscarriage, is sheer loneliness, and the nostalgia for lost ways of life. The characters created by Pangborn, Benét, Bradbury, Zelazny, Swanwick, Clarke, and Aikin—in stories which follow—all mourn, as do the inhabitants of Dante's Hell, for a lost world, and this makes me think of much post-Megawar fiction as a special case of the underworld myth. The fictional "underworld" is not always underground (in the Clarke story, it's in the sky), but it's the place of a dead civilization's afterlife; if you have an afterlife to spend, and have to spend it here, you'll pine and sigh for home like the shades of Virgil and Dante. After Megawar, as Edgar Pangborn tells it, human life goes on here and there, taking unpredictable turns in isolation, growing, shrinking, changing, reminiscing, and in the case of a master, practicing a way, the tao of his lost art.

A MASTER OF BABYLON
by Edgar Pangborn

For twenty-five years no one came.

In the seventy-sixth year of his life Brian Van Anda was still trying not to remember a happy boyhood. To do so was irrelevant and dangerous, although every instinct of his old age tempted him to reject the present and live in the lost times. He would recall stubbornly that the present year, for example, was 2096 according to the Christian calendar, that he had been born in 2020, seven years after the close of the civil war, fifty years before the last war, twenty-five years before the departure of the First Interstellar. The First and Second Interstellar would be still on the move, he supposed. It had been understood, obvious, long ago, that after radio contact faded out the world would not hear of them again for many lifetimes, if ever. They would be on the move, farther and farther away from a planet no longer capable of understanding such matters.

Brian sometimes recalled the place of birth, New Boston, the fine planned city far inland from the old metropolis which a rising sea had reclaimed after the earthquake of 1994. Such things, places and dates, were factual props, useful when Brian wanted to impose an external order on the vagueness of his immediate existence. He tried to make sure they became no more than that, to shut away the colors, the poignant sounds, the parks and the playgrounds of New Boston, the known faces (many of them loved), and the later years when he had experienced a curious intoxication called fame.

It was not necessarily better or wiser to reject these memories, but it was safer, and nowadays Brian was often sufficiently tired, sufficiently conscious of his growing weakness and lonely unimportance, to crave safety as a meadow mouse craves a burrow.

He tied his canoe to the massive window which for many years had been a port and a doorway. Lounging there with a suspended sense of time, he hardly knew he was listening. In a way, all the twenty-five years had been a listening. He watched Earth's patient star sink toward the rim of the forest on the Palisades. At this hour it was sometimes possible, if the sun-crimsoned water lay still, to cease grieving at the greater stillness.

There must be scattered human life elsewhere, he knew—probably a great deal of it. After twenty-five years alone, that also often seemed irrelevant. At other times than mild evenings—on hushed noons or in the mornings always so empty of human commotion— Brian might lapse into anger, fight the calm by yelling, resent the swift dying of his own echoes. Such moods were brief. A kind of humor remained in him, not to be ruined by any sorrow.

He remembered how, ten months or possibly ten years ago, he

had encountered a box turtle in a forest clearing, and had shouted at it: "They went thataway!" The turtle's rigidly comic face, fixed in a caricature of startled disapproval, had seemed to point up some truth or other. Brian had hunkered down on the moss and laughed uproariously until he observed that some of the laughter was weeping.

Today had been rather good. He had killed a deer on the Palisades, and with bow and arrow, not spending a bullet—irreplaceable toy of civilization.

Not that he needed to practice such economy. He could live, he supposed, another ten years at the outside. His rifles were in good condition, his hoarded ammunition would easily outlast him. So would the stock of canned and dried food stuffed away in his living quarters. But there was satisfaction in primitive effort, and no compulsion to analyze the why of it.

The stored food was more important than the ammunition; a time was coming soon enough when he would no longer have the strength for hunting. He would lose the inclination to depart from his fortress for trips to the mainland. He would yield to such timidity or laziness for days, then weeks. Sometime, after such an interlude, he might find himself too feeble to risk climbing the cliff wall into the forest. He would then have the good sense, he hoped, to destroy the canoe, thus making of his weakness a necessity.

There were books. There was the Hall of Music on the next floor above the water, probably safe from its lessening encroachment. To secure fresh water he need only keep track of the tides, for the Hudson had cleaned itself and now rolled down sweet from the lonely uncorrupted hills. His decline could be comfortable. He had provided for it and planned it.

Yet now, gazing across the sleepy water, seeing a broad-winged hawk circle in freedom above the forest, Brian was aware of the old thought moving in him: *If I could hear voices—just once, if I could hear human voices...*

The Museum of Human History, with the Hall of Music on what Brian thought of as the second floor, should also outlast his requirements. In the flooded lower floor and basement the work of slow destruction must be going on: here and there the unhurried waters could find their way to steel and make rust of it; the waterproofing of the concrete was nearly a hundred years old. But it ought to be good for another century or two.

Nowadays, the ocean was mild. There were moderate tides, winds no longer destructive. For the last six years there had been no more of the heavy storms out of the south; in the same period Brian had noted a rise in the water level of a mere nine inches. The window-sill, his port, stood six inches above high-tide mark this year. Perhaps Earth was settling into a new amiable mood. The climate had become delightful, about like what Brian remembered from a visit to southern Virginia in his childhood.

The last earthquake had come in 2082—a large one, Brian guessed, but its center could not have been close to the rock of Manhattan. The Museum had only shivered and shrugged—it had survived much worse than that, half a dozen times since 1994. Long after the tremor, a tall wave had thundered in from the south. Its force, like that of others, had mostly been dissipated against the barrier of tumbled rock and steel at the southern end of the submerged island—an undersea dam, man-made though not man-intended— and when it reached the Museum it did no more than smash the southern windows in the Hall of Music, which earlier waves had not been able to reach; then it passed on up the river enfeebled.

The windows of the lower floor had all been broken long before that. After the earthquake of '82 Brian had spent a month in boarding up all the openings on the south side of the Hall of Music—after all, it was home—with lumber painfully ferried over from mainland ruins. By that year he was sixty-two years old and not moving with the ease of youth. He deliberately left cracks and knotholes. Sunlight sifted through in narrow beams, like the bars of dusty gold Brian could remember in a hayloft at his uncle's farm in Vermont.

That hawk above the Palisades soared nearer over the river and receded. Caught in the evening light, he was himself a little sun, dying and returning.

The Museum had been finished in 2003. Manhattan, strangely enough, had never taken a bomb, although in the civil war two of the type called "small clean fission" had fallen on the Brooklyn and New Jersey sides—so Brian recalled from the jolly history books which had informed his adolescence that war was definitely a thing of the past. By the time of the next last war, in 2070, the sea, gorged on melting ice caps, had removed Manhattan Island from current history.

Everything left standing above the waters south of the Museum had been knocked flat by the tornadoes of 2057 and 2064. A few blobs of empty rock still demonstrated where Central Park and Mount Morris Park had been: not significant. Where Long Island once rose, there was a troubled area of shoals and small islands, probably a useful barrier of protection for the receding shore of Connecticut. Men had yielded their great city inch by inch, then foot by foot; a full mile in 2047, saying: "The flood years have passed their peak, and a return to normal is expected." Brian sometimes felt a twinge of sympathy for the Neanderthal experts who must have told each other to expect a return to normal at the very time when the Cro-Magnons were drifting in.

In 2057 the Island of Manhattan had to be yielded. New York City, half-new, half-ancient, sprawled stubborn and enormous upstream, on both sides of a river not done with its anger. Yet the Museum stood. Aided by sunken rubble of other buildings of its kind, aided also by men because they still had time to love it, the museum stood, and might for a long time yet—weather permitting.

The hawk floated out of sight above the Palisades into the field of the low sun.

The Museum of Human History covered an acre of ground north of 125th Street, rising a modest fifteen stories, its foundation secure in that layer of rock which mimics eternity. It deserved its name; here men had brought samples of everything man-made, literally everything known in the course of human creation since prehistory. Within human limits it was definitive.

No one had felt anything unnatural in the refusal of the Directors of the Museum to move the collection after the building weathered the storm of 2057. Instead, ordinary people donated money so that a mighty abutment could be built around the ground floor and a new entrance designed on the north side of the second. The abutment survived the greater tornado of 2064 without damage, although during those seven years the sea had risen another eight feet in its old ever-new game of making monkeys out of the wise. (It was left for Brian Van Anda, alone, in 2079, to see the waters slide quietly over the abutment, opening the lower regions for the use of fishes and the more secret water-dwellers who like shelter and privacy. In the '90s, Brian suspected the presence of an octopus or two in the vast vague territory that had once been parking lot, heating plant, storage space, air-raid shelter, etc. He couldn't prove it; it just seemed like a decent, comfortable place for an octopus.) In 2070 plans were under consideration for building a new causeway to the Museum from the still expanding city in the north. In 2070, also, the last war began and ended.

When Brian Van Anda came down the river late in 2071, a refugee from certain unfamiliar types of savagery, the Museum was empty of the living. He spent many days in exhaustive exploration of the building. He did this systematically, toiling at last up to the Directors' meeting room on the top floor. There he observed how they must have been holding a conference at the very time when a new gas was tried out over New York in a final effort to persuade the Western Federation that the end justifies the means. (Too bad, Brian sometimes thought, that he would never know exactly what had become of the Asian Empire. In the little splinter state called the Soviet of North America, from which Brian had fled in '71, the official doctrine was that the Asian Empire had won the war and the saviors of humanity would be flying in any day now. Brian had inadvertently doubted this out loud and then stolen a boat and gotten away safely under cover of night.)

Up in the meeting room, Brian had seen how that up-to-date neurotoxin had been no respecter of persons. An easy death, however, by the look of it. He observed also how some things endure. The Museum, for instance: virtually unharmed.

Brian often recalled those moments in the meeting room as a sort of island in time. They were like the first day of falling in love, the first hour of discovering that he could play Beethoven. And a little like the curiously cherished, more than life-size half-hour back there in Newburg, in that ghastly year of 2071, when he had briefly met and spoken with an incredibly old man, Abraham Brown. Brown had been President of the Western Federation at the time of the civil war. Later, retired from the uproar of public affairs, he had devoted himself to philosophy, unofficial teaching. In 2071, with the world he had loved in almost total ruin around him, Brown had spoken pleasantly to Brian Van Anda of small things—of chrysanthemums that would soon be blooming in the front yard of the house where he lived with friends, of a piano recital by Van Anda back in 2067 which the old man still remembered with warm enthusiasm.

Only a month later more hell was loose and Brian himself in flight.

Yes, the Museum Directors had died easily. Brooding in the evening sunlight, Brian reflected that now, all these years later, the innocent bodies would be perfectly decent. No vermin in the Museum. The doorways and the floors were tight, the upper windows unbroken.

One of the white-haired men had had a Ming vase on his desk. He had not dropped out of his chair, but looked as if he had fallen asleep in front of the vase with his head on his arms. Brian had left the vase untouched, but had taken one thing, moved by some stirring of his own never-certain philosophy and knowing that he would not return to this room, ever.

One of the Directors had been opening a wall cabinet when he fell; the key lay near his fingers. Their discussion had not been concerned only with war, perhaps not at all with war. After all, there were other topics. The Ming vase must have had a part in it. Brian wished he could know what the old man had meant to take from the cabinet. Sometimes he dreamed of conversations with that man, in which the Director told him the truth of this and other matters, but what was certainty in sleep was in the morning gone like childhood.

For himself Brian had taken a little image of rock-hard clay, blackened, two-faced, male and female. Prehistoric, or at any rate wholly savage, unsophisticated, meaningful like the blameless motion of an animal in sunlight. Brian had said: "With your permission, gentlemen." He had closed the cabinet and then, softly, the outer door.

"I'm old, too," Brian said to the red evening. He searched for the hawk and could no longer find it in the deepening sky. "Old, a little foolish—talk aloud to myself. I'll have some Mozart before supper."

He transferred the fresh venison from the canoe to a small raft hitched inside the window. He had selected only choice pieces, as much as he could cook and eat in the few days before it spoiled, leaving the rest for the wolves or any other forest scavengers which might need it. There was a rope strung from the window to the marble steps leading to the next floor of the Museum, which was home.

It had not been possible to save much from the submerged area, for its treasure was mostly heavy statuary. Through the still water, as he pulled the raft along the rope, the Moses of Michelangelo gazed up at him in tranquillity. Other faces watched him; most of them watched infinity. There were white hands that occasionally borrowed motion from ripples made by the raft. "I got a deer, Moses," said Brian Van Anda, smiling down in companionship, losing track of time.... "Good night, Moses." He carried his juicy burden up the stairway.

Brian's living quarters had once been a cloakroom for Museum attendants. Four close walls gave it a feel of security. A ventilating shaft now served as a chimney for the wood stove Brian had salvaged from a mainland farmhouse. The door could be tightly locked. There were no windows. You do not want windows in a cave.

Outside was the Hall of Music, a full acre, an entire floor of the Museum, containing an example of every musical instrument that was known or could be reconstructed in the twenty-first century. The library of scores and recordings lacked nothing—except electricity to make the recordings speak. A few might still be made to sound on a hand-cranked phonograph, but Brian had not bothered with that toy for years; the springs were probably rusted.

Brian sometimes took out orchestra and chamber music scores to read at random. Once, reading them, his mind had been able to furnish ensembles, orchestras, choirs of a sort, but lately the ability had weakened. He remembered a day, possibly a year ago, when his memory refused to give him the sound of oboe and clarinet in unison. He had wandered, peevish, distressed, unreasonably alarmed, among the racks and cases of woodwinds and brasses and violins. He tried to sound a clarinet; the reed was still good in the dust-proof case, but he had no lip. He had never mastered any instrument except the pianoforte.

He recalled—it might have been that same day—opening a chest of double basses. There was a three-stringer in the group, old, probably from the early nineteenth century, a trifle fatter than its more modern companions. Brian touched its middle string in an idle caress, not intending to make it sound, but it had done so. When in use, it would have been tuned to D; time had slackened the heavy murmur to A or something near it. That had throbbed in the silent room with finality, a sound such as a programmatic composer, say Tchaikovsky, might have used as a tonal symbol for the breaking of a heart. It stayed in the air as other instruments whispered a dim response. "All right, gentlemen," Brian said, "that was your A...."

Out in the main part of the hall, a place of honor was given to what may have been the oldest of the instruments, a seven-note marimba of phonolitic schist discovered in Indo-China in the twentieth century and thought to be at least five thousand years of age. The xylophone-type rack was modern. Brian for twenty-five years had obeyed a compulsion to keep it free of cobwebs. Sometimes he touched the singing stones, not for amusement but because there was comfort in it. They answered to the light tap of a fingernail. Beside them on a little table of its own he had placed the Stone Age god of two faces.

On the west side of the Hall of Music, a rather long walk from Brian's cave, was a small auditorium. Lectures, recitals, chamber music concerts had been given there in the old days. The pleasant room held a twelve-foot concert grand, made in 2043, probably the finest of the many pianos in the Hall of Music, a summit of technical achievement. Brian had done his best to preserve this beautiful artifact, prayerfully tuning it three times a year, robbing other pianos in the Museum to provide a reserve supply of strings, oiled and sealed against rust. When not in use his great piano was covered by stitched-together sheets. To remove the cover was a somber ritual. Before touching the keys, Brian washed his hands with needless fanatical care.

Some years ago he had developed the habit of locking the auditorium doors before he played. Yet even then he preferred not to glance toward the vista of empty seats, not much caring whether this inhibition derived from a Stone Age fear of finding someone there or from a flat civilized understanding that no one could be. It never occurred to him to lock the one door he used, when he was absent from the auditorium. The key remained on the inside; if he went in merely to tune the piano or to inspect the place, he never turned it.

The habit of locking it when he played might have started (he could not remember) back in the year 2076, when so many bodies had floated down from the north on the ebb tides. Full horror had somehow been lacking in the sight of all that floating death. Perhaps it was because Brian had earlier had his fill of horrors, or perhaps in 2076 he already felt so divorced from his own kind that what happened to them was like the photograph of a war in a distant country. Some had bobbed and floated quite near the Museum. Most of them had the gaping obvious wounds of primitive warfare, but some were oddly discolored—a new pestilence? So there was (or had been) more trouble up there in what was (or had been) the short-lived Soviet of North America, a self-styled "nation" that took in east central New York and most of New England. So ... Yes, that was probably the year when he had started locking the doors between his private concerts and an empty world.

He dumped the venison in his cave. He scrubbed his hands, showing high blue veins now, but still tough, still knowing. Mozart, he thought, and walked, not with much pleasure of anticipation but more like one externally driven, through the enormous hall that was so full and yet so empty and growing dim with evening, with dust, with age, with loneliness. Music should not be silent.

When the piano was uncovered, Brian delayed. He exercised his hands unnecessarily. He fussed with the candelabrum on the wall, lighting three candles, then blowing out two for economy. He admitted presently that he did not want the emotional clarity of Mozart at all, not now. The darkness of 2070 was too close, closer than he had felt it for a long time. It would never have occurred to Mozart, Brian thought, that a world could die. Beethoven could have entertained the idea soberly enough, and Chopin probably; even Brahms. Mozart, Hadyn, Bach would surely have dismissed it as somebody's bad dream, in poor taste. Andrew Carr, who lived and died in the latter half of the twentieth century, had endured the idea deep in his bloodstream from the beginning of his childhood.

The date of Hiroshima was 1945; Carr was born in 1951. The wealth of his music was written between 1969, when he was eighteen, and 1984, when he died among the smells of an Egyptian jail from injuries received in a street brawl.

"If not Mozart," said Brian Van Anda to his idle hands, "there is always the Project."

To play Carr's last sonata as it should be played—as Carr was supposed to have said he couldn't play it himself: Brian had been thinking of that as the Project for many years. It had begun teasing his mind long before the war, at the time of his triumphs in a civilized world which had been warmly appreciative of the polished interpretive artist (once he got the breaks) although no more awake than in any other age to the creative sort. Back there in the undestroyed society, Brian had proposed to program that sonata in the company of works that were older but no greater, and to play it— well, beyond his best, so that even music critics would begin to see its importance in history.

He had never done it, had never felt the necessary assurance that he had entered into the sonata and learned the depth of it. Now, when there was none to hear or care, unless the harmless brown spiders in the corners of the auditorium had a taste for music, there was still the Project. *I* hear, Brian thought. *I* care, and with myself for audience I wish to hear it once as it ought to be, a final statement for a world that was (I think) too good to die.

Technically, of course, he had it. The athletic demands Carr made on the performer were tremendous, but, given technique, there was nothing impossible about them. Anyone capable of concert work could at least play the notes at the required tempi. And any reasonably shrewd pianist could keep track of the dynamics, saving strength for the shattering finale. Brian had heard the sonata played by others two or three times in the old days—competently. Competency was not enough.

For example, what about the third movement, the mad scherzo, and the five tiny interludes of quiet scattered through its plunging fury? They were not alike. Related, but each one demanded a new climate of heart and mind—tenderness, regret, simple relaxation. Flowers on a flood—no. Window lights in a storm—no. The innocence of a child in a bombed city—no, not really. Something of all those. Much more, too, defying words.

What of the second movement, the largo, where in a way the pattern was reversed, the midnight introspection interrupted by moments of anger, or longing, or despair like the despair of an angel beating his wings against a prison of glass?

It was a work in which something of Carr's life, Carr's temperament, had to come into you, whether you dared welcome it or not; otherwise your playing was no more than reproduction of notes on a page. Carr's life was not for the contemplation of the timid.

The details were superficially well-known; the biographies were like musical notation, meaningless without interpretation and insight. Carr was a drunken roarer, a young devil-god with such a consuming hunger for life that he choked to death on it. His friends hated him for the way he drained their lives, loving them to distraction and the next moment having no time for them because he loved his work more. His enemies must have had times of helplessly admiring him if only because of a translucent honesty that made him more and less than human. A rugged Australian, not tall but built like a hero, a face all forehead and jaw and glowing hyperthyroid eyes. He wept only when he was angry, the biographic storytellers said. In one minute of talk he might shift from gutter obscenity to some extreme of altruistic tenderness, and from that perhaps to a philosophic comment of cold intelligence. He passed his childhood on a sheep farm, ran away on a freighter at thirteen, was flung out of two respectable conservatories for drunkenness and "public lewdness," then studied like a slave in London with single-minded desperation, as if he knew the time was short. He was married twice and twice divorced. He killed a man in a silly brawl on the New Orleans docks, and wrote his First Symphony while he was in jail for that. He died of stab wounds from a broken bottle in a Cairo jail, and was recognized by the critics. It all had relevancy; relevant or not, if the sonata was in your mind, so was the life.

You had to remember also that Andrew Carr was the last of civilization's great composers. No one in the twenty-first century approached him—they ignored his explorations and carved cherrystones. He belonged to no school, unless you wanted to imagine a school of music beginning with Bach, taking in perhaps a dozen along the way, and ending with Carr himself. His work was a summary as well as an advance along the mainstream into the unknown; in the light of the year 2070, it was also a completion.

Brian was certain he could play the first movement of the sonata as he wished to. Technically it was not revolutionary, and remained rather close to the ancient sonata form. Carr had even written in a double bar for a repeat of the entire opening statement, something that had made his cerebral contemporaries sneer with great satisfaction; it never occurred to them that Carr was inviting the performer to use his head.

The bright-sorrowful second movement, unfashionably long, with its strange pauses, unforseen recapitulations, outbursts of savage change—that was where Brian's troubles began. ("Reminiscent of

Franck," said the hunters for comparisons whom we have always with us.) It did not help Brian to be old, remembering the inner storms of forty years ago and more.

His single candle fluttered. For once Brian had forgotten to lock the door into the Hall of Music. This troubled him, but he did not rise from the piano chair. He chided himself instead for the foolish neuroses of aloneness—what could it matter? Let it go. He shut his eyes. The sonata had long ago been memorized; printed copies were safe in the library. He played the opening of the first movement as far as the double bar, opened his eyes to the friendly black-and-white of clean keys, and played the repetition with new light, new emphasis. Better than usual, he thought—

Yes. Good.... Now that naive-appearing modulation into A major, which only Carr would have wanted just there in that sudden obvious way, like the opening of a door on shining fields. On toward the climax—*I am playing it, I think*—through the intricate revelations of development and recapitulation. And the conclusion, lingering, half-humorous, not unlike a Beethoven *I'm-not-gone-yet* ending, but with a questioning that was all Andrew Carr. After that—

"No more tonight," said Brian aloud. "Some night, though...Not competent right now, my friend." He replaced the cover of the piano and blew out the candle. He had brought no torch, long use having taught his feet every inch of the small journey. It was quite dark. The never-opened western windows of the auditorium were dirty, most of the dirt on the outside, crusted windblown salt.

In this partial darkness something was wrong.

At first Brian found no source for the faint light, dim orange with a hint of motion. He peered into the gloom of the auditorium, fixing his eyes on the oblong of blacker shadow that was the doorway into the Hall of Music. The windows, of course!—he had almost forgotten there were any. The light, hardly deserving the name of light, was coming through them. But sunset was surely past. He had been here a long time, delaying and brooding before he played. Sunset should not flicker.

So there was some kind of fire on the mainland. There had been no thunderstorm. How could fire start, over there where no one ever came?

He stumbled a few times, swearing petulantly, locating the doorway again and groping through it into the Hall of Music. The windows out here were just as dirty; no use trying to see through them. There must have been a time when he had looked through them, enjoyed looking through them. He stood shivering in the marble silence, trying to remember.

Time was a gradual, continual dying. Time was the growth of dirt and ocean salt, sealing in, covering over. He stumbled for his cloak-room cave, hurrying now, and lit two candles. He left one by the cold stove and used the other to light his way down the stairs to his raft; once down there, he blew it out, afraid. The room a candle makes in the darkness is a vulnerable room. Having no walls, it closes in a blindness. He pulled the raft by the guide-rope, gently, for fear of noise.

He found his canoe tied as he had left it. He poked his white head slowly beyond the sill, staring west.

Merely a bonfire gleaming, reddening the blackness of the cliff.

Brian knew the spot, a ledge almost at water level, at one end of the troublesome path he usually followed in climbing to the forest at the top of the Palisades. Usable driftwood was often there, the supply renewed by the high tides.

"No," Brian said. "Oh, no!..."

Unable to accept or believe, or not believe, he drew his head in, resting his forehead on the coldness of the sill, waiting for the dizziness to pass, reason to return.

It might have been a long time, a kind of blackout. Now he was again in command of his actions and even rather calm, once more leaning out over the sill. The fire still shone and was therefore not a disordered dream of old age. It was dying to a dull rose of embers.

He wondered about the time. Clocks and watches had stopped long ago; Brian had ceased to want them. A sliver of moon was hanging over the water to the east. He ought to be able to remember the phases, deduce the approximate time from that. But his mind was too tired or distraught to give him the data. Maybe it was somewhere around midnight.

He climbed on the sill and lifted the canoe over it to the motionless water inside. Useless, he decided, as soon as the grunting effort was finished. That fire had been lit before daylight passed; whoever lit it would have seen the canoe, might even have been watching Brian himself come home from his hunting. The canoe's disappearance in the night would only rouse further curiosity. But Brian was too exhausted to lift it back.

And why assume that the maker of the bonfire was necessarily hostile? Might be good company.... He pulled his raft through the darkness, secured it at the stairway, and groped back to his cave.

He locked the door. The venison was waiting; the sight made him ravenous. He lit a small fire in the stove, one that he hoped would not still be sending smoke from the ventilator shaft when morning came. He cooked the meat crudely and wolfed it down, all enjoyment gone at the first mouthful. He was shocked to discover the dirtiness of his white beard. He hadn't given himself a real bath in—weeks, was it? He searched for scissors and spent an absent-minded while in trimming the beard back to shortness. He ought to take some soap—valuabale stuff—down to Moses's room, and wash.

Clothes, too. People probably still wore clothes. He had worn none for years, except for sandals. He used a carrying satchel for trips to the mainland. He had enjoyed the freedom at first, and especially the discovery that in his rugged fifties he did not need clothes even for the soft winters, except perhaps a light covering when he slept. Later, total nakedness had become so natural it required no thought at all. But the owner of that bonfire could have inherited or retained the pruderies of the lost culture.

He checked his rifles. The .22 automatic, an Army model from the 2040s, was the best—any amount of death in that. The tiny bullets carried a paralytic poison: graze a man's finger and he was almost painlessly dead in three minutes. Effective range, with telescopic sights, three kilometers; weight, a scant five pounds. Brian sat a long time cuddling that triumph of military science, listening for sounds that never came. Would it be two o'clock? He wished he could have seen the Time Satellite, renamed in his mind the Midnight Star, but when he was down there at his port, he had not once looked up at the night sky. Delicate and beautiful, bearing its everlasting freight of men who must have been dead now for twenty-five years and who would be dead a very long time—well, it was better than a clock, if you happened to look at the midnight sky at the right time of the month when the man-made star caught the moonlight. But he had missed it tonight.. Three o'clock?...

At some time during the long dark he put the rifle away on the floor. With studied, self-conscious contempt for his own weakness, he unlocked the door and strode out noisily into the Hall of Music, with a fresh-lit candle. This same bravado, he knew, might dissolve at the first alien noise. While it lasted, it was invigorating.

The windows were still black with night. As if the candle flame had found its own way, Brian was standing by the ancient marimba in the main hall, the gleam slanting carelessly away from his gaunt hand. And nearby sat the Stone Age god.

It startled him. He remembered clearly how he himself had placed it there, obeying a half-humorous whim. The image and the singing stones were both magnificently older than history, so why shouldn't they live together? Whenever he dusted the marimba, he dusted the image respectfully, and its table. It would not have needed much urging from the impulses of a lonely mind to make him place offerings before it—winking first, of course, to indicate that rituals suitable to a pair of aging gentlemen did not have to be sensible in order to be good.

The clay face remembering eternity was not deformed by the episode of civilization. Chipped places were simple honorable scars. The two faces stared mildly from the single head, uncommunicative, serene.

A wooden hammer of modern make rested on the marimba. Softly Brian tapped a few of the stones. He struck the shrillest one harder, waking many slow-dying overtones, and laid the hammer down, listening until the last murmur perished and a drop of wax hurt his thumb. He returned to his cave and blew out the candle, never thinking of the door, or if he thought, not caring.

Face down, he rolled his head and clenched his fingers into his pallet, seeking in pain, finding at last the relief of stormy childish weeping in the dark.

Then he slept.

They looked timid. The evidence of it was in their tense squatting pose, not in what the feeble light allowed Brian to see of their faces, which were blank as rock. Hunkered down just inside the doorway of the dim cloakroom cave, a morning grayness from the Hall of

Music behind them, they were ready for flight, and Brian's intelligence warned his body to stay motionless. Readiness for flight could also be readiness for attack. He studied them through slit eyelids knowing he was in deep shadow.

They were very young, sixteen or seventeen, firm-muscled, the boy slim but heavy in the shoulders, the girl a fully developed woman. They were dressed alike: loincloths of some coarse dull fabric, and moccasins that were probably deerhide. Their hair grew nearly to the shoulders and was cut off carelessly, but they were evidently in the habit of combing it. They appeared to be clean. Their complexion, so far as Brian could guess it in the meager light, was brown, like a heavy tan. With no immediate awareness of emotion, he decided they were beautiful, and then within his own poised and perilous silence Brian reminded himself that the young are always beautiful.

The woman muttered softly: "He wake."

A twitch of the man's head was probably meant to warn her to be quiet. He clutched the shaft of a javelin with a metal blade which had once belonged to a breadknife. The blade was polished, shining, lashed to a peeled stick. The javelin trailed, ready for use at a flick of the young man's arm. Brian sighed deliberately. "Good morning,"

The man, or boy, said: "Good morning, sa."

"Where do you come from?"

"Millstone." The man spoke automatically, but then his facial rigidity dissolved into astonishment and some kind of distress. He glanced at his companion, who giggled uneasily.

"The old man pretends to not know," she said, and smiled, and seemed to be waiting for the young man's permission to go on speaking. He did not give it, but she continued: "Sa, the old ones of Millstone are dead." She thrust her hand out and down, flat, a picture of finality, adding with nervous haste: "As the Old Man knows. He who told us to call him Jonas, she who told us to call her Abigail, dead. They are still-with-out-moving the full six days, then we do the burial as they told us. As the Old Man knows."

"But I don't know!" said Brian, and sat up on his pallet too quickly, startling them. But their motion was backward, a readying for flight. "Millstone? Where is Millstone?"

They looked wholly bewildered and dismayed. They stood up

with animal grace, stepping backward out of the cave, the girl whispering in the man's ear. Brian caught two words: "—is angry."

He jumped up. "Don't go! Please don't go!" He followed them out of the cave, slowly now, aware that he might be an object of terror in the half-dark, aware of his gaunt, graceless age, and nakedness, and dirty hacked-off beard. Almost involuntarily he adopted something of the flat stilted quality of their speech. "I will not hurt you. Do not go."

They halted. The girl smiled dubiously. The man said: "We need old ones. They die. He who told us to call him Jonas said, many days in the boat, not with the sun-path, he said, across the sun-path, he said, keeping land on the left hand. We need old ones, to speak the—to speak...The Old Man is angry?"

"No. I am not angry. I am never angry." Brian's mind groped, certain of nothing. No one came, for twenty-five years.

Millstone?

There was red-gold on the dirty eastern windows of the Hall of Music, a light becoming softness as it slanted down, touching the long rows of cases, the warm brown of an antique spinet, the clean gold of a twentieth century harp, the gray of singing stones five thousand years old and a two-faced god much older than that. "Millstone." Brian pointed in inquiry, southwest.

The girl nodded, pleased and not at all surprised that he should know, watching him now with a squirrel's stiff curiosity. Hadn't there been a Millstone River in or near Princeton, once upon a time? Brian thought he remembered that it emptied into the Raritan Canal. There was some moderately high ground there. Islands now, no doubt. Perhaps they would tell him. "There were old people in Millstone," he said, trying for peaceful dignity, "and they died. So now you need old ones to take their place."

The girl nodded vigorously many times. Her glance at the young man was shy, possessive, maybe amused. "He who told us to call him Jonas said no marriage without the words of Abraham."

"Abr—" Brian checked himself. If this was religion, it would not do to speak the name Abraham with a rising inflection. "I have been for a long time—" He checked himself again: A man old, ugly, and strange enough to be sacred should never stoop to explain anything.

They were standing by the seven-stone marimba. His hand dropped, his thumbnail clicking against the deepest stone and waking a murmur. The children drew back, alarmed. Brian smiled. "Don't be afraid." He tapped the other stones lightly. "It is only music. It will not hurt you." They were patient and respectful, waiting for more light. He said carefully: "He who told you to call him Jonas—he taught you all the things you know?"

"All things," the boy said, and the girl nodded three or four times, so that the soft brownness of her hair tumbled about her face, and she pushed it back in a small human motion as old as the clay image.

"Do you know how old you are?"

They looked blank. Then the girl said: "Oh—summers!" She held up her two hands with spread fingers, then one hand. "Three fives." She chuckled, and sobered quickly. "As the Old Man knows."

"I am very old," said Brian. "I know many things, but sometimes I wish to forget, and sometimes I wish to hear what others know, even though I may know it myself."

They looked uncomprehending and greatly impressed. Brian felt a smile on his face and wondered why it should be there. They were nice children. Born ten years after the death of a world; twenty, perhaps. *I think I am seventy-six, but what if I dropped a decade somewhere and never noticed the damned thing?* ... "He who told you to call him Jonas—he taught you all you know of Abraham?"

At the sound of the name, both made swift circular motions, first at the forehead, then at the breast. "He taught us all things," the young man said. "He, and she who told us to call her Abigail. The hours to rise, to pray, to wash, to eat. The laws for hunting, and I know the Abraham-words for that: Sol-Amra, I take this for my need."

Brian felt lost again, and looked down to the clay faces of the image for counsel, and found none. "They who told you to call them Jonas and Abigail, they were the only ones who lived with you?— the only old ones?"

Again that look of bewilderment and disappointment. "The only ones, sa," the young man said. "As the Old Man knows."

I could never persuade them that, being old, I know very nearly nothing. . . .

Brian straightened to his full great height. The young people were not tall. Though stiff and worn with age, Brian knew he was still overpowering. Once, among men, he had gently enjoyed being more than life-size. As a shield for loneliness and fright within, he now adopted a phony sternness. "I wish to examine you for your own good, my children, about Millstone and your knowledge of Abraham. How many others live at Millstone, tell me."

"Two fives, sa," said the boy promptly, "and I the one who may be called Jonason and this girl who may be called Paula. Two fives and two. We are the biggest. The others are only children, but the one who may be called Jimi has killed his deer; he sees after them now while we go across the sun-path."

Under Brian's questioning, more of the story came, haltingly, obscured by the young man's conviction that the Old Man already knew everything. Sometime, probably in the middle 2080s, Jonas and Abigail (whoever they were) had come on a group of twelve wild children who were keeping alive somehow in a ruined town where their elders had all died. Jonas and Abigail had brought them all to an island they called Millstone. Jonas and Abigail came originally from "up across the sun-path"—the boy seemed to mean north—and they were very old, which might mean, Brian guessed, anything between thirty and ninety. In teaching the children primitive means of survival, Jonas and Abigail had brought off a brilliant success: Jonason and Paula were well-fed, shining with health and the strength of wildness, and clean. Their speech, limited and odd though it was, had not been learned from the ignorant. Its pronunciation faintly suggested New England, so far as it had any local accent. "Did they teach you reading and writing?" Brian asked, and made writing motions on the flat of his palm, which the two watched in vague alarm.

The boy asked: "What is that?"

"Never mind." *I could quarrel with some of your theories, Mister-whom-I-may-call-Jonas.* But maybe, he thought, there had been no books, no writing materials, no way to get them. What's the minimum of technology required to keep the human spirit alive?... "Well—well, tell me what they taught you of Abraham. I wish to hear how well you remember."

Both made again the circular motion at forehead and breast, and the young man said with the stiffness of recitation: "Abraham was the Son of Heaven who died that we might live." The girl, her obligation discharged with the religious gesture, tapped the marimba shyly, fascinated, and drew her finger back, smiling up at Brian in apology for naughtiness. "He taught the laws, the everlasting truth of all time," the boy gabbled, "and was slain on the wheel at Nuber by the infidels; therefore since he died for us, we look up across the sun-path when we pray to Abraham Brown who will come again." The boy Jonason sighed and relaxed.

Abraham—Brown? But—

But I knew him. I met him. Nuber? Newburg, temporary capital of the Soviet of—oh, damn that ... Met him, 2071—the concert of mine he remembered ... The wheel? The wheel? "And when did Abraham die, boy?"

"Oh—" Jonason moved fingers helplessly, embarrassed. Dates would be no part of the doctrine. "Long ago. A—a—" He glanced up hopefully. "A thousand years? I think—he who told us to call him Jonas did not teach us that."

"I see. Never mind. You speak well, boy." *Oh, my good Doctor, ex-President—after all! Artist, statesman, student of ethics, agnostic philosopher—all that long life you preached charity and skepticism, courage without the need of faith, the positive uses of the suspended judgment. All so clear, simple, obvious—needing only that little bit more of patience and courage which your human hearers were not ready to give. You must have known they were not, but did you know this would happen?*

Jonas and Abigail—some visionary pair, Brian supposed, full of this theory and that, maybe gone a bit foolish under the horrors of those years. Unthinking admirers of Brown, or perhaps not even that, perhaps just brewing their own syncretism because they thought a religion was needed, and using Brown's name—why? Because it was easy to remember? They probably felt some pride of creation in the job; possibly belief even grew in their own minds as they found the children accepting it and building a ritual life around it.

It was impossible, Brian thought, that Jonas and Abigail could have met the living Abraham Brown. Brown accepted mysteries because he faced the limitations of human intelligence; he had only contempt for the needless making of mysteries. He was without arrogance. No one could have talked five minutes with him without hearing a tranquil: "I don't know."

The *wheel* at Nuber?—but Brian realized he would never learn how Brown actually died. *I hope you suffered no more than most prophets....*

He was pulled from the pit of abstraction by the girl's awed question: "What is that?"

She was pointing to the clay image in its dusty sunlight. Brian was almost deaf to his own words until they were past recovering: "Oh, that—that is very old. Very old and very sacred." She nodded, round-eyed, and stepped back a pace or two. "And that was all they taught you of Abraham Brown?"

Astonished, the boy asked: "Is it not enough?"

There is always the Project. "Why, perhaps—"

"We know all the prayers, Old Man."

"Yes, yes, I'm sure you do."

"The Old Man will come with us." It was not a question.

"Eh?" *There is always the Project....* "Come with you?"

"We look for old ones." There was a new note in the young man's fine firm voice, and it was impatience. "We traveled many days, up across the sun-path. We want you to speak the Abraham-words for marriage. The old ones said we must not mate as the animals do without the words. We want—"

"Marry, of course," Brian grumbled. *Poor old Jonas and Abigail, faithful to your century, such as it was!* Brian felt tired and confused, and rubbed a great long-fingered hand across his face so that the words might have come out blurred and dull. "Naturally, kids. Beget. Replenish the earth. I'm damned tired. I don't know any special hocus-pocus—I mean, any Abraham-words—for marriage. Just go ahead and breed. Try again—"

"But the Old Ones said—"

"Wait!" Brian cried. "Wait! Let me think.... Did he—he who told you to call him Jonas—did he teach you anything about the world as it was in the old days, before you were born?"

"Before—the Old Man makes fun of us."

"No, no." Since he now had to fight down a certain physical fear as well as confusion, Brian spoke more harshly than he intended: "Answer my question! What do you know of the old days? I was a young man once, do you understand that?—as young as you. What do you know about the world I lived in?"

The young man laughed. There was newborn suspicion in him as well as anger, stiffening his shoulders, narrowing his innocent gray eyes. "There was always the world," he said, "ever since God made it a thousand years ago."

"Was there?...I was a musician. Do you know what a musician is?"

The young man shook his head lightly, watching Brian, too alertly, watching his hands, aware of him in a new way, no longer humble. Paula sensed the tension and did not like it. She said worriedly, politely: "We forget some of the things they taught us, sa. They were Old Ones. Most of the days they were away from us in places where we were not to go, praying. Old Ones are always praying."

"I will hear this Old Man pray," said Jonason. The butt of the javelin rested against Jonason's foot, the blade swaying from side to side, a waiting snake's head. A misstep, a wrong word—any trifle, Brian knew, could make them decide he was evil and not sacred. Their religion would inevitably require a devil.

He thought also: *It would merely be one of the ways of dying, not the worst.*

"You shall hear me make music," he said sternly, "and you shall be content with that. Come this way!" In fluctuating despair, he was wondering if any good might come of anger. "Come this way! You shall hear a world you never knew." Naked and ugly, he stalked across the Hall of Music, not looking behind him, though he sensed every glint of light from that bread-knife javelin. "This way!" he shouted. "Come in here!" He flung open the door of the auditorium and strode up on the platform. "Sit down!" he roared at them. "Sit down over there and be quiet, be quiet!"

He thought they did—he could not look at them. He knew he was muttering between his noisy outbursts as he twitched the cover off the piano and raised the lid, muttering bits and fragments from the old times and the new: "They went thataway.... Oh, Mr. Van Anda, it just simply goes right through me—I can't express it. Madam, such was my intention, or as Brahms is supposed to have said on a slightly different subject, any ass knows that.... Brio, Rubato, and Schmalz went to sea in a—Jonason, Paula, this is a pianoforte; it will not hurt you. Sit there, be quiet, and I pray you listen...."

He found calm. *Now, if ever, when there is living proof that human nature, some sort of human nature, is continuing—now if ever, the Project—*

With the sudden authority that was natural to Andrew Carr, Andrew Carr took over. In the stupendous opening chords of the introduction, Brian very nearly forgot his audience. Not quite. The children had sat down out there in the dusty region where none but ghosts had lingered for twenty-five years, but the piano's first sound brought them to their feet. Brian played through the first four bars, piling the chords like mountains, then held the last one with the pedal and waved his right hand at Jonason and Paula in a furious downward motion.

He thought they understood. He thought he saw them sit down again. But he could pay them no more attention, for the sonata was coming alive under his fingers, waking, growing, rejoicing.

He did not forget the children. They were important, too important, terrifying at the fringe of awareness. But he could not look toward them any more, and presently he shut his eyes.

He had never played like this in the flood of his prime, in the old days, before audiences that loved him. Never.

His eyes were still closed, holding him secure in a world that was not all darkness, when he ended the first movement, paused very briefly, and moved on with complete assurance to explore the depth and height of the second. This was true statement. This was Andrew Carr; he lived, even if after this late morning he might never live again.

And now the third, the storm and the wrath, the interludes of calm, the anger, denials, affirmations....

Without hesitation, without awareness of self, of age or pain or danger or loss, Brian was entering on the broad reaches of the last movement when he glanced out into the auditorium and understood the children were gone.

Too big. It had frightened them away. He could visualize them, stealing out with backward looks of panic, and remembering apparently to close the exit door. To them it was incomprehensible thunder. Children—savages—to see or hear or comprehend the beautiful, you must first desire it. He could not think much about them now, when Andrew Carr was still with him. He played on with the same assurance, the same sense of victory. Children and savages, so let them go, with leave and goodwill.

Some external sound troubled him, something that must have begun under cover of these rising, pealing octave passages—storm waves, each higher than the last, until even the superhuman swimmer must be exhausted. It was some indefinable alien noise, a humming. Wind perhaps. Brian shook his head in irritation, not interrupting the work of his hands. It couldn't matter—everything was here, in the labors his hands still had to perform. The waves were growing more quiet, subsiding, and he must play the curious arpeggios he had never quite understood—but for this interpretation he understood them. Rip them out of the piano like showers of sparks, like distant lightning moving farther and farther away across a world that could never be at rest.

The final section at last. Why, it was a variation—and why had he never quite recognized it?—on a a theme of Brahms, from the German Requiem. Quite plain, simple—Brahms would have approved. *Blessed are the dead....* Something more remained to be said, and Brian searched for it through the mighty unfolding of the finale. No hurrying, no crashing impatience any more, but a moving through time without fear of time, through radiance and darkness with no fear of either. *That they may rest from their labors, and their works do follow after them.*

Brian stood up, swaying and out of breath. So the music was over, and the children were gone, but a jangling, humming confusion was filling the Hall of Music out there—hardly a wind—distant but entering with some violence even here, now that the piano was silent. He moved stiffly out of the small auditorium, more or less knowing what he would find.

The noise became immense, the unchecked overtones of the marimba fuming and quivering as the smooth, high ceiling of the Hall of Music caught them and flung them about against the answering strings of pianos and harps and violins, the sulky membranes of drums, the nervous brass of cymbals.

The girl was playing it. Brian laughed once, softly, in the shadows, and was not heard. She had hit on a primeval rhythm natural for children or savages and needed nothing else, banging it out on one stone and another, wanting no rest or variation.

The boy was dancing, slapping his feet and pounding his chest, thrusting out his javelin in time to the clamor, edging up to his companion, grimacing, drawing back in order to return. Neither one was laughing, or close to laughter. Their faces were savage-solemn, grim with the excitement and healthy lust. All as spontaneous as the drumming of partridges. It was a long time before they saw Brian in the shadows.

Reaction was swift. The girl dropped the hammer. The boy froze, his javelin raised, then jerked his head at Paula, who snatched at something—only moments later did Brian understand she had taken the clay image before she fled.

Jonason covered her retreat, stepping backward, his face blank and dangerous with fear. So swiftly, so easily, by grace of great civilized music and a few wrong words, had a Sacred Old One become a Bad Old One.

They were gone, down the stairway, leaving the echo of Brian's voice crying: "Don't go! Please don't go!"

Brian followed them. Unwillingly. He was slow to reach the bottom of the stairway; there he looked across the shut-in water to his raft, which they had used and left at the windowsill port. Brian had never been a good swimmer, and would not attempt it now, but clutched the rope and hitched himself hand over hand to the windowsill, collapsing awhile until he found strength to scramble into his canoe and grope for the paddle.

The children's canoe was already far off. Heading up the river, the boy paddling with deep powerful strokes. Up the river, of course. They had to find the right kind of Old Ones. Up across the sun-path.

Brian dug his blade in the quiet water. For a time his rugged, ancient muscles were willing. There was sap in them yet. Perhaps he was gaining. He shouted hugely: "Bring back my two-faced god! And what about my music? You? Did you like it? Speak up!"

They must have heard his voice booming at them. At least the girl looked back, once. The boy, intent on his paddling, did not. Brian roared: "Bring back my little god!"

He was not gaining on them. After all they had a mission. They had to find an Old One with the right Abraham-words. Brian thought: *Damn it, hasn't MY world some rights? We'll see about this!*

He lifted his paddle like a spear, and flung it, knowing even as his shoulder winced with the backlash of the thrust that his action was at the outer limit of absurdity. The children were so far away that even an arrow from a bow might not have reached them. The paddle splashed in the water. Not far away. A small infinity.

It swung about, adjusting to the current, the heavy end pointing downstream, obeying the river and the ebb tide. It nuzzled companionably against a gray-faced chunk of driftwood, diverting it, so that presently the chunk floated into Brian's reach. He flung it back toward the paddle, hoping it might fall on the other side and send the paddle near him, but it fell short. In his unexpectedly painless extremity Brian was not surprised, but merely watched the gray face floating and bobbing along beside him out of reach, and his irritation became partly friendliness. The driftwood fragment suggested the face of a music critic he had once met—New Boston, was it? Denver? London?—no matter.

"Why," he said aloud, detachedly observing the passage of his canoe beyond the broad morning shadow of the Museum, "why, I seem to have killed myself."

"Mr. Van Anda has abundantly demonstrated a mastery of the instrument and of the"—*Oh, go play solfeggio on your linotype!*— "literature of both classic and contemporary repertory. While we cannot endorse the perhaps overemotional quality of his Bach, and there might easily be two views of his handling of the passage in double thirds which—"

"I can't swim it, you know," said Brian. "Not against the ebb, that's for sure."

"—so that on the whole one feels he has earned himself a not discreditable place among—" Gaining on the canoe, passing it, the gray-faced chip moved on benignly twittering toward the open sea, where the canoe must follow. With a final remnant of strength Brian inched forward to the bow and gathered the full force of his lungs to shout up the river to the children: "Go in peace!"

They could not have heard him. They were too far away, and a new morning wind was blowing, fresh and sweet, out of the northwest.

12_____

Getting back to the problems of heredity and fertility brought on by irradiated genes, Jody and Paul and Myra and Ben and Littleboy and the children of tomorrow have not, up to now, achieved a consensus about the problem, or thought of solving it. Once a problem is defined, a committee can be created, given special powers to act, and trusted to find a solution, as in "Game Preserve." In the East, this is known as multiplying karma. And with those sneaky recessive genes, how can one be sure the solution is final? Hitler could be sure, because there is no such thing as a Jewish gene in the first place. But in Elf's case...

GAME PRESERVE
by Rog Phillips

"Hi-hi-hi!" Big One shouted, and heaved erect with the front end of It.

"Hi-hi-hi," Fat One and the dozen others echoed more mildly, lifting wherever they could get a hold on It.

It was lifted and borne forward in a half-crouching trot.

"Hi-hi hi-hi-hihihi," Elf chanted, running and skipping alongside the panting men and their massive burden.

224

It was carried forward through the lush grass for perhaps fifty feet.

"Ah-ah-ah," Big One sighed loudly, slowly letting the front end of It down until it dug into the soft black soil.

"Ahhh," Fat One and the others sighed, letting go and standing up, stretching aching back muscles, rubbing cramped hands.

"Ah-ah-ah-ah-ah-ah," Elf sang, running around and in between the resting men. He came too close to Big One and was sent sprawling by a quick, good-humored push.

Everyone laughed, Big One laughing the loudest. Then Big One lifted Elf to his feet and patted him on the back affectionately, a broad grin forming a toothy gap at the top of his bushy black beard.

Elf answered the grin with one of his own, and at that moment his ever present yearning to grow up to be the biggest and the strongest like Big One flowed through him with new strength.

Abruptly Big One leaped to the front end of It, shouting "Hi-hi-HI!"

"Hi-hi-hi," the others echoed, scrambling to their places. Once again It was borne forward for fifty feet—and again and again, across the broad meadowland.

A vast matting of blackberry brambles came into view off to one side. Big One veered his course toward it. The going was uphill now, so the forward surges shortened to forty feet, then thirty. By the time they reached the blackberries they were wet and glossy with sweat.

It was a healthy patch, loaded with large ripe berries. The men ate hungrily at first, then more leisurely, pointing to one another's stained beards and laughing. As they denuded one area they leaped to It, carried it another ten feet and started stripping another section, never getting more than a few feet from It.

Elf picked his blackberries with first one then another of the men. When his hunger was satisfied he became mischievous, picking a handful of berries and squashing them against the back or the chest of the nearest man and running away, laughing. It was dangerous sport, he knew, because if one of them caught him he would be tossed into the brambles.

Eventually they all had their fill, and thanks to Elf looked as though they were oozing blackberry juice from every pore. The sun was in its midafternoon position. In the distance a line of white-barked trees could be seen—evidence of a stream.

"Hi-hi-hi!" Big One shouted.

The journey toward the trees began. It was mostly downhill, so the forward spurts were often as much as a hundred feet.

Before they could hear the water they could smell it. They grunted their delight at the smell, a rich fish odor betokening plenty of food. Intermingled with this odor was the spicy scent of eucalyptus.

They pushed forward with renewed zeal so that the sweat ran down their skins, dissolving the berry juices and making rivulets that looked like purple blood.

When less than a hundred yards from the stream, which was still hidden beyond the tall grasses and the trees lining its bank, they heard the sound of high-pitched voices—women's voices. They became uneasy and nervous. Their surges forward shortened to ten feet, their rest periods became longer, they searched worriedly for signs of motion through the trees.

They changed their course to arrive a hundred yards downstream from the source of the women's voices. Soon they reached the edge of the tree belt. It was more difficult to carry It through the scatterings of bushes. Too, they would get part way through the trees and run into trees too close together to get It past them, and have to back out and try another place. It took almost two hours to work through the trees to the bank of the stream.

Only Elf recognized the place they finally broke through as the place they had left more than two days before. In that respect he knew he was different, not only from Big One and other grownups, but also all other Elfs except one, a girl Elf. He had known it as long as he could remember. He had learned it from many little things. For example, he had recognized the place when they reached it. Big One and the others never remembered anything for long. In getting It through the trees they blundered as they always had, and got through by trial and error with no memory of past blunderings.

Elf was different in another way, too. He could make more sounds than the others. Sometimes he would keep a little It with him until it gave him a feeling of security almost as strong as the big It, then wander off alone with It and play with making sounds, "Bz-bz. Walla-walla-walla-rue-rue-la-lo-hi. Da!" and all kinds of sounds. It excited him to be able to make different sounds and put them together so that they pleased his hearing, but such sounds made the others avoid him and look at him from a safe distance with worried expressions, so he had learned not to make *different* sounds within earshot of the others.

The women and Elfs were upstream a hundred yards, where they always remained. From the way they were milling around and acting alarmed it was evident to Elf they could no more remember the men having been here a few days before than the men could remember it themselves. It would be two or three days before they slowly lost their fear of one another. It would be the women and their Elfs who would cautiously approach, holding their portable Its clutched for security, until, finally losing all fear, they would join into one big group for a while.

Big One and the others carried It right to the water's edge so they could get into the water without ever being far from It. They shivered and shouted excitedly as they bathed. Fat One screamed with delight as he held a squirming fish up for the others to see. He bit into it with strong white teeth, water dripping from his heavy brown beard. Renewed hunger possessed him. He gobbled the fish and began searching for another. He always caught two fish for any other man's one, which was why he was fat.

Elf himself caught a fish. After eating it he lay on the grassy bank looking up at the white billowing clouds in the blue sky. The sun was now near the horizon, half hidden behind a cloud, sending divergent ramps of light downward. The clouds on the western horizon were slowly taking on color until red, orange, and green separated into definite areas. The soft murmur of the stream formed a lazy background to the excited voices of the men. From upstream, faintly, drifted the woman and Elf sounds.

Here, close to the ground, the rich earthy smell was stronger than that of the stream. After a time a slight breeze sprang up, bringing with it other odors, that of distant pines, the pungent eucalyptus, a musky animal scent.

Big One and the others were out of the water finally. Half-asleep, Elf watched them move It up to dry ground. As though that were what the sun had been waiting for, it sank rapidly below the horizon.

The clouds where the sun had been seemed now to blaze for a time with a smoldering redness that cooled to black. The stars came out, one by one.

A multitude of snorings erupted into the night. Elf crept among the sleeping forms until he found Big One, and settled down for the night, his head against Big One's chest, his right hand resting against the cool smooth metal of It.

Elf awoke with the bright morning sun directly in his eyes. Big One was gone, already wading in the stream after fish. Some of the others were with him. A few were still sleeping.

Elf leaped to his feet, paused to stretch elaborately, then splashed into the stream. As soon as he caught a fish he climbed out onto the bank and ate it. Then he turned to his search for a little It. There were many lying around, all exactly alike. He studied several, not touching some, touching and even nudging others. Since they all looked alike it was more a matter of *feel* than any real difference that he looked for. One and only one seemed to be the It. Elf returned his attention to it several times.

Finally he picked it up and carried it over to the big It, and hid it underneath. Big One, with shouts of sheer exuberance, climbed up onto the bank dripping water. He grinned at Elf.

Elf looked in the direction of the women and other Elfs. Some of them were wandering in his direction, each carrying an It of some sort, many of them similar to the one he had chosen.

In sudden alarm at the thought that someone might steal his new It, Elf rescued it from its hiding place. He tried to hide it behind him when any of the men looked his way. They scorned an individual It and, as men, preferred an It too heavy for one person.

As the day advanced, women and Elfs approached nearer, pretending to be unaware at times that the men were here, at other times openly fleeing back, overcome by panic.

The men never went farther than twenty feet from the big It. But as the women came closer the men grew surly toward one another. By noon two of them were trying to pick a fight with anyone who would stand up to them.

Elf clutched his little It closely and moved cautiously downstream until he was twenty feet from the big It. Tentatively he went another few feet—farther than any of the men dared go from the big It. At first he felt secure, then panic overcame him and he ran back, dropping the little It. He touched the big It until the panic was gone. After a while he went to the little It and picked it up. He walked around, carrying it, until he felt secure with it again. Finally he went downstream again, twenty feet, twenty-five feet, thirty... He felt panic finally, but not overwhelmingly. When it became almost unendurable he calmly turned around and walked back.

Confidence came to him. An hour later he went downstream until he was out of sight of the big It and the men. Security seemed to flow warmly from the little It.

Excitement possessed Elf. He ran here and there, clutching It closely so as not to drop it and lose it. He felt *free*.

"Bdlboo," he said aloud, experimentally. He liked the sounds. "Bdlboo-bdlboo-bdlboo." He saw a berry bush ahead and ran to it to munch on the delicious fruit. "Riddle piddle biddle," he said. It sounded nice.

He ran on, and after a time he found a soft, grassy spot and stretched out on his back, holding It carelessly in one hand. He looked up and up, at a layer of clouds going in one direction and another layer above it going in another direction.

Suddenly he heard voices.

At first he thought the wind must have changed so that it was carrying the voices of the men to him. He lay there listening. Slowly he realized these voices were different. They were putting sounds together like those he made himself.

A sense of wonder possessed him. How could there be anyone besides himself who could do that?

Unafraid, yet filled with caution, he clutched It closely to his chest and stole in the direction of the sounds.

After going a hundred yards he saw signs of movement through the trees. He dropped to the ground and lay still for a moment, then gained courage to rise cautiously, ready to run. Stooping low, he stole forward until he could see several moving figures. Darting from tree to tree he moved closer to them, listening with greater excitement than he had ever known to the smoothly flowing variety of beautiful sounds they were making.

This was something new, a sort of game they must be playing. One voice would make a string of sounds then stop, another would make a string of different sounds and stop, a third would take it up. They were good at it, too.

But the closer he got to them the more puzzled he became. They were shaped somewhat like people, they carried Its, they had hands and faces like people. That's as far as the similarity went. Their feet were solid, their arms, legs, and body were not skin at all but strangely colored and unliving in appearance. Their faces were smooth like women's, their hair short like babies', their voices deep like men's.

And the Its they carried were unlike any Elf had ever seen. Not only that, each of them carried more than one.

That was an *idea!* Elf became so excited he almost forgot to keep hidden. If you had more than one It, then if something happened to one you would still feel secure!

He resisted the urge to return to the stream and search for another little It to give him extra security. If he did that he might never again find these creatures that were so like men and yet so different. So instead, he filed the idea away to use at the earliest opportunity and followed the strange creatures, keeping well hidden from them.

Soon Elf could hear the shouts of the men in the distance. From the behavior of the creatures ahead, they had heard those shouts too. They changed their direction so as to reach the stream a hundred yards or more downstream at about the spot where Elf had left. They made no voice sounds now that Elf could hear. They clutched their strangely shaped, long Its before them tensely as though feeling greater security that way, their heads turning this way and that as they searched for any movement ahead.

They moved purposefully. An overwhelming sense of kinship brought tears to Elf's eyes. These creatures were *his kind.* Their differences from him were physical and therefore superficial, and even if those differences were greater it wouldn't have mattered.

He wanted, suddenly, to run to them. But the thought of it sent fear through him. Also they might run in panic from him if he suddenly revealed himself.

It would have to be a mutual approach, he felt. He was used to seeing them now. In due time he would reveal himself for a brief moment to them. Later he would stay in the open and watch them, making no move to approach until they got used to his being around. It might take days, but eventually, he felt sure, he could join them without causing them to panic.

After all, there had been the time when he absented himself from the men for three whole days and when he returned they had forgotten him, and his sudden appearance in their midst had sent even Big One into spasms of fear. Unable to flee from the security of the big It, and unable to bear his presence among them without being used to him, they had all fallen on the ground in a fit. He had had to retreat and wait until they recovered. Then, slowly, he had let them get used to his being in sight before approaching again. It had taken two full days to get to the point where they would accept him once more.

That experience, Elf felt, would be valuable to remember now. He wouldn't want to plunge these creatures into fits or see them scatter and run away.

Also, he was too afraid right now to reveal himself even though every atom of his being called for their companionship.

Suddenly he made another important discovery. Some of the Its these creatures carried had something like pliable vines attached to them so they could be hung about the neck! The thought was so staggering that Elf stopped and examined his It to see if that could be done to it. It was twice as long as his hand and round one way, tapering to a small end that opened to the hollow inside. It was too smooth to hold with a pliable vine unless—He visualized pliable vines woven together to hold It. He wasn't sure how it could be done, but maybe it could.

He set the idea aside for the future and caught up with the creatures again, looking at them with a new emotion, awe. The ideas he got just from watching them were so staggering he was getting dizzy!

Another new thought hit him. He rejected it at once as being too fantastic. It returned. Leaves are thin and pliable and can be wrapped around small objects like pebbles. Could it be that these creatures were really men of some sort, with bodies like men, covered with something thin like leaves are thin? It was a new and dizzy height in portable securities, and hardly likely. No. He rejected the idea with finality and turned his mind to other things.

He knew now where they could reach the stream. He decided to circle them and get ahead of them. For the next few minutes this occupied his full attention, leaving no room for crazy thoughts.

He reached the stream and hid behind some bushes where he would have a quick line of retreat if necessary. He clutched It tightly and waited. In a few moments he saw the first of the creatures emerge a hundred feet away. The others soon joined the first. Elf stole forward from concealment to concealment until he was only fifteen feet from them. His heart was pounding with a mixture of fear and excitement. His knuckles were white from clutching It.

The creatures were still carrying on their game of making sounds, but now in an amazing new way that made them barely audible. Elf listened to the incredibly varied sounds, enraptured.

"This colony seems to have remained pure."

"You never can tell."

"No, you never can tell. Get out the binoculars and look, Joe."

"Not just yet, Harold. I'm looking to see if I can spot one whose behavior shows intelligence."

Elf ached to imitate some of the beautiful combinations of sounds. He wanted to experiment and see if he could make the softly muted voices. He had an idea how it might be done, not make a noise in your throat but breathe out and form the sounds with your mouth just like you were uttering them aloud.

One of the creatures fumbled at an It hanging around his neck. The top of it hinged back. He reached in and brought out a gleaming It and held it so that it covered his eyes. He was facing toward the men upstream and stood up slowly.

"See something, Joe?"

Suddenly Elf was afraid. Was this some kind of magic? He had often puzzled over the problem of whether things were there when he didn't look at them. He had experimented, closing his eyes and then opening them suddenly to see if things were still there, and they always were; but maybe this was magic to make the men not be there. Elf waited, watching upstream, but Big One and the others did not vanish.

The one called Joe chuckled. "The toy the adult males have would be a museum piece if it were intact. A 1960 Ford, I think. Only one wheel on it, right front."

Elf's attention jerked back. One of the creatures was reaching over his shoulder, lifting on the large It fastened there. The top of the It pulled back. He reached inside, bringing out something that made Elf almost exclaim aloud. It was shaped exactly like the little It Elf was carrying, but it glistened in the sunlight and its interior was filled with a rich brown fluid.

"Anyone else want a Coke?"

"This used to be a picnic area," the one called Joe said, not taking his eyes from the binoculars. "I can see a lot of pop bottles lying around in the general area of that wreck of a Ford."

While Elf watched, breathless, the creature reached inside the skin of his hip and brought out a very small It and did something to the small end of the hollow It. Putting the very small It back under the skin of his hip, he put the hollow It to his lips and tilted it. Elf watched the brown liquid drain out. Here was magic. Such an It—the very one he carried—could be filled with water from the stream and carried around to drink any time!

When the It held no more liquid the creature dropped it to the ground. Elf could not take his eyes from it. He wanted it more than he had ever wanted anything. They might forget it. Sometimes the women dropped their Its and forgot them, picking up another one instead, and these creatures had beardless faces like women. Besides, each of them carried so many Its that they would feel just as secure without this one.

So many Its! One of the creatures held a flat white It in one hand and a very slim It shaped like a straight section of a bush stem, pointed at one end, with which he scratched on the white It at times, leaving black designs.

"There're fourteen males," the one called Joe whispered. The other wrote it down.

The way these creatures did things, Elf decided, was very similar to the way Big One and the other men went at moving the big It. They were very much like men in their actions, these creatures.

"Eighty-five or -six females."

"See any signs of intelligent action yet?"

"No. A couple of the males are fighting. Probably going to be a mating free-for-all tomorrow or next day. There's one! Just a minute, I want to make sure. It's a little girl, maybe eight or nine years old. Good forehead. Her eyes definitely lack that large marble-like quality of the submoron parent species. She's intelligent, all right. She's drawing something in the sand with a stick. Give me your rifle, Bill, it's got a better telescope sight on it than mine, and I don't want her to suffer."

That little It, abandoned on the ground. Elf wanted it. One of the creatures would be sure to pick it up. Elf worried. He would never get it then. If only the creatures would go, or not notice him. If only—

The creature with the thing over his eyes put it back where he had gotten it out of the thing hanging from his shoulder. He had taken one of the long slim things from another of the creatures and placed the thick end against his shoulder, the small end pointed upstream. The others were standing, their backs to Elf, all of them looking upstream. If they would remain that way, maybe he could dart out and get the little It. In another moment they might lose interest in whatever they were watching.

Elf darted out from his concealment and grabbed the It off the ground, and in the same instant an ear-shattering sound erupted from the long slim thing against the creature's shoulder.

"Got her!" the creature said.

Paralyzed with fright, Elf stood motionless. One of the creatures started to turn his way. At the last instant Elf darted back to his place of concealment. His heart was pounding so loudly he felt sure they would hear it.

"You sure, Joe?"

"Right through the head. She never knew what happened."

Elf held the new It close to him, ready to run if he were discovered. He didn't dare look at it yet. It wouldn't notice if he just held it and felt it without looking at it. It was cold at first, colder than the water in the stream. Slowly it warmed. He dared to steal a quick glance at it. It gleamed at him as though possessed of inner life. A new feeling of security grew within him, greater than he had ever known. The other It, the one half-filled with dried mud and deeply scratched from the violent rush of water over it when the stream went over its banks, lay forgotten at his feet.

"Well, that finishes the survey trip for this time."

Elf paid little attention to the voice whispers now, too wrapped up in his new feelings.

"Yes, and quite a haul. Twenty-two colonies—three more than ten years ago. Fourteen of them uncontaminated, seven with only one or two intelligent offspring to kill, only one colony so contaminated we had to wipe it out altogether. And one renegade."

"The renegades are growing scarcer every time. Another ten or twenty years and they'll be extinct."

"Then there won't be any more intelligent offspring in these colonies."

"Let's get going. It'll be dark in another hour or so."

The creatures were hiding some of their Its under their skin, in their carrying cases. There was a feeling about them of departure. Elf waited until they were on the move, back the way they had come, then he followed at a safe distance.

He debated whether to show himself now or wait. The sun was going down in the sky now. It wouldn't be long until it went down for the night. Should he wait until the morning to let them get their first glimpse of him?

He smiled to himself. He had plenty of time. Tomorrow and tomorrow. He would never return to Big One and the other men. Men or creatures, he would join with these new and wonderful creatures. They were *his kind.*

He thought of the girl Elf. They were her kind, too. If he could only get her to come with him.

On sudden impulse he decided to try. These creatures were going back the same way they had come. If he ran, and if she came right with him, they could catch up with the creatures before they went so far they would lose them.

He turned back, going carefully until he could no longer see the creatures, then he ran. He headed directly toward the place where the women and Elfs stayed. They would not be so easily alarmed as the men because there were so many of them they couldn't remember one another, and one more or less of the Elfs went unnoticed.

When he reached the clearing he slowed to a walk, looking for her. Ordinarily he didn't have to look much. She would see him and come to him, smiling in recognition of the fact that he was the only one like her.

He became a little angry. Was she hiding? Then he saw her. He went to her. She was on her stomach, motionless as though asleep, but something was different. There was a hole in one side of her head, and on the opposite side it was torn open, red and grayish white, with—He knelt down and touched her. She had the same inert feel to her that others had had who never again moved.

He studied her head curiously. He had never seen anything like this. He shook her. She remained limp. He sighed. He knew what would happen now. It was already happening. The odor was very faint yet, but she would not move again, and day after day the odor would get stronger. No one liked it.

He would have to hurry or he would lose the creatures. He turned and ran, never looking back. Once he started to cry, then stopped in surprise. Why had he been crying, he wondered. He hadn't hurt himself.

He caught up with the creatures. They were hurrying now, their long slender Its balanced on one shoulder, the big end resting in the palm of the hand. They no longer moved cautiously. Shortly it was new country. Elf had never been this far from the stream. Big One more or less led the men, and always more or less followed the same route in cross-country trips.

The creatures didn't spend hours stumbling along impossible paths. They looked ahead of them and selected a way, and took it. Also they didn't have a heavy It to trasnport, fifty feet at a time. Elf began to sense they had a destination in mind. Probably the place they lived.

Just ahead was a steep bank, higher than a man, running in a long line. The creatures climbed the bank and vanished on the other side. Cautiously Elf followed them, heading toward a large stone with It qualities at the top of the bank from whose concealment he could see where they had gone without being seen. He reached it and cautiously peeked around it. Just below him were the creatures, but what amazed Elf was the sight of the big It.

It was very much like the big It the men had, except that there were differences in shape, and instead of one round thing at one corner, it had one at each corner and rested on them so that it was held off the ground. It glistened instead of being dull. It had a strange odor that was quite strong.

The creatures were putting some of their Its into it; two of them had actually climbed into it—something neither Elf nor the men had ever dared to do with their own big It.

Elf took his eyes off of it for a moment to marvel at the ground. It seemed made of stone, but such stone as he had never before seen. It was an even width with edges going in straight lines that paralleled the long narrow hill on which he stood, and on the other side was a similar hill, extending as far as the eye could see.

He returned his attention to the creatures and their big It. The creatures had all climbed into it now. Possibly they were settling down for the night, though it was still early for that...

No matter. There was plenty of time. Tomorrow and tomorrow. Elf would show himself in the morning, then run away. He would come back again after a while and show himself a little longer, giving them time to get used to him so they wouldn't panic.

They were playing their game of making voice sounds to one another again. It seemed their major preoccupation. Elf thought how much fun it would be to be one of them, making voice sounds to his heart's content.

"I don't see why the government doesn't wipe out the whole lot," one of them was saying. "It's hopeless to keep them alive. Feeble-mindedness is dominant in them. They can't be absorbed into the race again, and any intelligent offspring they get from mating with a renegade would start a long line of descendants, at least one fourth of whom would be mindless idiots."

"Well," another of them said, "it's one of those things where there is no answer. Wipe them out, and next year it would be all the blond-haired people to be wiped out to keep the race of dark-haired people pure, or something. Probably in another hundred years nature will take care of the problem by wiping them out for us. Meanwhile we game wardens must make the rounds every two years and weed out any of them we can find that have intelligence." He looked up the embankment but did not notice Elf's head, concealed partially by the grass around the concrete marker. "It's an easy job. Any of them we missed seeing this time, we'll probably get next time. In the six or eight visits we make before the intelligent ones can become adults and mate we always find them."

"What I hate is when they see us, those intelligent ones," a third voice said. "When they walk right up to us and want to be friends with us it's too much like plain murder, except that they can't talk, and only make moronic sounds like 'Bdl-bdl-bdl.' Even so, it gets me when we kill them." The others laughed.

Suddenly Elf heard a new sound from the big It. It was not a voice sound, or if it was it was one that Elf felt he could not possibly match exactly. It was a growling, "RRrrRRrrRRrr." Suddenly it was replaced by still a different sound, a "p-p-p-p-p" going very rapidly. Perhaps it was the way these creatures snored. It was not unpleasant. Elf cocked his head to one side, listening to the sound, smiling. How exciting it would be when he could join with these creatures! He wanted to so much.

The big It began to move. In the first brief second Elf could not believe his senses. How could it move without being carried? But it was moving, and the creatures didn't seem to be aware of it! Or perhaps they were too overcome by fear to leap out!

Already the big It was moving faster than a walk, and was moving faster with every heartbeat. How could they remain unaware of it and not leap to safety?

Belatedly Elf abandoned caution and leaped down the embankment to the flat ribbon of rock, shouting. But already the big It was over a hundred yards away, and moving faster now than birds in flight!

He shouted, but the creatures didn't hear him—or perhaps they were so overcome with fright that they were frozen. Yes, that must be it.

Elf ran after the big It. If he could only catch up with it he would gladly join the creatures in their fate. Better to die with them than to lose them!

He ran and ran, refusing to believe he could never overtake the big It, even when it disappeared from view, going faster than the wind. He ran and ran until his legs could lift no more.

Blinded by tears, he tripped and sprawled full length on the wide ribbon of stone. His nose bled from hitting the hard surface. His knees were scraped and bleeding. He was unaware of this.

He was aware only that the creatures were gone, to what unimaginable fate he could not guess, but lost to him, perhaps forever.

Sobs welled up within him, spilled out, shaking his small naked body. He cried as he hadn't cried since he was a baby.

And the empty Coca-Cola bottle, clutched forgotten in his hand, glistened with the rays of the setting sun...

13————

No Jewish gene exists, to be sure, but there go the *Herrenvolk* genes
in the jeep. The Communist dies without an heir, the capitalist dies
likewise, but the fascist lives forever. We all have that Hitler-gene; it
shows up clearly in ad hoc committees.

Phillips's story reminds me again of the role of Logos as the snake in
Eden. Elf's tribe, or their genes, have forgotten that original "sin" of
speech, which enabled logic, which enabled science, which enabled
Megawar. It won't do to let those innocent, Logos-free genes spread
around.

The percentage of the world's population that had *consciously*
adopted the fascist persuasion was hovering near one of its historic
maxima when Stephen Vincent Benét wrote "By the Waters of
Babylon," and the bloody antics of these militarists must have been
much in his mind at the time. They were much in my mind, too,
about the time he published it, as I was engaged in a serious but
sporadic BB-gun war with a bunch of Minorcans across the alley that
year. That Benét should write a post-holocaust story may seem a bit
strange, for Benét died two years before Hiroshima. Of course, by that
time every graduate physics student had heard of Hahn and Strassman
and the splitting of uranium 235, had realized the implications, and
knew that something hush-hush was going on. But Benét published
this story in 1937 before the Hahn–Strassman experiments.

While my gang was shooting at the Minorcan gang with BB-guns
and getting as good as we got, Hitler's Luftwaffe was pounding civilian

targets such as Guernica (see Picasso), and Mussolini's air force was raining mustard gas and other like-minded gifts on Ethiopian camel cavalry who shot back with muzzle-loaders before dying like flies, as the stories said. Our gang was getting plenty of lessons from the fascists, but we didn't take them; our role models were from the First World War, so we dug a long, deep trench in the vacant lot next to my house and covered part of it with boards, palm fronds, and dirt to make a bunker. The French had been doing the same thing on the Rhine with the Maginot Line, and today Reagan is persuading us to dig a star-wars Maginot in the sky, but fortunately for our gang back then, the Minorcan gang lacked the military genius to come around our flank on bikes, or under it in submarines, or up our beaches with 68-pound backpack bombs, and they just dug their own trench in their own vacant lot; the BBs stung and left welts, but nobody was blinded. Benét was of course quite a bit older than I at the time, and took quite a different view of the world's reviving militarism. Here's what he thought he saw, after a World War *Two* as he imagined it.

BY THE WATERS OF BABYLON
by Stephen Vincent Benét

> How doth the city sit solitary, that was full of people! how is she become as a widow! she that was great among the nations, and princess among the provinces, how is she become tributary!
> —Jeremiah, 1:1 (605 B.C.)

The north and the west and the south are good hunting ground, but it is forbidden to go east. It is forbidden to go to any of the Dead Places except to search for metal and then he who touches the metal must be a priest or the son of a priest. Afterwards, both the man and the metal must be purified. These are the rules and the laws; they are well made. It is forbidden to cross the great river and look upon the place that was the Place of the Gods—this is most strictly forbidden. We do not even say its name though we know its name. It is there that spirits live, and demons—it is there are the ashes of the Great Burning. These things are forbidden—they have been forbidden since the beginning of time.

My father is a priest; I am the son of a priest. I have been in the Dead Places near us, with my father—at first, I was afraid. When my father went into the house to search for the metal, I stood by the door and my heart felt small and weak. It was a dead man's house, a spirit house. It did not have the smell of man, though there were old bones in a corner. But it is not fitting that a priest's son should show fear. I looked at the bones in the shadow and kept my voice still.

Then my father came out with the metal—a good, strong piece. He looked at me with both eyes but I had not run away. He gave me the metal to hold—I took it and did not die. So he knew that I was truly his son and would be a priest in my time. That was when I was very young—nevertheless my brothers would not have done it, though they are good hunters. After that, they gave me the good piece of meat and the warm corner by the fire. My father watched over me—he was glad that I should be a priest. But when I boasted or wept without reason, he punished me more strictly than my brothers. That was right.

After a time, I myself was allowed to go into the dead houses and search for metal. So I learned the ways of those houses—and if I saw bones, I was no longer afraid. The bones are light and old—sometimes they will fall into dust if you touch them. But that is a great sin.

I was taught the chants and the spells—I was taught how to stop the running of blood from a wound and many secrets. A priest must know many secrets—that was what my father said. If the hunters think we do all things by chants and spells, they may believe so—it does not hurt them. I was taught how to read in the old books and how to make the old writings—that was hard and took a long time. My knowledge made me happy—it was like a fire in my heart. Most of all, I liked to hear of the Old Days and the stories of the gods. I asked myself many questions that I could not answer, but it was good to ask them. At night, I would lie awake and listen to the wind—it seemed to me that it was the voice of the gods as they flew through the air.

We are not ignorant like the Forest People—our women spin

wool on the wheel, our priests wear a white robe. We do not eat grubs from the tree, we have not forgotten the old writings, although they are hard to understand. Nevertheless, my knowledge and my lack of knowledge burned in me—I wished to know more. When I was a man at last, I came to my father and said, "It is time for me to go on my journey. Give me your leave."

He looked at me for a long time, stroking his beard, then he said at last, "Yes. It is time." That night, in the house of the priesthood, I asked for and received purification. My body hurt but my spirit was a cool stone. It was my father himself who questioned me about my dreams.

He bade me look into the smoke of the fire and see—I saw and told what I saw. It was what I have always seen—a river, and, beyond it, a great Dead Place and in it the gods walking. I have always thought about that. His eyes were stern when I told him— he was no longer my father but a priest. He said, "This is a strong dream."

"It is mine," I said, while the smoke waved and my head felt light. They were singing the Star song in the outer chamber and it was like the buzzing of bees in my head.

He asked me how the gods were dressed and I told him how they were dressed. We know how they were dressed from the book, but I saw them as if they were before me. When I had finished, he threw the sticks three times and studied them as they fell.

"This is a very strong dream," he said. "It may eat you up."

"I am not afraid," I said and looked at him with both eyes. My voice sounded thin in my ears but that was because of the smoke.

He touched me on the breast and the forehead. He gave me the bow and the three arrows.

"Take them," he said. "It is forbidden to travel east. It is forbidden to cross the river. It is forbidden to go to the Place of the Gods. All these things are forbidden."

"All these things are forbidden," I said, but it was my voice that spoke and not my spirit. He looked at me again.

"My son," he said. "Once I had young dreams. If your dreams do not eat you up, you may be a great priest. If they eat you, you are still my son. Now go on your journey."

I went fasting, as is the law. My body hurt but not my heart. When the dawn came, I was out of sight of the village. I prayed and purified myself, waiting for a sign. The sign was an eagle. It flew east.

Sometimes signs are sent by bad spirits. I waited again on the flat rock, fasting, taking no food. I was very still—I could feel the sky above me and the earth beneath. I waited till the sun was beginning to sink. Then three deer passed in the valley, going east— they did not wind me or see me. There was a white fawn with them—a very great sign.

I followed them, at a distance, waiting for what would happen. My heart was troubled about going east, yet I knew that I must go. My head hummed with my fasting—I did not even see the panther spring upon the white fawn. But, before I knew it, the bow was in my hand. I shouted and the panther lifted his head from the fawn. It is not easy to kill a panther with one arrow but the arrow went through his eye and into his brain. He died as he tried to spring— he rolled over, tearing at the ground. Then I knew I was meant to go east—I knew that was my journey. When the night came, I made my fire and roasted meat.

It is eight suns' journey to the east and a man passes by many Dead Places. The Forest People are afraid of them but I am not. Once I made my fire on the edge of a Dead Place at night and, next morning, in the dead house, I found a good knife, little rusted. That was small to what came afterward but it made my heart feel big. Always when I looked for game, it was in front of my arrow, and twice I passed hunting parties of the Forest People without their knowing. So I knew my magic was strong and my journey clean, in spite of the law.

Toward the setting of the eighth sun, I came to the banks of the great river. It was half a day's journey after I had left the god-road— we do not use the god-roads now for they are falling apart into great blocks of stone, and the forest is safer going. A long way off, I had seen the water through trees but the trees were thick. At last, I came out upon an open place at the top of a cliff. There was the great river below, like a giant in the sun. It is very long, very wide. It could eat all the streams we know and still be thirsty. Its name in Ou-dis-sun, the Sacred, the Long. No man of my tribe had seen it, not even my father, the priest. It was magic and I prayed.

Then I raised my eyes and looked south. It was there, the Place of the Gods.

How can I tell what it was like—you do not know. It was there, in the red light, and they were too big to be houses. It was there with the red light upon it, mighty and ruined. I knew that in another moment the gods would see me. I covered my eyes with my hands and crept back into the forest.

Surely, that was enough to do, and live. Surely it was enough to spend the night upon the cliff. The Forest People themselves do not come near. Yet, all through the night, I knew that I should have to cross the river and walk in the Place of the Gods, although the gods ate me up. My magic did not help me at all and yet there was a fire in my bowels, a fire in my mind. When the sun rose, I thought, "My journey has been clean. Now I will go home from my journey." But, even as I thought so, I knew I could not. If I went to the Place of the Gods, I would surely die, but, if I did not go, I could never be at peace with my spirit again. It is better to lose one's life than one's spirit, if one is a priest and the son of a priest.

Nevertheless, as I made the raft, the tears ran out of my eyes. The Forest People could have killed me without fight, if they had come upon me then, but they did not come. When the raft was made, I said the sayings for the dead and painted myself for death. My heart was cold as a frog and my knees like water, but the burning in my mind would not let me have peace. As I pushed the raft from the shore, I began my death song—I had the right. It was a fine song.

> "I am John, son of John," I sang. "My people are the Hill People.
>   They are the men.
> I go into the Dead Places but I am not slain.
> I take the metal from the Dead Places but I am not blasted.
> I travel upon the god-roads and am not afraid. E-yah! I have killed
>   the panther, I have killed the fawn!
> E-yah! I have come to the great river. No man has come there
>   before.
> It is forbidden to go east, but I have gone, forbidden to go on the
>   great river, but I am there.
> Open your hearts, you spirits, and hear my song.
> Now I go to the Place of the Gods, I shall not return.
> My body is painted for death and my limbs weak, but my heart is
>   big as I go to the Place of the Gods!"

All the same, when I came to the Place of the Gods, I was afraid, afraid. The current of the great river is very strong—it gripped my raft with its hands. That was magic, for the river itself is wide and calm. I could feel evil spirits about me, in the bright morning; I could feel their breath on my neck as I was swept down the stream. Never have I been so much alone—I tried to think of my knowledge, but it was a squirrels' heap of winter nuts. There was no strength in my knowledge anymore and I felt small and naked as a new-hatched bird—alone upon the great river, the servant of the gods.

Yet, after a while, my eyes were opened and I saw. I saw both banks of the river—I saw that once there had been god-roads across it, though now they were broken and fallen like broken vines. Very great they were, and wonderful and broken—broken in the time of the Great Burning when the fire fell out of the sky. And always the current took me nearer to the Place of the Gods, and the huge ruins rose before my eyes.

I do not know the customs of rivers—we are the People of the Hills. I tried to guide my raft with the pole but it spun around. I thought the river meant to take me past the Place of the Gods and out into the Bitter Water of the legends. I grew angry then—my heart felt strong. I said aloud, "I am a priest and the son of a priest!" The gods heard me—they showed me how to paddle with the pole on one side of the raft. The current changed itself—I drew near to the Place of the Gods.

When I was very near, my raft struck and turned over. I can swim in our lakes—I swam to the shore. There was a great spike of rusted metal sticking out into the river—I hauled myself up upon it and sat there, panting. I had saved my bow and two arrows and the knife I found in the Dead Place but that was all. My raft went whirling downstream toward the Bitter Water. I looked after it, and thought if it had trod me under, at least I would be safely dead. Nevertheless, when I had dried my bowstring and restrung it, I walked forward to the Place of the Gods.

It felt like ground underfoot; it did not burn me. It is not true what some of the tales say, that the ground there burns forever, for I have been there. Here and there were the marks and stains of the Great Burning, on the ruins, that is true. But they were old marks and old stains. It is not true either, what some of our priests say, that it is an island covered with fogs and enchantments. It is not. It is a great Dead Place—greater than any Dead Place we know. Everywhere in it there are god-roads, though most are cracked and broken. Everywhere there are the ruins of the high towers of the gods.

How shall I tell what I saw? I went carefully, my strung bow in my hand, my skin ready for danger. There should have been the wailings of spirits and the shrieks of demons, but there were not. It was very silent and sunny where I had landed—the wind and the rain and the birds that drop seeds had done their work—the grass grew in the cracks of the broken stone. It is a fair island—no wonder the gods built there. If I had come there, a god, I also would have built.

How shall I tell what I saw? The towers are not all broken—here and there one still stands, like a great tree in a forest, and the birds nest high. But the towers themselves look blind, for the gods are gone. I saw a fish hawk, catching fish in the river. I saw a little dance of white butterflies over a great heap of broken stones and columns. I went there and looked about me—there was a carved stone with cut letters, broken in half. I can read letters but I could not understand these. They said UBTREAS. There was also the shattered image of a man or a god. It had been made of white stone and he wore his hair tied back like a woman's. His name was ASHING, as I read on the cracked half of a stone. I thought it wise to pray to ASHING, though I do not know that god.

How shall I tell what I saw? There was no smell of man left, on stone or metal. Nor were there many trees in that wilderness of stone. There are many pigeons, nesting and dropping in the towers—the gods must have loved them, or, perhaps, they used them for sacrifices. There are wild cats that roam the god-roads, green-eyed, unafraid of man. At night they wail like demons but they are not demons. The wild dogs are more dangerous, for they hunt in a a pack, but them I did not meet till later. Everywhere there are carved stones, carved with magical numbers or words.

I went north—I did not try to hide myself. When a god or a demon saw me, then I would die, but meanwhile I was no longer afraid. My hunger for knowledge burned in me—there was so much that I could not understand. After a while, I knew that my belly was hungry. I could have hunted for my meat, but I did not hunt. It is known that the gods did not hunt as we do—they got their food from enchanted boxes and jars. Sometimes these are still found in the Dead Places—once, when I was a child and foolish, I opened such a jar and tasted it and found the food sweet. But my father found out and punished me for it strictly, for, often, that food is death. Now, though, I had long gone past what was forbidden, and I entered the likeliest towers, looking for the food of the gods.

I found it at last in the ruins of a great temple in the mid-city. A mighty temple it must have been, for the roof was painted like the sky at night with its stars—that much I could see, though the colors were faint and dim. It went down into great caves and tunnels— perhaps they kept their slaves there. But when I started to climb down, I heard the squeaking of rats, so I did not go—rats are un- clean, and there must have been many tribes of them, from the squeaking. But near there, I found food, in the heart of a ruin, behind a door that still opened. I ate only the fruits from the jars—they had a very sweet taste. There was drink, too, in bottles of glass— the drink of the gods was strong and made my head swim. After I had eaten and drunk, I slept on the top of a stone, my bow at my side.

When I woke, the sun was low. Looking down from where I lay, I saw a dog sitting on his haunches. His tongue was hanging out of his mouth; he looked as if he were laughing. He was a big dog, with a gray-brown coat, as big as a wolf. I sprang up and shouted at him but he did not move—he just sat there as if he were laughing. I did not like that. When I reached for a stone to throw, he moved swiftly out of the way of the stone. He was not afraid of me; he looked at me as if I were meat. No doubt I could have killed him with an arrow, but I did not know if there were others. Moreover, night was falling.

I looked about me—not far away there was a great, broken god- road, leading north. The towers were high enough, but not so high, and while many of the dead houses were wrecked, there were some that stood. I went toward this god-road, keeping to the heights of the ruins, while the dog followed. When I had reached the god- road, I saw that there were others behind him. If I had slept later, they would have come upon me asleep and torn out my throat. As it was, they were sure enough of me; they did not hurry. When I went into the dead-house, they kept watch at the entrance—doubtless they thought they would have a fine hunt. But a dog cannot open a door and I knew, from the books, that the gods did not like to live on the ground but on high.

I had just found a door I could open when the dogs decided to rush. Ha! They were surprised when I shut the door in their faces— it was a good door, of strong metal. I could hear their foolish baying beyond it but I did not stop to answer them. I was in darkness—I found stairs and climbed. There were many stairs, turning around till my head was dizzy. At the top was another door—I found the knob and opened it. I was in a long small chamber—on one side of it was a bronze door that could not be opened, for it had no handle. Perhaps there was a magic word to open it but I did not have the word. I turned to the door in the opposite side of the wall. The lock of it was broken and I opened it and went in.

Within, there was a place of great riches. The god who lived there must have been a powerful god. The first room was a small ante-room—I waited there for some time, telling the spirits of the place that I came in peace and not as a robber. When it seemed to me that they had had time to hear me, I went on. Ah, what riches! Few, even, of the windows had been broken—it was all as it had been. The great windows that looked over the city had not been broken at all though they were dusty and streaked with many years. There were coverings on the floors, the colors not greatly faded, and the chairs were soft and deep. There were pictures upon the walls, very strange, very wonderful—I remember one of a bunch of flowers in a jar—if you came close to it, you could see nothing but bits of color, but if you stood away from it, the flowers might have been picked yesterday. It made my heart feel strange to look at this pic-ture—and to look at the figure of a bird, in some hard clay, on a table and see it so like our birds. Everywhere there were books and writings, many in tongues that I could not read. The god who lived there must have been a wise god and full of knowledge. I felt I had a right there, as I sought knowledge also.

Nevertheless, it was strange. There was a washing-place but no water—perhaps the gods washed in air. There was a cooking-place but no wood, and though there was a machine to cook food, there was no place to put fire in it. Nor were there candles or lamps— there were things that looked like lamps but they had neither oil nor wick. All these things were magic, but I touched them and lived—the magic had gone out of them. Let me tell one thing to show. In the washing-place, a thing said "Hot" but it was not hot to the touch—another thing said "Cold" but it was not cold. This must have been a strong magic but the magic was gone. I do not understand—they had ways—I wish that I knew.

It was close and dry and dusty in their house of the gods. I have said the magic was gone but that is not true—it had gone from the magic things but it had not gone from the place. I felt the spirits about me, weighing upon me. Nor had I ever slept in a Dead Place before—and yet, tonight, I must sleep there. When I thought of it, my tongue felt dry in my throat, in spite of my wish for knowledge. Almost I would have gone down again and faced the dogs, but I did not.

I had not gone through all the rooms when the darkness fell. When it fell, I went back to the big room looking over the city and made fire. There was a place to make fire and a box with wood in it, though I do not think they cooked there. I wrapped myself in a floor covering and slept in front of the fire—I was very tired.

Now I tell what is very strong magic. I woke in the midst of the night. When I woke, the fire had gone out and I was cold. It seemed to me that all around me there were whisperings and voices. I closed my eyes to shut them out. Some will say that I slept again, but I do not think that I slept. I could feel the spirits drawing my spirit out of my body as a fish is drawn on a line.

Why should I lie about it? I am a priest and the son of a priest. If there are spirits, as they say, in the small Dead Places near us, what spirits must there not be in that great Place of the Gods? And would not they wish to speak? After such long years? I know that I felt myself drawn as a fish is drawn on a line. I had stepped out of my body—I could see my body asleep in front of the cold fire, but it was not I. I was drawn to look out upon the city of the gods.

It should have been dark, for it was night, but it was not dark. Everywhere there were lights—lines of light—circles and blurs of light—ten thousand torches would not have been the same. The sky itself was alight—you could barely see the stars for the glow in the sky. I thought to myself, "This is strong magic," and trembled. There was a roaring in my ears like the rushing of rivers. Then my eyes grew used to the light and my ears to the sound. I knew that I was seeing the city as it had been when the gods were alive.

That was a sight indeed—yes, that was a sight: I could not have seen it in the body—my body would have died. Everywhere went the gods, on foot and in chariots—there were gods beyond number and counting and their chariots blocked the streets. They had turned night to day for their pleasure—they did not sleep with the sun. The noise of their coming and going was the noise of many waters. It was magic what they could do—it was magic what they did.

I looked out of another window—the great vines of their bridges were mended and the god-roads went east and west. Restless, restless, were the gods and always in motion! They burrowed tunnels under rivers—they flew in the air. With unbelievable tools they did giant works—no part of the earth was safe from them, for, if they wished for a thing, they summoned it from the other side of the world. And always, as they labored and rested, as they feasted and made love, there was a drum in their ears—the pulse of the giant city, beating and beating like a man's heart.

Were they happy? What is happiness to the gods? They were great, they were mighty, they were wonderful and terrible. As I looked upon them and their magic, I felt like a child—but a little more, it seemed to me, and they would pull down the moon from the sky. I saw them with wisdom beyond wisdom and knowledge beyond knowledge. And yet not all they did was well done—even I could see that—and yet their wisdom could not but grow until all was peace.

Then I saw their fate come upon them and that was terrible past speech. It came upon them as they walked the streets of their city. I have been in fights with the Forest People—I have seen men die. But this was not like that. When gods war with gods, they use weapons we do not know. It was fire falling out of the sky and a mist that poisoned. It was the time of the Great Burning and the Destruction. They ran about like ants in the streets of their city— poor gods, poor gods! Then the towers began to fall. A few escaped—yes, a few. The legends tell it. But, even after the city had become a Dead Place, for many years the poison was still in the ground. I saw it happen, I saw the last of them die. It was darkness over the broken city and I wept.

All this, I saw. I saw it as I have told it, though not in the body. When I woke in the morning, I was hungry, but I did not think first of my hunger for my heart was perplexed and confused. I knew the reason for the Dead Places but I did not see why it happened. It seemed to me it should not have happened, with all the magic they had. I went through the house looking for an answer. There was so much in the house I could not understand—and yet I am a priest and the son of a priest. It was like being on one side of the great river, at night, with no light to show the way.

Then I saw the dead god. He was sitting in his chair, by the window, in a room I had not entered before and, for the first moment, I thought that he was alive. Then I saw the skin on the back of his hand—it was like dry leather. The room was shut, hot and dry— no doubt that had kept him as he was. At first I was afraid to approach him—then the fear left me. He was sitting looking out over the city—he was dressed in the clothes of the gods. His age was neither young nor old—I could not tell his age. But there was wisdom in his face and great sadness. You could see that he would have not run away. He had sat at his window, watching his city die—then he himself had died. But it is better to lose one's life than one's spirit—and you could see from the face that his spirit had not been lost. I knew that if I touched him, he would fall into dust—and yet, there was something unconquered in the face.

That is all of my story, for then I knew he was a man—I knew then that they had been men, neither gods nor demons. It is a great knowledge, hard to tell and believe. They were men—they went a dark road, but they were men. I had no fear after that—I had no fear going home, though twice I fought off the dogs and once I was hunted for two days by the Forest People. When I saw my father again, I prayed and was purified. He touched my lips and my breast; he said, "You went away a boy. You come back a man and a priest." I said, "father, they were men! I have been in the Place of the Gods and seen it! Now slay me, if it is the law—but still I know that they were men."

He looked at me out of both eyes. He said, "The law is not always the same shape—you have done what you have done. I could not have done it in my time, but you come after me. Tell!"

I told and he listened. After that, I wished to tell all the people but he showed me otherwise. He said, "Truth is a hard deer to hunt. If you eat too much truth at once, you may die of the truth. It was not idly that our fathers forbade the Dead Places." He was right— it is better the truth should come little by little. I have learned that, being a priest. Perhaps, in the old days, they ate knowledge too fast.

Nevertheless, we make a beginning. It is not for the metal alone we go to the Dead Places now—there are the books and the writings. They are hard to learn. And the magic tools are broken—but we can look at them and wonder. At least, we make a beginning. And, when I am chief priest we shall go beyond the great river. We shall go to the Place of the Gods—the place new-york—not one man but a company. W shall look for the images of the gods and find the god ASHING and the others—gods Lincoln and Biltmore and Moses. But they were men who built the city, not gods or demons. They were men. I remember the dead man's face. They were men who were here before us. We must build again.

14_____

Except for a few technical details, and that optimistic last line, it might have been about nuclear Megawar. Sunday supplement writers in those days tried to tell us what a second world war would be like, and most were as mistaken as Benét. There was to be widespread use of incendiary and chemical weapons against civilian populations— Benet's "fire from the sky" and "poison in the ground"—and possibly even ray-guns; although lasers were still unknown, everybody knew about radium emission. Take comfort, if you wish, in the fact that the writers of those days did not accurately describe the coming global war. But perhaps those writers were one war ahead of us. You can be sure their modern counterparts are no better as prophets, but neither are the fearless leaders at the Pentagon or in the Kremlin. It's a law in the stock market, as in war, that what everybody bets will happen can't possibly happen in the expected way. Instead of doing what experts are betting on, the institutions will suddenly discover there's nobody left to sell their IBM (or whatever) stock to except each other, and start panic-dumping on trivial bad news; or else the uncouth Huns will come around your Maginot Line on motorcycles. And maybe Allah-fearing backpackers with 68-pound nukes will thumb a ride from our beaches to their targets with the driver of a semitrailer filled with Florida oranges, or a submarine will squirt Cruise missiles (immune to laser defenses) at Atlanta, Orlando, and Cape Canaveral from just inside Jacksonville harbor. (Don't tell me they can't get in there; they got into a secret naval installation in Sweden). If global conflict comes

253

again, it won't come in the way we've bet all our billions on for "defense."

After it's over and the grief is gone, still a great nostalgia endures—for places or things or people lost.

The two Bradbury stories that follow are paired, because they seem complementary, although thirteen years separate their publication dates. In the first, nostalgia for man seems to linger in man's *things*.

THERE WILL COME SOFT RAINS
by Ray Bradbury

In the living room the voice-clock sang, *Tick-tock, seven o'clock, time to get up, time to get up, seven o'clock!* as if it were afraid that nobody would. The morning house lay empty. The clock ticked on, repeating and repeating its sounds into the emptiness. *Seven-nine, breakfast time, seven-nine!*

In the kitchen the breakfast stove gave a hissing sigh and ejected from its warm interior eight pieces of perfectly browned toast, eight eggs sunnyside up, sixteen slices of bacon, two coffees, and two cool glasses of milk

"Today is August 4, 2026," said a second voice from the kitchen ceiling, "in the city of Allendale, California." It repeated the date three times for memory's sake. "Today is Mr. Featherstone's birthday. Today is the anniversary of Tilita's marriage. Insurance is payable, as are the water, gas, and light bills."

Somewhere in the walls, relays clicked, memory tapes glided under electric eyes.

Eight-one, tick-tock, eight-one o'clock, off to school, off to work, run, run, eight-one! But no doors slammed, no carpets took the soft tread of rubber heels. It was raining outside. The weather box on the front door sang quietly: "Rain, rain, go away; rubbers, raincoats for today..." And the rain tapped on the empty house, echoing.

Outside, the garage chimed and lifted its door to reveal the waiting car. After a long wait the door swung down again.

At eight-thirty the eggs were shriveled and the toast was like stone. An aluminum wedge scraped them into the sink, where hot water whirled them down a metal throat which digested and flushed them away to the distant sea. The dirty dishes were dropped into a hot washer and emerged twinkling dry.

Nine-fifteen, sang the clock, *time to clean.*

Out of warrens in the wall, tiny robot mice darted. The rooms were acrawl with the small cleaning animals, all rubber and metal. They thudded against chairs, whirling their mustached runners, kneading the rug nap, sucking gently at hidden dust. Then, like mysterious invaders, they popped into their burrows. Their pink electric eyes faded. The house was clean.

Ten o'clock. The sun came out from behind the rain. The house stood alone in a city of rubble and ashes. This was the one house left standing. At night the ruined city gave off a radioactive glow which could be seen for miles.

Ten-fifteen. The garden sprinklers whirled up in golden founts, filling the soft morning air with scatterings of brightness. The water pelted windowpanes, running down the charred west side where the house had been burned evenly free of its white paint. The entire west face of the house was black, save for five places. Here the silhouette in paint of a man mowing a lawn. Here, as in a photograph, a woman bent to pick flowers. Still farther over, their images burned on wood in one titanic instant, a small boy, hands flung into the air; higher up, the image of a thrown ball, and opposite him a girl, hands raised to catch a ball which never came down.

The five spots of paint—the man, the woman, the children, the ball—remained. The rest was a thin charcoaled layer.

The gentle sprinkler rain filled the garden with falling light.

Until this day, how well the house had kept its peace. How carefully it had inquired, "Who goes there? What's the password?" and, getting no answer from lonely foxes and whining cats, it had shut up its windows and drawn shades in an old-maidenly preoccupation with self-protection which bordered on a mechanical paranoia.

It quivered at each sound, the house did. If a sparrow brushed a window, the shade snapped up. The bird, startled, flew off! No, not even a bird must touch the house!

The house was an altar with ten thousand attendants, big, small, servicing, attending, in choirs. But the gods had gone away, and the ritual of the religion continued senselessly, uselessly.

Twelve noon.

A dog whined, shivering, on the front porch.

The front door recognized the dog voice and opened. The dog, once huge and fleshy, but now gone to bone and covered with sores, moved in and through the house, tracking mud. Behind it whirred angry mice, angry at having to pick up mud, angry at inconvenience.

For not a leaf fragment blew under the door but what the wall panels flipped open and the copper scrap rats flashed swiftly out. The offending dust, hair, or paper, seized in miniature steel jaws, was raced back to the burrows. There, down tubes which fed into the cellar, it was dropped into the sighing vent of an incinerator which sat like evil Baal in a dark corner.

The dog ran upstairs, hysterically yelping to each door, at last realizing, as the house realized, that only silence was here.

It sniffed the air and scratched the kitchen door. Behind the door, the stove was making pancakes which filled the house with a rich baked odor and the scent of maple syrup.

The dog frothed at the mouth, lying at the door, sniffing, its eyes turned to fire. It ran wildly in circles, biting at its tail, spun in a frenzy, and died. It lay in the parlor for an hour.

Two o'clock, sang a voice.

Delicately sensing decay at last, the regiments of mice hummed out as softly as blown gray leaves in an electrical wind.

Two-fifteen.

The dog was gone.

In the cellar, the incinerator glowed suddenly and a whirl of sparks leaped up the chimney.

Two thirty-five.

Bridge tables sprouted from patio walls. Playing cards fluttered onto pads in a shower of pips. Martinis manifested on an oaken bench with egg-salad sandwiches. Music played.

But the tables were silent and the cards untouched.

At four o'clock the tables folded like great butterflies back through the paneled walls.

Four-thirty.

The nursery walls glowed.

Animals took shape: yellow giraffes, blue lions, pink antelopes, lilac panthers cavorting in crystal substance. The walls were glass. They looked out upon color and fantasy. Hidden films clocked through well-oiled sprockets, and the walls lived. The nursery floor was woven to resemble crisp, cereal meadow. Over this ran aluminum roaches and iron crickets, and in the hot still air butterflies of delicate red tissue wavered among the sharp aroma of animal spoors! There was the sound like a great matted yellow hive of bees within a dark bellows, the lazy bumble of a purring lion. And there was the patter of okapi feet and the murmur of a fresh jungle rain, like other hoofs, falling upon the summer-starched grass. Now the walls dissolved into distances of parched weed, mile on mile, and warm endless sky. The animals drew away into thorn brakes and water holes.

It was the children's hour.

Five-o'clock. The bath filled with clear hot water.

Six, seven, eight o'clock. The dinner dishes manipulated like magic tricks, and in the study a *click.* In the metal stand opposite the hearth where a fire now blazed up warmly, a cigar popped out, half an inch of soft gray ash on it, smoking, waiting.

Nine o'clock. The beds warmed their hidden circuits, for nights were cool here.

*Nine-five.*A voice spoke from the study ceiling:

"Mrs. McClellan, which poem would you like this evening?"

The house was silent.

The voice said at last, "Since you express no preference, I shall select a poem at random." Quiet music rose to back the voice. "Sara Teasdale. As I recall, your favorite....

"There will come soft rains and the smell of the ground,
And swallows circling with their shimmering sound;

And frogs in the pools singing at night,
And wild plum trees in tremulous white;

Robins will wear their feathery fire,
Whistling their whims on a low fence-wire;

And not one will know of the war, not one
Will care at last when it is done.

Not one would mind, neither bird nor tree,
If mankind perished utterly;

And Spring herself, when she woke at dawn
Would scarcely know that we were gone."

The fire burned on the stone hearth and the cigar fell away into a mound of quiet ash on its tray. The empty chairs faced each other between the silent walls, and the music played.

At ten o'clock the house began to die.

The wind blew. A falling tree bough crashed through the kitchen window. Cleaning solvent, bottled, shattered over the stove. The room was ablaze in an instant.

"Fire!" screamed a voice. The house lights flashed, water pumps shot water from the ceilings. But the solvent spread on the linoleum, licking, eating, under the kitchen door, while voices took it up in chorus: "Fire, fire, fire!"

The house tried to save itself. Doors sprang tightly shut, but the windows were broken by the heat and the wind blew and sucked upon the fire.

The house gave ground as the fire in ten billion angry sparks moved with flaming ease from room to room and then up the stairs, while scurrying water rats squeaked from the walls, pistoled their water, and ran for more. And the wall sprays let down showers of mechanical rain.

But too late. Somewhere, sighing, a pump shrugged to a stop. The quenching rain ceased. The reserve water supply which had filled baths and washed dishes for many quiet days was gone.

The fire crackled up the stairs. It fed upon Picassos and Matisses in the upper halls, like delicacies, baking off the oily flesh, tenderly crisping the canvases into black shavings.

Now the fire lay in beds, stood in windows, changed the colors of drapes!

And then, reinforcements.

From attic trapdoors, blind robot faces peered down with faucet mouths gushing green chemical.

The fire backed off, as even an elephant must at the sight of a dead snake. Now there were twenty snakes whipping over the floor, killing the fire with a clear cold venom of green froth.

But the fire was clever. It had sent flame outside the house, up through the attic to the pumps there. An explosion! The attic brain which directed the pumps was shattered into bronze shrapnel on the beams.

The fire rushed back into every closet and felt of the clothes hung there. The house shudderred, oak bone on bone, its bared skeleton cringing from the heat, its wire, its nerves revealed as if a surgeon had torn the skin off to let the red veins and capillaries quiver in the scalded air. Help, help! Fire! Run, run! Heat snapped mirrors like the first brittle winter ice. And the voices wailed Fire, fire, run, run, like a tragic nursery rhyme, a dozen voices, high, low, like children dying in a forest alone, alone. And the voices fading as the wires popped their sheathings like hot chestnuts. One, two, three, four, five voices died.

In the nursery the jungle burned. Blue lions roared, purple giraffes bounded off. The panthers ran in circles, changing color, and ten million animals, running before the fire, vanished off toward a distant steaming river....

Ten more voices died. In the last instant under the fire avalanche, other choruses, oblivious, could be heard announcing the time, playing music, cutting the lawn by remote-control mower, or setting an umbrella frantically out and in the slamming and opening front door, a thousand things happening, like a clock shop when each clock strikes the hour insanely before or after the other, a scene of maniac confusion, yet unity; singing, screaming, a few last cleaning mice darting bravely out to carry the horrid ashes away! And one voice, with sublime disregard for the situation, read poetry aloud in the fiery study, until all the film spools burned, until all the wires withered and the circuits cracked.

The fire burst the house and let it slam flat down, puffing out skirts of spark and smoke.

In the kitchen, an instant before the rain of fire and timber, the stove could be seen making breakfasts at a psychopathic rate, ten dozen eggs, six loaves of toast, twenty dozen bacon strips, which, eaten by fire, started the stove working again, hysterically hissing!

The crash. The attic smashing into kitchen and parlor. The parlor into cellar, cellar into sub-cellar. Deep freeze, armchair, film tapes, circuits, beds, and all like skeletons thrown in a cluttered mound deep under.

Smoke and silence. A great quantity of smoke.

Dawn showed faintly in the east. Among the ruins, one wall stood alone. Within the wall, a last voice said, over and over again and again, even as the sun rose to shine upon the heaped rubble and steam:

"Today is August 5, 2026, today is August 5, 2026, today is..."

15_____

When, on the other hand, man survives but can't get his *things* back...

TO THE CHICAGO ABYSS
by Ray Bradbury

Under a pale April sky in a faint wind that blew out of a memory of winter, the old man shuffled into the almost empty park at noon. His slow feet were bandaged with nicotine-stained swathes, his hair was wild, long, and gray as was his beard which enclosed a mouth which seemed always atremble with revelation.

Now he gazed back as if he had lost so many things he could not begin to guess there in the tumbled ruin, the toothless skyline of the city. Finding nothing he shuffled on until he found a bench where sat a woman alone. Examining her, he nodded and sat to the far end of the bench and did not look at her again.

He remained, eyes shut, mouth working, for three minutes, head moving as if his nose were printing a single word on the air. Once written, he opened his mouth to pronounce it in a clear, fine voice:

"Coffee."

The woman gasped and stiffened.

The old man's gnarled fingers tumbled in pantomime on his unseen lap.

"Twist the key! Bright red, yellow-letter can! Compressed air. Hisss! Vacuum pack. Ssst! Like a snake!"

The woman snapped her head about as if slapped to stare in dreadful fascination at the old man's moving tongue.

"The scent, the odor, the smell. Rich, dark, wondrous Brazilian beans, fresh ground!"

Leaping up, reeling as if gunshot, the woman tottered.

The old man flicked his eyes wide. "No! I—"

But she was running, gone.

The old man sighed and walked on through the park until he reached a bench where sat a young man completely involved with wrapping dried grass in a small square of thin tissue paper. His thin fingers shaped the grass tenderly, in an almost holy ritual, trembling as he rolled the tube, put it to his mouth, and, hypnotically, lit it. He leaned back, squinting deliciously, communing with the strange rank air in his mouth and lungs. The old man watched the smoke blow away on the noon wind and said:

"Chesterfields."

The young man gripped his knees, tight.

"Raleighs," said the old man. "Lucky Strikes."

The young man stared at him.

"Kent. Kools. Marlboro," said the old man, not looking at him. "Those were the names. White, red, amber packs grass-green, sky-blue, pure gold with the red slick small ribbon that ran around the top that you pulled to zip away the crinkly cellophane, and the blue government tax-stamp—"

"Shut up," said the young man.

"Buy them in drug-stores, fountains, subways—"

"Shut up!"

"Gently," said the old man. "It's just, that smoke of yours made me think—"

"Don't think!" The young man jerked so violently his home-made cigarette fell in chaff to his lap. "Now look what you made me do!"

"I'm sorry. It was such a nice friendly day—"

"I'm no friend!"

"We're all friends now, or why live?"

"Friends?" the young man snorted, aimlessly plucking at the shredded grass and paper. "Maybe there were 'friends' back in 1970, but now—"

"1970. You must have been a baby then. They still had Butter-fingers then in bright yellow wrappers. Baby Ruths. Clark Bars in orange paper. Milky Ways...swallow a universe of stars, comets, meteors. Nice—"

"It was never nice." The young man stood suddenly. "What's wrong with you?"

"I remember limes, and lemons, that's what's wrong with me. Do you remember oranges?"

"Damn right. Oranges, hell. You calling me a liar? You want me to feel bad? You nuts? Don't you know the law? You know I could turn you in, you?"

"I know, I know," said the old man, shrugging. "The weather fooled me. It made me want to compare—"

"Compare rumors, that's what they'd say, the Police, the Special Cops, they'd say it, rumors, you trouble-making bastard, you—"

He seized the old man's lapels which ripped so he had to grab another handful, yelling down into his face.

"Why don't I just blast the living Jesus out of you. I ain't hurt no one in so long, I—"

He shoved the old man. Which gave him the idea to pummel and when he pummeled he began to punch and punching made it easy to strike and soon he rained blows upon the old man, who stood like one caught in thunder and down-poured storm, using only his fingers to ward off the blows that fleshed his cheeks, shoulders, his brow, his chin, as the young man shrieked cigarettes, moaned can-dies, yelled smokes, cried sweets until the old man fell to be kick-rolled and shivering. The young man stopped and began to cry. At the sound, the old man, cuddled, clenched into his pain, took his fingers away from his broken mouth and opened his eyes to gaze with astonishment at his assailant. The young man wept.

"Please..." begged the old man.

The young man wept louder, tears falling from his eyes.

"Don't cry," said the old man. "We won't be hungry forever. We'll rebuild the cities. Listen, I didn't mean for you to cry, only to think where are we going, what are we doing, what've we done? You weren't hitting me. You meant to hit something else, but I was handy. Look, I'm sitting up. I'm okay."

The young man stopped crying and blinked down at the old man who forced a bloody smile.

"You...you can't go around," said the young man, "making people unhappy. I'll find someone to fix you!"

"Wait!" The old man struggled to his knees. "No!"

But the young man ran wildly off out of the park, yelling.

Crouched alone, the old man felt his bones, found one of his teeth lying red amongst the strewn gravel, handled it sadly.

"Fool," said a voice.

The old man glanced over and up.

A lean man of some forty years stood leaning against a tree nearby, a look of pale weariness and curiosity on his long face.

"Fool," he said again.

The old man gasped. "You were there, all the time, and did *noth-ing?*"

"What, fight one fool to save another? No." The stranger helped him up and brushed him off. "I do my fighting where it pays. Come on. You're going home with me."

The old man gasped again. "Why?"

"That boy'll be back with the police any second. I don't want you stolen away, you're a very precious commodity. I've heard of you, looked for you for days now. Good Grief, and when I find you you're up to your famous tricks. What did you say to the boy made him mad?"

"I said about oranges and lemons, candy, cigarettes. I was just getting ready to recollect in detail wind-up toys, briar-pipes and back-scratchers, when he dropped the sky on me."

"I almost don't blame him. Half of me wants to hit you, itself. Come on, double-time. There's a siren, quick!"

And they went swiftly, another way, out of the park.

He drank the home-made wine because it was easiest. The food must wait until his hunger overcame the pain in his broken mouth. He sipped, nodding.

"Good, many thanks, good."

The stranger who had walked him swiftly out of the park sat across from him at the flimsy dining room table as the stranger's wife placed broken and mended plates on the worn cloth.

"The beating," said the husband, at last. "How did it happen?"

At this, his wife almost dropped a plate.

"Relax," said the husband. "No one followed us. Go ahead, old man, tell us, why do you behave like a saint panting after martyrdom? You're famous, you know. Everyone's heard about you. Many would like to meet you. Myself, first, I want to know what makes you tick. Well?"

But the old man was only entranced with the vegetables on the chipped plate before him. Twenty-six, no, twenty-eight peas! He counted the impossible sum! He bent to the incredible vegetables like a man praying over his quietest beads. Twenty-eight glorious green peas, plus a few graphs of half-raw spaghetti announcing that today business was fair. But under the line of pasta, the cracked line of the plate showed where business for years now was more than terrible. The old man hovered counting above the food like a great and inexplicable buzzard, crazily fallen and roosting in this cold apartment, watched by his samaritan hosts until at last he said:

"These twenty-eight peas remind me, of a film I saw as a child. A comedian—do you know the word?—a funny man met a lunatic in a midnight house in this film and—"

The husband and wife laughed quietly.

"No, that's not the joke yet, sorry," the old man apologized. "The lunatic sat the comedian down to an empty table, no knives, no forks, no food. 'Dinner is served!' he cried. Afraid of murder, the comedian fell in with the make believe. 'Great!' he cried, pretending to chew steak, vegetables, dessert. He bit nothings. 'Fine!' he swallowed air. 'Wonderful!' Eh...you may laugh now."

But the husband and wife, grown still, only looked at their sparsely strewn plates.

The old man shook his head and went on. "The comedian, thinking to impress the madman, exclaimed, 'And these spiced brandy peaches! Superb!' 'Peaches?' screamed the madman, drawing a gun. 'I served no peaches! You must be insane!' And shot the comedian in the behind!"

The old man, in the silence which ensued, picked up the first pea and weighed its lovely bulk upon his bent tin fork. He was about to put it in his mouth when—

There was a sharp rap on the door.

"Special Police!" a voice cried.

Silent but trembling, the wife hid the extra plate.

The husband rose calmly to lead the old man to a wall where a panel hissed open and he stepped in and the panel hissed shut and he stood in darkness hidden away as, beyond, unseen, the apartment door opened. Voices murmured excitedly. The old man could imagine the Special Policeman in his midnight blue uniform, with drawn gun, entering to see only the flimsy furniture, the bare walls, the echoing linoleum floor, the glassless, cardboarded-over windows, this thin and oily film of civilization left on an empty shore when the storm tide of war went away.

"I'm looking for an old man," said the tired voice of authority beyond the wall. Strange, thought the old man, even the Law sounds tired now. "Patched clothes—" But, thought the old man, I thought everyone's clothes were patched! "Dirty. About eighty years old..." but isn't everyone dirty, everyone old? the old man cried out, to himself. "If you turn him in, there's a week's rations as reward," said the police voice. "Plus ten cans of vegetables, five cans of soup, bonus."

Real tin cans with bright printed labels, thought the old man. The cans flashed like meteors rushing by in the dark over his eyelids. What a fine reward! Not TEN THOUSAND DOLLARS, not TWENTY THOUSAND DOLLARS, no, no, but... five incredible cans of real not imitation soup, and ten, count them, ten brilliant circus-colored cans of exotic vegetables like string beans and sun-yellow corn! Think of it! *Think!*

There was a long silence in which the old man almost thought he heard faint murmurs of stomachs turning uneasily, slumbered but dreaming of dinners much finer than the hairballs of old illusion gone nightmare and politics gone sour in the long twilight since A.D., Annihilation Day.

"Soup. Vegetables," said the police voice, a final time. "Fifteen solid-pack cans!"

The door slammed.

The boots stomped away through the ramshackle tenement

pounding coffin lid doors to stir other Lazarus souls alive to cry aloud of bright tins and real soups. The poundings faded. There was a last banging slam.

And at last the hidden panel whispered up. The husband and wife did not look at him as he stepped out. He knew why and wanted to touch their elbows.

"Even I," he said gently. "Even *I* was tempted to turn myself in, to claim the reward, to eat the soup..."

Still they would not look at him.

"Why," he asked. "Why didn't you hand me over? Why?"

The husband, as if suddenly remembering, nodded to his wife. She went to the door, hesitated, her husband nodded again, impatiently, and she went out, noiseless as a puff of cobweb. They heard her rustling along the hall, scratching softly at doors, which opened to gasps and murmurs.

"What's she up to? What are *you* up to?" asked the old man.

"You'll find out. Sit. Finish your dinner," said the husband. "Tell me why you're such a fool you make us fools who seek you out and bring you here."

"Why am I such a fool?" The old man sat. The old man munched slowly, taking peas one at a time from the plate which had been returned to him. "Yes, I am a fool. How did I start my foolishness? Years ago I looked at the ruined world, the dictatorships, the desicated states and nations, and said, "What can I do? Me, a weak old man, what? Rebuild a devastation? Ha! But lying half asleep one night an old phonograph record played in my head. Two sisters named Duncan sang out of my childhood a song called *REMEM-BERING*. 'Remembering, is all I do, dear, so try and remember, too.' I sang the song and it wasn't a song but a way of life. What did I have to offer a world that was forgetting? My memory! How could this help? By offering a standard of comparison. By telling the young *what once was*, by considering our losses. I found the more I remembered, the more I *could* remember! Depending on who I sat down with I remembered imitation flowers, dial telephones, refrigerators, kazoos (you ever *play* a kazoo?!), thimbles, bicycle clips, not bicycles, no, but bicycle *clips!* isn't that wild and strange? Antimacassars. Do you know them? Never mind. Once a man asked me to remember just the dashboard dials on a Cadillac. I remembered. I told him in detail. He listened. He cried great tears down his face. Happy tears? or sad? I can't say. I only remember. Not literature, no, I never had a head for plays or poems, they slip away, they die. All I am, really, is a trash-heap of the mediocre, the third-best hand-me-down useless and chromed-over slush and junk of a racetrack civilization that ran 'last' over a precipice. So all I offer really is scintillant junk, the clamored-after chronometers and absurd machineries of a never-ending river of robots and robot-mad owners. Yet, one way or another, civilization *must* get back on the road. Those who can offer fine butterfly poetry, let them remember, let them offer. Those who can weave and build butterfly *nets*, let them weave, let them build. My gift is smaller than both, and perhaps, contemptible in the long hoist, climb, jump toward the old and amiably silly peak. But I *must* dream myself worthy. For the things, silly or not, that people remember are the things they will search for again. I will, then, ulcerate their half-dead desires with vinegar-gnat memory. Then perhaps they'll rattle bang the Big Clock together again, which is the city, the state, and then the World. Let one man want wine, another lounge chairs, a third a batwing glider to soar the March winds on and build bigger electro-pterodactyls to scour even greater winds, with even greater peoples. Someone wants moron Christmas trees and some wise man goes to cut them. Pack this all together, wheel in want, want in wheel, and I'm just there to oil them, but oil them I do. Ho, once I would have raved, 'only the best is best, only quality is true!' But roses grow from blood manure. Mediocre must be, so most-excellent can bloom. So I shall be the *best* mediocre there is and fight all who say slide under, sink back, dust-wallow, let brambles scurry over your living grave. I shall protest the roving apeman tribes, the sheep-people munching the far fields preyed on by the feudal land-baron wolves who rarefy themselves in the few skyscraper summits and horde unremembered foods. And these villains I will kill with canopener and corkscrew. I shall run them down with ghosts of Buick, Kissel-Kar, and Moon, thrash them with licorice whips until they cry for some sort of unqualified mercy. Can I *do* all this? One can only try."

The old man rummaged the last pea, with the last words, in his mouth, while his samaritan host simply looked at him with gently amazed eyes, and far off up through the house people moved, doors tapped open and shut, and there was a gathering outside the door of this apartment where now the husband said:

"And *you* asked why we didn't turn you in? Do you hear that out there?"

"It sounds like everyone in the apartment house—"

"Everyone. Old man, old fool, do you remember—motion picture houses, or better, drive-in movies?"

The old man smiled. "Do *you?*"

"Almost. Look, listen, today, now, if you're going to be a fool, if you want to run risks, do it in the aggregate, in one fell blow. Why waste your breath on one, or two, or even three if—"

The husband opened the door and nodded outside. Silently, one at a time, and in couples, the people of the house entered. Entered this room as if entering a synagogue or church or the kind of church known as a movie or the kind of movie known as a drive-in, and the hour was growing late in the day, with the sun going down the sky, and soon in the early evening hours, in the dark, the room would be dim and in the one light the voice of the old man would speak and these would listen and hold hands and it would be like the old days with the balconies and the dark, or the cars and the dark, and just the memory, the words, of popcorn, and the words for the gum and the sweet drinks and candy, but the words, anyway, the words...

And while the people were coming in and settling on the floor, and the old man watched them, incredulous that he had summoned them here without knowing, the husband said:

"Isn't this better than taking a chance in the open?"

"Yes. Strange. I hate pain. I hate being hit and chased. But my tongue moves. I must hear what it has to say. But this is better."

"Good." The husband pressed a red ticket into his palm. "When this is all over, an hour from now, here is a ticket from a friend of mine in Transportation. One train crosses the country each week. Each week I get a ticket for some idiot I want to help. This week, it's you."

The old man read the destination on the folded red paper:

"*CHICAGO ABYSS*," and added, "Is the Abyss still there?"

"This time next year Lake Michigan may break through the last crust and make a new lake in the pit where the city once was.

There's life of sorts around the crater rim, and a branch train goes west once a month. Once you leave here, keep moving, forget you met or know us. I'll give you a small list of people like ourselves. A long time from now, look them up, out in the wilderness. But, for God's sake, in the open, alone, for a year, declare a moratorium. Keep your wonderful mouth shut. And here—" The husband gave him a yellow card. "A dentist I know. Tell him to make a new set of teeth that will only open at meal times."

A few people, hearing, laughed, and the old man laughed quietly and the people were in now, dozens of them, and the day was late, and the husband and wife shut the door and stood by it and turned and waited for this last special time when the old man might open his mouth.

The old man stood up.

His audience grew very still.

The train came, rusty and loud at midnight, into a suddenly snow-filled station. Under a cruel dusting of white, the ill-washed people crowded into and through the ancient chair cars mashing the old man along the corridor and into an empty compartment that had once been a lavatory. Soon the floor was a solid mass of bedroll on which sixteen people twisted and turned in darkness, fighting their way into sleep.

The train rushed forth to white emptiness.

The old man thinking: "quiet, shut up, no, don't speak, nothing, no, stay still, think! careful! cease!" found himself now swayed, joggled, hurled this way and that as he half-crouched against a wall. He and just one other were upright in this monster room of dreadful sleep. A few feet away, similarly shoved against the wall, sat an eight-year-old boy with a drawn sick paleness escaping from his cheeks. Full awake, eyes bright, he seemed to watch, he *did* watch, the old man's mouth. The boy gazed because he must. The train hooted, roared, swayed, yelled, and ran.

Half an hour passed in a thunderous grinding passage by night under the snow-hidden moon, and the old man's mouth was tight-nailed shut. Another hour, and still boned shut. Another hour, and the muscles around his cheeks began to slacken. Another, and his lips parted to wet themselves. The boy stayed awake. The boy saw.

The boy waited. Immense sifts of silence came down the night air outside, tunneled by avalanche train. The travelers, very deep in invoiced terror, numbed by flight, slept each separate, but the boy did not take his eyes away and at last the old man leaned forward, softly.

"Sh. Boy. Your name?"

"Joseph."

The train swayed and groaned in its sleep, a monster floundering through timeless dark toward a morn that could not be imagined.

"Joseph..." The old man savored the word, bent forward, his eyes gentle and shining. His face filled with pale beauty. His eyes widened until they seemed blind. He gazed at a distant and hidden thing. He cleared his throat ever so softly. "Ah..."

The train roared round a curve. The people rocked in their snowing sleep.

"Well, Joseph," whispered the old man. He lifted his fingers softly in the air. "Once upon a time..."

16

Nobody here is poor in spirit.

Nor is Buddhist detachment a virtue of the man Carlson in the next story. He too is a compulsive flasher, but his photophiliac tendencies apparently do not lead him to molest strangers in a strange city obviously depopulated by some weapon other than a hydrogen warhead. When this story appeared, people were talking a lot about neutron bombs, which kill without demolishing much property, but I suppose cobra-venom influenza could do the job as well.

LUCIFER
by Roger Zelazny

Carlson stood on the hill in the silent center of the city whose people had died.

He stared up at the Building—the one structure that dwarfed every hotel-grid, skyscraper-needle, or apartment-cheesebox packed into all the miles that lay about him. Tall as a mountain, it caught the rays of the bloody sun. Somehow it turned their red into golden halfway up its height.

Carlson suddenly felt that he should not have come back.

272

It had been over two years, as he figured it, since last he had been here. He wanted to return to the mountains now. One look was enough. Yet still he stood before it, transfixed by the huge Building, by the long shadow that bridged the entire valley. He shrugged his thick shoulders then, in an unsuccessful attempt to shake off memories of the days, five (or was it six?) years ago, when he had worked within the giant unit.

Then he climbed the rest of the way up the hill and entered the high, wide doorway.

His fiber sandals cast a variety of echoes as he passed through the deserted offices and into the long hallway that led to the belts.

The belts, of course, were still. There were no thousands riding them. There was no one alive to ride. Their deep belly-rumble was only a noisy phantom in his mind as he climbed onto the one nearest him and walked ahead into the pitchy insides of the place.

It was like a mausoleum. There seemed no ceiling, no walls, only the soft *pat-pat* of his soles on the flexible fabric of the belt.

He reached a junction and mounted a cross-belt, instinctively standing still for a moment and waiting for the forward lurch as it sensed his weight.

Then he chuckled silently and began walking again.

When he reached the lift, he set off to the right of it until his memory led him to the maintenance stairs. Shouldering his bundle, he began the long, groping ascent.

He blinked at the light when he came into the Power Room. Filtered through its hundred high windows, the sunlight trickled across the dusty acres of machinery.

Carlson sagged against the wall, breathing heavily from the climb. After a while he wiped a workbench clean and set down his parcel.

Then he removed his faded shirt, for the place would soon be stifling. He brushed his hair from his eyes and advanced down the narrow metal stair to where the generators stood, row on row, like an army of dead, black beetles. It took him six hours to give them all a cursory check.

He selected three in the second row and systematically began tearing them down, cleaning them, soldering their loose connections with the auto-iron, greasing them, oiling them and sweeping away all the dust, cobwebs, and pieces of cracked insulation that lay at their bases.

Great rivulets of perspiration ran into his eyes and down along his sides and thighs, spilling in little droplets onto the hot flooring and vanishing quickly.

Finally, he put down his broom, remounted the stair and returned to his parcel. He removed one of the water bottles and drank off half its contents. He ate a piece of dried meat and finished the bottle. He allowed himself one cigarette then, and returned to work.

He was forced to stop when it grew dark. He had planned on sleeping right there, but the room was too oppressive. So he departed the way he had come and slept beneath the stars, on the roof of a low building at the foot of the hill.

It took him two more days to get the generators ready. Then he began work on the huge Broadcast Panel. It was in better condition than the generators, because it had last been used two years ago. Whereas the generators, save for the three he had burned out last time, had slept for over five (or was it six?) years.

He soldered and wiped and inspected until he was satisfied. Then only one task remained.

All the maintenance robots stood frozen in mid-gesture. Carlson would have to wrestle a three-hundred-pound power cube without assistance. If he could get one down from the rack and onto a cart without breaking a wrist he would probably be able to convey it to the Igniter without much difficulty. Then he would have to place it within the oven. He had almost ruptured himself when he did it two years ago, but he hoped that he was somewhat stronger—and luckier—this time.

It took him ten minutes to clean the Igniter oven. Then he located a cart and pushed it back to the rack.

One cube was resting at just the right height, approximately eight inches above the level of the cart's bed. He kicked down the anchor chocks and moved around to study the rack. The cube lay on a downward-slanting shelf, restrained by a two-inch metal guard. He pushed at the guard. It was bolted to the shelf.

Returning to the work area, he searched the tool boxes for a wrench. Then he moved back to the rack and set to work on the nuts.

The guard came loose as he was working on the fourth nut. He heard a dangerous creak and threw himself back out of the way, dropping the wrench on his toes.

The cube slid forward, crushed the loosened rail, teetered a bare moment, then dropped with a resounding crash onto the heavy bed of the cart. The bed surface bent and began to crease beneath its weight; the cart swayed toward the outside. The cube continued to slide until over half a foot projected beyond the edge. Then the cart righted itself and shivered into steadiness.

Carlson sighed and kicked loose the chocks, ready to jump back should it suddenly give way in his direction. It held.

Gingerly, he guided it up the aisle and between the rows of generators, until he stood before the Igniter. He anchored the cart again, stopped for water and a cigarette, then searched up a pinch bar, a small jack and a long, flat metal plate.

He laid the plate to bridge the front end of the cart and the opening to the oven. He wedged the far end in beneath the Igniter's doorframe.

Unlocking the rear chocks, he inserted the jack and began to raise the back end of the wagon, slowly, working with one hand and holding the bar ready in the other.

The cart groaned as it moved higher. Then a sliding, grating sound began and he raised it faster.

With a sound like the stroke of a cracked bell the cube tumbled onto the bridgeway; it slid forward and to the left. He struck at it with the bar, bearing to the right with all his strength. About half an inch of it caught against the left edge of the oven frame. The gap between the cube and the frame was widest at the bottom.

He inserted the bar and heaved his weight against it—three times.

Then it moved forward and came to rest within the Igniter.

He began to laugh. He laughed until he felt weak. He sat on the broken cart, swinging his legs and chuckling to himself, until the sounds coming from his throat seemed alien and out of place. He stopped abruptly and slammed the door.

The Broadcast Panel had a thousand eyes, but none of them winked back at him. He made the final adjustments for Transmit, then gave the generators their last checkout.

After that, he mounted a catwalk and moved to a window.

There was still some daylight to spend, so he moved from window to window pressing the "Open" button set below each sill.

* * *

He ate the rest of his food then, and drank a whole bottle of water and smoked two cigarettes. Sitting on the stair, he thought of the days when he had worked with Kelly and Murchison and Djizinsky, twisting the tails of electrons until they wailed and leapt out over the walls and fled down into the city.

The clock! He remembered it suddenly—set high on the wall, to the left of the doorway, frozen at 9:33 (and forty-eight seconds).

He moved a ladder through the twilight and mounted it to the clock. He wiped the dust from its greasy face with a sweeping, circular movement. Then he was ready.

He crossed to the Igniter and turned it on. Somewhere the ever-batteries came alive, and he heard a click as a thin, sharp shaft was driven into the wall of the cube. He raced back up the stairs and sped hand-over-hand up to the catwalk. He moved to a window and waited.

"God," he murmured, "don't let them blow! Please don't—"

Across an eternity of darkness the generators began humming. He heard a crackle of static from the Broadcast Panel and he closed his eyes. The sound died.

He opened his eyes as he heard the window slide upward. All around him the hundred high windows opened. A small light came on above the bench in the work area below him, but he did not see it.

He was staring out beyond the wide drop of the acropolis and down into the city. His city.

The lights were not like the stars. They beat the stars all to hell. They were the gay, regularized constellation of a city where men made their homes: even rows of streetlamps, advertisements, lighted windows in the cheesebox-apartments, a random solitaire of bright squares running up the sides of skyscraper-needles, a searchlight swiveling its luminous antenna through cloudbanks that hung over the city.

He dashed to another window, feeling the high night breezes comb at his beard. Belts were humming below; he heard their wry monologues rattling through the city's deepest canyons. He pictured the people in their homes, in theaters, in bars—talking to each other, sharing a common amusement, playing clarinets, holding hands, eating an evening snack. Sleeping ro-cars awakened and rushed past each other on the levels above the belts; the background hum of the city told him its story of production, of function, of movement and service to its inhabitants. The sky seemed to wheel overhead, as though the city were its turning hub and the universe its outer rim.

Then the lights dimmed from white to yellow and he hurried, with desperate steps, to another window.

"No! Not so soon! Don't leave me yet!" he sobbed.

The windows closed themselves and the lights went out. He stood on the walk for a long time, staring at the dead embers. A smell of ozone reached his nostrils. He was aware of a blue halo about the dying generators.

He descended and crossed the work area to the ladder he had set against the wall.

Pressing his face against the glass and squinting for a long time he could make out the position of the hands.

"Nine thirty-five, and twenty-one seconds," Carlson read.

"Do you hear that?" he called out, shaking his fist at anything. "Ninety-three seconds! I made you live for ninety-three seconds!"

Then he covered his face against the darkness and was silent.

After a long while he descended the stairway, walked the belt, and moved through the long hallway and out of the Building. As he headed back toward the mountains he promised himself—again— that he would never return.

17 _____

Humor in post-Megawar fiction is usually irony. In "Eastward Ho!"
William Tenn assumes, as did Ballard, that the Megawar has been a
Mini, with a lot of survivors. And yet conditions are not yet politically
settled in this land of the brave. A lost tribe of Israel is returning to its
former lands, and the White Man finds himself in need of a Caucasian
Marcus Garvey. Theme music from *Exodus* here, please.

EASTWARD HO!
by William Tenn

The New Jersey Turnpike had been hard on the horses. South of
New Brunswick the potholes had been so deep, the scattered boulders so plentiful, that the two men had been forced to move at a
slow trot, to avoid crippling their three precious animals. And, of
course, this far south, farms were nonexistent: they had been able
to eat nothing but the dried provisions in the saddlebags, and last
night they had slept in a roadside service station, suspending their
hammocks between the tilted, rusty gas pumps.

But it was still the best, the most direct route, Jerry Franklin
knew. The Turnpike was a government road: its rubble was cleared

278

semiannually. They had made excellent time and come through without even developing a limp in the pack horse. As they swung out on the last lap, past the riven tree stump with the words TRENTON EXIT carved on its side, Jerry relaxed a bit. His father, his father's colleagues, would be proud of him. And he was proud of himself.

But the next moment, he was alert again. He roweled his horse, moved up alongside his companion, a young man of his own age.

"Protocol," he reminded. "I'm the leader here. You know better than to ride ahead of me this close to Trenton."

He hated to pull rank. But facts were facts, and if a subordinate got above himself he was asking to be set down. After all, he was the son—and the oldest son, at that—of the Senator from Idaho; Sam Rutherford's father was a mere Undersecretary of State and Sam's mother's family was pure post office clerk all the way back.

Sam nodded apologetically and reined his horse back the proper couple of feet. "Thought I saw something odd," he explained. "Looked like an advance party on the side of the road—and I could have sworn they were wearing buffalo robes."

"Seminole don't wear buffalo robes, Sammy. Don't you remember your sophomore political science?"

"I never had any political science, Mr. Franklin: I was an engineering major. Digging around in ruins has always been my dish. But, from the little I know, I didn't *think* buffalo robes went with the Seminole. That's why I was—"

"Concentrate on the pack horse," Jerry advised. "Negotiations are my job."

As he said this, he was unable to refrain from touching the pouch upon his breast with rippling fingertips. Inside it was his commission, carefully typed on one of the last precious sheets of official government stationery (and it was not one whit less official because the reverse side had been used years ago as a scribbled interoffice memo) and signed by the President himself. In ink!

The existence of such documents was important to a man in later life. He would have to hand it over, in all probability, during the conferences, but the commission to which it attested would be on file in the capital up north. And, when his father died, and he took over one of the two hallowed Idaho seats, it would give him enough stature to make an attempt at membership on the Appropriations

Committee. Or, for that matter, why not go the whole hog—the Rules Committee itself? No Senator Franklin had ever been a member of the Rules Committee....

The two envoys knew they were on the outskirts of Trenton when they passed the first gangs of Jerseyites working to clear the road. Frightened faces glanced at them briefly, and quickly bent again to work. The gangs were working without any visible supervision. Evidently the Seminole felt that simple instructions were sufficient.

But as they rode into the blocks of neat ruins that were the city proper and still came across nobody more important than white men, another explanation began to occur to Jerry Franklin. This all had the look of a town still at war, but where were the combatants? Almost certainly on the other side of Trenton, defending the Delaware River—that was the direction from which the new rulers of Trenton might fear attack—not from the north where there was only the United States of America.

But if that were so, who in the world could they be defending against? Across the Delaware to the south there was nothing but more Seminole. Was it possible—was it possible that the Seminole had at last fallen to fighting among themselves?

Or was it possible that Sam Rutherford had been right? Fantastic. Buffalo robes in Trenton! There should be no buffalo robes closer than a hundred miles westward, in Harrisburg.

But when they turned onto State Street, Jerry bit his lip in chagrin. Sam had seen correctly, which made him one up.

Scattered over the wide lawn of the gutted state capitol were dozens of wigwams. And the tall, dark men who sat impassively, or strode proudly among the wigwams, all wore buffalo robes. There was no need even to associate the paint on their faces with a remembered lecture in political science: these were Sioux.

So the information that had come drifting up to the government about the identity of the invader was totally inaccurate—as usual. Well, you couldn't expect communication miracles over this long a distance. But that inaccuracy made things difficult. It might invalidate his commission for one thing: his commission was addressed directly to Osceola VII, Ruler of All the Seminoles. And if Sam Rutherford thought this gave him a right to preen himself—

He looked back dangerously. No, Sam would give no trouble. Sam knew better than to dare an I-told-you-so. At his leader's look, the son of the Undersecretary of State dropped his eyes ground-wards to immediate humility.

Satisfied, Jerry searched his memory for relevant data on recent political relationships with the Sioux. He couldn't recall much— just the provisions of the last two or three treaties. It would have to do.

He drew up before an important-looking warrior and carefully dismounted. You might get away with talking to a Seminole while mounted, but not the Sioux. The Sioux were very tender on matters of protocol with white men.

"We come in peace," he said to the warrior standing as impassively straight as the spear he held, as stiff and hard as the rifle on his back. "We come with a message of importance and many gifts to your chief. We come from New York, the home of our chief." He thought a moment, then added: "You know, the Great White Father?"

Immediately, he was sorry for the addition. The warrior chuckled briefly; his eyes lit up with a lightning-stroke of mirth. Then his face was expressionless again, and serenely dignified as befitted a man who had counted coup many times.

"Yes," he said. "I have heard of him. Who has not heard of the wealth and power and far dominions of the Great White Father? Come. I will take you to our chief. Walk behind me, white man."

Jerry motioned Sam Rutherford to wait.

At the entrance to a large, expensively decorated tent, the Indian stood aside and casually indicated that Jerry should enter.

It was dim inside, but the illumination was rich enough to take Jerry's breath away. Oil lamps! Three of them! These people lived well.

A century ago, before the whole world had gone smash in the last big war, his people had owned plenty of oil lamps themselves. Better than oil lamps, perhaps, if one could believe the stories the engineers told around the evening fires. Such stories were pleasant to hear, but they were glories of the distant past. Like the stories of overflowing granaries and chock-full supermarkets, they made you proud of the history of your people, but they did nothing for you now. They made your mouth water, but they didn't feed you.

The Indians whose tribal organization had been the first to adjust to the new conditions, in the all-important present, the Indians had the granaries, the Indians had the oil lamps. And the Indians...

There were two nervous white men serving food to the group squatting on the floor. An old man, the chief, with a carved, chunky body. Three warriors, one of them surprisingly young for council. And a middle-aged Negro, wearing the same bound-on rags as Franklin, except that they looked a little newer, a little cleaner.

Jerry bowed low before the chief, spreading his arms apart, palms down.

"I come from New York, from our chief," he mumbled. In spite of himself, he was more than a little frightened. He wished he knew their names so that he could relate them to specific events. Although he knew what their names would be like—approximately. The Sioux, the Seminole, all the Indian tribes renaissant in power and numbers, all bore names garlanded with anachronism. That queer mixture of several levels of the past, overlaid always with the cocky, expanding present. Like the rifles *and* the spears, one for the reality of fighting, the other for the symbol that was more important than reality. Like the use of wigwams on campaign, when, according to the rumors that drifted smokily across country, their slave artisans could now build the meanest Indian noble a damp-free, draftproof dwelling such as the President of the United States, lying on his special straw pallet, did not dream about. Like paint-spattered faces peering through newly reinvented, crude microscopes. What had microscopes been like? Jerry tried to remember the Engineering Survey Course he'd taken in his freshman year—and drew a blank. All the same, the Indians were so queer, *and* so awesome. Sometimes you thought that destiny had meant them to be conquerors, with a conqueror's careless inconsistency. Sometimes...

He noticed that they were waiting for him to continue. "From our chief," he repeated hurriedly. "I come with a message of importance and many gifts."

"Eat with us," the old man said. "Then you will give us your gifts and your message."

Gratefully, Jerry squatted on the ground a short distance from them. He was hungry, and among the fruit in the bowls he had seen something that must be an orange. He had heard so many arguments about what oranges tasted like!

After a while, the old man said, "I am Chief Three Hydrogen Bombs. This"—pointing to the young man—"is my son, Makes

Much Radiation. And this"—pointing to the middle-aged Negro—
"is a sort of compatriot of yours."

At Jerry's questioning look, and the chief's raised finger of permission, the Negro explained. "Sylvester Thomas. Ambassador to
the Sioux from the Confederate States of America."

"The Confederacy? She's still alive? We heard ten years ago—"

"The Confederacy is very much alive, sir. The Western Confederacy, that is, with its capital at Jackson, Mississippi. The Eastern
Confederacy, the one centered at Richmond, Virginia, did go down
under the Seminole. We have been more fortunate. The Arapahoe,
the Cheyenne, and"—with a nod to the chief—"especially the Sioux,
if I may say so, sir, have been very kind to us. They allow us to live
in peace, so long as we till the soil quietly and pay our tithes."

"Then would you know, Mr. Thomas—" Jerry began eagerly. "That
is...the Lone Star Republic—Texas—Is it possible that Texas,
too...?"

Mr. Thomas looked at the door of the wigwam unhappily. "Alas,
my good sir, the Republic of the Lone Star Flag fell before the
Kiowa and the Comanche long years ago when I was still a small
boy. I don't remember the exact date, but I do know it was before
even the last of California was annexed by the Apache and the
Navajo, and well before the nation of the Mormons under the august
leadership of—"

Makes Much Radiation shifted his shoulders back and forth and
flexed his arm muscles. "All this talk," he growled. "Paleface talk.
Makes me tired."

"Mr. Thomas is not a paleface," his father told him sharply. "Show
respect! He's our guest and an accredited ambassador—you're not
to use a word like paleface in his presence!"

One of the other, older warriors near the child spoke up. "In
ancient days, in the days of the heroes, a boy of Makes Much
Radiation's age would not dare raise his voice in council before
his father. Certainly not to say the things he just has. I cite as refer-
ence, for those interested, Robert Lowie's definitive volume, *The
Crow Indians*, and Lesser's fine piece of anthropological insight,
Three Types of Siouan Kinship. Now, whereas we have not yet
been able to reconstruct a Siouan kinship pattern on the classic
model described by Lesser, we have developed a working arrangement that—"

"The trouble with you, Bright Book Jacket," the warrior on his left broke in, "is that you're too much of a classicist. You're always trying to live in the Golden Age instead of the present, and a Golden Age that really has little to do with the Sioux. Oh, I'll admit that we're as much Dakotan as the Crow, from the linguist's point of view at any rate, and that, superficially, what applies to the Crow should apply to us. But what happens when we quote Lowie in so many words and try to bring his precepts into daily life?"

"Enough," the chief announced. "Enough, Hangs A Tale. And you, too, Bright Book Jacket—enough, enough! These are private tribal matters. Though they do serve to remind us that the paleface was once great before he became sick and corrupt and frightened. These men whose holy books teach us the lost art of being real Sioux, men like Lesser, men like Robert H. Lowie, were not these men palefaces? And in memory of them should we not show tolerance?"

"A-ah!" said Makes Much Radiation impatiently. "As far as I'm concerned, the only good paleface is a dead paleface. And that's that." He thought a bit. "Except their women. Paleface women are fun when you're a long way from home and feel like raising a little hell."

Chief Three Hydrogen Bombs glared his son into silence. Then he turned to Jerry Franklin. "Your message and your gifts. First your message."

"No, Chief," Bright Book Jacket told him respectfully but definitely. "First the gifts. *Then* the message. That's the way it was done."

"I'll have to get them. Be right back." Jerry walked out of the tent backwards and ran to where Sam Rutherford had tethered the horses. "The presents," he said urgently. "The presents for the chief."

The two of them tore at the pack straps. With his arms loaded, Jerry returned through the warriors who had assembled to watch their activity with quiet arrogance. He entered the tent, set the gifts on the ground and bowed low again.

"Bright beads for the chief," he said, handing over two star sapphires and a large white diamond, the best that the engineers had evacuated from the ruins of New York in the past ten years.

"Cloth for the chief," he said, handing over a bolt of linen and a bolt of wool, spun and loomed in New Hampshire especially for this occasion and painfully, expensively carted to New York.

"Pretty toys for the chief," he said, handing over a large, only slightly rusty alarm clock and a precious typewriter, both of them put in operating order by batteries of engineers and artisans working in tandem (the engineers interpreting the brittle old documents to the artisans) for two and a half months.

"Weapons for the chief," he said, handing over a beautifully decorated cavalry saber, the prized hereditary possession of the Chief of Staff of the United States Air Force, who had protested its requisitioning most bitterly ("Damn it all, Mr. President, do you expect me to fight these Indians with my bare hands?" "No, I don't, Johnny, but I'm sure you can pick up one just as good from one of your eager junior officers").

Three Hydrogen Bombs examined the gifts, particularly the typewriter, with some interest. Then he solemnly distributed them among the members of his council, keeping only the typewriter and one of the sapphires for himself. The sword he gave to his son.

Makes Much Radiation tapped the steel with his fingernail. "Not so much," he stated. "*Not-so-much*. Mr. Thomas came up with better stuff than this from the Confederate States of America for my sister's puberty ceremony." He tossed the saber negligently to the ground. "But what can you expect from a bunch of lazy, good-for-nothing whiteskin stinkards?"

When he heard the last word, Jerry Franklin went rigid. That meant he'd have to fight Makes Much Radiation—and the prospect scared him right down to the wet hairs on his legs. The alternative was losing face completely among the Sioux.

"Stinkard" was a term from the Natchez system and was applied these days indiscriminately to all white men bound to field or factory under their aristocratic Indian overlords. A "stinkard" was something lower than a serf, whose one value was that his toil gave his masters the leisure to engage in the activities of full manhood: hunting, fighting, thinking.

If you let someone call you a stinkard and didn't kill him, why, then you *were* a stinkard—and that was all there was to it.

"I am an accredited representative of the United States of America," Jerry said slowly and distinctly, "and the oldest son of the Senator from Idaho. When my father dies, I will sit in the Senate in his place. I am a free-born man, high in the councils of my nation, and anyone who calls me a stinkard is a rotten, no-good, foul-mouthed liar!"

There—it was done. He waited as Makes Much Radiation rose to his feet. He noted with dismay the well-fed, well-muscled sleekness of the young warrior. He wouldn't have a chance against him. Not in hand-to-hand combat—which was the way it would be.

Makes Much Radiation picked up the sword and pointed it at Jerry Franklin. "I could chop you in half right now like a fat onion," he observed. "Or I could go into a ring with you knife to knife and cut your belly open. I've fought and killed Seminole, I've fought Apache, I've even fought and killed Comanche. But I've never dirtied my hands with paleface blood, and I don't intend to start now. I leave such simple butchery to the overseers of our estates. Father, I'll be outside until the lodge is clean again." Then he threw the sword ringingly at Jerry's feet and walked out.

Just before he left, he stopped, and remarked over his shoulder: "The oldest son of the Senator from Idaho! Idaho has been part of the estates of my mother's family for the past forty-five years! When will these romantic children stop playing games and start living in the world as it is now?"

"My son," the old chief murmured. "Younger generation. A bit wild. Highly intolerant. But he means well. Really does. Means well."

He signaled to the white serfs who brought over a large chest covered with great splashes of color.

While the chief rummaged in the chest, Jerry Franklin relaxed inch by inch. It was almost too good to be true: he wouldn't have to fight Makes Much Radiation, and he hadn't lost face. All things considered, the whole business had turned out very well indeed.

And as for the last comment—well, why expect an Indian to understand about things like tradition and the glory that could reside forever in a symbol? When his father stood up under the cracked roof of Madison Square Garden and roared across to the Vice-President of the United States: "The people of the sovereign state of Idaho will never in all conscience consent to a tax on potatoes. From time immemorial, potatoes have been associated with Idaho, potatoes have been the pride of Idaho. The people of Boise say *no* to a tax on potatoes, the people of Pocatello say *no* to a tax on potatoes, the very rolling farmlands of the Gem of the Mountain say *no, never,* a thousand times *no,* to a tax on potatoes!"—when his father spoke like that, he *was* speaking for the people of Boise and Pocatello. Not the crushed Boise or desolate Pocatello of today, true, but the magnificent cities as they had been of yore...and the rich farms on either side of the Snake River....And Sun Valley, Moscow, Idaho Falls, American Falls, Weiser, Grangeville, Twin Falls....

"We did not expect you, so we have not many gifts to offer in return," Three Hydrogen Bombs was explaining. "However, there is this one small thing. For you."

Jerry gasped as he took it. It was a pistol, a real, brand-new pistol! And a small box of cartridges. Made in one of the Sioux slave workshops of the Middle West that he had heard about. But to hold it in his hand, and to know that it belonged to him!

It was a Crazy Horse .45, and, according to all reports, far superior to the Apache weapon that had so long dominated the West, the Geronimo .32. This was a weapon a General of the Armies, a President of the United States, might never hope to own—and it was his!

"I don't know how—Really, I—I—"

"That's all right," the chief told him genially. "Really it is. My son would not approve of giving firearms to palefaces, but I feel that palefaces are like other people—it's the individual that counts. You look like a responsible man for a paleface: I'm sure you'll use the pistol wisely. Now your message."

Jerry collected his faculties and opened the pouch that hung from his neck. Reverently, he extracted the precious document and presented it to the chief.

Three Hydrogen Bombs read it quickly and passed it to his warriors. The last one to get it, Bright Book Jacket, wadded it up into a ball and tossed it back at the white man.

"Bad penmanship," he said. "And 'receive' is spelled three different ways. The rule is: 'i before e, except after c.' But what does it have to do with us? It's addressed to the Seminole chief, Osceola VII, requesting him to order his warriors back to the southern bank of the Delaware River, or to return the hostage given him by the Government of the United States as an earnest of good will and peaceful intentions. We're not Seminole: why show it to us?"

As Jerry Franklin smoothed out the wrinkles in the paper with painful care and replaced the document in his pouch, the Confederate Ambassador, Sylvester Thomas, spoke up. "I think I might explain," he suggested, glancing inquiringly from face to face. "If you gentlemen don't mind...? It is obvious that the United States Government has heard that an Indian tribe finally crossed the Delaware at this point, and assumed it was the Seminole. The last movement of the Seminole, you will recall, was to Philadelphia, forcing the evacuation of the capital once more and its transfer to New York City. It was a natural mistake: the communications of the American States, whether Confederate or United"—a small, coughing, diplomatic laugh here—"have not been as good as might have been expected in recent years. It is quite evident that neither this young man nor the government he represents so ably and so well, had any idea that the Sioux had decided to steal a march on his majesty, Osceola VII, and cross the Delaware at Lambertville."

"That's right," Jerry broke in eagerly. "That's exactly right. And now, as the accredited emissary of the President of the United States, it is my duty formally to request that the Sioux nation honor the treaty of eleven years ago as well as the treaty of fifteen—I *think* it was fifteen—years ago, and retire once more behind the banks of the Susquehanna River. I must remind you that when we retired from Pittsburgh, Altoona, and Johnstown, you swore that the Sioux would take no more land from us and would protect us in the little we had left. I am certain that the Sioux want to be known as a nation that keeps its promises."

Three Hydrogen Bombs glanced questioningly at the faces of Bright Book Jacket and Hangs A Tale. Then he leaned forward and placed his elbows on his crossed legs. "You speak well, young man," he commented. "You are a credit to your chief.... Now, then. Of course the Sioux want to be known as a nation that honors its treaties and keeps its promises. And so forth and so forth. But we have an expanding population. You don't have an expanding population. We need more land. You don't use most of the land you have. Should we sit by and see the land go to waste—worse yet, should we see it acquired by the Seminole who already rule a domain stretching from Philadelphia to Key West? Be reasonable. You can retire to—to other places. You have most of New England left and a large part of New York State. Surely you can afford to give up New Jersey."

In spite of himself, in spite of his ambassadorial position, Jerry

Franklin began yelling. All of a sudden it was too much. It was one thing to shrug your shoulders unhappily back home in the blunted ruins of New York, but here on the spot where the process was actually taking place—no, it was too much.

"What else can we afford to give up? Where else can we retire to? There's nothing left of the United States of America but a handful of square miles, and still we're supposed to move back! In the time of my forefathers, we were a great nation, we stretched from ocean to ocean, so say the legends of my people, and now we are huddled in a miserable corner of our land, starving, filthy, sick, dying, and ashamed. In the North, we are oppressed by the Ojibway and the Cree, we are pushed southward relentlessly by the Montaignais; in the South, the Seminole climb up our land yard by yard; and in the West, the Sioux take a piece more of New Jersey, and the Cheyenne come up and nibble yet another slice out of Elmira and Buffalo. When will it stop—where are we to go?"

The old man shifted uncomfortably at the agony in his voice. "It *is* hard; mind you, I don't deny that it *is* hard. But facts are facts, and weaker peoples always go to the wall. . . . Now, as to the rest of your mission. If we don't retire as you request, you're supposed to ask for the return of your hostage. Sounds reasonable to me. You ought to get something out of it. However, I can't for the life of me remember a hostage. Do we have a hostage from you people?"

His head hanging, his body exhausted, Jerry muttered in misery, "Yes. All the Indian nations on our borders have hostages. As earnests of our good will and peaceful intentions."

Bright Book Jacket snapped his fingers. "That girl. Sarah Cameron—Canton—what's-her-name."

Jerry looked up. "Calvin?" he asked. "Could it be *Calvin?* Sarah Calvin? The Daughter of the Chief Justice of the United States Supreme Court?"

"Sarah Calvin. That's the one. Been with us for five, six years. You remember, chief? The girl your son's been playing around with?"

Three Hydrogen Bombs looked amazed. "Is *she* the hostage? I thought she was some paleface female he had imported from his plantations in southern Ohio. Well, well, well. Makes Much Radiation is just a chip off the old block, no doubt about it." He became suddenly serious. "But that girl will never go back. She rather goes for Indian loving. Goes for it all the way. And she has the idea that my son will eventually marry her. Or some such."

He looked Jerry Franklin over. "Tell you what, my boy. Why don't you wait outside while we talk this over? And take the saber. Take it back with you. My son doesn't seem to want it."

Jerry wearily picked up the saber and trudged out of the wigwam.

Dully, uninterestedly, he noticed the band of Sioux warriors around Sam Rutherford and his horses. Then the group parted for a moment, and he saw Sam with a bottle in his hand. Tequila! The damned fool had let the Indians give him tequila—he was drunk as a pig.

Didn't he know that white men couldn't drink, didn't dare drink? With every inch of their unthreatened arable land under cultivation for foodstuffs, they were all still on the edge of starvation. There was absolutely no room in their economy for such luxuries as intoxicating beverages—and no white man in the usual course of a lifetime got close to so much as a glassful of the stuff. Give him a whole bottle of tequila and he was a stinking mess.

As Sam was now. He staggered back and forth in dipping semicircles, holding the bottle by its neck and waving it idiotically. The Sioux chuckled, dug each other in the ribs and pointed. Sam vomited loosely down the rags upon his chest and belly, tried to take one more drink, and fell over backwards. The bottle continued to pour over his face until it was empty. He was snoring loudly. The Sioux shook their heads, made grimaces of distaste, and walked away.

Jerry looked on and nursed the pain in his heart. Where could they go? What could they do? And what difference did it make? Might as well be as drunk as Sammy there. At least you wouldn't be able to feel.

He looked at the saber in one hand, the bright new pistol in the other. Logically, he should throw them away. Wasn't it ridiculous when you came right down to it, wasn't it pathetic—a white man carrying weapons?

Sylvester Thomas came out of the tent. "Get your horses ready, my dear sir," he whispered. "Be prepared to ride as soon as I come back. Hurry!"

The young man slouched over to the horses and followed instructions—might as well do that as anything else. Ride where? Do what?

He lifted Sam Rutherford up and tied him upon his horse. Go back home? Back to the great, the powerful, the respected capital of what had once been the United States of America?

Thomas came back with a bound and gagged girl in his grasp. She wriggled madly. Her eyes crackled with anger and rebellion. She kept trying to kick the Confederate Ambassador.

She wore the rich robes of an Indian princess. Her hair was braided in the style currently fashionable among Sioux women. And her face had been stained carefully with some darkish dye.

Sarah Calvin. The daughter of the Chief Justice. They tied her to the pack horse.

"Chief Three Hydrogen Bombs," the Negro explained. "He feels his son plays around too much with paleface females. He wants this one out of the way. The boy has to settle down, prepare for the responsibilities of chieftainship. This may help. And listen, the old man likes you. He told me to tell you something."

"I'm grateful. I'm grateful for every favor, no matter how small, how humiliating."

Sylvester Thomas shook his head decisively. "Don't be bitter, young sir. If you want to go on living you have to be alert. And you can't be alert and bitter at the same time. The Chief wants you to know there's no point in your going home. He couldn't say it openly in council, but the reason the Sioux moved in on Trenton has nothing to do with the Seminole on the other side. It has to do with the Ojibway-Cree-Montaignais situation in the North. They've decided to take over the Eastern Seaboard—that includes what's left of your country. By this time, they're probably in Yonkers or the Bronx, somewhere inside New York City. In a matter of hours, your government will no longer be in existence. The Chief had advance word of this and felt it necessary for the Sioux to establish some sort of bridgehead on the coast before matters were permanently stabilized. By occupying New Jersey he is preventing an Ojibway–Seminole junction. But he likes you, as I said, and wants you warned against going home."

"Fine, but where *do* I go? Up a rain cloud? Down a well?"

"No," Thomas admitted without smiling. He hoisted Jerry up on his horse. "You might come back with me to the Confederacy—" He paused, and when Jerry's sullen expression did not change, he went on, "Well, then, may I suggest—and mind you, this is my advice, not the Chief's—head straight out to Asbury Park. It's not far away—you can make it in reasonable time if you ride hard. According to reports I've overheard, there should be units of the United States Navy there, the Tenth Fleet, to be exact."

"Tell me," Jerry asked, bending down. "Have you heard any other news? Anything about the rest of the world? How has it been with those people—the Russkies, the Sovietskis, whatever they were called—the ones the United States had so much to do with years and years ago?"

"According to several of the chief's councilors, the Soviet Russians were having a good deal of difficulty with people called Tatars. I *think* they were called Tatars. But, my good sir, you should be on your way."

Jerry leaned down further and grasped his hand. "Thanks," he said. "You've gone to a lot of trouble for me. I'm grateful."

"That's quite all right," said Mr. Thomas earnestly. "After all, by the rocket's red glare, and all that. We were a single nation once."

Jerry moved off, leading the other two horses. He set a fast pace, exercising the minimum of caution made necessary by the condition of the road. By the time they reached Route 33, Sam Rutherford, though not altogether sober or well, was able to sit in his saddle. They could then untie Sarah Calvin and ride with her between them.

She cursed and wept. "Filthy paleface! Foul, ugly, stinking whiteskins! I'm an Indian, can't you see I'm an Indian? My skin isn't white—it's brown, brown!"

They kept riding.

Asbury Park was a dismal clatter of rags and confusion and refugees. There were refugees from the north, from Perth Amboy, from as far as Newark. There were refugees from Princeton in the west, flying before the Sioux invasion. And from the south, from Atlantic City—even, unbelievably, from distant Camden—were still other refugees, with stories of a sudden Seminole attack, an attempt to flank the armies of Three Hydrogen Bombs.

The three horses were stared at enviously, even in their lathered, exhausted condition. They represented food to the hungry, the fastest transportation possible to the fearful. Jerry found the saber very useful. And the pistol was even better—it had only to be exhibited.

Few of these people had ever seen a pistol in action: they had a mighty, superstitious fear of firearms.

With this fact discovered, Jerry kept the pistol out nakedly in his right hand when he walked into the United States Naval Depot on the beach at Asbury Park. Sam Rutherford was at his side; Sarah Calvin walked sobbing behind.

He announced their family backgrounds to Admiral Milton Chester. The son of the Undersecretary of State. The daughter of the Chief Justice of the Supreme Court. The oldest son of the Senator from Idaho. "And now. Do you recognize the authority of this document?"

Admiral Chester read the wrinkled commission slowly, spelling out the harder words to himself. He twisted his head respectfully when he had finished, looking first at the seal of the United States on the paper before him, and then at the glittering pistol in Jerry's hand.

"Yes," he said at last. "I recognize its authority. Is that a real pistol?"

Jerry nodded. "A Crazy Horse .45. The latest. *How* do you recognize its authority?"

The admiral spread his hands. "Everything is confused out here. The latest word I've received is that there are Ojibway warriors in Manhattan—that there is no longer any United States Government. And yet this"—he bent over the document once more—"this is a commission by the President himself, appointing you full plenipotentiary. To the Seminole, of course. But full plenipotentiary. The last official appointment, to the best of my knowledge, of the President of the United States of America."

He reached forward and touched the pistol in Jerry Franklin's hand curiously and inquiringly. He nodded to himself, as if he'd come to a decision. He stood up, and saluted with a flourish.

"I hereby recognize you as the last legal authority of the United States Government. And I place my fleet at your disposal."

"Good." Jerry stuck the pistol in his belt. He pointed with the saber. "Do you have enough food and water for a long voyage?"

"No, sir," Admiral Chester said. "But that can be arranged in a few hours at most. May I escort you aboard, sir?"

He gestured proudly down the beach and past the surf to where the three forty-five-foot gaff-rigged schooners rode at anchor. "The United States Tenth Fleet, sir. Awaiting your orders."

Hours later when the three vessels were standing out to sea, the admiral came to the cramped main cabin where Jerry Franklin was resting. Sam Rutherford and Sarah Calvin were asleep in the bunks above.

"And the orders, sir...?"

Jerry Franklin walked out on the narrow deck, looked up at the taut, patched sails. "Sail east."

"East, sir? *Due* east?"

"Due east all the way. To the fabled lands of Europe. To a place where a white man can stand at last on his own two legs. Where he need not fear persecution. Where he need not fear slavery. Sail east, Admiral, until we discover a new and hopeful world—a world of freedom!"

18_____

The downfall of the White Man is a premise, not an outcome, of Michael Swanwick's "The Feast of Saint Janis." If the effects of a limited Megawar prove less devastating to the southern than the northern hemisphere, the centers of political and economic power will shift to the Third World, humanity's last hope. Swanwick's story has rich overtones. It's about so many things: music, freedom, feminism, politics, evil, suffering, sexuality, mob insanity, self-sacrifice and fascist exploitation, kindness, and the personality of a late, great singer. Listen to "The Full Tilt Boogie" (Pearl) before you read it if you don't remember Janis very well.

THE FEAST OF SAINT JANIS
by Michael Swanwick

> Take a load off, Janis,
> And
> You put the load right on me...
> —"The Wait" (trad.)

Wolf stood in the early morning fog watching the *Yankee Clipper* leave Baltimore harbor. His elbows rested against a cool, clammy wall, its surface eroded smooth by the passage of countless hands, almost certainly dating back to before the Collapse. A metallic gray sparkle atop the foremast drew his eye to the dish antenna that linked the ship with the geosynchronous *Trickster* seasats it relied on to plot winds and currents.

To many the wooden *Clipper*, with its computer-designed hydrofoils and hand-sewn sails, was a symbol of the New Africa. Wolf, however, watching it merge into sea and sky, knew only that it was going home without him.

He turned and walked back into the rick-a-rack of commercial buildings crowded against the waterfront. The clatter of hand-drawn carts mingled with a mélange of exotic cries and shouts, the alien music of a dozen American dialects. Workers, clad in coveralls most of them, swarmed about, grunting and cursing in exasperation when an iron wheel lurched in a muddy pothole. Yet there was something furtive and covert about them, as if they were hiding an ancient secret.

Craning to stare into the dark recesses of a warehouse, Wolf collided with a woman clad head to foot in chador. She flinched at his touch, her eyes glaring above the black veil, then whipped away. Not a word was exchanged.

A citizen of Baltimore in its glory days would not have recognized the city. Where the old buildings had not been torn down and buried, shanties crowded the streets, taking advantage of the space automobiles had needed. Sometimes they were built *over* the streets, so that alleys became tunnelways, and sometimes these collapsed, to the cries and consternation of the natives.

It was another day with nothing to do. He could don a filter mask and tour the Washington ruins, but he had already done that, and besides the day looked like it was going to be hot. It was unlikely he'd hear anything about his mission, not after months of waiting on American officials who didn't want to talk with him. Wolf decided to check back at his hostel for messages, then spend the day in the bazaars.

Children were playing in the street outside the hostel. They scattered at his approach. One, he noted, lagged behind the others, hampered by a malformed leg. He mounted the unpainted wooden steps, edging past an old man who sat at the bottom. The old man was laying down tarot cards with a slow and fatalistic disregard for what they said; he did not look up.

The bell over the door jangled notice of Wolf's entry. He stepped into the dark foyer.

Two men in the black uniforms of the Political Police appeared, one to either side of him. "Wolfgang Hans Mbikana?" one asked. His voice had the dust of ritual on it; he knew the answer. "You will come with us," the other said.

"There is some mistake," Wolf objected.

"No, sir, there is no mistake," one said mildly. The other opened the door. "After you, Mr. Mbikana."

The old man on the stoop squinted up at them, looked away, and slid off the step.

The police walked Wolf to an ancient administrative building. They went up marble steps sagging from centuries of foot-scuffing, and through an empty lobby. Deep within the building they halted before an undistinguished-looking door. "You are expected," the first of the police said.

"I beg your pardon?"

The police walked away, leaving him there. Apprehensive, he knocked on the door. There was no answer, so he opened it and stepped within.

A woman sat at a desk just inside the room. Though she was modernly dressed, she wore a veil. She might have been young; it was impossible to tell. A flick of her eyes, a motion of one hand, directed him to the open door of an inner room. It was like following an onion to its conclusion, a layer of mystery at a time.

A heavy-set man sat at the final desk. He was dressed in the traditional suit and tie of American businessmen. But there was nothing quaint or old-fashioned about his mobile, expressive face or the piercing eyes he turned on Wolf.

"Sit down," he grunted, gesturing toward an old, overstuffed chair. Then: "Charles DiStephano. Comptroller for Northeast Regional. You're Mbikana, right?"

"Yes, sir." Wolf gingerly took the proffered chair, which did not seem all that clean. It was becoming clear to him now; DiStephano was one of the men on whom he had waited these several months, the biggest of the lot, in fact. "I represent—"

"The Southwest Africa Trade Company." DiStephano lifted some documents from his desk. "Now this says you're prepared to offer— among other things—resource data from your North American *Coyote* landsat in exchange for the right to place students in Johns

Hopkins. I find that an odd offer for your organization to make."

"Those are my papers," Wolf objected. "As a citizen of Southwest Africa, I'm not used to this sort of cavalier treatment."

"Look, kid, I'm a busy man, I have no time to discuss your rights. The papers are in my hands, I've read them, the people that sent you knew I would. Okay? So I know what you want and what you're offering. What I want to know is *why* you're making this offer."

Wolf was disconcerted. He was used to a more civilized, a more leisurely manner of doing business. The oldtimers at SWATC had warned him that the pace would be different here, but he hadn't had the experience to decipher their veiled references and hints. He was painfully aware that he had gotten the mission, with its high salary and the promise of a bonus, only because it was not one that appealed to the older hands.

"America was hit hardest," he said, "but the Collapse was worldwide." He wondered whether he should explain the system of corporate social responsibility that African business was based on. Then decided that if DiStephano didn't know, he didn't want to. "There are still problems. Africa has a high incidence of birth defects." *Because America exported its poisons; its chemicals and pesticides and foods containing a witch's brew of preservatives.* "We hope to do away with the problem; if a major thrust is made, we can clean up the gene pool in less than a century. But to do this requires professionals—eugenicists, embryonic surgeons—and while we have these, they are second-rate. The very best still come from your nation's medical schools."

"We can't spare any."

"We don't propose to steal your doctors. We'd provide our own students—fully trained doctors who need only the specialized training."

"There are only so many openings at Hopkins," DiStephano said. "Or at U of P or the UVM Medical College, for that matter."

"We're prepared to—" Wolf pulled himself up short. "It's in the papers. We'll pay enough that you can expand to meet the needs of twice the number of students we require." The room was dim and oppressive. Sweat built up under Wolf's clothing.

"Maybe so. You can't buy teachers with money, though." Wolf said nothing. "I'm also extremely reluctant to let your people *near* our medics. You can offer them money, estates—things our country cannot afford. And we *need* our doctors. As it is, only the very rich can get the corrective surgery they require."

"If you're worried about our pirating your professionals, there are ways around that. For example, a clause could be written—" Wolf went on, feeling more and more in control. He was getting somewhere. If there wasn't a deal to be made, the discussion would never have gotten this far.

The day wore on. DiStephano called in aides and dismissed them. Twice, he had drinks sent in. Once, they broke for lunch. Slowly the heat built, until it was sweltering. Finally, the light began to fail, and the heat grew less oppressive.

DiStephano swept the documents into two piles, returned one to Wolf, and put the other inside a desk drawer. "I'll look these over, have our legal boys run a study. There shouldn't be any difficulties. I'll get back to you with the final word in—say a month. September twenty-first. I'll be in Boston then, but you can find me easily enough, if you ask around."

"A month? But I thought..."

"A month. You can't hurry City Hall," DiStephano said firmly. "Ms. Corey!"

The veiled woman was at the door, remote, elusive. "Sir."

"Drag Kaplan out of his office. Tell him we got a kid here he should give the VIP treatment to. Maybe a show. It's a Hopkins things, he should earn his keep."

"Yes, sir." She was gone.

"Thank you," Wolf said, "but I don't really need..."

"Take my advice, kid, take all the perks you can get. God knows there aren't many left. I'll have Kaplan pick you up at your hostel in an hour."

Kaplan turned out to be a slight, balding man with nervous gestures, some sort of administrative functionary for Hopkins. Wolf never did get the connection. But Kaplan was equally puzzled by Wolf's status, and Wolf took petty pleasure in not explaining it. It took some of the sting off of having his papers stolen.

Kaplan led Wolf through the evening streets. A bright sunset circled the world and the crowds were much thinner. "We won't be leaving the area that's zoned for electricity," Kaplan said. "Otherwise I'd advise against going out at night at all. Lot of jennie-deafs out then."

"Jennie-deafs?"

"Mutes. Culls. The really terminal cases. Some of them can't pass themselves off in daylight even wearing coveralls. Or chador—a lot are women." A faintly perverse expression crossed the man's face, leaving not so much as a greasy residue.

"Where are we going?" Wolf asked. He wanted to change the subject. A vague presentiment assured him he did not want to know the source of Kaplan's expression.

"A place called Peabody's. You've heard of Janis Joplin, our famous national singer?"

Wolf nodded, meaning no.

"The show is a recreation of her act. Woman name of Maggie Horowitz does the best impersonation of Janis I've ever seen. Tickets are almost impossible to get, but Hopkins has special influence in this case because—ah, here we are."

Kaplan led him down a set of concrete steps and into the basement of a dull, brick building. Wolf experienced a moment of dislocation. It was a bookstore. Shelves and boxes of books and magazines brooded over him, a packrat's clutter of paper.

Wolf wanted to linger, to scan the ancient tomes, remnants of a time and culture fast sinking into obscurity and myth. But Kaplan brushed past them without a second glance and he had to hurry to keep up.

They passed through a second roomful of books, then into a hallway where a gray man held out a gnarled hand and said, "Tickets, please."

Kaplan gave the man two crisp pasteboard cards, and they entered a third room.

It was a cabaret. Wooden chairs clustered about small tables with flickering candles at their centers. The room was lofted with wood beams, and a large, unused fireplace dominated one wall. Another wall had obviously been torn out at one time to make room for a small stage. Over a century's accumulation of memorabilia covered the walls or hung from the rafters, like barbarian trinkets from toppled empires.

"Peabody's is a local institution," Kaplan said. "In the twentieth century it was a speakeasy. H. L. Mencken himself used to drink here." Wolf nodded, though the name meant nothing to him. "The bookstore was a front and the drinking went on here in back."

The place was charged with a feeling of the past. It invoked America's bygone days as a world power. Wolf half-expected to see Theodore Roosevelt or Henry Kissinger come striding in. He said something to this effect and Kaplan smiled complacently.

"You'll like the show, then," he said.

A waiter took their orders. There was barely time to begin on the drinks when a pair of spotlights came on, and the stage curtain parted.

A woman stood alone in the center of the stage. Bracelets and bangles hung from her wrists, gaudy necklaces from her throat. She wore large tinted glasses and a flowered granny gown. Her nipples pushed against the thin dress. Wolf stared at them in horrified fascination. She had an extra set, immediately below the first pair.

The woman stood perfectly motionless. Wolf couldn't stop staring at her nipples; it wasn't just the number, it was the fact of their being visible at all. So quickly had he taken on this land's taboos.

The woman threw her head back and laughed. She put one hand on her hip, thrust the hip out at an angle, and lifted the microphone to her lips. She spoke, and her voice was harsh and raspy.

"About a year ago I lived in a rowhouse in Newark, right? Lived on the third floor, and I thought I had my act together. But nothing was going right, I wasn't getting any...action. Know what I mean? No talent comin' around. And there was this chick down the street, didn't have much and she was doing okay, so I say to myself: *What's wrong, Janis?* How come she's doing so good and you ain't gettin' any? So I decided to check it out, see what she had that I didn't. And one day I get up early, look out the window, and I see this chick out there *hustling!* I mean, she was doing the streets at *noon!* So I said to myself, Janis, honey, you ain't even trying. And when ya want action, ya gotta try. Yeah. Try just a little bit harder."

The music swept up out of nowhere, and she was singing: "Try-iiii, Try-iiii, Just a little bit harder..."

And unexpectedly, it was good. It was like nothing he had ever heard, but he understood it, almost on an instinctual level. It was world-culture music. It was universal.

Kaplan dug fingers into Wolf's arm, brought his mouth up to Wolf's ear. "You see? You see?" he demanded. Wolf shook him off impatiently. He wanted to hear the music.

The concert lasted forever, and it was done in no time at all. It left Wolf sweaty and emotionally spent. Onstage, the woman was energy personified. She danced, she strutted, she wailed more power into her songs than seemed humanly possible. Not knowing the original, Wolf was sure it was a perfect recreation. It had that feel.

The audience loved her. They called her back for three encores, and then a fourth. Finally, she came out, gasped into the mike, "I love ya, honeys, I truly do. But please—no more. I just couldn't do it." She blew a kiss, and was gone from the stage.

The entire audience was standing, Wolf among them, applauding furiously. A hand fell on Wolf's shoulder, and he glanced to his side, annoyed. It was Kaplan. His face was flushed and he said, "Come on." He pulled Wolf free of the crowd and backstage to a small dressing room. It's door was ajar and people were crowded into it.

One of them was the singer, hair stringy and out-of-place, laughing and gesturing widely with a Southern Comfort bottle. It was an antique, its label lacquered to the glass, and three-quarters filled with something amber-colored.

"Janis, this is—" Kaplan began.

"The name is Maggie," she sang gleefully. "Maggie Horowitz. I ain't no *dead* blues singer. And don't you forget it."

"This is a fan of yours, Maggie. From Africa." He gave Wolf a small shove. Wolf hesitantly stumbled forward, grimacing apologetically at the people he displaced.

"Whee-howdy!" Maggie whooped. She downed a slug from her bottle. "Pleased ta meetcha, Ace. Kinda light for an African, aintcha?"

"My mother's people were descended from German settlers." And it was felt that a light-skinned representative could handle the touchy Americans better, but he didn't say that.

"Whatcher name, Ace?"

"Wolf."

"Wolf'!" Maggie crowed. "Yeah, you look like a real heartbreaker, honey. Guess I'd better be careful around you, huh? Likely to sweep me off my feet and deflower me." She nudged him with an elbow. "That's a joke, Ace."

Wolf was fascinated. Maggie was *alive*, a dozen times more so than her countrymen. She made them look like zombies. Wolf was also a little afraid of her.

"*Hey*. Whatcha think of my singing, hah?"

"It was excellent," Wolf said. "It was—" he groped for words "—

in my land the music is quieter, there is not so much emotion."

"Yeah, well *I* think it was fucking good, Ace. Voice's never been in better shape. So tell 'em that at Hopkins, Kaplan. Tell 'em I'm giving them their money's worth."

"Of course you are," Kaplan said.

"Well, I *am*, goddammit. Hey, this place is like a morgue! Let's ditch this matchbox dressing room and hit the bars. Hey? Let's party."

She swept them all out of the dressing room, out of the building, and into the street. They formed a small, boisterous group, noisily wandering the city, looking for bars.

"There's one a block thataway," Maggie said. "Let's hit it. Hey, Ace, I'd likeya ta meet Cynthia. Sin, this is Wolf. Sin and I are like one person inside two skins. Many's the time we've shared a piece of talent in the same bed. "Hey?" She cackled, and grabbed at Cynthia's ass.

"Cut it out, Maggie." Cynthia smiled when she said it. She was a tall, slim, striking woman.

"Hey, this town is *dead!*" Maggie screamed the last word, then gestured them all to silence so they could listen for the echo. "There it is." She pointed and they swooped down on the first bar.

After the third bar, Wolf lost track. At some point he gave up on the party and somehow made his way back to his hostel. The last he remembered of Maggie she was calling after him, "Hey, Ace, don't be a party poop." Then: "At least be sure to come back tomorrow, goddammit."

Wolf spent most of the next day in his room, drinking water and napping. His hangover was all but gone by the time evening took the edge off the day's heat. He thought of Maggie's half-serious invitation, dismissed it and decided to go to the Club.

The Uhuru Club was ablaze with light by the time he wandered in, a beacon in a dark city. Its frequenters, after all, were all African foreign service, with a few commercial reps such as himself forced in by the insular nature of American society, and the need for polite conversation. It was *de facto* exempt from the power-use laws that governed the natives.

"Mbikana! Over here, lad, let me set you up with a drink." Nnamdi of the consulate waved him over to the bar. Wolf complied, feeling conspicious as he always did in the Club. His skin stood out here. Even the American servants were dark, though whether this was a gesture of deference or arrogance on the part of the local authorities, he could not guess.

"Word is that you spent the day closeted with the comptroller." Nnamdi had a gin-and-tonic set up. Wolf loathed the drink, but it was universal among the service people. "Share the dirt with us." Other faces gathered around; the service ran on gossip.

Wolf gave an abridged version of the encounter and Nnamdi applauded. "A full day with the Spider King and you escaped with your balls intact. An auspicious beginning for you, lad."

"Spider King?"

"Surely you were briefed on regional autonomy—how the country was broken up when it could no longer be managed by a central directorate? There *is* no higher authority than DiStephano in this part of the world, boy."

"Boston," Ajuji sniffed. Like most of the expatriates, she was a failure; unlike many, she couldn't hide the fact from herself. "That's exactly the sort of treatment one comes to expect from these savages."

"Now, Ajuji," Nnamdi said mildly. "These people are hardly savages. Why, before the Collapse they put men on the moon."

"Technology! Hard-core technology, that's all it was, of a piece with the kind that almost destroyed us all. If you want a measure of a people, you look at how they live. These—*Yanks*," she hissed the word to emphasize its filthiness, "live in squalor. Their streets are filthy, their cities are filthy, and even the ones who aren't rotten with genetic disease are filthy. A child can be taught to clean up after itself. What does that make them?"

"Human beings, Ajuji."

"Hogwash, Nnamdi."

Wolf followed the argument with acute embarrassment. He had been brought up to expect well from people with social standing. To hear gutter language and low prejudice from them was almost beyond bearing. Suddenly it *was* beyond bearing. He stood, his stool making a scraping noise as he pushed it back. He turned his back on them all, and left.

"Mbikana! You mustn't—" Nnamdi called after him.

"Oh, let him go." Ajuji cut in, with a satisfied tone, "you mustn't expect better. After all, he's practically one of *them*."

Well, maybe he was.

Wolf wasn't fully aware of where he was going until he found himself at Peabody's. He circled the building, and found a rear door. He tried the knob; it turned loosely in his hand. Then the door swung open and a heavy, bearded man in coveralls leaned out. "Yes?" he said in an unfriendly tone.

"Uh," Wolf said. "Maggie Horowitz told me I could drop by."

"Look, pilgrim, there are a lot of people try to get backstage. My job is to keep them out unless I know them. I don't know you."

Wolf tried to think of some response to this, and failed. He was about to turn away when somebody unseen said, "Oh, let him in, Deke."

It was Cynthia. "Come on," she said in a bored voice. "Don't clog up the doorway." The guard moved aside, and he entered.

"Thank you," he said.

"*Nada*," she replied. "As Maggie would say. The dressing room is that way, pilgrim."

"Wolf, honey!" Maggie shrieked. "How's it going, Ace? Ya catch the show?"

"No, I—"

"You shoulda. I was good. Really good. Janis herself was never better. Hey, gang! Let's split, hah? Let's go somewhere and get down and boogie."

A group of twenty ended up taking over a methane-lit bar outside the zoned-for-electricity sector. Three of the band had brought along their instruments, and they talked the owner into letting them play. The music was droning and monotonous. Maggie listened appreciatively, grinning and moving her head to the music.

"Whatcha think of that, Ace? Pretty good, hey? That's what we call Dead music."

Wolf shook his head. "I think it's well named."

"Hey, guys, you hear that? Wolf here just made a funny. There's hope for you yet, honey." Then she sighed. "Can't get behind it, huh? That's really sad, man. I mean they played *good* music back then; it was real. We're just echoes, man. Just playing away at them old songs. Got none of our own worth singing."

"Is that why you're doing the show, then?" Wolf asked, curious.

Maggie laughed. "Hell no. I do it because I got the chance. DiStephano got in touch with me—"

"DiStephano? The comptroller?"

"One of his guys, anyway. They had this gig all set up and they needed someone to play Janis. So they ran a computer search and came up with my name. And they offered me money, and I spent a month or two in Hopkins being worked over, and here I am. On the road to fame and glory." Her voice rose and warbled and mocked itself on the last phrase.

"Why did you have to go to Hopkins?"

"You don't think I was *born* looking like this? They had to change my face around. Changed my voice too, for which God bless. They brought it down lower, widened out my range, gave it the strength to hold onto them high notes and push 'em around."

"Not to mention the mental implants," Cynthia said.

"Oh, yeah, the 'plants so I could talk in a bluesy sorta way without falling out of character," Maggie said. "But that was minor."

Wolf was impressed. He had known that Hopkins was good, but this—! "What I don't understand is why your government did all this. What possible benefit is there for them?"

"Beats the living hell out of me, lover-boy. Don't know, don't care, and don't ask. That's my motto."

A long-haired, pale young man sitting nearby said, "The government is all hacked up on social engineering. They do a lot of weird things, and you never find out why. You learn not to ask questions."

"Hey, listen, Hawk, bringing Janis back to life isn't weird. It's a beautiful thing to do," Maggie objected. "Yeah, I only wish they could *really* bring her back. Sit her down next to me. Love to talk with that lady."

"You two would tear each other's eyes out," Cynthia said.

"What? Why?"

"Neither one of you'd be willing to give up the spotlight to the other."

Maggie cackled. "Ain't it the truth? Still, she's one broad I'd love to have met. A *real* star, see? Not a goddammed echo like me."

Hawk broke in, said, "You, Wolf. Where does your pilgrimage take you now? The group goes on tour the day after tomorrow; what are your plans?"

"I don't really have any," Wolf said. He explained his situation. "I'll probably stay in Baltimore until it's time to go up north. Maybe I'll take a side trip or two."

"Why don't you join the group, then?" Hawk asked. "We're planning to make the trip one long party. And we'll slam into Boston in just less than a month. The tour ends there."

"That," said Cynthia, "is a real bright idea. All we need is another nonproductive person on board the train."

Maggie bristled. "So what's wrong with that? Not like we're paying for it, is it? What's wrong with it?"

"Nothing's wrong with it. It's just a dumb idea."

"Well, *I* like it. How about it, Ace? You on the train or off?"

"I—" He stopped. Well, why not? "Yes. I would be pleased to go along."

"Good." She turned to Cynthia. "*Your* problem, sweets, is that you're just plain jealous."

"Oh Christ, here we go again."

"Well, don't bother. It won't do any good. Hey, you see that piece of talent at the far end of the bar?"

"Maggie, that 'piece of talent,' as you call him, is eighteen years old. At most."

"Yeah. Nice though." Maggie stared wistfully down the bar. "He's kinda pretty, ya know?"

Wolf spent the next day clearing up his affairs and arranging for letters of credit. The morning of departure day, he rose early and made his way to Baltimore Station. A brief exchange with the guards let him into the walled trainyard.

The train was an ungainly steam locomotive with a string of rehabilitated cars behind it. The last car had the word PEARL painted on it, in antique psychedelic lettering.

"Hey, Wolf! Come lookit this mother." A lone figure waved at him from the far end of the train. Maggie.

Wolf joined her. "What do you think of it, hah?"

He searched for something polite to say. "It is very impressive," he said finally. The word that leapt to mind was grotesque.

"Yeah. Runs on garbage, you know that? Just like me."

"Garbage?"

"Yeah, there's a methane processing plant nearby. Hey, lookit me! Up and awake at eight in the morning. Can ya take it? Had to get behind a little speed to do it, though."

The idiom was beyond him. "You mean—you were late waking up?"

"What? Oh, hey, man, you can be—look, forget I said a thing. No." She pondered a second. "Look, Wolf. There's this stuff called 'speed,' it can wake you up in the morning, give you a little boost, get you going. Ya know?"

Awareness dawned. "You mean amphetamines."

"Yeah, well this stuff ain't exactly legal, dig? So I'd just as soon you didn't spread the word around. I mean, I trust you, man, but I wanna be sure you know what's happening before you go shooting off your mouth."

"I understand," Wolf said. "I won't say anything. But you know that amphetamines are—"

"Gotcha, Ace. Hey, you gotta meet the piece of talent I picked up last night. Hey, Dave! Get your ass over here, lover."

A young, sleepy-eyed blond shuffled around the edge of the train. He wore white shorts, defiantly it seemed to Wolf, and a loose blouse buttoned up to his neck. Giving Maggie a weak hug around the waist, he nodded to Wolf.

"Davie's got four nipples, just like me. How about that? I mean, it's gotta be a pretty rare mutation, hah?"

Dave hung his head, half blushing. "Aw, Janis," he mumbled. Wolf waited for Maggie to correct the boy, but she didn't. Instead she led them around and around the train, chatting away madly, pointing out this, that, and the other thing.

Finally, Wolf excused himself, and returned to his hostel. He left Maggie prowling about the train, dragging her pretty boy after her. Wolf went out for a long lunch, picked up his bags, and showed up at the train earlier than most of the entourage.

The train lurched, and pulled out of the station. Maggie was in constant motion, talking, laughing, directing the placement of luggage. She darted from car to car, never still. Wolf found a seat and stared out the window. Children dressed in rags ran alongside the tracks, holding out hands and begging for money. One or two of the party threw coins; more laughed and threw bits of garbage.

The children were gone, and the train was passing through end-less miles of weathered ruins. Hawk sat down beside Wolf. "It'll be a slow trip," he said. "The train has to go around large sections of land it's better not to go through." He stared moodily at the broken-windowed shells that were once factories and warehouses. "Look out there, pilgrim, *that's* my country," he said in a disgusted voice. "Or the corpse of it."

"Hawk, you're close to Maggie."

"Now if you go out to the center of the continent..." Hawk's voice grew distant. "There's a cavern out there, where they housed radioactive waste. It was formed into slugs and covered with solid gold—anything else deteriorates too fast. The way I figure it, a man with a lead suit could go into that cavern and shave off a fortune. There's tons of the stuff there." He sighed. "Someday I'm going to rummage through a few archives and go."

"Hawk, you've got to *listen* to me."

Hawk held up a hand for silence. "It's about the drugs, right? You just found out and you want me to warn her."

"Warning her isn't good enough. Someone has to stop her."

"Yes, well. Try to understand. Maggie was in Hopkins for *three months* while they performed some very drastic surgery on her. She didn't look a thing like she does now, and she could sing, but her voice wasn't anything to rave about. Not to mention the mental implants.

"Imagine the pain she went through. Now ask yourself what are the two most effective painkillers in existence?"

"Morphine and heroin. But in my country, when drugs are re-sorted to, the doctors wean the patients off them before their re-lease."

"That's not the point. Consider this—Maggie could have had Hopkins remove the extra nipples. They could have done it. But she wasn't willing to go through the pain."

"She seems proud of them."

"She talks about them a lot, at least."

The train lurched and stumbled. Three of the musicians had uncrated their guitars and were playing more "Dead" music. Wolf chewed his lip in silence for a time, then said, "So what is the point you're making?"

"Simply that Maggie was willing to undergo the greater pain so that she could become Janis. So when I tell you she only uses drugs as painkillers, you have to understand that I'm not necessarily talking about physical pain." Hawk got up and left.

Maggie danced into the car. "Big time!" she whooped. "We made it into the big time, boys and girls. Hey, let's party!"

The next ten days were one extended party, interspersed with concerts. The reception in Wilmington was phenomenal. Thousands came to see the show; many were turned away. Maggie was unsteady before the first concert, achingly afraid of failure. But she played a rousing set, and was called back time and time again. Finally exhausted and limp, her hair sticking to a sweaty forehead, she stood up front and gasped, "That's all there is, boys and girls. I love ya and I wish there was more to give ya, but there ain't. You used it all up." And the applause went on and on...

The four shows in Philadelphia began slowly, but built up big. A few seats were unsold at the first concert; people were turned away for the second. The last two were near-riots. The group entrained to Newark for a day's rest and put on a Labor Day concert that made the previous efforts look pale. They stayed in an obscure hostel for an extra day's rest.

Wolf spent his rest day sightseeing. While in Philadelphia he had hired a native guide and prowled through the rusting refinery buildings at Breeze Point. They rose to the sky forever in tragic magnificence, and it was hard to believe there had been enough oil in the world to fill the holding tanks there. In Wilmington, he let the local guide lead him to a small Italian neighborhood to watch a religious festival.

The festival was a parade, led first by a priest trailed by eight altar girls, with incense burners and fans. Then came twelve burly men carrying the flower-draped body of an ancient Cadillac. After them came the faithful, in coveralls and chador, singing.

Wolf followed the procession to the river, where the car was placed in a hole in the ground, sprinkled with holy water, and set afire.

He asked the guide what story lay behind the ritual, and the boy shrugged. It was old, he was told, very very old.

It was late when Wolf returned to the hostel. He was expecting a party, but found it dark and empty. Cynthia stood in the foyer, hands behind her back, staring out a barred window at black nothingness.

"Where is everybody?" Wolf asked. It was hot. Insects buzzed about the coal-oil lamp, batting against it frenziedly.

Cynthia turned, studied him oddly. Her forehead was beaded with sweat. "Maggie's gone home—she's attending a mid-school reunion. She's going to show her old friends what a hacking big star she's become. The others?" She shrugged. "Off wherever puppets go when there's no one to bring them to life. Their rooms, probably."

"Oh." Cynthia's dress clung damply to her legs and sides. Dark stains spread out from under her armpits. "Would you like to play a game of chess or—something?"

Cynthia's eyes were strangely intense. She took a step closer to him. "Wolf, I've been wondering. You've been celibate on this trip. Is there a problem? No? Maybe a girlfriend back home?"

"There was, but she won't wait for me." Wolf made a deprecating gesture. "Maybe that was part of the reason I took this trip."

She took one of his hands, placed it on her breast. "But you *are* interested in girls?" Then, before he could shape his answer into clumsy words, she whispered, "Come on," and led him to her room.

Once inside, Wolf seized Cynthia and kissed her, deeply and long. She responded with passion, then drew away and with a little shove toppled him onto the bed. "Off with your clothes," she said. She shucked her blouse in a complex, fluid motion. Pale breasts bobbled, catching vague moonlight from the window.

After an instant's hesitation, Wolf doffed his own clothing. By contrast with Cynthia he felt weak and irresolute, and it irked him to feel that way. Determined to prove he was nothing of the kind, he reached for Cynthia as she dropped onto the bed beside him. She evaded his grasp.

"Just a moment, pilgrim." She rummaged through a bag by the headboard. "Ah. Care for a little treat first? It'll enhance the sensations."

"Drugs?" Wolf asked, feeling an involuntary horror.

"Oh, come down off your high horse. Once won't melt your genes. Give a gander at what you're being so critical of."

"What is it?"

"Vanilla ice cream," she snapped. She unstoppered a small vial and meticulously dribbled a few grains of white powder onto a thumbnail. "This is expensive, so pay attention. You want to breathe it all in with one snort. Got that? So by the numbers: Take a deep breath and breathe out slowly. That's it. Now in. Now out and hold."

Cynthia laid her thumbnail beneath Wolf's nose, pinched one nostril shut with her free hand. "Now in fast, Yeah!"

He inhaled convulsively and was flooded with sensations. A crisp, clean taste filled his mouth, and a spray of fine white powder hit the back of his throat. It tingled pleasantly. His head felt spacious. He moved his jaw, suspiciously searching about with his tongue.

Cynthia quickly snorted some of the powder herself, restoppering the vial.

"Now," she said. "Touch me. Slowly, slowly, we've got all night. That's the way. Ahhhh." She shivered. "I think you've got the idea."

They worked the bed for hours. The drug, whatever it was, made Wolf feel strangely clearheaded and rational, more playful and more prone to linger. There was no urgency to their lovemaking; they took their time. Three, perhaps four times they halted for more of the powder, which Cynthia doled out with careful ceremony. Each time they returned to their lovemaking with renewed interest and resolution to take it slowly, to postpone each climax to the last possible instant.

The evening grew old. Finally, they lay on the sheets, not touching, weak and exhausted. Wolf's body was covered with a fine sheen of sweat. He did not care to even think of making love yet another time. He refrained from saying this.

"Not bad," Cynthia said softly. "I must remember to recommend you to Maggie."

"Sin, why do you do that?"

"Do what?"

"We've just—been as intimate as two human beings can be. But as soon as it's over, you say something cold. Is it that you're afraid of contact?"

"Christ." It was an empty syllable, devoid of religious content, and flat. Cynthia fumbled in her bag, found a flat metal case, pulled a cigarette out, and lit it. Wolf flinched inwardly. "Look, pilgrim, what are you asking for? You planning to marry me and take me away to your big, clean African cities to meet your momma? Hah?

"Didn't think so. So what do you want from me? Mental souvenirs to take home and tell your friends about? I'll give you one: I spent years saving up enough to go see a doctor, find out if I could have any brats. Went to one last year and what do you think he tells me? I've got red-cell dyscrasia, too far gone for treatment, there's nothing to do but wait. Lovely, hah? So one of these days it'll just stop working and I'll die. Nothing to be done. So long as I eat right, I won't start wasting away, so I can keep my looks up to the end. I could buy a little time if I gave up drugs like this"—she waved the cigarette, and an ash fell on Wolf's chest. He brushed it away quickly—"and the white powder, and anything else that makes life worth living. But it wouldn't buy me enough time to do anything worth doing." She fell silent. "Hey. What time is it?"

Wolf climbed out of bed, rummaged through his clothing until he found his timepiece. He held it up to the window, squinted. "Um. Twelve ... fourteen."

"Oh, *nukes*." Cynthia was up and scrabbling for her clothes. "Come on, get dressed. Don't just stand there."

Wolf dressed himself slowly. "What's the problem?"

"I promised Maggie I'd get some people together to walk her back from that damned reunion. It ended *hours* ago, and I lost track of the time." She ignored his grin. "Ready? Come on, we'll check her room first and then the foyer. God, is she going to be mad."

They found Maggie in the foyer. She stood in the center of the room, haggard and bedraggled, her handbag hanging loosely from one hand. Her face was livid with rage. The sputtering lamp made her face look old and evil.

"Well!" she snarled. "Where have you two been?"

"In my room, balling," Cynthia said calmly. Wolf stared at her, appalled.

"Well that's just beautiful. That's really beautiful, isn't it? Do you know where I've been while my two best friends were upstairs humping their brains out? Hey? Do you want to know?" Her voice reached a hysterical peak. "I was being *raped by two jennie-deafs*, that's where!"

She stormed past them, half-cocking her arm as if she were going to assault them with her purse, then thinking better of it. They heard her run down the hall. Her door slammed.

Bewildered, Wolf said, "But I—"

"Don't let her dance on your head," Cynthia said. "She's lying."

"Are you certain?"

"Look, we've lived together, bedded the same men—I know her. She's all hacked off at not having an escort home. And Little Miss Sunshine has to spread the gloom."

"We should have been there," Wolf said dubiously. "She could have been killed, walking home alone."

"Whether Maggie dies a month early or not doesn't make a bit of difference to me, pilgrim. I've got my own problems."

"A month—? Is Maggie suffering from a disease too?"

"We're all suffering, we all— Ah, the hell with you too." Cynthia spat on the floor, spun on her heel and disappeared down the hallway. It had the rhythm and inevitability of a witch's curse.

The half-day trip to New York left the troupe with playtime before the first concert, but Maggie stayed in seclusion, drinking. There was talk about her use of drugs, and this alarmed Wolf, for they were all users of drugs themselves.

There was also gossip about the reunion. Some held that Maggie had dazzled her former friends—who had not treated her well in her younger years—had been glamorous and gracious. The predominant view, however, was that she had been soundly snubbed, that she was still a freak and an oddity in the eyes of her former contemporaries. That she had left the reunion alone.

Rumors flew about the liaison between Wolf and Cynthia too. The fact that she avoided him only fed the speculation.

Despite everything the New York City concerts were a roaring success. All four shows were sold out as soon as tickets went on sale. Scalpers made small fortunes that week, and for the first time the concerts were allowed to run into the evening. Power was diverted from a section of the city to allow for the lighting and amplification. And Maggie sang as she had never sung before. Her voice roused the audiences to a frenzy, and her blues were enough to break a hermit's heart.

They left for Hartford on the tenth, Maggie sequestered in her compartment in the last car. Crew members lounged about idly. Some strummed guitars, never quite breaking into a recognizable tune. Others talked quietly. Hawk flipped tarot cards into a heap, one at a time.

"Hey, this place is fucking *dead!*" Maggie was suddenly in the car, her expression an odd combination of defiance and guilt. "Let's party! Hey? Let's hear some music." She fell into Hawk's lap and nibbled on an ear.

"Welcome back, Maggie," somebody said.

"*Janis!*" she shouted happily. "The lady's name is Janis!"

Like a rusty machine starting up, the party came to life. Music jelled. Voices became animated. Bottles of alcohol appeared and were passed around. And for the remainder of the two days that the train spent making wide, looping detours to avoid the dangerous stretches of Connecticut and New York, the party never died.

There were tense undertones to the party, however, a desperate quality in Maggie's gaiety. For the first time, Wolf began to feel trapped, to count the days that separated him from Boston and the end of the tour.

The dressing room for the first Hartford concert was cramped, small, badly lit—like every other dressing room they'd encountered. "Get your ass over here, Sin," Maggie yelled. "You've gotta make me up so I look strung out, like Janis did."

Cynthia held Maggie's chin, twisted it to the left, to the right. "Maggie, you don't *need* makeup to look strung out."

"Goddammit, yes I *do.* Let's get it on. Come on, come on—I'm a star, I shouldn't have to put up with this shit."

Cynthia hesitated, then began dabbing at Maggie's face, lightly accentuating the lines, the bags under her eyes.

Maggie studied the mirror. "Now *that's* grim," she said. "That's really grotesque."

"That's what you look like, Maggie."

"You cheap bitch! You'd think *I* was the one who nodded out last night before we could get it on." There was an awkward silence. "Hey, Wolf!" She spun to face him. "What do *you* say?"

"Well," Wolf began, embarrassed, "I'm afraid Cynthia's..."

"You see? Let's get this show on the road." She grabbed her cherished Southern Comfort bottle and upended it.

"That's not doing you any good either."

Maggie smiled coldly. "Shows what *you* know. Janis always gets smashed before a concert. Helps her voice." She stood, made her way to the curtains. The emcee was winding up his pitch.

"Ladies and gentlemen...Janis!"

Screams arose. Maggie sashayed up to the mike, lifted it, laughed into it.

"Heyyy. Good ta see ya." She swayed and squinted at the crowd, and was off and into her rap. "Ya know, I went ta see a doctor the other week. Told him I was worried about how much drinking I was doing. Told him I'd been drinkin' heavy since I was twelve. Get up in the morning and have a few Bloody Marys with breakfast. Polish off a fifth before lunch. Have a few drinks at dinner, and really get into it when the partying begins. Told him how much I drank for how many years. So I said, 'Look, Doc, none of this ever hurt me any, but I'm kinda worried, ya know? Give it to me straight, have I got a problem? And he said, 'Man, *I* don't think you've got a problem. *I* think you're doing just *fine!*'" Cheers from the audience. Maggie smiled smugly. "Well, honey, *everybody's* got problems, and I'm no exception." The music came up. "But when I got problems, I got an answer, 'cause I can sing dem ole-time blues. Just sing my problems away." She launched into "Ball and Chain" and the audience went wild.

Backstage, Wolf was sitting on a stepladder. He had bought a cup of water from a vendor and was nursing it, taking small sips. Cynthia came up and stood beside him. They both watched Maggie strutting on stage, stamping and sweating, writhing and howling.

"I can never get over the contrast," Wolf said, not looking at Cynthia. "Out there everybody is excited. Back here, it's calm and peaceful. Sometimes I wonder if we're seeing the same thing the audience does."

"Sometimes it's hard to see what's right in front of your face." Cynthia smiled a sad, cryptic smile and left. Wolf had grown used to such statements, and gave it no more thought.

The second and final Hartford show went well. However, the first two concerts in Providence were bad. Maggie's voice and timing were off, and she had to cover with theatrics. At the second show she had to order the audience to dance—something that had never been necessary before. Her onstage raps became bawdier and more graphic. She moved her body as suggestively as a stripper, employing bumps and grinds. The third show was better, but the earthy elements remained.

The cast wound up in a bar in a bad section of town, where guards with guns covered the doorway from fortified booths. Maggie got drunk and ended up crying. "Man, I was so blitzed when I went onstage—you say I was good?"

"Sure, Maggie," Hawk mumbled. Cynthia snorted.

"You were very good," Wolf assured her.

"I don't remember a goddamned thing," she wailed. "You say I was good? It ain't fair, man. If I was good, I deserve to be able to remember it. I mean, what's the point otherwise? Hey?"

Wolf patted her shoulder clumsily. She grabbed the front of his dashiki and buried her face in his chest. "Wolf, Wolf, what's gonna *happen* to me?" she sobbed.

"Don't cry," he said, patting her hair.

Finally, Wolf and Hawk had to lead her back to the hostel. No one else was willing to quit the bar.

They skirted an area where all the buildings had been torn down but one. It stood alone, with great gaping holes where plate-glass had been, and large nonfunctional arches on one side.

"It was a fast-food building," Hawk explained when Wolf asked. He sounded embarrassed.

"Why is it still standing?"

"Because there are ignorant and superstitious people everywhere," Hawk muttered. Wolf dropped the subject.

The streets were dark and empty. They went back into the denser areas of town, and the sound of their footsteps bounced off the buildings. Maggie was leaning half-conscious on Hawk's shoulder, and he almost had to carry her.

There was a stirring in the shadows. Hawk tensed. "Speed up a bit, if you can," he whispered.

Something shuffled out of the darkness. It was large and only vaguely human. It moved toward them. "What—?" Wolf whispered.

"Jennie-deaf," Hawk whispered back. "If you know any clever tricks, this is the time to use 'em." The thing broke into a shambling run.

Wolf thrust a hand into a pocket and whirled to face Hawk. "Look," he said in a loud, angry voice. "I've taken *enough* from you! I've got a *knife* and I don't care *what* I do!" The jennie-deaf halted. From the corner of his eye, Wolf saw it slide back into the shadows.

Maggie looked up with a sleepy, quizzical expression. "Hey, what..."

"Never mind," Hawk muttered. He upped his pace, half-dragging Maggie after him. "That was arrogant," he said approvingly.

Wolf forced his hand from his pocket. He found he was shivering from aftershock. "*Nada,*" he said. Then: "That is the correct term?"

"Yeah."

"I wasn't certain that jennie-deafs really existed."

"Just some poor mute with gland trouble. Don't think about it."

Autumn was just breaking out when the troupe hit Boston. They arrived to find the final touches being put on the stage on Boston Common. A mammoth concert was planned; dozens of people swarmed about making preparations.

"This must be how America was all the time before the Collapse," Wolf said, impressed. He was ignored.

The morning of the concert, Wolf was watching canvas being hoisted above the stage, against the chance of rain, when a gripper ran up and said, "You, pilgrim, have you seen Janis?"

"Maggie," he corrected automatically. "No, not recently."

"Thanks," the man gasped, and ran off. Not long after, Hawk hurried by and asked, "Seen Maggie lagging about?"

"No. Wait, Hawk, what's going on? You're the second person to ask me that."

Hawk shrugged. "Maggie's disappeared. Nothing to scream about."

"I hope she'll be back in time for the show."

"The local police are hunting for her. Anyway, she's got the implants; if she can move she'll be on stage. Never doubt it." He hurried away.

The final checks were being run, and the first concertgoers beginning to straggle in when Maggie finally appeared. Uniformed men held each arm; she looked sober and angry. Cynthia took charge, dismissed the police, and took Maggie to the trailer that served as a dressing room.

Wolf watched from a distance, decided he could be of no use. He ambled about the Common aimlessly, watching the crowd grow. The people coming in found places to sit, took them, and waited. There was little talk among them, and what there was was quiet. They were dressed brightly, but not in their best. Some carried winejugs or blankets.

They were an odd crew. They did not look each other in the eye; their mouths were grim, their faces without expression. Their speech was low, but with an undercurrent of tension. Wolf wandered among them, eavesdropping, listening to fragments of their talk.

"Said that her child was going to..."

"...needed that. Nobody needed that."

"Couldn't have paid it away..."

"...tasted odd, so I didn't..."

"Had to tear down three blocks..."

"...blood."

Wolf became increasingly uneasy. There was something about their expressions, their tones of voice. He bumped into Hawk, who tried to hurry past.

"Hawk, there is something very wrong happening."

Hawk's face twisted. He gestured toward the light tower. "No time," he said, "the show's beginning. I've got to be at my station." Wolf hesitated, then followed the man up the ladders of the light tower.

All of the Common was visible from the tower. The ground was thick with people, hordes of ant-specks against the brown of trampled earth. Not a child among them, and that felt wrong too. A gold and purple sunset smeared itself three-quarters of the way around the horizon.

Hawk flicked lights on and off, one by one, referring to a sheet of paper he held in one hand. Sometimes he cursed and respliced wires. Wolf waited. A light breeze ruffled his hair, though there was no hint of wind below.

"This is a sick country," Hawk said. He slipped a headset on, played a red spot on the stage, let it wink out. "You there, Patrick? The kliegs go on in two." He ran a check on all the locals manning lights, addressing them by name. "Average life span is something like forty-two—*if* you get out of the delivery room alive. The birth-rate has to be very high to keep the population from dwindling away to nothing." He brought up all the red and blue spots. The stage was bathed in purple light. The canvas above looked black in contrast. An obscure figure strolled to the center mike.

"Hit it, Patrick." A bright pool of light illuminated the emcee. He coughed, went into his spiel. His voice boomed over the crowd, relayed away from the stage by a series of amps with timed delay along each rank, so that his voice reached the distant listeners in synchronization with the further amplification. The crowd moved sluggishly about the foot of the tower, set in motion by latecomers straggling in. "So the question you should ask yourself is why the government is wasting its resources on a goddamned show."

"All right," Wolf said. "Why?" He was very tense, very still. The breeze swept away his sweat, and he wished he had brought along a jacket. He might need one later.

"Because their wizards said to—the damn social engineers and their machines," Hawk answered. "Watch the crowd."

"...*Janis!*" the loudspeakers boomed. And Maggie was on stage, rapping away, handling the microphone suggestively, obviously at the peak of her form. The crowd exploded into applause. Offerings of flowers were thrown through the air. Bottles of liquor were passed hand over hand and deposited on the stage.

From above it could not be seen how the previous month had taken its toll on Maggie. The lines on her face, the waxy skin, were hidden by the colored light. The kliegs bounced off her sequined dress dazzlingly.

Halfway through her second song, Maggie came to an instrumental break and squinted out at the audience. "Hey, what the fuck's the matter with you guys? Why ain't you *dancing?*" At her cue, scattered couples rose to their feet. "Ready on the kliegs," Hawk murmured into his headset. "Three, four, and five on the police." Bright lights pinpointed three widely separated parts of the audience, where uniformed men were struggling with dancers. A single klieg stayed on Maggie, who pointed an imperious finger at one struggling group and shrieked, "Why are you trying to stop them from dancing? I want them to dance. I *command* them to dance!"

With a roar, half the audience were on their feet. "Shut down three. Hold four and five to the count of three, then off. One—Two—Three! Good." The police faded away, lost among the dancers.

"That was prearranged," Wolf said. Hawk didn't so much as glance at him.

"It's part of the legend. You, Wolf, over to your right." Wolf looked where Hawk was pointing, saw a few couples at the edge of the crowd slip from the light into the deeper shadows.

"What am I seeing?"

"Just the beginning." Hawk bent over his control board.

By slow degrees the audience became drunk and then rowdy. As the concert wore on, an ugly, excited mood grew. Sitting far above it all, Wolf could still feel the hysteria grow, as well as see it. Women shed chador and danced atop it, not fully dressed. Men ripped free of their coveralls. Here and there, spotted through the crowd, couples made love. Hawk directed lights onto a few, held them briefly; in most cases the couples went on, unheeding.

Small fights broke out, and were quelled by police. Bits of trash were gathered up and set ablaze, so that small fires dotted the landscape. Wisps of smoke floated up. Hawk played colored spots on the crowd. By the time darkness was total, the lights and the bestial noise of the revelers combined to create the feel of a Witch's Sabbath.

"Pretty nasty down there," Hawk observed. "And all most deliberately engineered by government wizards."

"But there is no true feeling involved," Wolf objected. "It is nothing but animal lust. No—no involvement."

"Yeah." Onstage, Maggie was building herself up into a frenzy. And yet her blues were brilliant—she had never been better. "Not so much different from the other concerts. The only difference is that tonight nobody waits until they go home."

"Your government can't believe that enough births will result from this night to make any difference."

"Not tonight, no. But all these people will have memories to keep them warm over the winter." Then he spat over the edge of the platform. "Ahhhh, why should I spout their lies for them? It's just bread and circuses is all, just a goddamned release for the masses."

Maggie howled with delight. "Whee-ew, man! I'm gettin' horny just looking at you. Yeah, baby, get it on, that's right!" She was strutting up and down the stage, a creature of boundless energy, while the band filled the night with music, fast and urgent.

"Love it!" She stuck her tongue out at the audience and received howls of approval. She lifted her Southern Comfort bottle, took a gigantic swig, her hips bouncing to the music. More howls. She caressed the neck of the bottle with her tongue.

"Yeah! Makes me horny as sin, 'deed it does. Ya know," she paused a beat, then continued, "that's something I can really understand, man. 'Cause I'm just a horny little hippie chick myself. Yeah." Wolf suddenly realized that she was competing against the audience itself for its attention, that she was going to try to outdo everybody present.

Maggie stroked her hand down the front of her dress, lingering between her breasts, then between her legs. She shook her hair back from her eyes, the personification of animal lust. "I mean, shit. I mean, hippie chicks don't even wear no underwear." More ribald howls and applause. "Don't believe me, do ya?"

Wolf stared, was unable to look away as Maggie slowly spread her legs wide and squatted, giving the audience a good look up her skirt. Her frog face leered, and it was an ugly, lustful thing. She lowered a hand to the stage behind her for support, and beckoned. "Come to momma," she crooned.

It was like knocking the chocks out from a dam. There was an instant of absolute stillness, and then the crowd roared and surged forward. An ocean of humanity converged on the stage, smashing through the police lines, climbing up on the wooden platform. Wolf had a brief glimpse of Maggie trying to struggle to her feet, before she was overrun. There was a dazed, disbelieving expression on her face.

"Mother of Sin," Wolf whispered. He stared at the mindless, evil mob below. They were in furious motion, straining, forcing each other in great swirling eddies. He waited for the stage to collapse, but it did not. The audience kept climbing atop it, pushing one another off its edge, and it did not collapse. It would have been a mercy if it had.

A hand waved above the crowd, clutching something that sparkled. Wolf could not make it out at first. Then another hand waved a glittering rag, and then another, and he realized that these were shreds of Maggie's dress.

Wolf wrapped his arms around a support to keep from falling into the horror below. The howling of the crowd was a single, chaotic noise; he squeezed his eyes shut, vainly trying to fend it off. "Right on cue," Hawk muttered. "Right on goddamned cue." He cut off all the lights, and placed a hand on Wolf's shoulder.

"Come on. Our job is done here."

Wolf twisted to face Hawk. The act of opening his eyes brought on a wave of vertigo, and he slumped to the platform floor, still clutching the support desperately. He wanted to vomit and couldn't. "It's—they—Hawk, did you *see* it? Did you see what they did? Why didn't someone—?" He choked on his words.

"Don't ask me," Hawk said bitterly. "I just play the part of Judas Iscariot in this little drama." He tugged at Wolf's shoulders. "Let's go, pilgrim. We've got to go down now." Wolf slowly weaned himself of the support, allowed himself to be coaxed down from the tower.

There were men in black uniforms at the foot of the tower. One of them addressed Hawk. "Is this the African national?" Then, to Wolf: "Please come with us, sir. We have orders to see you safely to your hostel."

Tears flooded Wolf's eyes and he could not see the crowd, the Common, the men before him. He allowed himself to be led away, as helpless and as trusting as a small child.

In the morning, Wolf lay in bed staring at the ceiling. A fly buzzed somewhere in the room, and he did not look for it. In the streets iron-wheeled carts rumbled by, and children chanted a counting-out game.

After a time he rose, dressed, and washed his face. He went to the hostel's dining room for breakfast.

There, finishing off a piece of toast, was DiStephano.

"Good morning, Mr. Mbikana. I was beginning to think I'd have to send for you." He gestured to a chair. Wolf looked about, took it. There were at least three of the political police seated nearby.

DiStephano removed some documents from his jacket pocket, handed them to Wolf. "Signed, sealed, and delivered. We made some minor changes in the terms, but nothing your superiors will object to." He placed the last corner of toast in the side of his mouth. "I'd say this was a rather bright beginning to your professional career."

"Thank you," Wolf said automatically. He glanced at the documents, could make no sense of them, dropped them in his lap.

"If you're interested, the *African Genesis* leaves port tomorrow morning. I've made arrangements that a berth be ready for you, should you care to take it. Of course, there will be another passenger ship in three weeks if you wish to see more of our country."

"No," Wolf said hastily. Then, because that seemed rude, "I'm most anxious to see my home again. I've been away far too long."

DiStephano dabbed at the corners of his mouth with a napkin, let it fall to the tablecloth. "Then that's that." He started to rise.

"Wait," Wolf said. "Mr. DiStephano, I...I would very much like an explanation."

DiStephano sat back down. He did not pretend not to understand the request. "The first thing you must know," he said, "is that Ms. Horowitz was not our first Janis Joplin."

"No," Wolf said.

"Nor the second."

Wolf looked up.

"She was the twenty-third, not counting the original. The show is sponsored every year, always ending in Boston on the Equinox. So far, it has always ended in the same fashion."

Wolf wondered if he should try to stab the man with a fork, if he should rise up and attempt to strangle him. There should be rage, he knew. He felt nothing. "Because of the brain implants."

"No. You must believe me when I say that I wish she had lived. The implants helped her keep in character, nothing more. It's true that she did not recall the previous women who played the part of Janis. But her death was not planned. It's simply something that—happens."

"Every year."

"Yes. Every year Janis offers herself to the crowd. And every year they tear her apart. A sane woman would not make the offer; a sane people would not respond in that fashion. I'll know that my country is on the road to recovery come the day that Janis lives to make a second tour." He paused. "Or the day we can't find a woman willing to play the role, knowing how it ends."

Wolf tried to think. His head felt dull and heavy. He heard the words, and he could not guess whether they made sense or not. "One last question," he said. "Why me?"

DiStephano rose. "One day you may return to our nation," he said. "Or perhaps not. But you will certainly rise to a responsible position within the Southwest Africa Trade Company. Your decision will affect our economy." Four men in uniform also rose from their chairs. "When that happens, I want you to understand one thing about our land: *We have nothing to lose.* Good day, and a long life to you, sir."

DiStephano's guards followed him out.

It was evening. Wolf's ship rode in Boston harbor, waiting to carry him home. Away from this magic nightmare land, with its ghosts and walking dead. He stared at it and he could not make it real; he had lost all capacity for belief.

The ship's dinghy was approaching. Wolf picked up his bags.

19 _____

For music to think about it by afterwards, I found Stravinsky's *Le Sacre du printemps* just right.

In *The Golden Bough* Frazer tells of an Aztec fertility rite involving the selection of a Corn Maiden every year, and what a great honor it was for a girl to be chosen. They worshipped her as Miss Maize of 1485 (Aztec equivalent) until a certain time of year when they cut off her head, skinned her, and splashed her blood about the temple and on the seed-corn and on the people to insure the general fertility of everything and everybody. Apparently the farmers liked the results at harvest time, for they kept doing it annually until the Catholics came and put a stop to it. The Corn Goddess was smart enough to join the conqueror's church, however. I have a picture of her now on my office wall; she's a 1984 calendar girl for "Tamales by Bargas," an Austin establishment. She appears as a timid maiden standing on a crescent menstrual moon (the fertility connection, still), she's wearing a pink smock and a gold-trimmed robe surrounded by light, two baby angels are crowning her queen of the universe, and the title proclaims her *La Virgen de Guadalupe*. In A.D. 1531, Miss Maize showed herself to an ex-Aztec named Juan Diego at the site of the old Corn-Goddess temple, introduced herself by another name, and told him to have the bishop build her a church there. Finally the Pope (who also takes a new name when first elected) made her the patroness of Mexico, and the Aztecs don't have to kill a young girl as goddess-surrogate every year, for she has become the Mother of God and sells tamales and

326

other corn-based delicacies for Bargas, besides doing miracles for those who light votive candles before her altar.

I don't think Swanwick had Frazer or Aztecs in mind at all when he wrote about Saint Janis. He didn't need to. When you strike an archetype, related myths begin to vibrate in resonance. Persephone stirs in Hades and prepares to return fertility to the earth in the spring. "The Feast of Saint Janis" is underworld myth, and so are the next three stories.

"IF I FORGET THEE, OH EARTH..."
by Arthur C. Clarke

When Marvin was ten years old, his father took him through the long, echoing corridors that led up through Administration and Power, until at last they came to the uppermost levels of all and were among the swiftly growing vegetation of the Farmlands. Marvin liked it here: it was fun watching the great, slender plants creeping with almost visible eagerness towards the sunlight as it filtered down through the plastic domes to meet them. The smell of life was everywhere, awakening inexpressible longings in his heart: no longer was he breathing the dry, cool air of the residential levels, purged of all smells but the faint tang of ozone. He wished he could stay here for a little while, but father would not let him. They went onwards until they had reached the entrance to the Observatory, which he had never visited: but they did not stop, and Marvin knew with a sense of rising excitement that there could be only one goal left. For the first time in his life, he was going Outside.

There were a dozen of the surface vehicles, with their wide balloon tires and pressurized cabins, in the great servicing chamber. His father must have been expected, for they were led at once to the little scout car waiting by the huge circular door of the airlock. Tense with expectancy, Marvin settled himself down in the cramped cabin while his father started the motor and checked the controls. The inner door of the lock slid open and then closed behind them:

he heard the roar of the great air-pumps fade slowly as the pressure dropped to zero. Then the "Vacuum" sign flashed on, the outer door parted, and before Marvin lay the land which he had never yet entered.

He had seen it in photographs, of course: he had watched it imaged on television screens a hundred times. But now it was lying all around him, burning beneath the fierce sun that crawled so slowly across the jet-black sky. He stared into the west, away from the blinding splendor of the sun—and there were the stars, as he had been told but had never quite believed. He gazed at them for a long time, marveling that anything could be so bright and yet so tiny. They were intense unscintillating points, and suddenly he remembered a rhyme he had once read in one of his father's books:

> Twinkle, twinkle, little star,
> How I wonder what you are.

Well, *he* knew what the stars were. Whoever asked that question must have been very stupid. And what did they mean by "twinkle"? You could see at a glance that all the stars shone with the same steady, unwavering light. He abandoned the puzzle and turned his attention to the landscape around him.

They were racing across a level plain at almost a hundred miles an hour, the great balloon tires sending up little spurts of dust behind them. There was no sign of the Colony: in the few minutes while he had been gazing at the stars, its domes and radio towers had fallen below the horizon. Yet there were other indications of man's presence, for about a mile ahead Marvin could see the curiously shaped structures clustering round the head of a mine. Now and then a puff of vapor would emerge from a squat smokestack and would instantly disperse.

They were past the mine in a moment: father was driving with a reckless, and exhilarating skill as if—it was a strange thought to come into a child's mind—he was trying to escape from something. In a few minutes they had reached the edge of the plateau on which the Colony had been built. The ground fell sharply away beneath them in a dizzying slope whose lower stretches were lost in shadow. Ahead, as far as the eye could reach, was a jumbled wasteland of craters, mountain ranges, and ravines. The crests of the mountains, catching the low sun, burned like islands of fire in a sea of darkness: and above them the stars still shone as steadfastly as ever.

There could be no way forward—yet there was. Marvin clenched his fists as the car edged over the slope and started the long descent. Then he saw the barely visible track leading down the mountainside, and relaxed a little. Other men, it seemed, had gone this way before.

Night fell with a shocking abruptness as they crossed the shadow line and the sun dropped below the crest of the plateau. The twin searchlights sprang into life, casting blue-white bands on the rocks ahead, so that there was scarcely need to check their speed. For hours they drove through valleys and past the feet of mountains whose peaks seemed to comb the stars, and sometimes they emerged for a moment into the sunlight as they climbed over higher ground.

And now on the right was a wrinkled, dusty plain, and on the left, its ramparts and terraces rising mile after mile into the sky, was a wall of mountains that marched into the distance until its peaks sank from sight below the rim of the world. There was no sign that men had ever explored this land, but once they passed the skeleton of a crashed rocket, and beside it a stone cairn surmounted by a metal cross.

It seemed to Marvin that the mountains stretched on forever: but at last, many hours later, the range ended in a towering, precipitous headland that rose steeply from a cluster of little hills. They drove down into a shallow valley that curved in a great arc toward the far side of the mountains: and as they did so, Marvin slowly realized that something very strange was happening in the land ahead.

The sun was now low behind the hills on the right: the valley before them should be in total darkness. Yet it was awash with a cold white radiance that came spilling over the crags beneath which they were driving. Then, suddenly, they were out in the open plain, and the source of the light lay before them in all its glory.

It was very quiet in the little cabin now that the motors had stopped. The sound was the faint whisper of the oxygen feed and an occasional metallic crepitation as the outer walls of the vehicle radiated away their heat. For no warmth at all came from the great silver crescent that floated low above the far horizon and flooded all this land with pearly light. It was so brilliant that minutes passed before Marvin could accept its challenge and look steadfastly into its glare, but at last he could discern the outlines of continents, the hazy border of the atmosphere, and the white islands of cloud. And even at this distance, he could see the glitter of sunlight on the polar ice.

It was beautiful, and it called to his heart across the abyss of space. There in that shining crescent were all the wonders that he had never known—the hues of sunset skies, the moaning of the sea on pebbled shores, the patter of falling rain, the unhurried benison of snow. These and a thousand others should have been his rightful heritage, but he knew them only from the books and ancient records, and the thought filled him with the anguish of exile.

Why could they not return? It seemed so peaceful beneath those lines of marching cloud. Then Marvin, his eyes no longer blinded by the glare, saw that the portion of the disk that should have been in darkness was gleaming faintly with an evil phosphorescence: and he remembered. He was looking upon the funeral pyre of a world—upon the radioactive aftermath of Armageddon. Across a quarter of a million miles of space, the glow of dying atoms was still visible, a perennial reminder of the ruinous past. It would be centuries yet before that deadly glow died from the rocks and life could return again to fill that silent, empty world.

And now father began to speak, telling Marvin the story which until this moment had meant no more to him than the fairy-tales he had heard in childhood. There were many things he could not understand: it was impossible for him to picture the glowing, multicolored pattern of life on the planet he had never seen. Nor could he comprehend the forces that had destroyed it in the end, leaving the Colony, preserved by its isolation, as the sole survivor. Yet he could share the agony of those final days, when the Colony had learned at last that never again would the supply ships come flaming down through the stars with gifts from home. One by one the radio stations had ceased to call: on the shadowed globe the lights of the cities had dimmed and died, and they were alone at last, as no men had ever been alone before, carrying in their hands the future of the race.

Then had followed the years of despair, and the longdrawn battle for survival in this fierce and hostile world. That battle had been won, though barely: this little oasis of life was safe against the worst that Nature could do. But unless there was a goal, a future toward which it could work, the Colony would lose the will to live and neither machines nor skill nor science could save it then.

So, at last, Marvin understood the purpose of this pilgrimage. He would never walk beside the rivers of that lost and legendary world, or listen to the thunder raging above its softly rounded hills. Yet one day—how far ahead?—his children's children would return to claim their heritage. The winds and the rains would scour the poisons from the burning lands and carry them to the sea, and in the depths of the sea they would waste their venom until they could harm no living things. Then the great ships that were still waiting here on the silent, dusty plains could lift once more into space, along the road that led to home.

That was the dream: and one day, Marvin knew with a sudden flash of insight, he would pass it on to his own son, here at this same spot with the mountain behind him and the silver light from the sky streaming into his face.

He did not look back as they began the homeward journey. He could not bear to see the cold glory of the crescent Earth fade from the rocks around him, as he went to rejoin his people in their long exile.

20_____

It's quite a view of here from there, as you now know, but in 1951, when the story appeared, not even astronomer Clarke had seen the planet Gaia against that background of space. When Father Hesburgh of Notre Dame moderated the conference of American and Russian scientists after the showing of *Threads* earlier this year, the visual center of the set was a large color photograph of Earth intended as background. It was eerily effective as a religious symbol, and I wonder who thought of hanging the mother of life there to preside over of that discussion of universal death. A good photograph of Earth in space has a numinous power, it seems to me, because it is a new vision for the human species of an ancient archetype: the Earth Mother, now appearing as a global image of Self in a heavenly pantheon, like a painting of the Assumption of the Virgin—of which it is a photograph. Lovelock's hypothesis that she's alive is fascinating, but why call her Gaia? It was fitting to name dead planets after dead gods, but Earth is still struggling to stay alive, so why not rename her for a goddess to whom men still pray? Why not rename her Miriam[1] in the West, and Kuan Yin in the East? She may become a barren and dusty Gaia soon enough.

In "A Boy and His Dog," the underworld is really the underworld,

---

[1]Teilhard once called the mother of Jesus "the True Demeter." Demeter was the Corn Maiden of the Greeks, and the name seems to mean "earth mother." Gaia was the mother of the Cyclops.

but something seems upside down. Warning: parental guidance is suggested for children younger than forty. Ladies are admitted free, but whether they can get out again alive is a question. This powerful (and gruesome) story, which was written in anger after the Kent State shootings, won Nebula and Hugo awards. As in "The Feast of Saint Janis," a female is victim, but there's a difference. The story appears here as a worst-case finale for civilization in collapse. When a civilization collapses, barbarians *do* fall on women first, as every place becomes a war zone and no rules exist.

Case 113: Ch'iu-Ch'iu's Wow

A monk asked Abbot Ch'iu-Ch'iu, "Teacher, is there Buddha nature in a dog?"

"Bow!" said Ch'iu-Ch'iu.

The monk bowed.

"Wow!" said Ch'iu-Ch'iu.

The monk looked up in silence.

"Do you understand?" asked Ch'iu-Ch'iu.

The monk trotted on all fours around the Abbot's meditation seat, then sat back on his haunches with his forepaws up and begged, "Teach me, O Master."

Ch'iu-Ch'iu threw his staff across the room and said, "Fetch!"

The student brought it back at once. Ch'iu-Ch'iu hit him with it, crying "Wild fox!" and hit him again. The student hurried out.

Brother Pseudo comments:

> Tell me, why hit him only twice?
> This monk has heard of Chao Chou[2] and comes rehearsed,
> but incurs a beating for his trouble.
> Ch'iu-Ch'iu in his grandmotherly kindness
> Wastes two words instead of one. "Bow!"
> The monk knows how to grovel and roll over well enough,
> But is driven away all the same.
> Is there Buddha nature in the dog?
> "Wow!"

from THE YELLOW CLIFF RECORD

[2]Who answered the same question with a simple *Wu!*

A BOY AND HIS DOG

I

I was out with Blood, my dog. It was his week for annoying me; he kept calling me Albert. He thought that was pretty damned funny. Payson Terhune: ha ha.

I'd caught a couple of water rats for him, the big green and ocher ones, and someone's manicured poodle, lost off a leash in one of the downunders.

He'd eaten pretty good, but he was cranky. "Come on, son of a bitch," I demanded, "find me a piece of ass."

Blood just chuckled, deep in his dog-throat. "You're funny when you get horny," he said.

Maybe funny enough to kick him upside his sphincter asshole, that refugee from a dingo-heap.

"Find! I ain't kidding!"

"For shame, Albert. After all I've taught you. Not 'I *ain't* kidding'. I'm *not* kidding."

He knew I'd reached the edge of my patience. Sullenly, he started casting. He sat down on the crumbled remains of the curb, and his eyelids flickered and closed, and his hairy body tensed. After a while he settled down on his front paws, and scraped them forward till he was lying flat, his shaggy head on the outstretched paws. The tenseness left him and he began trembling, almost the way he trembled just preparatory to scratching a flea. It went on that way for almost a quarter of an hour, and finally he rolled over and lay

335

on his back, his naked belly toward the night sky, his front paws folded mantislike, his hind legs extended and open. "I'm sorry," he said. "There's nothing."

I could have gotten mad and booted him, but I knew he had tried. I wasn't happy about it, I really wanted to get laid, but what could I do? "Okay," I said, with resignation, "forget it."

He kicked himself onto his side and quickly got up.

"What do you want to do?" he asked.

"Not much we *can* do, is there?" I was more than a little sarcastic. He sat down again, at my feet, insolently humble.

I leaned against the melted stub of a lamppost, and thought about girls. It was painful. "We can always go to a show," I said. Blood looked around the street, at the pools of shadow lying in the weed-overgrown craters, and didn't say anything. The whelp was waiting for me to say okay, let's go. He liked movies as much as I did.

"Okay, let's go."

He got up and followed me, his tongue hanging, panting with happiness. Go ahead and laugh, you eggsucker. No popcorn for *you!*

Our Gang was a roverpak that had never been able to cut it simply foraging, so they'd opted for comfort and gone a smart way to getting it. They were movie-oriented kids, and they'd taken over the turf where the Metropole Theater was located. No one tried to bust their turf, because we all needed the movies, and as long as Our Gang had access to films, and did a better job of keeping the films going, they provided a service, even for solos like me and Blood. *Especially* for solos like us.

They made me check my .45 and the Browning .22 long at the door. There was a little alcove right beside the ticket booth. I bought my tickets first; it cost me a can of Oscar Mayer Philadelphia Scrapple for me, and a tin of sardines for Blood. Then the Our Gang guards with the bren guns motioned me over to the alcove and I checked my heat. I saw water leaking from a broken pipe in the ceiling and I told the checker, a kid with big leathery warts all over his face and lips, to move my weapons where it was dry. He ignored me. "Hey you! Motherfuckin' toad, move my stuff over the other side ... it goes to rust fast ... an' it picks up any spots, man, I'll break your bones!"

He started to give me jaw about it, looked at the guards with the brens, knew if they tossed me out I'd lose my price of admission whether I went in or not, but they weren't looking for any action, probably understrength, and gave him the nod to let it pass, to do what I said. So the toad moved my Browning to the other end of the gun rack, and pegged my .45 under it.

Blood and me went into the theater.

"I want popcorn."

"Forget it."

"Come on, Albert. Buy me popcorn."

"I'm tapped out. You can live without popcorn."

"You're just being a shit."

I shrugged: sue me.

We went in. The place was jammed. I was glad the guards hadn't tried to take anything but guns. My spike and knife felt reassuring, lying-up in their oiled sheaths at the back of my neck. Blood found two together, and we moved into the row, stepping on feet. Someone cursed and I ignored him. A Doberman growled. Blood's fur stirred, but he let it pass. There was always *some* hardcase on the muscle, even on neutral ground like the Metropole.

(I heard once about a get-it-on they'd had at the old Loew's Granada, on the South Side. Wound up with ten or twelve rovers and their mutts dead, the theater burned down and a couple of good Cagney films lost in the fire. After that was when the roverpaks had got up the agreement that movie houses were sanctuaries. It was better now, but there was always somebody too messed in the mind to come soft.)

It was a triple feature. "Raw Deal" with Dennis O'Keefe, Claire Trevor, Raymond Burr and Marsha Hunt was the oldest of the three. It'd been made in 1948, eighty-six years ago; god only knows how the damn thing'd hung together all that time; it slipped sprockets and they had to stop the movie all the time to re-thread it. But it was a good movie. About this solo who'd been japped by his roverpak and was out to get revenge. Gangsters, mobs, a lot of punching and fighting. Real good.

The middle flick was a thing made during the Third War, in '92, twenty-seven years before I was even born, thing called "Smell of a Chink." It was mostly gut-spilling and some nice hand-to-hand. Beautiful scene of skirmisher greyhounds equipped with napalm throwers, jellyburning a Chink town. Blood dug it, even though we'd seen this flick before. He had some kind of phony shuck going that these were ancestors of his, and *he* knew and *I* knew he was making it up.

"Wanna burn a baby, hero?" I whispered to him. He got the barb and just shifted in his seat, didn't say a thing, kept looking pleased as the dogs worked their way through the town. I was bored stiff.

I was waiting for the main feature.

Finally it came on. It was a beauty, a beaver flick made in the late 1970s. It was called "Big Black Leather Splits." Started right out very good. These two blondes in black leather corsets and boots laced all the way up to their crotches, with whips and masks, got this skinny guy down and one of the chicks sat on his face while the other one went down on him. It got really hairy after that.

All around me there were solos playing with themselves. I was about to jog it a little myself when Blood leaned across and said, real soft, the way he does when he's onto something unusually smelly, "There's a chick in here."

"You're nuts," I said.

"I tell you I smell her. She's in here, man."

Without being conspicuous, I looked around. Almost every seat in the theater was taken with solos or their dogs. If a chick had slipped in there'd have been a riot. She'd have been ripped to pieces before any single guy could have gotten into her. "Where?" I asked, softly. All around me, the solos were beating-off, moaning as the blondes took off their masks and one of them worked the skinny guy with a big wooden ram strapped around her hips.

"Give me a minute," Blood said. He was really concentrating. His body was tense as a wire. His eyes were closed, his muzzle quivering. I let him work.

It was possible. Just maybe possible. I knew that they made really dumb flicks in the downunders, the kind of crap they'd made back in the 1930s and '40s, real clean stuff with even married people sleeping in twin beds. Myrna Loy and George Brent kind of flicks. And I knew that once in a while a chick from one of the really strict middle-class downunders would cumup, to see what a hairy flick was like. I'd heard about it, but it'd never happened in any theater *I'd* ever been in.

And the chances of it happening in the Metropole, particularly, were slim. There was a lot of twisty trade came to the Metropole. Now, understand, I'm not specially prejudiced against guys corning one another...hell, I can understand it. There just aren't enough chicks anywhere. But I can't cut the jockey-and-boxer scene because it gets some weak little boxer hanging on you, getting jealous, you have to hunt for him and all he thinks he has to do is bare his ass to get all the work done for him. It's as bad as having a chick dragging along behind. Made for a lot of bad blood and fights in the bigger roverpaks, too. So I just never swung that way. Well, not *never*, but not for a long time.

So with all the twisties in the Metropole, I didn't think a chick would chance it. Be a toss-up who'd tear her apart first; the boxers or the straights.

And if she *was* here, why couldn't any of the other dogs smell her...?

"Third row in front of us," Blood said. "Aisle seat. Dressed like a solo."

"How's come *you* can whiff her and no other dog's caught her?"

"You forget who I am, Albert."

"I didn't forget, I just don't believe it."

Actually, bottom-line, I guess I *did* believe it. When you'd been as dumb as I'd been and a dog like Blood'd taught me so much, a guy came to believe *everything* he said. You don't argue with your teacher.

Not when he'd taught you how to read and write and add and subtract and everything else they used to know that meant you were smart (but doesn't mean much of anything now, except it's good to know it, I guess).

(The reading's a pretty good thing. It comes in handy when you can find some canned goods someplace, like in a bombed-out supermarket; makes it easier to pick out stuff you like when the pictures are gone off the labels. Couple of times the reading stopped me from taking canned beets. Shit, I *hate* beets!)

So I guess I *did* believe why he could whiff a maybe chick in there, and no other mutt could. He'd told me all about *that* a million times. It was his favorite story. History he called it. Christ, I'm not *that* dumb! I knew what history was. That was all the stuff that happened before now.

But I liked hearing history straight from Blood, instead of him making me read one of those crummy books he was always dragging in. And *that* particular history was all about him, so he laid it on me over and over, till I knew it by heart...no, the word was *rote.* Not *wrote,* like writing, that was something else. I knew it by rote, like it means you got it word-for-word.

And when a mutt teaches you everything you know, and he tells you something rote, I guess finally you *do* believe it. Except I'd never let that leg-lifter know it.

II

What he'd told me rote was:

Over sixty-five years ago, in Los Angeles, before the Third War even got going completely, there was a man named Buesing who lived in Cerritos. He raised dogs as watchmen and sentries and attackers. Dobermans, Danes, schnauzers and Japanese akitas. He had one four-year-old German shepherd bitch named Ginger. She worked for the Los Angeles Police Department's narcotics division. She could smell out marijuana. No matter how well it was hidden. They ran a test on her: there were 25,000 boxes in an auto parts warehouse. Five of them had been planted with marijuana sealed in cellophane, wrapped in tin foil and heavy brown paper, and finally hidden in three separate sealed cartons. Within seven minutes Ginger found all five packages. At the same time that Ginger was working, ninety-two miles farther north, in Santa Barbara, cetologists had drawn and amplified dolphin spinal fluid and injected it into Chacma baboons and dogs. Altering surgery and grafting had been done. The first successful product of this cetacean experimentation had been a two-year-old male Puli named Ahbhu, who had communicated sense-impressions telepathically. Cross-breeding and continued experimentation had produced the first skirmisher dogs, just in time for the Third War. Telepathic over short distances, easily trained, able to track gasoline or troops or poison gas or radiation when linked with their human controllers, they had become the shock commandos of a new kind of war. The selective traits had bred true. Dobermans, greyhounds, akitas, pulis and schnauzers had become steadily more telepathic.

Ginger and Ahbhu had been Blood's ancestors.

He had told me so, a thousand times. Had told me the story just that way, in just those words, a thousand times, as it had been told to him. I'd never believed him till now.

Maybe the little bastard *was* special.

I checked out the solo scrunched down in the aisle seat three rows ahead of me. I couldn't tell a damned thing. The solo had his (her?) cap pulled way down, fleece jacket pulled way up.

"Are you sure?"

"As sure as I can be. It's a girl."

"If it is, she's playing with herself just like a guy."

Blood snickered. "Surprise," he said sarcastically.

The mystery solo sat through "Raw Deal" again. It made sense, if that was a girl. Most of the solos and all of the members of roverpaks left after the beaver flick. The theater didn't fill up much more, it gave the streets time to empty, he/she could make his/her way back to wherever he/she had come from. I sat through "Raw Deal" again myself. Blood went to sleep.

When the mystery solo got up, I gave him/her time to get weapons if any'd been checked, and started away. Then I pulled Blood's big shaggy ear and said, "Let's do it." He slouched after me, up the aisle.

I got my guns and checked the street. Empty.

"Okay, nose," I said, "where'd he go?"

"Her. To the right."

I started off, loading the Browning from my bandolier. I still didn't see anyone moving among the bombed-out shells of the buildings. This section of the city was crummy, really bad shape. But then, with Our Gang running the Metropole, they didn't have to repair anything else to get their livelihood. It was ironic; the Dragons had to keep an entire power plant going to get tribute from the other roverpaks; Ted's Bunch had to mind the reservoir; the Bastinados worked like fieldhands in the marijuana gardens; the Barbados Blacks lost a couple of dozen members every year cleaning out the radiation pits all over the city; and Our Gang only had to run that movie house.

Whoever their leader had been, however many years ago it had been that the roverpaks had started forming out of foraging solos, I had to give it to him: he'd been a flinty sharp mother. He knew what services to deal in.

"She turned off here," Blood said.

I followed him as he began loping, toward the edge of the city and the bluish-green radiation that still flickered from the hills. I knew he was right, then. The only things out here were screamers and the access dropshaft to the downunder. It was a girl, all right.

The cheeks of my ass tightened as I thought about it. I was going to get laid. It had been almost a month, since Blood had whiffed that solo chick in the basement of the Market Basket. She'd been filthy, and I'd gotten the crabs from her, but she'd been a woman, all right, and once I'd tied her down and clubbed her a couple of times she'd been pretty good. She'd liked it, too, even if she did spit on me and tell me she'd kill me if she ever got loose. I left her tied up, just to be sure. She wasn't there when I went back to look, week before last.

"Watch out," Blood said, dodging around a crater almost invisible against the surrounding shadows. Something stirred in the crater.

Trekking across the nomansland I realized why it was that all but a handful of solos or members of roverpaks were guys. The War had killed off most of the girls, and that was the way it always was in wars...at least that's what Blood told me. The things getting born were seldom male *or* female, and had to be smashed against a wall as soon as they were pulled out of the mother.

The few chicks who hadn't gone downunder with the middle-classers were hard, solitary bitches like the one in the Market Basket; tough and stringy and just as likely to cut off your meat with a razor blade once they let you get in. Scuffing for a piece of ass had gotten harder and harder, the older I'd gotten.

But every once in a while a chick got tired of being roverpak property, or a raid was got-up by five or six roverpaks and some unsuspecting downunder was taken, or—like this time, yeah—some middle-class chick from a downunder got hot pants to find out what a beaver flick looked like, and cumup.

I was going to get laid. Oh boy, I couldn't wait!

III

Out here it was nothing but empty corpses of blasted buildings. One entire block had been stomped flat, like a steel press had come down from Heaven and given one solid wham! and everything was powder under it. The chick was scared and skittish, I could see that. She moved erratically, looking back over her shoulder and to either side. She knew she was in dangerous country. Man, if she'd only known *how* dangerous.

There was one building standing all alone at the end of the smash-flat block, like it had been missed and chance let it stay. She ducked inside, and a minute later I saw a bobbing light. Flashlight? Maybe.

Blood and I crossed the street and came up into the blackness surrounding the building. It was what was left of a YMCA.

That meant "Young Men's Christian Association." Blood taught me to read.

So what the hell was a young men's christian association? Sometimes being able to read makes more questions than if you were stupid.

I didn't want her getting out; inside there was as good a place to screw her as any, so I put Blood on guard right beside the steps leading up into the shell, and I went around the back. All the doors and windows had been blown out, of course. It wasn't no big trick getting in. I pulled myself up to the ledge of a window, and dropped down inside. Dark inside. No noise, except the sound of her, moving around on the other side of the old YMCA. I didn't know if she was heeled or not, and I wasn't about to take any chances. I bowslung the Browning and took out the .45 automatic. I didn't have to snap back the action—there was always a slug in the chamber.

I started moving carefully through the room. It was a locker room of some kind. There was glass and debris all over the floor, and one entire row of metal lockers had the paint blistered off their surfaces; the flash blast had caught them through the windows, a lot of years ago. My sneakers didn't make a sound coming through the room.

The door was hanging on one hinge, and I stepped over—through the inverted triangle. I was in the swimming pool area. The big pool was empty, with tiles buckled down at the shallow end. It stunk bad in there; no wonder, there were dead guys, or what was left of them, along one wall. Some lousy cleaner-up had stacked them, but hadn't buried them. I pulled my bandanna up around my nose and mouth and kept moving.

Out the other side of the pool place, and through a little passage with popped light bulbs in the ceiling. I didn't have any trouble seeing. There was moonlight coming through busted windows and a chunk was out of the ceiling. I could hear her real plain now, just on the other side of the door at the end of the passage. I hung close to the wall, and stepped down to the door. It was open a crack, but blocked by a fall of lath and plaster from the wall. It would make noise when I went to pull it open, that was for certain. I had to wait for the right moment.

Flattened against the wall, I checked out what she was doing in there. It was a gymnasium, big one, with climbing ropes hanging down from the ceiling. She had a squat, square, eight-cell flashlight sitting up on the croup of a vaulting horse. There were parallel bars and a horizontal bar about eight feet high, the tempered steel all rusty now. There were swinging rings and a trampoline and a big wooden balancing beam. Over to one side there were wall-bars and balancing benches, horizontal and oblique ladders, and a couple of stacks of vaulting boxes. I made a note to remember this joint. It was better for working-out than the jerry-rigged gym I'd set up in an old auto wrecking yard. A guy has to keep in shape, if he's going to be a solo.

She was out of her disguise. Standing there in the skin, shivering. Yeah, it was chilly, and I could see a pattern of chicken-skin all over her. She was maybe five-six or -seven, with nice tits and kind of skinny legs. She was brushing out her hair. It hung way down the back. The flashlight didn't make it clear enough to tell if she had red hair or chestnut, but it wasn't blonde, which was good, and that was because I dug redheads. She had nice tits, though. I couldn't see her face, the hair was hanging down all smooth and wavy and cut off her profile.

The crap she'd been wearing was thrown around on the floor, and what she was going to put on was up on the vaulting horse. She was standing in little shoes with a kind of funny heel on them.

I couldn't move. I suddenly realized I couldn't move. She was nice, really nice. I was getting a real big kick out of just standing there and seeing the way her waist fell inward and her hips fell outward, the way the muscles at the side of her tits pulled up when she reached to the top of her head to brush all that hair down. It was really weird the kick I was getting out of standing and just staring at a chick do that. Kind of very, well, woman stuff. I liked it a lot.

I'd never ever stopped and just looked at a chick like that. All the ones I'd ever seen had been scumbags that Blood had smelled out for me, and I'd snatchn'grabbed them. Or the big chicks in the beaver flicks. Not like this one, kind of soft and very smooth, even with the goose bumps. I could have watched her all night.

She put down the brush, and reached over and took a pair of panties off the pile of clothes and wriggled into them. Then she got her bra and put it on. I never knew the way chicks did it. She put it on backwards, around her waist, and it had a hook on it. Then she slid it around till the cups were in front, and kind of pulled it up under and scooped herself into it, first one, then the other; then she pulled the straps over her shoulder. She reached for her dress, and I nudged some of the lath and plaster aside, and grabbed the door to give it a yank.

She had the dress up over her head, and her arms up inside the material, and when she stuck her head in, and was all tangled there for a second, I yanked the door and there was a crash as chunks of wood and plaster fell out of the way, and a heavy scraping, and I jumped inside and was on her before she could get out of the dress.

She started to scream, and I pulled the dress off her with a ripping sound, and it all happened for her before she knew what that crash and scrape was all about.

Her face was wild. Just wild. Big eyes: I couldn't tell what color they were because they were in shadow. Real fine features, a wide mouth, little nose, cheekbones just like mine, real high and prominent, and a dimple in her right cheek. She stared at me really scared.

And then...and this is really weird...I felt like I should *say* something to her. I don't know what. Just something. It made me uncomfortable, to see her scared, but what the hell could I do about *that*, I mean, I was going to rape her, after all, and I couldn't very well tell her not to be shrinky about it. She was the one cumup, after all. But even so, I wanted to say hey, don't be scared, I just want to lay you. (That never happened before. I never wanted to *say* anything to a chick, just get in, and that was that.)

But it passed, and I put my leg behind hers and tripped her back, and she went down in a pile. I leveled the .45 at her, and her mouth kind of opened in a little o shape. "Now I'm gonna go over there and get one of them wrestling mats, so it'll be better, comfortable, uh-huh? You make a move off that floor and I shoot a leg out from under you, and you'll get screwed just the same, except you'll be without a leg." I waited for her to let me know she was onto what I was saying, and she finally nodded real slow, so I kept the automatic on her, and went over to the big dusty stack of mats, and pulled one off.

I dragged it over to her, and flipped it so the cleaner side was up, and used the muzzle of the .45 to maneuver her onto it. She just sat there on the mat, with her hands behind her, and her knees bent, and stared at me.

I unzipped my pants and started pulling them down off one side, when I caught her looking at me real funny. I stopped with the jeans. "What're *you* lookin' at?"

I was mad. I didn't know why I was mad, but I was.

"What's your name?" she asked. Her voice was very soft, and kind of furry, like it came up through her throat that was all lined with fur or something.

She kept looking at me, waiting for me to answer.

"Vic," I said. She looked like she was waiting for more.

"Vic what?"

I didn't know what she meant for a minute, then I did. "Vic. Just Vic. That's all."

"Well, what're your mother and father's names?"

Then I started laughing, and working my jeans down again. "Boy, are you a dumb bitch," I said, and laughed some more. She looked hurt. It made me mad again. "Stop lookin' like that, or I'll bust out your teeth!"

She folded her hands in her lap.

I got the pants around my ankles. They wouldn't come off over the sneakers. I had to balance on one foot and scuff the sneaker off the other foot. It was tricky, keeping the .45 on her and getting the sneaker off at the same time. But I did it.

I was standing there buck-naked from the waist down and she had sat forward a little, her legs crossed, hands still in her lap. "Get that stuff off," I said.

She didn't move for a second, and I thought she was going to give me trouble. But then she reached around behind and undid the bra. Then she tipped back and slipped the panties off her ass.

Suddenly, she didn't look scared any more. She was watching me very close and I could see her eyes were blue now. Now this is the really weird thing...

I couldn't do it. I mean, not exactly. I mean, I *wanted* to fuck her, see, but she was all soft and pretty and she kept *looking* at me, and no solo I ever met would believe me, but I heard myself *talking* to her, still standing there like some kind of wetbrain, one sneaker off and jeans down around my ankles. "What's *your* name?"

"Quilla June Holmes."

"That's a weird name."

"My mother says it's not that uncommon, back in Oklahoma."

"That where your folks come from?"

She nodded. "Before the Third War."

"They must be pretty old by now."

"They are, but they're okay. I guess."

We were just frozen there, talking to each other. I could tell she was cold, because she was shivering. "Well," I said, sort of getting ready to drop down beside her, "I guess we better—"

Damn it! That damned Blood! Right at that moment he came crashing in from outside. Came skidding through the lath, and plaster, raising dust, slid along on his ass till he got to us. "*Now* what?" I demanded.

"Who're you talking to?" the girl asked.

"Him. Blood."

"*The dog!?!*"

Blood stared at her and then ignored her. He started to say something but the girl interrupted him. "Then it's true what they say ... you can all talk to animals ..."

"You going to listen to her all night, or do you want to hear why I came in?"

"Okay, why're you here?"

"You're in trouble, Albert."

"Come *on*, forget the mickeymouse. What's up?"

Blood twisted his head toward the front door of the YMCA. "Roverpak. Got the building surrounded. I make it fifteen or twenty, maybe more."

"How the hell'd they know we was here?"

Blood looked chagrined. He dropped his head.

"Well?"

"Some other mutt must've smelled her in the theater."

"Great."

"Now what?"

"Now we stand 'em off, that's what. You got any better sugges-
tions?"

"Just one."

I waited. He grinned.

"Pull your pants up."

IV

The girl, this Quilla June, was pretty safe. I made her a kind of a
shelter out of wrestling mats, maybe a dozen of them. She wouldn't
get hit by a stray bullet, and if they didn't go right for her, they
wouldn't find her. I climbed one of the ropes hanging down from
the girders and laid out up there with the Browning and a couple
of handfuls of reloads. I wished to God I'd had an automatic, a bren
or a Thompson. I checked the .45, made sure it was full, with one
in the chamber, and set the extra clips down on the girder. I had a
clear line-of-fire all around the gym.

Blood was lying in shadow right near the front door. He'd suggested I try and pick off any dogs with the roverpak first, if I could.
That would allow him to operate freely.

That was the least of my worries.

I'd wanted to hole up in another room, one with only a single
entrance, but I had no way of knowing if the rovers were already
in the building, so I did the best I could with what I had.

Everything was quiet. Even that Quilla June. It'd taken me valuable minutes to convince her she'd damned well better hole up
and not make any noise; she was better off with me than with twenty
of *them*. "If you ever wanna see your mommy and daddy again," I
warned her. After that she didn't give me no trouble, packing her
in with mats.

Quiet.

Then I heard two things, both at the same time. From back in
the swimming pool I heard boots crunching plaster. Very soft. And
from one side of the front door, I heard a tinkle of metal striking
wood. So they were going to try a yoke. Well, I was ready.

Quiet again.

I sighted the Browning on the door to the pool room. It was still
open from when I'd come through. Figure him at maybe five-ten,
and drop the sights a foot and a half, and I'd catch him in the chest.

I'd learned long ago you don't try for the head. Go for the widest part of the body: the chest and stomach. The trunk.

Suddenly, outside, I heard a dog bark, and part of the darkness near the front door detached itself and moved inside the gym. Directly opposite Blood. I didn't move the Browning.

The rover at the front door moved a step along the wall, away from Blood. Then he cocked back his arm and threw something—a rock, a piece of metal, something—across the room to draw fire. I didn't move the Browning.

When the thing he'd thrown hit the floor, two rovers jumped out of the swimming pool door, one on either side of it, rifles down, ready to spray. Before they could open up, I'd squeezed off the first shot, tracked across and put a second shot into the other one. They both went down. Dead hits, right in the heart. Bang, they were down, neither one moved.

The mother by the door turned to split, and Blood was on him. Just like that, out of the darkness, riiiip!

Blood leaped, right over the crossbar of the guy's rifle held at ready, and sank his fangs into the rover's throat. The guy screamed, and Blood dropped, carrying a piece of the guy with him. The guy was making awful bubbling sounds and went down on one knee. I put a slug into his head, and he fell forward.

It went quiet again.

Not bad. Not bad atall atall. Three takeouts and they still didn't know our positions. Blood had fallen back into the murk by the entrance. He didn't say a thing, but I knew what he was thinking: maybe that was three out of seventeen, or three out of twenty, or twenty-two. No way of knowing; we could be faced-off in here for a week and never know if we'd gotten them all, or some, or none. They could go and get poured full again, and I'd find myself run out of slugs and no food and that girl, that Quilla June, crying and making me divide my attention, and daylight—and they'd be still laying out there, waiting till we got hungry enough to do something dumb, or till we ran out of slugs; and then they'd cloud up and rain all over us.

A rover came dashing straight through the front door at top speed, took a leap, hit on his shoulders, rolled, came up going in a different direction, and snapped off three rounds into different corners of the room before I could track him with the Browning. By that time he was close enough under me where I didn't have to waste a .22 slug. I picked up the .45 without a sound and blew the back off his head. Slug went in neat, came out and took most of his hair with it. He fell right down.

"Blood! The rifle!"

Came out of the shadows, grabbed it up in his mouth and dragged it over to the pile of wrestling mats in the far corner. I saw an arm poke out from the mass of mats, and a hand grabbed the rifle, dragged it inside. Well, it was at least safe there, till I needed it. Brave little bastard: he scuttled over to the dead rover and started worrying the ammo bandolier off his body. It took him a while; he could have been picked off from the doorway or outside one of the windows, but he did it. Brave little bastard. I had to remember to get him something good to eat when we got out of this. I smiled, up there in the darkness: *if* we got out of this, I wouldn't have to worry about getting him something tender. It was lying all over the floor of that gymnasium.

Just as Blood was dragging the bandolier back into the shadows, two of them tried it with their dogs. They came through a ground floor window, one after another, hitting and rolling and going in opposite directions, as the dogs—a mother-ugly akita, big as a house, and a Doberman bitch the color of a turd—shot through the front door and split in the unoccupied two directions. I caught one of the dogs, the akita, with the .45, and it went down thrashing. The Doberman was all over Blood.

But firing, I'd given away my position. One of the rovers fired from the hip and .30–06 soft-nosed slugs spanged off the girders around me. I dropped the automatic, and it started to slip off the girder as I reached for the Browning. I made a grab for the .45 and that was the only thing saved me. I fell forward to clutch at it, it slipped away and hit the gym floor with a crash, and the rover fired at where I'd been. But I was flat on the girder, arm dangling, and the crash startled him. He fired at the sound, and right at that instant I heard another shot, from a Winchester, and the other rover, who'd made it safe into the shadows, fell forward holding a big pumping hole in his chest. That Quilla June had shot him, from behind the mats.

I didn't even have time to figure out what the fuck was happening

...Blood was rolling around with the Doberman and the sounds they were making were awful...the rover with the .30–06 chipped off another shot and hit the muzzle of the Browning, protruding over the side of the girder, and wham it was gone, falling down. I was naked up there without clout, and the sonofabitch was hanging back in shadow waiting for me.

Another shot from the Winchester, and the rover fired right into the mats. She ducked back behind, and I knew I couldn't count on her for anything more. But I didn't need it; in that second, while he was focused on her, I grabbed the climbing rope, flipped myself over the girder, and howling like a burnpit-screamer, went sliding down, feeling the rope cutting my palms. I got down far enough to swing, and kicked off. I swung back and forth, whipping my body three different ways each time, swinging out and over, way over, each time. The sonofabitch kept firing, trying to track a trajectory, but I kept spinning out of his line of fire. Then he was empty, and I kicked back as hard as I could, and came zooming in toward his corner of shadows, and let loose all at once and went ass-over-end into the corner, and there he was, and I went right into him and he spanged off the wall, and I was on top of him, digging my thumbs into his eyesockets. He was screaming and the dogs were screaming and that girl was screaming, and I pounded the motherfucker's head against the floor till he stopped moving, then I grabbed up the empty .30–06 and whipped his head till I knew he wasn't gonna give me no more aggravation.

Then I found the .45 and shot the Doberman.

Blood got up and shook himself off. He was cut up bad. "Thanks," he mumbled, and went over to lie down in the shadows to lick himself off.

I went and found that Quilla June, and she was crying. About all the guys we'd killed. Mostly about the one *she'd* killed. I couldn't get her to stop bawling so I cracked her across the face and told her she'd saved my life, and that helped some.

Blood came dragassing over. "How're we going to get out of this, Albert?"

"Let me think."

I thought and knew it was hopeless. No matter how many we got, there'd be more. And it was a matter of *macho* now. Their honor.

"How about a fire?" Blood suggested.

"Get away while it's burning?" I shook my head. "They'll have the place staked-out all around. No good."

"What if we don't leave? What if we burn up with it?"

I looked at him. Brave...and smart as hell.

V

We gathered all the lumber and mats and scaling ladders and vaulting boxes and benches and anything else that would burn, and piled the garbage against a wooden divider at one end of the gym. Quilla June found a can of kerosene in a storeroom, and we set fire to the whole damn pile. Then we followed Blood to the place he'd found for us. The boiler room way down under the YMCA. We all climbed into the empty boiler, and dogged down the door, leaving a release vent open for air. We had one mat in there with us, and all the ammo we could carry, and the extra rifles and sidearms the rovers'd had on them.

"Can you catch anything?" I asked Blood.

"A little. Not much. I'm reading one guy. The building's burning good."

"You be able to tell when they split?"

"Maybe. *If* they split."

I settled back. Quilla June was shaking from all that had happened. "Just take it easy," I told her. "By morning the place'll be down around our ears, and they'll go through the rubble and find a lot of dead meat, and maybe they won't look too hard for a chick's body. And everything'll be all right...if we don't get choked off in here."

She smiled, very thin, and tried to look brave. She was okay, that one. She closed her eyes and settled back on the mat and tried to sleep. I was beat. I closed my eyes, too.

"Can you handle it?" I asked Blood.

"I suppose. You better sleep."

I nodded, eyes still closed, and fell on my side. I was out before I could think about it.

When I came back, I found the girl, that Quilla June, snuggled up under my armpit, her arm around my waist, dead asleep. I could hardly breathe. It was like a furnace; hell, it *was* a furnace. I reached out a hand and the wall of the boiler was so damned hot I couldn't touch it. Blood was up on the mattress with us. That mat had been the only thing'd kept us from being singed good. He was asleep, head buried in his paws. She was asleep, still naked.

I put a hand on her tit. It was warm. She stirred and cuddled into me closer. I got a hard-on.

Managed to get my pants off, and rolled on top of her. She woke up fast when she felt me pry her legs apart, but it was too late by then. "Don't... *stop*... what are you doing... no, don't..."

But she was half-asleep, and weak, and I don't think she really wanted to fight me anyhow.

She cried when I broke her, of course, but after that it was okay. There was blood all over the wrestling mat. And Blood just kept sleeping.

It was really different. Usually, when I'd get Blood to track something down for me, it'd be grab it and punch it and pork it and get away fast before something bad could happen. But when she came, she rose up off the mat, and hugged me around the back so hard I thought she'd crack my ribs, and then she settled back down slow slow slow, like I do when I'm doing leg-lifts in the makeshift gym I rigged in the auto wrecking yard. And her eyes were closed, and she was relaxed looking. And happy. I could tell.

We did it a lot of times, and after a while it was her idea, but I didn't say no. And then we lay out side-by-side and talked.

She asked me about how it was with Blood, and I told her how the skirmisher dogs had gotten telepathic, and how they'd lost the ability to hunt food for themselves, so the solos and roverpaks had to do it for them, and how dogs like Blood were good at finding chicks for solos like me. She didn't say anything to that.

I asked her about what it was like where she lived, in one of the downunders.

"It's nice. But it's always very quiet. Everyone is very polite to everyone else. It's just a small town."

"Which one you live in?"

"Topeka. It's real close to here."

"Yeah, I know. The access dropshaft is only about half a mile from here. I went out there once, to take a look around."

"Have you ever been in a downunder?"

"No. But I don't guess I want to be, either."

"Why? It's very nice. You'd like it."

"Shit."

"That's very crude."

"*I'm* very crude."

"Not all the time."

I was getting mad. "Listen, you ass, what's the matter with you? I grabbed you and pushed you around, I raped you half a dozen times, so what's so good about me, huh? What's the matter with you, don't you even have enough smarts to know when somebody's—"

She was smiling at me. "I didn't mind. I liked doing it. Want to do it again?"

I was really shocked. I moved away from her. "What the hell is wrong with you? Don't you know that a chick from a downunder like you can be really mauled by solos? Don't you know chicks get warnings from their parents in the downunders, 'Don't cumup, you'll get snagged by them dirty, hairy, slobbering solos!' Don't you know that?"

She put her hand on my leg and started moving it up, the fingertips just brushing my thigh. I got another hard-on. "My parents never said that about solos," she said. Then she pulled me over her again, and kissed me, and I couldn't stop from getting in her again.

God, it just went on like that for hours. After a while Blood turned around and said, "I'm not going to keep pretending I'm asleep. I'm hungry. And I'm hurt."

I tossed her off me—she was on top by this time—and examined him. The Doberman had taken a good chunk out of his right ear, and there was a rip right down his muzzle, and blood-matted fur on one side. He was a mess. "Jesus, man, you're a mess," I said.

"You're no fucking rose garden yourself, Albert!" he snapped. I pulled my hand back.

"Can we get out of here?" I asked him.

He cast around, and then shook his head. "I can't get any readings. Must be a pile of rubble on top of this boiler. I'll have to go out and scout."

We kicked that around for a while, and finally decided if the building was razed, and had cooled a little, the roverpak would have gone through the ashes by now. The fact that they hadn't tried the boiler indicated that we were probably buried pretty good.

Either that, or the building was still smoldering overhead. In which case, they'd still be out there, waiting to sift the remains.

"Think you can handle it, the condition you're in?"

"I guess I'll *have* to, won't I?" Blood said. He was really surly. "I mean, what with you busy coitusing your brains out, there won't be much left for staying alive, will there?"

I sensed real trouble with him. He didn't like Quilla June. I moved around him and undogged the boiler hatch. It wouldn't open. So I braced my back against the side, and jacked my legs up, and gave it a slow, steady shove.

Whatever had fallen against it from outside resisted for a minute, then started to give, then tumbled away with a crash. I pushed the door open all the way, and looked out. The upper floors had fallen in on the basement, but by the time they'd given, they'd been mostly cinder and lightweight rubble. Everything was smoking out there. I could see daylight through the smoke.

I slipped out, burning my hands on the outside lip of the hatch. Blood followed. He started to pick his way through the debris. I could see that the boiler had been almost completely covered by the gunk that had dropped from above. Chances were good the roverpack had taken a fast look, figured we'd been fried, and moved on. But I wanted Blood to run a recon anyway. He started off, but I called him back. He came.

"What is it?"

I looked down at him. "I'll tell you what it is, man. You're acting very shitty."

"Sue me."

"Goddammit, dog, what's got your ass up?"

"Her. That nit chick you've got in there."

"So what? Big deal ... I've had chicks before."

"Yeah, but never any that hung on like this one. I warn you, Albert, she's going to make trouble."

"Don't be dumb!" He didn't reply. Just looked at me with anger, and then limped off to check out the scene. I crawled back inside and dogged the hatch. She wanted it again. I said I didn't want to; Blood had brought me down. I was bugged. And I didn't know which one to be pissed off at.

But God she was pretty.

She kind of pouted and settled back with her arms wrapped around her. "Tell me some more about the downunder," I said.

At first she was cranky, wouldn't say much, but after a while she opened up and started talking freely. I was learning a lot. I figured I could use it some time, maybe.

There were only a couple of hundred downunders in what was left of the United States and Canada. They'd been sunk on the sites of wells or mines or other kinds of deep holes. Some of them, out in the west, were in natural cave formations. They went way down, maybe two to five miles. They were like big caissons, stood on end. And the people who'd settled them were squares of the worst kind. Southern Baptists, Fundamentalists, lawanorder goofs, real middle-class squares with no taste for the wild life. And they'd gone back to a kind of life that hadn't existed for a hundred and fifty years. They'd gotten the last of the scientists to do the work, invent the how and why, and then they'd run them out. They didn't want any progress, they didn't want any dissent, they didn't want anything that would make waves. They'd had enough of that. The best time in the world had been just before the First War, and they figured if they could keep it like that, they could live quiet lives and survive. Shit! I'd go nuts in one of the downunders.

Quilla June smiled, and snuggled up again, and this time I didn't turn her off. She started touching me again, down there and all over, and then she said, "Vic?"

"Uh-huh."

"Have you ever been in love?"

"What?"

"In love? Have you ever been in love with a girl?"

"Well, I damn well guess I haven't!"

"Do you know what love is?"

"Sure. I guess I do."

"But if you've never been in love...?"

"Don't be dumb. I mean, I've never had a bullet in the head, and I know I wouldn't like it."

"You don't know what love is, I'll bet."

"Well, if it means living in a downunder, I guess I just don't wanna find out." We didn't go on with the conversation much after that. She pulled me down and we did it again. And when it was over, I heard Blood scratching at the boiler. I opened the hatch, and he was standing out there. "All clear," he said.

"You sure?"

"Yeah, yeah, I'm sure. Put your pants on," he said it with a sneer in the tone, "and come out here. We have to talk some stuff."

I looked at him, and he wasn't kidding. I got my jeans and sneakers on, and climbed down out of the boiler.

He trotted ahead of me, away from the boiler over some blacksoot beams, and outside the gym. It was down. Looked like a rotted stump tooth.

"Now what's lumbering you?" I asked him.

He scampered up on a chunk of concrete till he was almost nose-level with me.

"You're going dumb on me, Vic."

I knew he was serious. No Albert shit, straight Vic. "How so?"

"Last night, man. We could have cut out of there and left her for them. *That* would have been smart."

"I wanted her."

"Yeah, I know. That's what I'm talking about. It's today now, not last night. You've had her about a half a hundred times. Why're we hanging around?"

"I want some more."

Then he got angry. "Yeah, well, listen, chum . . . *I* want a few things myself. I want something to eat, and I want to get rid of this pain in my side, and I want away from this turf. Maybe they *don't* give up this easy."

"Take it easy. We can handle all that. Don't mean she can't go with us."

"*Doesn't* mean," he corrected me. "And so *that's* the new story. Now we travel three, is that right?"

I was getting really uptight myself. "You're starting to sound like a damn poodle!"

"And you're starting to sound like a boxer."

I hauled back to crack him one. He didn't move. I dropped the hand. I'd never hit Blood. I didn't want to start now.

"Sorry," he said, softly.

"That's okay."

But we weren't looking at each other.

"Vic, man, you've got a responsibility to me, you know."

"You don't have to tell me that."

"Well, I guess maybe I do. Maybe I have to remind you of some stuff. Like the time that burnpit-screamer came up out of the street and made a grab for you."

I shuddered. The motherfucker'd been green. Righteous stone green, glowing like fungus. My gut heaved, just thinking.

"And I went for him, right?"

I nodded. Right, mutt, right.

"And I could have been burned bad, and died, and that would've been all of it for me, right or wrong, isn't that true?" I nodded again. I was getting pissed off proper. I didn't like being made to feel guilty. It was a fifty-fifty with Blood and me. He knew that. "But I did it, right?" I remembered the way the green thing had screamed. Christ, it was all ooze and eyelashes.

"Okay, okay, don't hanger me."

"*Harangue*, not hanger."

"Well, WHATEVER!" I shouted. "Just knock off the crap, or we can forget the whole fucking arrangement!"

Then Blood blew. "Well, maybe we *should*, you simple *dumb putz!*"

"What's a *putz*, you little turd... is that something bad... yeah, it must be... you watch your fucking mouth, son of a bitch; or I'll kick your ass!"

We sat there and didn't talk for fifteen minutes. Neither one of us knew which way to go.

Finally, I backed off a little. I talked soft and I talked slow. I was about up to here with him, but told him I was going to do right by him, like I always had, and he threatened me, saying I'd damned well better because there were a couple of very hip solos making it around the city, and they'd be delighted to have a sharp tail-scent like him. I told him I didn't like being threatened, and he'd better watch his fucking step or I'd break his leg. He got furious and stalked off. I said screw you and went back to the boiler to take it out on that Quilla June again.

But when I stuck my head inside the boiler, she was waiting, with a pistol one of the dead rovers had supplied. She hit me good and solid over the right eye with it, and I fell straight forward across the hatch, and was out cold.

VI

"I told you she was no good." He watched me as I swabbed out the cut with disinfectant from my kit and painted the gash with iodine. He smirked when I flinched.

I put away the stuff, and rummaged around in the boiler, gathering up all the spare ammo I could carry, and ditching the Browning in favor of the heavier .30–06. Then I found something that must've slipped out of her clothes.

It was a little metal plate, about three inches long and an inch-and-a-half high. It had a whole string of numbers on it, and there were holes in it, in random patterns. "What's this?" I asked Blood.

He looked at it, sniffed it.

"Must be an identity card of some kind. Maybe it's what she used to get out of the downunder."

That made my mind up.

I jammed it in a pocket and started out. Toward the access dropshaft.

"Where the hell are you going?" Blood yelled after me.

"Come on back, you'll get killed out there!

"I'm hungry, dammit! I'm wounded!

"Albert, you sonofabitch! Come back here!"

I kept right on walking. I was gonna find that bitch and brain her. Even if I had to go downunder to find her.

It took me an hour to walk to the access dropshaft leading down to Topeka. I thought I saw Blood following, but hanging back a ways. I didn't give a damn. I was mad.

Then, there it was. A tall, straight, featureless pillar of shining black metal. It was maybe twenty feet in diameter, perfectly flat on top, disappearing straight into the ground. It was a cap, that was all. I walked straight up to it, and fished around in my pocket for that metal card. Then something was tugging at my right pants leg.

"Listen, you moron, you can't go down there!"

I kicked him off, but he came right back.

"Listen to me!"

I turned around and stared at him.

Blood sat down; the powder puffed up around him. "Albert..."

"My name is Vic, you little eggsucker."

"Okay, okay, no fooling around. Vic." His tone softened. "Vic.

Come on, man." He was trying to get through to me. I was really boiling, but he was trying to make sense. I shrugged, and crouched down beside him.

"Listen, man," Blood said, "this chick has bent you way out of shape. You *know* you can't go down there. It's all square and settled, and they know everyone; they hate solos. Enough roverpaks have raided downunder, and raped their women, and stolen their food, they'll have defenses set up. They'll *kill* you, Vic!"

"What the hell do you care? You're always saying you'd be better off without me." He sagged at that.

"Vic, we've been together almost three years. Good and bad. But this can be the worst. I'm scared, man. Scared you won't come back. And I'm hungry, and I'll have to go find some dude who'll take me on... and you know most solos are in paks now, I'll be low mutt. I'm not that young any more. And I'm hurt pretty bad."

I could dig it. He was talking sense. But all I could think of was how that bitch, that Quilla June, had rapped me. And then there were images of her soft tits, and the way she made little sounds when I was in her, and I shook my head, and knew I had to go get even.

"I got to do it, Blood. *I got to.*"

He breathed deep and sagged a little more. He knew it was useless. "You don't even see what she's done to you, Vic. That metal card, it's too easy, as if she *wanted* you to follow."

I got up. "I'll try to get back quick. Will you wait...?"

He was silent a long while, and I waited. Finally, he said, "For a while. Maybe I'll be here, maybe not."

I understood. I turned around and started walking around the pillar of black metal. Finally I found a slot in the pillar, and slipped the metal card into it. There was soft humming sound, then a section of the pillar dilated. I hadn't even seen the lines of the sections. A circle opened and I took a step through. I turned and there was Blood, watching me. We looked at each other, all the while that pillar was humming.

"So long, Vic."

"Take care of yourself, Blood."

"Hurry back."

"Do my best."

"Yeah. Right."

Then I turned around and stepped inside. The access portal irised closed behind me.

VII

I should have known. I should have suspected. Sure, every once in a while a chick came up to see what it was like on the surface, what had happened to the cities; sure, it happened. Why, I'd believed her when she'd told me, cuddled up beside me in that steaming boiler, that she'd wanted to see what it was like when a girl did it with a guy, that all the flicks she'd seen in Topeka were sweet and solid and dull, and the girls in her school'd talked about beaver flicks, and one of them had a little eight-page comic book and she'd read it with wide eyes... sure, I'd believed her. It was logical. I should have suspected something when she left that metal I.D. plate behind. It was too easy. Blood'd tried to tell me. Dumb? Yeah!

The second that access iris swirled closed behind me, the humming got louder, and some cool light grew in the walls. Wall. It was a circular compartment with only two sides to the wall: *in*side and *out*side. The wall pulsed up light and the humming got louder, and the deckplate I was standing on dilated just the way the outside port had done. But I was standing there, like a mouse in a cartoon, and as long as I didn't look down I was cool, I wouldn't fall.

Then I started settling. Dropped through the floor, the iris closed overhead, I was dropping down the tube, picking up speed but not too much, just dropping steadily. Now I knew what a dropshaft was.

Down and down I went and every once in a while I'd see something like 10 LEV or ANTIPOLL 55 or BREEDER-CON or PUMP SE 6 on the wall, faintly I could make the sectioning of an iris... but I never stopped dropping.

Finally, I dropped all the way to the bottom, and there was TOPEKA CITY LIMITS POP. 22,860 on the wall, and I settled down without any strain, bending a little from the knees to cushion the impact, but even that wasn't much.

I used the metal plate again, and the iris—a much bigger one this time—swirled open, and I got my first look at a downunder.

It stretched away in front of me, twenty miles to the dim shining horizon of tin can metal where the wall behind me curved and curved and curved till it made one smooth, encircling circuit and came back around around around to where I stood, staring at it. I was down at the bottom of a big metal tube that stretched up to a ceiling an eighth of a mile overhead, twenty miles across. And in the bottom of that tin can, someone had built a town that looked for all the world like a photo out of one of the water-logged books in the library on the surface. I'd seen a town like this in the books. Just like this. Neat little houses, and curvy little streets, and trimmed lawns, and a business section and everything else that a Topeka would have.

Except a sun, except birds, except clouds, except rain, except snow, except cold, except wind, except ants, except dirt, except mountains, except oceans, except big fields of grain, except stars, except the moon, except forests, except animals running wild, except...

Except freedom.

They were canned down here, like dead fish. Canned.

I felt my throat tighten up. I wanted to get out. Out! I started to tremble, my hands were cold and there was sweat on my forehead. This had been insane, coming down here. I had to get out. *Out!*

I turned around to get back in the dropshaft, and then it grabbed me.

That bitch Quilla June! I shoulda suspected!

The thing was low, and green, and boxlike, and had cables with mittens on the ends instead of arms, and it rolled on tracks, and it grabbed me.

It hoisted me up on its square flat top, holding me with them mittens on the cables, and I couldn't move, except to try kicking at the big glass eye in the front, but it didn't do any good. It didn't bust. The thing was only about four feet high, and my sneakers almost reached the ground, but not quite, and it started moving off into Topeka, hauling me along with it.

People were all over the place. Sitting in rockers on their front porches, raking their lawns, hanging around the gas station, sticking pennies in gumball machines, painting a white stripe down the middle of the road, selling newspapers on a corner, listening to an oompah band on a shell in a park, playing hopscotch and pussy-in-the-corner, polishing a fire engine, sitting on benches reading, washing windows, pruning bushes, tipping hats to ladies, collecting milk bottles in wire carrying racks, grooming horses, throwing a stick for a dog to retrieve, diving into a communal swimming pool, chalking vegetable prices on a slate outside a grocery, walking hand-in-hand with a girl, all of them watching me go past on that metal motherfucker.

I could hear Blood speaking, saying just what he'd said before I'd entered the dropshaft: *It's all square and settled and they know everyone; they hate solos. Enough roverpaks have raided down-unders, and raped their women and stolen their food, they'll have defenses set up. They'll kill you, Vic!*

Thanks, mutt.

Goodbye.

VIII

The green box tracked through the business section and turned in at a shopfront with the words BETTER BUSINESS BUREAU on the window. It rolled right inside the open door, and there were half a dozen men and old men and very old men in there, waiting for me. Also a couple of women. The green box stopped.

One of them came over and took the metal plate out of my hand. He looked at it, then turned around and gave it to the oldest of the old men, a withered toad wearing baggy pants and a green eyeshade and garters that held up the sleeves of his striped shirt. "Quilla June, Lew," the guy said to the old man. Lew took the metal plate and put it in the top left drawer of a rolltop desk. "Better take his guns, Aaron," the old coot said. And the guy who'd taken the plate cleaned me.

"Let him loose, Aaron," Lew said.

Aaron stepped around the back of the green box and something clicked, and the cable-mittens sucked back inside the box, and I got down off the thing. My arms were numb where the box had held me. I rubbed one, then the other, and I glared at them.

"Now, boy..." Lew started.

"Suck wind, asshole!"

The women blanched. The men tightened their faces.

"I told you it wouldn't work," another of the old men said to Lew.

"Bad business, this," said one of the younger ones.

Lew leaned forward in his straight-back chair and pointed a crumbled finger at me. "Boy, you better be nice."

"I hope all your fuckin' children are hare-lipped!"

"This is no good, Lew!" another man said.

"Guttersnipe," a woman with a beak snapped.

Lew stared at me. His mouth was a nasty little black line. I knew the sonofabitch didn't have a tooth in his crummy head that wasn't rotten and smelly. He stared at me with vicious little eyes. God, he was ugly, like a toad ready to snaffle a fly off the wall with his tongue. He was getting set to say something I wouldn't like. "Aaron, maybe you'd better put the sentry back on him." Aaron moved to the green box.

"Okay, hold it," I said, holding up my hand.

Aaron stopped, looked at Lew, who nodded. Then Lew leaned real far forward again, and aimed that bird-claw at me. "You ready to behave yourself, son?"

"Yeah, I guess."

"You'd better be dang sure."

"Okay. I'm *dang* sure. Also *fuckin'* sure!"

"And you'll watch your mouth."

I didn't reply. Old coot.

"You're a bit of an experiment for us, boy. We tried to get one of you down here other ways. Sent up some good folks to capture one of you little scuts, but they never came back. Figgered it was best to lure you down to us."

I sneered. That Quilla June. I'd take care of her!

One of the women, a little younger than Bird-Beak, came forward and looked into my face. "Lew, you'll never get this one to kowtow. He's a filthy little killer. Look at those eyes."

"How'd you like the barrel of a rifle jammed up your ass, bitch?" She jumped back. Lew was angry again. "Sorry," I said real quickly, "I don't like bein' called names. *Macho*, y'know?"

He settled back and snapped at the woman. "Mez, leave him alone. I'm tryin' to talk a bit of sense here. You're only making it worse."

Mez went back and sat with the others. Some Better Business Bureau these creeps were!

"As I was saying, boy: you're an experiment for us. We've been down here in Topeka close to thirty years. It's nice down here.

Quiet, orderly, nice people, who respect each other, no crime, respect for the elders, and just all around a good place to live. We're growin' and we're prosperin'."

I waited.

"But, well, we find now that some of our folks can't have no more babies, and the women that do, they have mostly girls. We need some men. Certain special kind of men."

I started laughing. This was too good to be true. They wanted me for stud service. I couldn't stop laughing.

"Crude!" one of the women said, scowling.

"This's awkward enough for us, boy, don't make it no harder." Lew was embarrassed.

Here I'd spent most of Blood's and my time aboveground hunting up tail, and down here they wanted me to service the local ladyfolk. I sat down on the floor and laughed till tears ran down my cheeks.

Finally, I got up and said, "Sure. Okay. But if I do, there's a couple of things *I* want."

Lew looked at me close.

"The first thing I want is that Quilla June. I'm gonna fuck her blind, and then I'm gonna bang her on the head the way she did me!"

They huddled for a while, then came out and Lew said, "We can't tolerate any violence down here, but I s'pose Quilla June's as good a place to start as any. She's capable, isn't she, Ira?"

A skinny, yellow-skinned man nodded. He didn't look happy about it. Quilla June's old man, I bet.

"Well, let's get started," I said. "Line 'em up." I started to unzip my jeans.

The women screamed, the men grabbed me, and they hustled me off to a boarding house where they gave me a room, and they said I should get to know Topeka a little bit before I went to work because it was, uh, er, well, awkward, and they had to get the folks in town to accept what was going to have to be done ... on the assumption, I suppose, that if I worked out okay they'd import a few more young bulls from aboveground and turn us loose.

So I spent some time in Topeka, getting to know the folks, seeing what they did, how they lived.

It was nice, real nice.

They rocked in rockers on the front porches, they raked their lawns, they hung around the gas station, they stuck pennies in gumball machines, they painted white stripes down the middle of the road, they sold newspapers on the corners, they listened to oompah bands in a shell in the park, they played hopscotch and pussy-in-the-corner, they polished fire engines, they sat on benches reading, they washed windows and pruned bushes, they tipped their hats to ladies, they collected milk bottles in wire carrying racks, they groomed horses and threw sticks for their dogs to retrieve, they dove into the communal swimming pool, they chalked vegetable prices on a slate outside the grocery, they walked hand-in-hand with some of the ugliest chicks I've ever seen, *and they bored the ass off me.*

Inside a week I was ready to scream.

I could feel that tin can closing in on me.

I could feel the weight of the earth over me.

They ate artificial shit: artificial peas and fake meat and make-believe chicken and ersatz corn and bogus bread, and it all tasted like chalk and dust to me.

Polite? Christ, you could puke from the lying, hypocritical crap they called civility. Hello Mr. This and Hello Mrs. That. And how are you? And how is little Janie? And how is business? Are you going to the sodality meeting Thursday? And I started gibbering in my room at the boarding house.

The clean, sweet, neat, lovely way they lived was enough to kill a guy. No wonder the men couldn't get it up and make babies that had balls instead of slots.

The first few days, everyone watched me like I was about to explode and cover their nice whitewashed fences with shit. But after a while, they got used to seeing me. Lew took me over to the Mercantile, and got me fitted out with a pair of bib overalls and a shirt that any solo could've spotted a mile away. That Mez, that dippy bitch who'd called me a killer, she started hanging around, finally said she wanted to cut my hair, make me look civilized. But I was hip to where she was at. Wasn't a bit of the mother in her.

"What'sa'matter, cunt," I pinned her. "Your old man isn't taking care of you?"

She tried to stick her fist in her mouth, and I laughed like a loon. "Go chop off *his* balls, baby. My hair stays the way it is." She cut and run. Went like she had a diesel tail-pipe.

It went on like that for a while. Me just walking around, them coming and feeding me, keeping all their young meat out of my way till they got the town stacked-away for what was coming with me.

Jugged like that, my mind wasn't right for a while. I got all claustrophobed, clutched, went and sat under the porch in the dark at the rooming house. Then that passed, and I got piss-mean, snapped at them, then surly, then quiet, then just mud dull. Quiet.

Finally, I started getting hip to the possibilities of getting out of there. It began with me remembering the poodle I'd fed Blood one time. It had to come from a downunder. And it couldn't have got up through the dropshaft. So that meant there were other ways out.

They gave me pretty much the run of the town, as long as I kept my manners around me and didn't try anything sudden. That green sentry box was always somewhere nearby.

So I found the way out. Nothing so spectacular; it just had to be there, and I found it.

Then I found out where they kept my weapons, and I was ready. Almost.

IX

It was a week to the day when Aaron and Lew and Ira came to get me. I was pretty goofy by that time. I was sitting out on the back porch of the boarding house, smoking a corncob pipe with my shirt off, catching some sun. Except there wasn't no sun. Goofy.

They came around the house, "Morning, Vic," Lew greeted me. He was hobbling along with a cane, the old fart. Aaron gave me a big smile. The kind you'd give a big black bull about to stuff his meat into a good breed cow. Ira had a look that you could chip off and use in your furnace.

"Well, howdy, Lew. Mornin', Aaron, Ira."

Lew seemed right pleased by that.

Oh, you lousy bastards, just you wait!

"You 'bout ready to go meet your first lady?"

"Ready as I'll ever be, Lew," I said, and got up.

"Cool smoke, ain't it?" Aaron said.

I took the corncob out of my mouth. "Pure dee-light." I smiled. I hadn't even lit the fucking thing.

They walked me over to Marigold Street and as we came up on a little house with yellow shutters and a white picket fence, Lew said, "This's Ira's house. Quilla June is his daughter."

"Well, land sakes," I said, wide-eyed.

Ira's lean jaw muscles jumped.

We went inside.

Quilla June was sitting on the settee with her mother, an older version of her, pulled thin as a withered muscle. "Miz Holmes," I said and made a little curtsey. She smiled. Strained, but smiled.

Quilla June sat with her feet right together, and her hands folded in her lap. There was a ribbon in her hair. It was blue.

Matched her eyes.

Something went thump in my gut.

"Quilla June," I said.

She looked up. "Mornin', Vic."

Then everyone sort of stood around looking awkward, and finally Ira began yapping and yipping about get in the bedroom and get this unnatural filth over with so they could go to Church and pray the Good Lord wouldn't Strike All Of Them Dead with a bolt of lightning in the ass, or some crap like that.

So I put out my hand, and Quilla June reached for it without looking up, and we went in the back, into a small bedroom, and she stood there with her head down.

"You didn't tell 'em, did you?" I asked.

She shook her head.

And suddenly, I didn't want to kill her at all. I wanted to hold her. Very tight. So I did. And she was crying into my chest, and making little fists beating on my back, and then she was looking up at me and running her words all together: "Oh, Vic, I'm sorry, so sorry, I didn't mean to, I had to, I was sent out to, I was so scared, and I love you, and now they've got you down here, and it isn't dirty, is it, it isn't the way my Poppa says it is, is it?"

I held her and kissed her and told her it was okay, and then I asked her if she wanted to come away with me, and she said yes yes yes she really did. So I told her I might have to hurt her Poppa to get away, and she got a look in her eyes that I knew real well.

For all her propriety, Quilla June Holmes didn't much like her prayer-shouting Poppa.

I asked her if she had anything heavy, like a candlestick or a club, and she said no. So I went rummaging around in that back bedroom and found a pair of her Poppa's socks in a bureau drawer. I pulled the big brass balls off the headboard of the bed and dropped them into the sock. I hefted it. Oh. Yeah.

She stared at me with big eyes. "What're you going to do?"

"You want to get out of here?"

She nodded.

"Then just stand back behind the door. No, wait a minute. I got a better idea. Get on the bed."

She lay down on the bed. "Okay," I said, "now pull up your skirt, pull off your pants, and spread out." She gave me a look of pure horror. "Do it," I said. "If you want out."

So she did it, and I rearranged her so her knees were bent and her legs open at the thighs, and I stood to one side of the door, and whispered to her, "Call your Poppa. Just him."

She hesitated a long moment, then she called out in a voice she didn't have to fake, "Poppa! Poppa, come here, please!" Then she clamped her eyes shut tight.

Ira Holmes came through the door, took one look at his secret desire, his mouth dropped open, I kicked the door closed behind him and walloped him as hard as I could. He squished a little, and spattered the bedspread, and went very down.

She opened her eyes when she heard the thunk! and when the stuff spattered her legs, she leaned over and puked on the floor. I knew she wouldn't be much good to me in getting Aaron into the room, so I opened the door, stuck my head around, looked worried, and said, "Aaron, would you come here a minute, please?" He looked at Lew, who was rapping with Mrs. Holmes about what was going on in the back bedroom, and when Lew nodded him on, he came into the room. He took a look at Quilla June's naked bush, at the blood on the wall and bedspread, at Ira on the floor, and opened his mouth to yell just as I whacked him. It took two more to get him down, and then I had to kick him in the chest to put him away. Quilla June was still puking.

I grabbed her by the arm and swung her up off the bed. At least she was being quiet about it, but man, did she stink.

"Come on!"

She tried to pull back, but I held on and opened the bedroom door. As I pulled her out, Lew stood up, leaning on his cane. I kicked the cane out from under the old fart and down he went in a heap. Mrs. Holmes was staring at us, wondering where her old man was. "He's back in there," I said, heading for the front door. "The Good Lord got him in the head."

Then we were out in the street, Quilla June stinking along behind me, dry-heaving and bawling and probably wondering what had happened to her underpants.

They kept my weapons in a locked case at the Better Business Bureau, and we detoured around by my boarding house where I pulled the crowbar I'd swiped from the gas station out from under the back porch. Then we cut across behind the Grange and into the business section, and straight into the BBB. There was a clerk who tried to stop me, and I split his gourd with the crowbar. Then I pried the latch off the cabinet in Lew's office and got the .30–06 and my .45 and all the ammo, and my spike and my knife and my kit, and loaded up. By that time Quilla June was able to make some sense.

"Where we gonna go, where we gonna go, oh Poppa Poppa Popp...!"

"Hey, listen, Quilla June, Poppa me no Poppas. You said you wanted to be with me...well, I'm goin'! *Up*, baby, and if you wanna go with me, you better stick close."

She was too scared to object.

I stepped out the front of the shopfront, and there was that green box sentry, coming on like a whippet. It had its cables out, and the mittens were gone. It had hooks.

I dropped to one knee, wrapped the sling of the .30–06 around my forearm, sighted clean, and fired dead at the big eye in the front. One shot, spang!

Hit that eye, the thing exploded in a shower of sparks, and the green box swerved and went through the front window of The Mill End Shoppe, screeching and crying and showering the place with flames and sparks. Nice.

I turned around to grab Quilla June, but she was gone. I looked off down the street, and here came all the vigilantes, Lew hobbling along with his cane like some kind of weird grasshopper.

And right then the shots started. Big, booming sounds. The .45 I'd given Quilla June. I looked up, and on the porch around the second floor, there she was, the automatic down on the railing like a pro, sighting into that mob and snapping off shots like maybe Wild Bill Elliott in a '40s Republic flick.

But dumb! Mother, dumb! Wasting time on that, when we had to get away.

I found the outside staircase going up there, and took it three steps at a time. She was smiling and laughing, and every time she'd pick one of those boobs out of the pack her little tonguetip would peek out of the corner of her mouth, and her eyes would get all slick and wet and wham! down the boob would go.

She was really into it.

Just as I reached her, she sighted down on her scrawny mother. I slammed the back of her head, and she missed the shot, and the old lady did a little dance-step and kept coming. Quilla June whipped her head around at me, and there was kill in her eyes. "You made me miss." The voice gave me a chill.

I took the .45 away from her. Dumb. Wasting ammunition like that.

Dragging her behind me, I circled the building, found a shed out back, dropped down onto it, and had her follow. She was scared at first, but I said, "Chick can shoot her old lady as easy as you do shouldn't be worried about a drop this small." She got out on the ledge, other side of the railing and held on. "Don't worry," I said, "you won't wet your pants. You haven't got any."

She laughed, like a bird, and dropped. I caught her, we slid down the shed door, and took a second to see if that mob was hard on us. Nowhere in sight.

I grabbed Quilla June by the arm and started off toward the south end of Topeka. It was the closest exit I'd found in my wandering, and we made it in about fifteen minutes, panting and weak as kittens.

And there it was.

A big air-intake duct.

I pried off the clamps with the crowbar, and we climbed up inside. There were ladders going up. There had to be. It figured. Repairs. Keep it clean. Had to be. We started climbing.

It took a long, long time.

Quilla June kept asking me, from down behind me, whenever she got too tired to climb, "Vic, do you love me?" I kept saying yes. Not only because I meant it. It helped her keep climbing.

X

We came up a mile from the access dropshaft. I shot off the filter covers and the hatch bolts, and we climbed out. They should have known better down there. You don't fuck around with Jimmy Cagney.

They never had a chance.

Quilla June was exhausted. I didn't blame her. But I didn't want to spend the night out in the open; there were things out there I didn't like to think about meeting even in daylight. It was getting on toward dusk.

We walked toward the access dropshaft.

Blood was waiting.

He looked weak. But he'd waited.

I stooped down and lifted his head. He opened his eyes, and very softly he said, "Hey."

I smiled at him. Jesus, it was good to see him. "We made it back, man."

He tried to get up, but he couldn't. The wounds on him were in ugly shape. "Have you eaten?" I asked.

"No. Grabbed a lizard yesterday...or maybe it was day before. I'm hungry, Vic."

Quilla June came up then, and Blood saw her. He closed his eyes. "We'd better hurry, Vic," she said. "Please. They might come up from the dropshaft."

I tried to lift Blood. He was dead weight. "Listen, Blood, I'll leg it into the city and get some food. I'll come back quick. You just wait here."

"Don't go in there, Vic," he said. "I did a recon the day after you went down. They found out we weren't fried in that gym. I don't know how. Maybe mutts smelled our track. I've been keeping watch, and they haven't tried to come out after us. I don't blame them. You don't know what it's like out here at night, man...you don't know..."

He shivered.

"Take it easy, Blood."

"But they've got us marked lousy in the city, Vic. We can't go back there. We'll have to make it someplace else."

That put it on a different stick. We couldn't go back, and with Blood in that condition we couldn't go forward. And I knew, good as I was solo, I couldn't make it without him. And there wasn't anything out here to eat. He had to have food at once, and some medical care. I had to do something. Something good, something fast.

"Vic," Quilla June's voice was high and whining, "come *on!* He'll be all right. We have to hurry."

I looked up at her. The sun was going down. Blood trembled in my arms.

She got a pouty look on her face. "If you love me, you'll come *on!*"

I couldn't make it alone out there without him. I knew it. If I loved her. She asked me, in the boiler, do you know what love is?

It was a small fire, not nearly big enough for any roverpak to spot from the outskirts of the city. No smoke. And after Blood had eaten his fill, I carried him to the air-duct a mile away, and we spent the night inside on a little ledge. I held him all night. He slept good. In the morning, I fixed him up pretty good. He'd make it; he was strong.

He ate again. There was plenty left from the night before. I didn't eat. I wasn't hungry.

We started off across the blast wasteland that morning. We'd find another city, and make it.

We had to move slow because Blood was still limping. It took a long time before I stopped hearing her calling in my head. Asking me, asking me: *do you know what love is?*

Sure I know.

A boy loves his dog.

21_____

For the future of intelligent life on Earth, may Blood find a smart bitch for himself.

It seems to me that the mathematics professor in the following story might have been an earlier patron of Sheckley's "Store of the Worlds," although his plight might have resulted from a social evolution that had its beginning either in Ellison's story or at the time of Wyndham's "The Wheel." Lao-tzu tells what comes from following Logos, and what comes from following Tao, but what comes from abandoning both and following Banana? Jim Aikin explains it all for us very clearly, but I don't quite understand. My thoughts are not very collected these days, and the world seems much less logical to me than it used to. I'm growing old.

MY LIFE IN THE JUNGLE
by Jim Aikin

At one time, incongruous as it must now seem, I was a professor of mathematics. I'm not sure that that fact is of any importance, though I *am* fairly certain that it's of no importance to anybody but me.

374

Perhaps I think and feel more deeply because of it. Perhaps my remembrance of the past provides me with a better perspective on the nature of events than those around me are privy to. But it's difficult to be certain—first, because I have no idea what those around me think and feel, if anything; and second, because I cannot quite imagine what I would think and feel if I were otherwise than I am.

There must be millions of us here, wandering perpetually in this desolation of heat and dust. We all, I'm sure, suffer the same torment. Nevertheless, I do feel that I'm different from the others in some subtle but important way because of my former circumstances. But while at one time I could recall my life as a professor of mathematics in great detail (indeed, such fond recollections of the tree-lined campus, the classrooms, the cool quiet of the library, the meticulously reasoned papers I wrote for academic journals, occupied at one time many happy hours), of late the memories have grown dim and fragmentary, and what I can still recall, I take no pleasure in. On the contrary—the contrast between my remembered life and my current situation is a source of further pain. If I remembered more of the details of the past, the pain would only be worse. Fortunately, those memories have been largely overlaid and blotted out by more recent, more brutal scenes, by more pressing needs and immediate concerns.

Bananas, for instance. As a professor of mathematics, I knew little about bananas, and cared less. They were yellow and grew on trees. I knew, in a general way, what one tasted like. Today, on the other hand, I can identify more than a dozen distinct varieties of bananas, including too green to eat, green but edible, overripe but edible, rotten, wormy but edible, lying on the ground forgotten but still edible, half-masticated and spit out, bitter for no apparent reason, and just right. Then there are somebody else's bananas, bananas stomped into the floor of the jungle and pulped by somebody who was angry, bananas smeared over the body, and bananas hanging too high in the tree to reach. Bananas are a subject of vast and consuming importance to all of us here, me along with the rest.

In recent weeks the band with which I am associated has shrunk by attrition to a fraction of its former size—which, considering the drastic alteration in our environment, is hardly surprising. Originally we numbered between twenty and twenty-five individuals.

Even then the number fluctuated from day to day as individuals wandered away and were replaced by others upon whom we happened in our travels. Today the happy state that we enjoyed in the weeks following my arrival is nearly as remote from me as the campus life that preceded it. I look back wistfully on the leafy paradise in which we roamed; nowhere now in this wasteland is such a luxuriant habitat to be found. Had I known then what deterioration would occur, surely I would have tried to find some way to prevent it. Probably nothing I could have done would have done any good. Perhaps, indeed, I would have found myself incapable of acting differently than I have. In any event, at the time I was too busy mourning my lost academic life to pay much attention to the direction in which events were tending. Thus, I did nothing.

Even in those days, it was difficult for me to reliably distinguish one individual of the band from another by sight; now, of course, the problem is compounded a thousandfold. Certain individuals did, however, possess characteristics that enabled me after a time to identify them. I gave them names, in my own mind. The one who was more or less our acknowledged leader I dubbed Blackie, because of the broad irregular stripe of black fur running down his back. In addition to Blackie, there was a particular nervous, excitable little fellow I called Phil; a toothless old female I called Granny (whose principal distinguishing feature was a severe chronic case of diarrhea); and—always at the center of my thoughts—a gentle, doe-eyed female I called Arabella. Ah, Arabella!

Perhaps I should call us a tribe, and Blackie our chief. Not that his chieftainship went unchallenged—far from it. We were constantly quarreling amongst ourselves. Indeed, next to foraging for bananas, quarreling has always been our chief occupation. Whenever we happened upon a band of strangers, we set aside our petty internal squabbles and put up a united front, screeching our challenge at them from the treetops and trampling and crushing whatever vegetation might be handy in order to demonstrate our ferocity and our utter contempt for them. They, of course, were simultaneously doing likewise. These noisy, destructive encounters were by far the grandest, most festive events punctuating our life in the jungle. But when no band of strangers was available, the young males not infrequently exhibited the same sort of aggressive behavior toward Blackie. He was not reluctant to reply in kind, and since he was larger and noisier than any of the rest, he inevitably emerged the victor, after which he would swagger around for hours with a self-satisfied smirk pasted on his repulsive features, deliberately bumping into anybody who was not quick enough to move out of his path and grabbing their bananas away from them.

These, then, were the parameters of the new life into which I was thrust—bananas and quarreling and roaming through the trees, or along the jungle floor when no trees were handy. At first the abruptness of the transition from the quiet life of a college professor left me shocked and appalled—only natural, I suppose, under the circumstances. For some weeks I remained in a rather befuddled state, and I am sure that I seemed odd and distant to the others. Fortunately the new body in which I found myself already knew the arts of the jungle survival, else I would surely have perished. Sitting on a limb peeling a banana (a task I executed as expertly as though I had devoted a life's intensive study to it, though I now possessed only incompletely opposable thumbs), I pondered how such a thing could possibly have happened; but I was unable to arrive at any very satisfactory answer. It seemed impossible; in point of fact, it still seems impossible.

Nevertheless, the clarity and reliability of my perceptions made it clear at once that I had not been precipitated into a hallucination or a dream. If I had gone to sleep at night a college professor and wakened the next morning in my present situation, I might have found the dream hypothesis more attractive, but the transition was not cloaked in unconsciousness, nor even accompanied by any sense of movement. At one moment, I was standing at a blackboard, explaining the techniques of differential calculus to a class of freshmen and sophomores, most of whom were thoroughly bored and trying to conceal the fact; and then, in the blink of an eye, the classroom, the students, all had vanished, and I was sitting on a limb peeling a banana. When I saw how far above the ground I was, I became dizzy and had to cling to the limb to keep from falling; but the dizziness was, I am convinced, a consequence of my reaction, not of the transition itself.

When, a few moments later, I first came face to face with my new companions, again I reacted badly. I was, I regret, somewhat less than cordial. Far from embracing them, I was seized by terror and turned and fled headlong through the jungle, screeching in alarm and confusion. I might easily have become separated from them and thus lost (hardly a serious matter, since I would sooner or later have been bound to stumble upon another virtually indistinguishable band); but when they saw me running, they instantly concluded that this was some grand new game in which I desired their participation, and without hesitation they followed after me, crashing loudly through the underbrush and screeching in concert. Hearing this commotion, I in turn naturally assumed that I was being pursued by those who wished me ill, and thus drove myself to greater exertion attempting to escape them. Eventually I would have outpaced them—except for the unfailing fascination of quarreling, their attention span was not long—but before me suddenly the jungle fell away, and I was brought up short at the edge of a wide grassy plain dotted with distant herds of elephants and zebras. Even then I would have continued, save that directly before me, lolling in the dust, was a family of lions. Before I quite realized what I was doing, I had altered the direction of my progress from the X to the Y axis and scampered up the nearest tree—where, of course, Blackie and the others speedily joined me. For some hours, until the lions moved off in search of game, we had no choice but to remain where we were. Given this opportunity to make an acquaintance with the band, I quickly lost my fear of them. Certainly they had their shortcomings, but I was not insensible of the fact that to be alone in the jungle is less desirable than to be with others with whom one has interests in common.

For some time after the transition, I did wonder whether I might shift back to the classroom as suddenly and unexpectedly as I had left it, whether I might begin shuttling back and forth as a regular thing, or perhaps with as little warning find myself in a third set of surroundings unrelated to either of the others. I no longer think this likely. I seem to be stuck very firmly and permanently where I am. I also wondered whether my new companions might be newly transplanted like myself; but their behavior has never given me any evidence to confirm this hypothesis. My attempts to communicate with them by means of grunts and gestures, by drawing signs in the dirt, were met with blank indifference, or on occasion with crude and mocking imitations of my behavior that could not possibly conceal anything of semantic significance.

I was forced, then, to consider whether *my* overt behavior, however precise or articulate my intentions, was any different than theirs. This is a question I still have not been able to lay to rest. I feel that I am far more intelligent than they, but as I have no method of observing myself from the outside, I am unable to determine whether this inner condition is manifest in any perceptible way. Conceivably, they are as intelligent as I, and we are all equally incapable of communication. As time goes on, admittedly, I am less inclined even to try to establish any meaningful interaction, and I acknowledge with regret that I am no longer much more attentive to matters of cleanliness than they. While I still think of myself as a professor of mathematics, so much time has passed that I might find it difficult to explain the calculus, should the occasion arise, or even to take a square root. I am reluctant, truth be told, to try to remember the details of such operations, for fear I might fail. As long as I don't dwell on the details, I can cling to the idea that I am in fact, if not in semblance, a professor of mathematics. If I tried to remember and failed, I would be forced to consider that after all, I may be no more than what I seem.

It is even possible, though I shudder to think of it, that my memories of that previous life are illusory. I may always have been as I am now. While I may consider myself a professor of mathematics, I would be hard pressed to offer any proof.

Once over the initial shock, I found that my new life offered certain consolations. For example, I no longer had any professional obligations. There were no faculty meetings to attend, no undergraduates to advise, no thesis proposals to approve, no examinations to administer, no appointment calendars or clocks to watch. My new environment, while perhaps less than idyllic, was in the main quite pleasant. The weather was uniformly warm, and although embarrassed at first, I shortly found that I didn't mind much going without constantly being chafed by clothing. I suffered somewhat from boredom, but not excessively. While the course of events was more narrowly circumscribed here, there were endless matters of detail—such as learning to distinguish the many varieties of bananas—to claim my attention. And most of all, by way of consolation, there was Arabella.

It was during my first days in the jungle, when I was still cautiously trying to discover the nature of my situation, that Arabella and I became aware of one another. Far from being impudently, raucously lewd like most of the other females, she was shy and retiring by nature, even fastidious in comparison with the others (though admittedly the general standards of grooming were deplorably lax, and her own accomplishments in this regard were relative rather than absolute). I no longer recall whether it was she who first approached me or vice versa, but before very long we had become steadfast companions.

Companionship among the tribe was a simple matter, consisting chiefly of long sessions spent picking lice from one another's fur—a necessary task if we were not all to succumb to terminal itching—and it was this activity that formed the primary basis of my relationship with Arabella. How well I remember the gentleness of her hands as they roamed delicately over my back and shoulders! I also from time to time offered her an especially delectable-looking banana; I wish I could report that she reciprocated, but alas, the exchange of such tokens of generosity seemed to be entirely unknown among the tribe. At most, she favored me perhaps with a fleeting glance of appreciation before devoting her attention to the matter at hand—that is, to the banana.

There was a time when I thought Arabella and I could be happy together. I pretended to myself that within her must reside, hidden, a soul akin to my own, though she never gave me any concrete evidence in support of this idea. I seemed to recall a student I had had once who possessed such soft, compassionate eyes, such a sweet disposition, and I fondly imagined that it was with this student that I was passing the hours in our leafy bower. I found, however, that I was unable to remember the student's name, and this dampened my enjoyment of the fantasy somewhat.

No matter. In the evenings, when the tribe had settled down for the night in the boughs of a banana grove, when the air was fragrant with the scent of wild orchards and the occasional sleepy roar of a lion could be heard in the distance, Arabella would come to me and pick the lice from my fur, and I the lice from hers. I am sure she would have allowed a greater degree of familiarity if I had sought it; couplings among the tribe were indulged in quite casually and openly, with no consideration whatever of propriety or decorum. But I could not quite bear to disturb the tranquility of our time together; nor, to be honest, could I ever wholly divest myself of the knowledge that I was after all a professor of mathematics, for whom such a scene must remain too grotesquely undignified ever to take part in.

I have no idea how long this period of arboreal contentment lasted. More than a year, surely; perhaps several. At one time I considered whether I might be able to fashion a crude calendar by carving every day a new notch in a convenient tree branch. But even had I possessed a suitable carving tool, it would have availed me nothing, for in our wanderings through the jungle, we rarely spent two nights in the same place. To have carved a single notch in a new tree every night would have been an exercise in futility.

All during this time, our encounters with other roving bands similar to ours continued. These were occasions of some devastation to the jungle, for when we saw strangers, so like us and yet so utterly unlike, we flew into paroxysms of rage. To demonstrate our ferocity, we uprooted whole bushes and young trees, or trampled them into the mud. If the strangers had not begun doing so before us, they imitated us without delay. This activity was accompanied by prolonged screeching, gnashing of teeth, rude gestures, and (though it shames me to admit it) the flinging of excrement. Actual hand-to-hand combat was a rarity, though we sometimes worked ourselves into such a frenzy that no other measures would do to slake our rage. Generally we preferred to take up a safe strategic position, from which, after a thorough display of animosity, we would begin pelting the enemy with bodily wastes—or, when none came readily to hand, with bananas. After a few hours of such excitement, both sides would retire grumbling, leaving behind a battlefield strewn with dung and trampled vegetation.

At first there seemed little harm in this enterprise. After all, the jungle was large, and the scars of battle quickly overgrown. As time went on, however, I noticed that our encounters with bands of strangers were becoming more frequent, and the injuries to the jungle slower to heal. Often in our migrations we came upon old battlegrounds, bedraggled and foul-smelling. On some of these occasions, I could recall that it was we who had participated in the depredation, while on others the geography was not one I recognized. I concluded therefore that we were not alone in provoking and relishing such hostilities.

Unquestionably, we did our share of the destructive work. There was one band in particular with whom we fought repeatedly, in a series of skirmishes that ranged up and down the jungle. If I had been transported originally into their midst rather than into Blackie's group, I don't suppose it would have made the slightest difference, for on the whole we were quite indistinguishable from one another. Nevertheless, we were bitter enemies. On one memorable occasion, we became rivals for a single strand of banana trees, an unusually large and fertile grove whose bananas were among the finest I had ever tasted. In truth, the grove was large enough easily to have fed both our group and the others, but there was no possibility of our reaching an accommodation. Arriving one morning at the grove simultaneously from opposite directions, we both took umbrage; each group was determined that it and it alone should occupy this entire site. As a result, we threw more bananas at one another than we ate, and tore more and more leaves from the banana trees in our furious displays of aggression.

When the trees on all sides were wholly denuded, we had no alternative but to uproot them; failure to do so would have been proof of cowardice. The labor of uprooting full-grown trees was prodigious, and required a greater degree of cooperation than our band had shown before, or has since. But we were determined, and when we finished, the trees lay about on the ground like matchsticks. We slammed them down, and grimaced and howled, and tore our fingers on the roots. I cannot say whether our group or the detested strangers uprooted more of the trees; it would have been a victory of sorts, if only symbolic, though I am bound to suppose that nobody but myself was even capable of counting. Perhaps my failure to keep a tally was, under the circumstances, a form of disloyalty. In any event, the upshot was that we completely destroyed the grove, and both tribes had to look elsewhere for sustenance.

One remarkable aspect of these battles was their effect on the one I called Phil. As if in compensation for the fact that he was unable to best Blackie in our domestic uproars (or, more accurately, that he was unwilling to challenge him), Phil became in our encounters with strangers the most hysterically aggressive of our band. He screeched the loudest, he trampled bushes the most enthusiastically, and he flung excrement with such glee that he generally got more on himself (it not having hardened enough to make proper missiles) than on the enemy. Not that the rest of us were immune from this unfortunate scattering effect. Phil, however, was nervous and excitable at the best of times, and these bouts did him no good. For hours after a battle, he would lie on the ground twitching, eyes rolling far back into his head and foam dribbling from his mouth. He was a pitiful sight, and would have been easy prey for a lion had one happened along. Fortunately for him, he was victimized only by the rest of the young males of our own tribe, who lost no opportunity to urinate on him and otherwise display their contempt while he was helpless.

Nor did I, to my everlasting shame, abstain from this ritual of debasement. Although I had only pity for poor Phil, I feared that to hang back when the rest of the tribe was so eagerly pressing forward would make me conspicuous, and might lead to my being singled out for the same sort of abuse. Even Granny, the aged and incontinent female, participated on these occasions. Since this was the only time she got the better of anybody, I found it hard to begrudge her the opportunity, though unquestionably it was a disgusting spectacle.

To an outsider it might have appeared that we were demonstrating our disapproval of Phil's extreme pugnacity, but nothing could have been further from the truth; our vociferousness in encounters with strangers was nearly equal to his. Rather, we were deflecting onto Phil the aggressive impulses we had been unable to vent on any less helpful victim. If the band of strangers had been so considerate as to lie down on the floor of the jungle and allow such treatment, our deepest longings would have been fulfilled.

It was on the evening following our destruction—with the collaboration of our habitual nemeses—of the banana grove, that I lost my Arabella. For some time before, to be sure, she had seemed somewhat distracted. Once or twice she actually pushed away a banana I was offering her. But until it was too late, I attached no significance to this. Perhaps if I had—well, such speculation is of no value now. It happened that during the battle, Blackie's usual consort, his favorite of the five or six upon whom he customarily lavished his attentions, had wandered away—where or why, I never learned. In her absence, his roving eye fell upon Arabella; and she, to my sorrow, seemed not to find his attentions distasteful. Disdaining even to undertake a preliminary picking of lice by way of courtship, he mounted her straightaway, as I watched in horror. The lust in his eyes was acid in my heart—and as for Arabella, she continued placidly eating a banana all the time he was at his business. A banana I had given her! Faithless Arabella! I fought him, naturally; I had no choice, if I were to salvage even a tattered remnant of honor. And of course he beat me soundly. I fear that I have always been too inhibited to screech and trample with necessary abandon.

But while I remained furious at Blackie, it was hard to hold Arabella blameless. Far from being distraught by the change, far from pining for me or casting longing glances in my direction, she took to the arrangement as placidly as she had to her life with me, and seemed to want nothing further to do with me. When I approached, humbly beckoning for her to search my back for lice, she pushed me away roughly. At night I was forced to listen to her grunts of pleasure mingled with his. Dismally depressed by this turn of events, I gorged myself on bananas for weeks. Briefly I considered leaving the tribe entirely and striking out through the jungle in search of new companions, but I knew I would carry the unhappy memory with me wherever I went, and would have no peace. As long as I stayed nearby, I could cherish the hope that eventually he would tire of her, or she of him. I was unsure whether I would wish to resume our former relations in that case, whether I would be capable of so blithely putting the past behind me, but it seemed wrong to deny myself the opportunity should it arise.

From this time on, it seemed, a change came over our life in the jungle. Or perhaps it was only that, no longer distracted by Arabella's sweet presence, I noticed for the first time a change that had already begun. Indeed, as I was searching for distractions, I may have noticed the change long before it became apparent to the others—if indeed it has ever become apparent to them. To this day, I sometimes think, they have not noticed the cataclysmic deterioration in our surroundings. They continue to behave exactly as they did before, though it is no longer appropriate (if it ever was). Perhaps they have no memory of what once was, and thus no way to measure the loss. Perhaps it is only I, among the millions here, who am aware of the disaster we have brought on ourselves. Could I have averted it, if I had acted in time? What could I have done?

We moved on, then, from the destroyed banana grove in search of unspoiled forage. But more and more, the groves we found were already in the possession of bands of strangers, whom we had to drive off in order to enjoy the bananas. The jungle was thick with evidence of past combats, and virgin stretches of wild growth increasingly rare. The first time we came upon two separate bands of strangers fighting for possession of a grove, we retreated in confusion, never having seen such a thing before. But before long we were inured to the sight. We learned that we could pitch in, making it a three-way fight, taking advantage of the fact that the others were already in a debilitated condition to promote our own cause, and on occasion we emerged the victors. For our victory celebration, naturally, we stuffed ourselves with bananas, whether or not they were ripe and continuing long after we had eaten our fill, continuing until we vomited up undigested banana and then reaching for more— for who knew when we might have the chance for such an orgy again? Just as often, we found ourselves unequal to the contest, and were driven off; if not initially, by those who had possession before us, then certainly at a later date, by those who came after. It proved impossible to retain control of any given grove for long, especially as the roving bands were becoming more numerous, and stands of banana trees scarcer. When we could secure victory only by uprooting the trees, naturally we did so; nor have I any reason to suppose we were alone in this improvident behavior. And always, sooner or later, we were compelled to move on, searching, ever searching for a grove where we could enter and eat and remain unmolested. It was after one of these raids that I noticed Arabella was gone. Though it galled me to look on her, now that she was another's, I found that I mourned her loss none the less keenly. I hoped that she had found a haven with another band like ours, new companions who would devotedly pick the lice from her fur. The thought that she might lie crushed under a fallen banana tree, her warm doe eyes forever cold and vacant, was for a long time a source of torment for me. I am compelled to wonder, however, whether such a fate might after all be better for her than to have survived. Our circumstances now are so wretched that, though I may wish she were here to ease my loneliness, I cannot in good conscience desire that she should suffer such pain. Perhaps, nevertheless, she has survived, and wanders here as we do. Perhaps someday I will stumble upon her, and not recognize her, and pass on. Perhaps I have done so already. Ah, Arabella, truly you are lost!

By now our encounters with bands of strangers are no longer

frequent; they are continual. Of the jungle, nothing remains. As far as I can see in every direction (which is not far, unless I climb for a moment onto somebody else's shoulders), there is nothing on this arid plain but thousands of bands like ourselves roaming through the dust and filth, screeching foul imprecations at one another, bespattering one another with excrement, stumbling occasionally over the dried bleached bones of a lion, seeking perpetually in vain for a leafy grove where grow bananas.

Of our group, only myself and Blackie and Granny remain. Wanting nothing to do with Granny, but needing release, Blackie has taken to mounting me instead. I find this humiliating, and rather painful, but I am powerless to prevent it. Also, he demands that I search his fur for lice, while showing no inclination whatever to reciprocate. I itch constantly, agonizingly. When I scratch, my fur comes out in clumps, leaving raw red sores behind. The heat of the sunlight is sufficient to raise blisters, and in the thick dust, I am dreadfully, excruciatingly thirsty. There being no trees left to uproot, some of the more foul-tempered among us have taken to tearing one another's limbs off and belaboring one another about the head with them. The delicious wetness of the blood as it spurts from these horrid wounds goads my thirst to unbearable agony. Once the blood has mingled with the dust, however, its usefulness as a means of allaying thirst is a thing of the past. I find myself wondering whether I could become so crazed by thirst as to do what I am contemplating. Am I actually capable of such savagery? I would like, even in this extremity, to feel that I still possess some measure of dignity, of rationality. After all, I was at one time a professor of mathematics.

by permission of Richard Curtis Associates, Inc. THE TERMINAL BEACH, by J.G. Ballard, copyright © 1964 by J.G. Ballard. Reprinted by permission of the Scott Meredith Literary Agency, Inc., 845 Third Avenue, New York, NY 10022. TOMORROW'S CHILDREN, by Poul Anderson, copyright © 1947 by Street & Smith Publications, Inc.; copyright © renewed 1975 by Poul Anderson. Reprinted by permission of the author and the author's agents, the Scott Meredith Literary Agency, 845 Third Avenue, New York, NY 10022. HEIRS APPARENT, by Robert Abernathy, copyright © 1954 by Fantasy House, Inc.; copyright © renewed 1982 by Robert Abernathy. Reprinted by permission of the author. A MASTER OF BABYLON, by Edgar Pangborn, copyright © 1954 by Galaxy Publishing Corporation; copyright renewed. Reprinted by permission of Richard Curtis Associates, Inc. GAME PRESERVE, by Rog Phillips, copyright © 1957 by Galaxy Publishing Corporation. Reprinted by permission of the Scott Meredith Literary Agency, 845 Third Avenue, New York, NY 10022. BY THE WATERS OF BABYLON, by Stephen Vincent Benet. From *The Selected Works of Stephen Vincent Benet*, Holt, Rhinehart & Winston, Inc. Copyright © 1937 by Stephen Vincent Benet; copyright © renewed 1964 by Thomas C. Benet, Stephanie B. Mahin and Rachel Benet Lewis. Reprinted by permission of Brandt & Brandt Literary Agents, Inc. THERE WILL COME SOFT RAINS, by Ray Bradbury, copyright © 1950 by Ray Bradbury; copyright © renewed 1978 by Ray Bradbury. Reprinted by permission of Don Congdon Associates, Inc. TO THE CHICAGO ABYSS, by Ray Bradbury, copyright © 1963 by Ray Bradbury. Reprinted by permission of Don Congdon Associates, Inc. LUCIFER, by Roger Zelazny, copyright © 1964 by Galaxy Publishing Corporation. Reprinted by permission of the author. EASTWARD HO!, by William Tenn, copyright © 1958 by Mercury Press, Inc. Reprinted by permission of the author and the author's agent, Virginia Kidd. THE FEAST OF SAINT JANIS, by Michael Swanwick, copyright © 1980 by Michael Swanwick. Reprinted by permission of the author and the author's agent, Virginia Kidd. "IF I FORGET THEE, OH EARTH . . . " by Arthur C. Clarke, copyright © 1951; copyright © renewed 1979 by Arthur C. Clarke. Reprinted by permission of the author and the author's agents, the Scott Meredith Literary Agency, 845 Third Avenue, New York, NY 10022. A BOY AND HIS DOG, by Harlan Ellison, originally appeared in a shorter version in *New Worlds*; copyright © 1969 by New Worlds Publishing (Great Britain); revised version copyright © 1969 by Harlan Ellison. Reprinted with the permission of, and by arrangement with, the author and the author's agent, Richard Curtis Associates, Inc., 164 East 64th Street, New York, NY 10021. All rights reserved. MY LIFE IN THE JUNGLE, by Jim Aiken, copyright © 1984 by Mercury Press, Inc. Reprinted by permission of the author and the author's agent, James Allen.

IN THE BEYOND ARMAGEDDON SERIES